Frances Paige has made herself one of the most popular writers of the decade with the publication of her ongoing saga about the McGraths of Sholton, but she has always had a large following for her many novels, written under a number of pseudonyms. Under the name Frances Paige she published two novels before embarking on her saga: *Three Girls* and *Lost Time*. The first book about the McGraths, *The Sholtie Burn*, was published in 1986, to be followed by *Maeve's Daughter* in 1987, *The Distaff Side* in 1988, *Men Who March Away* in 1989 and *The Sholtie Flyer* in 1990.

Born in Scotland, Frances Paige is married to a psychiatrist whose thinking, she admits, has greatly influenced her approach to characterization. She and her husband live in Lancashire and travel regularly to south-west France, her second love.

D0994076

By the same author

FRANCES PAIGE

The Sholtie Burn

This edition published by Diamond Books, 2000

Diamond Books is an imprint of
HarperCollins*Publishers*
77-85 Fulham Palace Road,
Hammersmith, London W6 8JB

This paperback edition first published
by Grafton Books 1988

First published in Great Britain by
Souvenir Press Ltd 1986

Copyright © Frances Paige & Souvenir Press 1986

ISBN 0 26 167389 0

Printed and bound in Great Britain by
Caledonian International Book Manufacturing Ltd, Glasgow

Set in Times

BOOK ONE
The Far Side
1851–1869

1

Maeve Muldoon sat at her window watching the wide sweep of the park in the moonlight. She had risen quietly at midnight when the house was still, bathed her face and hands from the rose-patterned ewer Deirdre had filled, dressed quickly. There were two hours still to go. She would have to possess her soul in patience. She made herself sit straight, clasped her hands loosely in her lap. If you forced yourself to sit quietly, your mind quietened.

Don't panic, she told herself. It's no worse than going over a high fence with Blackthorn. The one at the foot of Crow Wood had five bars. You had to keep yourself taut, hands steady, fight back the terror coiled inside you, ready to reduce you to a quivering nothing, like Phoebe Tynan with her yellow ringlets. Once when she had asked Kieran what he thought of Phoebe he had said, '*That* stuck-up miss with her china-blue eyes! Now yours are sea-blue in comparison. They go dark and light like the sea.' He was a poet, Kieran.

It was a pity about the moonlight. Sometimes it made Mama sleep fitfully, then summon Deirdre to bring her a warm drink. But it would not penetrate the dark drive to the house, with its laurel bushes on either side of it backed by the jungle of black branches towering behind them. In spite of herself she moaned. It's difficult to be brave all the time when you're just seventeen, she reassured herself. What we're doing is right. There's no other solution.

They had thought Crow Wood safe, a half-mile from the house. No one ever went there because of the

9

overgrown tangle of brambles, nettles and straggly shrubs. Even the Hunt had never penetrated it. Had they not lost the fox there just the other day and the horses had turned back? That terrible day . . .

She had clattered into the front drive afterwards, dishevelled and wet, her skirts soaked and clinging round her boots. Sean had been waiting to take Blackthorn round to the stables, since her father had forbidden her to go there. 'We lost the fox, Sean,' she had said as she dismounted. She thought the boy looked thinner than ever, his eyes dark in his white face. But then, his mother never gave him a proper meal, slut that she was. Peters was in the habit of slinking up to her house at nights. Peters . . . she drew in her breath as she thought of him.

'I heard that.' There were lines round his young mouth.

'It's not the end of the world,' she said, laughing at him.

'Miss Maeve.' She saw now he was shaking. 'Something terrible's happened! The Major's been at the stables, and, and . . .' he put his hand to his mouth.

'What is it, Sean?'

'And I heard Mr Peters telling him he saw you and Kieran in the old shack in Crow Wood!' His eyes were nearly falling out of his head.

'Is Kieran in the stables?' She felt the blood drain from her body and took hold of Blackthorn's reins to prevent herself from swaying.

'No . . . well, maybe now. He rode into the village for something . . .'

'What . . .' she had to summon all her courage to speak calmly. She was a sea of terror inside. 'What . . . did my father say?'

'Nothing at first, Miss. His face was red the way it goes, and then he asked Mr Peters if Kieran was there. He said

10

he'd gone for some horse physic from Mr Kilroy. Then the Major said, "Just as well. There would have been a murder . . ." Oh, Miss Maeve, will he be after finding out that I took messages from you and Kieran? I've never told a soul, just as Kieran told me.'

'No, no! How could he know that? Did my father go away then?'

'Yes, he said he'd go back to the house and decide what to do. His face was near to bursting and he kept hitting his gaiters with his whip.'

'Take Blackthorn and don't worry.' She hated to see the terror in his face. They should never have involved him. 'No harm will come to you. Off you go. Oh, and have a look at Blackthorn's off foreleg.'

She glanced up at the drawing-room windows. Was her father pacing up and down there this minute, telling her mother? Not that Mama would give him any help or even champion her. She would say she had a terrible headache and she would have to go to bed. She was suddenly shaking with anger at Peters. The sly evil toad, skulking about at night, spying on us, the dirty peeping Tom. But sick fear replaced her anger. Papa would kill Kieran. She had not got much time.

She went running round the back of the house, past the outhouses and the vegetable gardens, towards the stables. Old Mick was shutting up his greenhouses against the January frost. 'A bad hunt, then, was it, Miss Maeve?' He doffed his cap.

'Yes, bad, Mick, bad.' She scarcely stopped running, was aware of him staring after her. Pray God Kieran is there, pray God Kieran is there . . . Her heart was beating loudly in her ears. She stumbled and nearly fell.

He was in the yard sitting on a stool with Blackthorn's hoof on his knee. He looked up and his eyes were so full

11

of love when he saw her that she had to prevent herself from rushing into his arms. 'Maeve!' He must have seen the alarm in her face. 'What is it?' He got up.

'Did Sean speak to you?' She tried to signal a warning with her eyes. Peters could be skulking a few yards away.

'He didn't get time, the poor little runt. Peters whipped him away by the ear and told him to take the barrow to the dung-heap.' He took a step towards her, his eyes anxious. 'Something's happened, hasn't it? Peters looked . . .'

She put her finger to her lips, glanced towards the stable half-door. 'I've got to see you . . . *not in Crow Wood*.' She whispered the last words. 'Yes, something dreadful has happened. We've got to meet, to talk. Where? Think, Kieran . . .'

Peters was suddenly at her elbow. He moves as quietly as that fox that got away, she thought, sliding in and out of the shadows. She raised her chin, stared at him.

'Now, Miss Maeve, you know what your father said about you coming to the stables.'

'Mind your own business, Peters,' she said. 'I'm finding out what made Blackthorn lame.' She stood, tapping her foot, staring him out until he shrugged and went back to the harness room. She turned quickly to Kieran. '*Where*? Have you thought?' He was white, as if the enormity of the situation had just struck him.

'He said . . . I've to wait here till the Major sees me . . . after dinner.'

'Making you wait. That's cruel. No, he *mustn't* see you, not till we talk. We have to plan . . .' She was half-crying in her agitation.

'Listen.' He nodded once, then spoke softly and quickly. 'I've thought of a place. Halfway down the drive a path runs off it. It's marked by a fir but it's difficult to

12

see. The undergrowth hides it. I was looking for rabbits once when I . . .' she interrupted him.

'Yes, I know it. That'll do. When does Peters go for his tea?'

'In half-an-hour. It'll be dark then.'

'Half-an-hour. I'll be there.' She wanted to cling to him, to weep with fear in his arms. Instead she said in a loud voice for Peters' benefit, 'I hope I'll be able to ride Blackthorn tomorrow, McGrath.' She touched Kieran's hand with her own, met his eyes, then walked quickly away. She would stay in Mairi's kitchen until it was time. Father would never dare speak to her in front of the maids; his pride would not let him.

And Peters was too cowardly to tackle Kieran himself. He had hated him ever since Kieran had taken the whip out of his hand when he had come upon him beating Sean. The boy had been his willing slave since then – Sean at least had loyalties.

She sat amongst the clutter of Mairi's big kitchen table, drinking the cup of tea the old woman had poured out for her.

'Time you was upstairs having your bath, Miss Maeve.' The old woman bustled around her. 'You shouldn't sit about in those wet clothes. And look at your hair with the damp! All that nice red colour's gone from it.'

'Where are Mama and Papa, Mairi?'

'Closeted upstairs in the drawing-room, Deirdre tells me. Ructions. Himself's pacing about, herself's weeping. Not to be disturbed till dinner-time, the word goes.'

'I'll just drink this . . .' She sat, waiting for her heart to stop battering against her ribs. They would have to get away. She thought of Kieran, of coming across him in the yard just now, his curly head bent over Blackthorn's foot, thought how often it had rested on her breast in the old

13

shack in Crow Wood. All summer, creeping from her bedroom when the house was quiet, the terror and the wonder. It was over, over . . .

'My, what a sigh that was,' Mairi said, chopping up vegetables for the soup beside her. 'And is it those old onions that are making your eyes water?'

She moaned again, softly, sitting at the window of her bedroom. Not time yet. Not yet. If only Papa had not come down the drive that night! Perhaps Mama had had hysterics and he had wanted to get away from her. So she had thought at the time, but now, in her cold bedroom, she knew the truth. They had not been careful enough, Peters had overheard them in the stable yard and gone straight to his master. A flame of anger shot through her. I could murder him, she thought, twisting her hands.

What did it matter now? In spite of her quick temper she could plan, too, when the need arose. And pretend. Mama had thought she had given in, that she was ready to go to Aunt Maud's in Dublin tomorrow morning. Her trunk was packed. She looked at it standing near the door, ready for Mick to carry down in the morning, at the canvas bag by her feet, into which she had put a change of clothing. There would be no need for fine clothes where she was going, but at the last moment she had rolled up her new blue ball-gown and somehow managed to stuff it in. She had a moment's regret for the violet crinoline in the trunk, and its matching poke bonnet trimmed with violets. 'That will let Maud see that we know how to dress for Dublin,' Mama had said when she had been supervising the packing.

At least I've got my Brussels lace shawl, she thought. Her fingers caressed it for a moment under the heavy woollen one she was wearing, felt its soft silkiness.

It had been that bull terrier of Papa's, a sharp, sly

14

beast, like Peters, sniffing amongst the dead leaves, then breaking into a frenzy of barking when it discovered them behind the laurels. 'Keep quiet, Murphy!' she had whispered, agonized. The next second she had heard her father crashing through the bushes.

Would she ever forget his face as long as she lived, the darkness of it? It would have shown surging red with blood, she knew, if the moon had been able to penetrate the trees. He had stared at them, eyes bulging, unable to speak for a second, then the words had spilled out like an avalanche, like the Boyle itself in spate.

'My God! Come out of there! The blazing effrontery of it! A few yards from my own front door!' He was possessed with anger. He lifted his stick wildly, Kieran's arm went up to protect her, and the stick smashed down on his arm. He doubled up over it, his face twisted, and the dog threw itself at him, snarling.

'You've hurt him!' She was sobbing, distraught. 'Call off Murphy, Papa, please!'

'Hurt him! Hurt him, she says! You should count yourself lucky that I don't shoot him like the dog he is! Are you mad, miss? Cowering in the bushes with a stable boy . . . when you could have had James Tynan!'

'I told you I hate James Tynan! Call off Murphy!' Her voice was almost drowned by the furious barking of the dog. 'He only obeys you! Oh, call him off!' She heard herself wailing, saw Kieran trying to protect his injured arm as the dog flung itself at him again and again.

'When it suits me. I want to know what you have to say for yourself, McGrath.' He turned to Kieran. 'I could hardly believe my ears when . . . not so bold now, I see.'

'We love each other. We want to . . .' He swayed on his feet and she put her arm around him.

'Let me help him to the stables, please, Papa,

15

please . . .' The dog's incessant barking was piercing her ears, making it impossible to think.

'It's too late to plead with me, my girl. Take yourself off to your room this instant. We have something to discuss, this miserable . . . this *stable*-boy and I.'

'Go, for the love of God,' Kieran muttered, pulling himself away from her. She stood for a moment, looking at his bowed head, how he clutched his arm out of reach of the dog's still furious onslaughts, then turned from them and ran sobbing through the laurels, tearing her hands on the brambles, pulling her dress roughly free when it became entangled. The tears were running down her face, half in terror, half in self-pity. I'm not able to cope with this, she said to herself as she stumbled up the broad staircase to her room . . . but she knew she was. She bathed her face and dried her hair with a towel, and its colour sprang at her in the mirror, a rich dark red.

Sometimes, lying in the shack in Crow Wood, they had talked about running away to get married. 'We'll have to make plans,' she had said. 'If Papa ever found out about us, he'd half-kill you. When he loses his temper he's like a madman. And Mama's no help. All she'll do is have hysterics and beat her heels on the floor. She'd do the same for Waterford glasses that didn't arrive in time for a party. I've seen her.'

He had been so innocent. 'Let me go to your father. I'll tell him we're in love.'

'Will you stop talking as if you've taken leave of your senses?' She'd put her hand over his mouth. 'I told you, he'd half-kill you, and where should I be then and me loving you so much?'

'Then, let us run away to Dublin,' he had said.

'Dublin, is it now? That's not nearly far enough away. And doesn't my father know every corner of Dublin and

16

him a Trinity man?' And then, as she had looked at his beautiful face above hers, her sharpness had left her and she was weak with desire. 'Yes, I'd run away with you to the ends of the earth.'

'Would Scotland be far enough? The far side, it is.' He had smiled confidently. 'I'd get work there. I'd put a lamp on my head and go down into the bowels of the earth and hew coal.'

'But you're never off the back of a horse! What would you be knowing about hewing coal?'

'Well, I could look after the pit ponies. Would that suit your ladyship?' His hands had been tender on her.

I'm leaving my childhood, she thought, looking round the familiar room, as well as my parents, everything familiar to my life. If only Terence were here to talk to. For a bleak moment she saw clearly into the future. What would it hold for her if they went to Scotland, to the far side as Kieran called it? A poor sort of place, she had heard, all pits and folks working down them, or rearing mountains that would put the fear of God in you. And where she would be unknown as Major Muldoon's daughter of Woodlea. Would she come to regret it?

Kieran had some money saved and they would not be the first to leave Ireland. Many had gone away in the last few years because of the potato famine, but not people like the Muldoons. He had told her often of his Scottish relatives and the village where they lived. It was on the banks of the Sholtie Burn, he said, a tributary of the Clyde, pretty in itself, but in the middle of the mining area. He thought his uncle and cousins worked down the pits or in the ironworks nearby. He was vague when it came to details. The Clyde Valley, he said, was the place to be now, with all that work going on, making iron and steel for the great ships being built on the Clyde, hewing

17

coal for the foundries. He spoke with a countryman's innocent awe. His uncle had been a carter to begin with; horses were in the McGrath blood. He was sure there would be plenty of jobs going, not like here where the only thing was to work at the Big House, or go away.

But what sort of life would *she* have? It would not be like this where she had never done a hand's turn, had even been forbidden the kitchen when her mother had found her there rolling pastry under Mairi's tuition.

'But I want to know how things are done, Mama,' she had said.

'There will be no need for that. That's cook's job. Your place is in the drawing-room with me.'

'But I don't *like* sitting there like a stuffed hen, waiting for callers, and embroidering . . .'

'It's not what you like, it's what is expected of you. You're a lady. In Dublin . . .'

Young ladies were not expected to express opinions, they were there to look pretty, learn how to order servants about, sew, play the piano, sing duets with young men, and ride well. Papa had spoken sharply to her at the dinner table. 'Your mother tells me you're never out of the kitchen or the stables. I won't have you consorting with the lower orders.'

'They're human beings, too,' she had said. 'Besides, I want to learn things. You've taught me to ride, but Mama doesn't know anything about cooking, and I like it, just as I like to clean tackle and look after the horses.'

Mama had put up her hands in horror. 'Patrick! You must forbid her the stables! She'll pick up loose talk there, or worse!'

He had glowered at her. There was no love between them – Maeve had known that for a long time. Her sympathies were mostly with her father. 'There's some-

18

thing in what the girl says. We'd starve if old Mairi dropped dead tomorrow. You lie most of the day in that bedroom of yours, having the vapours about one damn' thing or another . . . now, don't start weeping, for God's sake!'

'There's nothing to get up for in this hole. In Dublin . . .'

'Ah, yes, Dublin. We've heard all that before.' He waved his hand, dismissing her. 'As for the stables,' he had looked sternly at Maeve, 'you're forbidden them from now on.'

'If I were your son instead of your daughter you wouldn't say that!' She knew how to wound him.

'Keep your brother out of it!' He had never got over Terence going off to America – it was five years ago now. And why would he ever want to come back, now that he had met and married a rich American girl called Caroline Grant? 'You're a young lady, not a young gentleman, and that is why you may not go to the harness room. You must only go to the stables when you wish to ride Blackthorn. If you disobey me, I'll stop you riding altogether.'

'Oh, no, Papa!' Not to ride Blackthorn would be unbearable. Was there anything more wonderful than clattering out of the stable yard in the early morning, along the road with the sun slanting in bars across it, making for the fields and the woods? The world at that time of day was new, fresh, the Curlew Mountains shrouded in mist. Her love of being alive and love of the land would envelop her, and she would urge Blackthorn to a gallop as if the soaring sensation could not be contained.

'I see that makes you think. Better seat than I have myself . . .' His face softened. 'You'll find a young man

19

who'll admire that in you, a man of your own kidney. But not in the stables. Remember your place. Treat them as servants and they'll treat you as their mistress.'

She had tossed her head but had not dared to reply. He was thinking of James Tynan, of course, that chinless skinny-malink! But she knew she had gone far enough. If he found out about Kieran, or even began to be suspicious, he was capable of thrashing him the way he thrashed the dogs. Kieran had not believed her.

I hate my father, she thought. He thinks dogs and servants are his property, to be treated in the same way. *And* sons and daughters. She remembered overhearing as a young girl the rows between him and Terence, how she had hidden her head under the blankets. If Terence and I hadn't crossed him, she thought, it would have been all right. But who wanted to be mamby-pamby like those awful Tynans?

And yet she felt a reluctant tenderness for him. He was an unhappy man. It permeated everything he did, showed in the grim lines of his face. Papa and Mama don't love each other, she thought. It's a loveless home. That's what drove Terence away, as well as the constant rows; is driving me away because Kieran can give me love. I can surround us with love, and the family we might have.

She peered out of the window. How cold and dark it was, the heavy branches swaying in the wind, the mountains hidden. Beyond them and across the sea there was an unknown country which was to be her home. She could never love it as much as Ireland which was in her bones, every square green mile of it, but there was no going back now.

Ever since that terrible happening behind the laurels she seemed to have only one friend in the house, old Mairi. Deirdre had been forbidden to speak to her and

Mama had been in bed with a sick headache for two days, of no use to herself or anyone else. 'Go away, you wicked girl,' she had said when Maeve had offered to fetch her a warm drink, 'as if I hadn't enough to contend with.' She had turned her face to the wall. There was a sour smell from her.

'You have to know this, girl.' Mairi had toiled up the stairs to her room where she was now confined by Papa's orders. 'And you won't like it. Kieran's been horse-whipped by the Major.'

She had sprung to her feet. 'That's why I'm locked up here! He knew I'd go to him if I heard. Oh, Mairi, I can't bear it! To whip him, to . . . insult him and humiliate him like that . . . oh, my heart's breaking!' She had put her face in her hands.

'Come to old Mairi.' She had taken her in her arms. 'That's right. Cry it out.'

'But he couldn't have done! Kieran would never let him!'

'Peters held him down, Sean is for telling me.'

'Oh, he's evil, that one, a slimy creeping toad of a man. That's what I call him to myself, Mairi.'

'Maybe so. Sean said the lad uttered never a word, but the blood was running from his lip where he'd bitten into it.'

'Where is he now?' She raised her face. 'I'm going to him! Where is he, Mairi?'

'Now, don't you go making matters worse than they are. He's locked up in the old tack room above the stables. Sure, and it's a prison this place is coming to. Sean's looking after him, slipping him nice bits of food from the kitchen. Like this nice custard I'm after bringing to you.'

She waved it away impatiently. 'What about his family?

21

Why didn't they try to stop this . . . this outrage?' She put her face in her hands again, feeling the hot tears against them.

'There now, cushla. It's a terrible thing for Mr McGrath, sure enough, and him a proud man.'

'Well, why didn't he come and *see* Papa?' She raised her head. 'Stand up to him?' She had to speak defiantly to hide her terror.

'It's not so easy. He'd be out on his ear without a house, and his wife and family depending on him. It belongs to the Major. Someone like you, brought up in a fine place like this, can't understand. Now put the whole matter out of your head and eat this fine custard. There's cream as well.'

'Don't treat me like a child with your custard! Take it away,' she said, 'I'll never eat again!'

Mairi lifted the tray. 'Like Master Terence, you are. Too high-spirited for your own good, a real Muldoon.' She sighed. 'Or maybe himself hasn't the touch . . . ach, I'm too old for all this bother.'

'Oh, Mairi.' She had flung herself into the old woman's arms again. 'I'm so unhappy. I can't bear to think of Kieran, hurt . . .'

'Don't you worry yourself about Kieran. Sure, it's no worse than a fall from a horse. He's a right strong lad. There'll be nothing but a few bruises.'

'But I love him, love him . . .'

'You should have known better, then, stepping out of your class.' She stroked Maeve's hair. 'That's what caused the damage.'

'He might be descended from the Kings of Ireland for all you know,' she said through her tears. 'His father has it all worked out. Don't talk about something you know nothing about, you old fool.'

'Fool, is it? My, but you've got the devil in you, right enough! A good slice of the Muldoon temper. But think on this, Miss. It's Kieran that's doing the suffering for your misdeeds.'

'I felt every blow as you told me! If I could have got the blood to run from *my* lip I would! I'm sorry I shouted at you, Mairi. I love him, love him. No one will believe me. Why does no one believe me?' She flung herself on her bed, sobbing.

'Because it's not natural for a fine young lady like yourself to take up with a groom of her father's.'

'Someday it won't matter. I'm so miserable! And I'm being packed off to Aunt Maud's in Dublin. Everyone persists in treating me like a child and I'm a woman, with a woman's feelings. Kieran and I belong to each other. There will never be anyone else for me.' Old Mairi had gone away, shaking her head. She had heard the key turning in the lock.

When Sean came in at night with the logs for her fire he had a note from Kieran. She snatched it from him, tore open the envelope. The words danced in front of her for a moment.

'I'm feeling fine now,' she read. 'No permanent damage done. Will you meet me at two in the morning at the foot of the drive? We'll be off to Scotland as we always planned. But only if you are willing, my love, remember. It seems I've brought you enough trouble. I'll understand if you say no.'

She said, looking up, 'Will you say yes to Kieran?' It would be safer not to write.

'I will that, Miss Maeve. That'll make him better quicker than anything else, though I've been rubbing horse liniment on his back every night.'

'Are you the only one who's seen him?'

23

'Except for Tommy, the ostler. There was something he needed to know from Kieran about one of the horses and Mr Peters said I could take him up. They had a long talk.'

She nodded calmly. 'Thank you, Sean. Now, go off and tell Kieran.' My clever Kieran, she thought. He'll have to ask Tommy to arrange horses for us. Yes, she was sure.

Mama had paid her a visit, her eyes wretched, great black holes in her face, her puffy cheeks powdered. 'What trouble you've brought on us with your wickedness! You *and* your brother. What have I done to deserve it? I can't stand it any more. I'll go back to Dublin. Your Papa goes on and on about the family name and I can't get a wink of sleep. On and on . . . my poor head!' She put her handkerchief to her eyes. 'And now he wants to know . . .' The sunken eyes raised to Maeve's brought a wave of pitying love to her for a second. Pour soul . . .

'What does he want to know, Mama?' She tried to speak gently.

'Why it should be *me* who should ask you, I can't think . . . he wants to know . . . if you're . . . you're . . . Oh, it isn't fair to put this on me with this drumming head of mine . . . If you and this stable lad . . . if you're . . . well, it's ridiculous, of course . . . going to have his child?'

'No, I'm not!' Her pity went, her temper flared. 'And if I were he'd *have* to let me marry Kieran!'

'Ah, that's where you're wrong, miss.' Her mother's chin lifted. 'Oh, dear no, put that notion out of your head! He'd pack you off to Dublin and get rid of it. He's done that before . . .'

'With Nellie, you mean?'

'Oh, your father's right! You have low tastes, listening to the tittle-tattle in the kitchen about a servant who gets herself into trouble with a married man in the village. It's

24

not suitable for your ears at all. Concentrate on your own disgrace, allowing yourself to become infatuated with a stable boy, and you Major Muldoon's daughter.'

'A *groom*, Mama.'

'They're all the same, smelling of horses and sweating into their shirts. Horrible talk about covering, and things like that. And those peasants in the village. You wouldn't get Phoebe Tynan consorting with people like that.'

'Because she's a worm like her brother!' she shouted, beside herself. 'Sidling about on their stomachs, ingratiating themselves with you and Papa. I'd rather die than marry into that family!'

She had wept bitterly when her mother went away. What luxury it would have been to confide in her, but that had never been possible. Everything always gave her a headache. 'If you knew the tenderness I feel for Kieran,' she would have said, 'you would intercede with Papa. It is his tenderness rather than his passion that has always overwhelmed me. Do you know, Mama, sometimes I feel I could die in his arms.'

But it's true what my father says, she thought again. And what's the matter with that, pray? I love Mairi, and I loved my old nurse, Kate, and Deirdre and Jenny, and Nellie who went away so quickly, poor soul, a married man in the village, and Mick and Kevin in the garden and the stable lads, Pat and Sean. And Kieran, my Kieran. I've always liked the lower orders as Papa calls them, because they've shown me kindness and love.

Once, when she and Kieran had talked about being married he had said that maybe, if they were frank with the Major, he would accept him. Now that Master Terence was in America, he could take his place and help Papa with the running of the farms and so on. 'We'd all

25

settle down together nicely,' he had said. She had laughed at him, loving him.

Kieran was a great believer in the settling down processes of the world. Sometimes she thought he was almost too equable, that he did not have a grasp of how other people's minds worked, that everyone thought well of everyone else. But then he had not had her advantages – a governess since she was five, then a tutor from England for Latin and French. Richard had said she had a good mind, had given her books to read, history and the like, plays by Molière and Racine. If she had not fallen in love with Kieran, maybe she would have become a blue stocking and travelled abroad. Maybe become a Trinity woman, if they had allowed it.

'Well, then,' he had said when she laughed at him, 'I could leave and get a good job with my cousin who works in the racing stables in County Meath. And when I'm rich and the owner of a fine horse that's running at the Curragh, I'll come back again and ask for your hand.'

He had never quite believed her that even if he won the Gold Cup her father would never agree to them being married. He had never been able to envisage, as she could, the depth of her father's anger, the insult it would be to him. He felt no inferiority. His skill lay in his hands, and sure to God didn't she know that, she who could thrill to the marrow just sitting here imagining his touch on her body.

Well, now he would believe her. She was glad she had not seen that beating. When her father had whipped a hound that had run away – steadily, remorselessly, as if he was getting rid of all his resentment against life on the poor beast – she had run screaming out of the yard, her hands over her ears.

My mind is more complex than Kieran's, she thought,

although he is four years older than I am. It was strange to be sitting in her bedroom in the middle of the night and thinking like this, as if she had never given herself time before. Maybe if she had . . . no, it was too late for thoughts like that. Besides, it was a different thing from loving him, and she would always do that.

But I have a greater sophistication. It could be a question of breeding. Was that what was in the back of her father's mind? He was passionate about their ancestry, just as he was passionate about the ancestry of horses. He would travel miles over Ireland to find the right stallion for a mare; no fair or show was too far. But then, she remembered, Kieran believes he's as good as us, if not better, that he was here before us.

I'm born out of my time, she thought, with the clarity of finality, of knowing that the die was cast. Someday it would be easier and men would listen to women. Terence had said in a letter that it was not the same in America, that everybody was as good as his neighbour. Caroline did not go on about her southern background the way father had done. 'It's a relief to be out of that rain-sodden, class-ridden West of Ireland,' he had written.

And yet, even if Kieran was as good as she was, she had scorned the idea of living with his family in their overcrowded cottage. That had been Kieran's third plan, and she had laughed most at that. That surly, proud father of his, she had thought, and his mother who would want to wipe the chair for her every time she sat down. He did not seem to understand that they would resent her . . .

What peculiar thoughts I'm having. She moved in her chair at the window. And wasn't it 'interesting' to be sitting here with all these thoughts going through her head? That was the word Richard had used. 'You'll find this an "interesting" book, Miss Maeve . . .' There would be no time for books in far-off Scotland. That was another world. Richard's world, one of the intellect. She would have liked to know it.

Once, long ago, when Papa had been in a soft mood, he had talked about their ancestry. They had been sitting at the crackling fire in the hall after a hunt that had gone well. The dogs were stretched on the black and white tiles. Through the arched window at the side of the fireplace she could see the greenness.

She knew she was taking Terence's place for him. 'Our family goes back a long way, Maeve. King James brought us from the Scottish Lowlands – we were gentry there, too – and gave us the land here. He thought we'd be able to skip about the bogs as well as the Irish.'

'When was that, Papa?' she had asked.

'At the beginning of the seventeenth century. All that time back. This land is in my bones. You can see why I want the best for it, and for you, always.'

'But you must have displaced someone who was here already?'

'There are those who think so.' He did not seem perturbed. 'I expect some would be ordered to quit, some would settle down somewhere or other, some might even have been here. Peasants.' He had laughed. 'I dare say there are those who bear a grudge against us.'

She had told Kieran. 'My father does, for one,' he had said quickly. 'He says the land around here is as much his as your father's.'

'Then, when we're rich and married somewhere we'll come back and buy it off him,' she had said.

She knew he loved his country with an even deeper love than hers although he never talked about the wrench it would be for him to leave it. He had a better feeling for nature than she had. He could describe a bird on the wing

28

or the hares leaping on the high fields, or the feeling at full gallop when you were stretched along the neck of a horse, and make his words seem like poetry.

Before she was forbidden the stables she had heard him sing often as he groomed the horses, not through his teeth like the other lads, but with proper words, some of them lilting, like 'Phil the Fluter's Ball', or plaintive: 'Oh, the Sound of the Kerry Dancers . . .' She had said to him later in Crow Wood, 'When we have our own house you'll sing to me all your songs. We'll teach our children to sing them, too, and it'll remind them of where their parents came from.'

It would be all right. They would go to Scotland and make their fortune in the dark satanic mills (she was pleased she remembered that phrase from her reading), and some day they would come back here. And they would keep it alive in their hearts. They would talk of the Curlew Mountains which were a different colour every day, and of their early morning rides when the frost was sharp in their nostrils; and of how, in the warm wet summers, the mountains disappeared in the mists rising from the river, so that you could believe in the old Irish tales of a far country beckoning you and that if you gave in to the beckoning, you would never come back.

Kieran liked the autumn best – the golden days, he called them – when the colours flamed like her hair. When they were rich, he promised, he would buy her a warm, golden velvet gown. 'But truth to tell,' he said, kissing her, 'although I've loved every day of my life here, I'd give it all up willingly for you.' Who would not give up the world for a man like that? Or Ireland?

The house was silent. Nearly two o'clock now. 'Remember and look out for the light,' Sean had said. 'And I'll slip up and unlock your door when Mairi's gone

29

to sleep.' She had not heard its soft click. Perhaps she had been too busy thinking.

'And how will Kieran get away?' she had asked. 'Peters isn't as daft as old Mairi.'

'Sure and isn't he the grand climber out of the windows?' the boy had said, 'and isn't it strange that there will just happen to be a ladder leaning against the wall?' She had laughed and patted his shoulder.

'When we get settled we'll send for you, Sean.'

'You'll not find me, Miss Maeve.' He had shaken his head. 'When Kieran goes, I go. There will be nothing for me here.' His face was white and pinched, closed-looking. At the door he had turned and said, 'Good luck to you both, you and Kieran.'

She listened again. Still silence. Everyone would now be sleeping soundly, the deep sleep before dawn. In a couple of hours the stable boys would be going about their duties; old Mairi would be lighting the kitchen fire and grumbling about her stiff knees as she always did; Deirdre would be setting out pretty trays for Papa and Mama; Jenny would be sweeping down the broad steps and one of the gardeners would be raking the gravel.

Morning in the kitchen had been the best time, before the family came down. Deirdre would give her a knock as she came running down from the attic, and she would not be long after her, dressing quickly and sweeping up her long hair with her hands to pin it on top of her head.

What good times she had had there, chatting to the stable lads as they came in for a sup of tea, laughing with Deirdre and Jenny as they stirred the porridge over the big hot range. And yet she had been a young lady when it suited her, leaving them, without an apology, to make a decorous entry into the dining-room, helping herself to breakfast from the silver dishes on the sideboard, sitting down quietly, listening to her father's talk about the new hunter he had bought, her mother's tittle-tattle (if she were there at all) of the balls at Dublin they were missing by being buried at Woodlea. Sometimes her father would look at her and smile, as if they shared a secret.

Tears rushed to her eyes. I'll miss him, she thought, even if he did thrash Kieran. On one level I know it was a terrible thing to do, but I understand him, his disappointment in Terence, and me, and how mother has never given him any support, or love. I understand his love of Woodlea and the horses, most of all his desire to be liked, under his short temper and lashing tongue. Nothing he has done has ever pleased Mama . . . Oh, she thought, the confusion there is in me, the sorrow for what I'm doing to them, as well as the determination, and the fear . . .

She sobbed her heart out, then she wiped her eyes, drew herself straight and sat quietly. When she saw the light moving in the drive she wrapped her cloak round her, lifted the canvas bag and stole softly downstairs. The key in the big door turned easily. Old Mick kept the locks well oiled and the clocks wound up. Papa was in the habit of standing in front of that long-case one every morning, checking his own watch by it . . .

She closed the door quietly behind her, ran down the steps and along the drive, keeping in the shadow of the laurel bushes. In five minutes she was in Kieran's arms. There was no confusion in her mind now.

2

Last night Kieran had spread newspapers systematically over the flagged floor of the kitchen. He had scrubbed it with a handful of washing soda in the water to make it soft. Maeve had laughed at him, lying swollen-bellied in the box bed, laughed because she was close to tears. 'You'd think you were back in the stables at Woodlea, all this scrubbing. Only it was straw there, not paper.'

'I've been a good midwife to many a mare, mavourneen.' And seeing her pouting mouth, 'No offence intended. Come on, it's a joke.' He had laughed with her, aware of her tears. He was afraid, too. 'There's an art in it, though, gentle coaxing, but firm. It goes through your hands to them, the reassurance. They trust you, that's the great thing about it. There are some words that are full of meaning, like trust, some empty words like . . . consolation. Consolation's a smarmy word, one of old Murdoch's at the kirk here.'

'I'm sure Dymphna and Kathleen and Philomel and all the others felt safe with you,' she had said, 'a lot safer than they ever did with Peters. Once I saw him dragging a foal from its mother. Papa had taken me to the stables, saying I was old enough now. I was horrified. Peters' face was red, bursting with frustration. He was cursing, "You mucky bitch, get on with it . . ." "Moderate your language in front of a young lady," Papa said to him. Peters threw me that sly, malicious look of his as he pulled and tugged. I still remember those red, cruel hands, red with the poor mare's blood . . .' She had shuddered, laughed again, 'All the same, I'm glad Mrs Lambie is going to be here tomorrow.'

That had been last night, she thought now, when she *could* laugh, when it seemed this thing was happening to another girl, not the late Miss Maeve Muldoon of Woodlea in the County of Roscommon, not even that young Irishwoman, Mrs McGrath, of 4, Colliers' Row, Sholton, Lanarkshire, Scotland.

But about four o'clock in the morning the fingers of reality had clutched her by the throat, then gathered her entrails together in a cruel grip, and she had been very frightened indeed. She had shaken Kieran from his heavy sleep, shaken him and shaken him, frantic with fear. He had been working double shifts down the pit to get a few extra pennies to buy clothes for the coming baby. He was always tired. His face in the dim light had been worn, hollow-cheeked, like an older man. He did not get enough to eat, pretended that he was not hungry these days . . .

'Kieran, it's begun!' I'm still only seventeen, she had thought. I should be studying the plays of Racine with Richard of the soft voice from England, going up to Dublin to balls with Mama, riding with the hunt. It was bafflement that she felt, even more than the reality. How in God's name had she landed herself into this? What was that force which had been strong enough to sweep her away from home nine months ago to this grim place, her taut slim figure gone, a child from this man inside her, struggling madly to get out?

He was out of bed in an instant, pulling on his trousers, and her bafflement went. This was Kieran, her lover, her husband. Everything about him she loved, the springing curls, the curving sweetness of his mouth, the way he held his head, the gentleness you felt when he met your eyes, the knowledge that he felt *her* pain, *her* bafflement, as if his heart beat with hers. 'Shall I get Mrs Cairns in from next door while I go for the guidwife?'

'No, no!' She did not like Mrs Cairns' suspicious looks, nor most of the other women, come to that: Mrs Haddow, the thin, shrewish one, Beenie Drummond, the fat one who giggled inanely behind her hand, hardly one single soul of them. The children she liked, feeling often like a child herself. 'Get on your way. I'll be all right.' She grimaced with a sudden sword-thrust of pain.

'Oh, my love . . .' His face mirrored her agony.

'Go on with you! But be sure and bring her back. I'll feel safer then.'

When he had gone she got up and walked gingerly about the room, terrified, and yet jubilant in a strange way. She had always liked a challenge – putting Black-thorn to a high fence, swimming far out at Louth when they visited Aunt Maud, and causing her to have scream-ing hysterics from her safe bench on the green cap of the cliffs. 'Maeve, Maeve, come out of there this instant!' She had directed the waddling woman in charge of the bathing cabins to wade out and shout to her. 'Miss, Miss! Your aunt's after taking a fit!'

You have to pay for loving, she told herself, feeling ungainly and unsteady, walking flat-footed, toes turned out like the waddling woman in charge of the bathing cabins. Maybe if she crouched down on the floor, like the animals did . . .

She was still there when Kieran came back and he went to her immediately. 'In the name of God, Maeve, what are you doing out of your bed?'

'I thought it would be better if I moved around. I once read that the natives just dropped their babies in the forest.' She smiled – hoped it was a smile. 'I was trying it out . . .'

34

'You're soaking with sweat, and you're shivering.' He put an arm round her shoulders and pushed her hair tenderly back from her brow, but she impatiently shook herself free.

'Where's Mrs Lambie? If you were doing your job properly you would have brought her back with you!' She was shrill, shrewish, a new Maeve, divorced from him by the vice that gripped her.

'She had to step out. A premature child, it seems. Mr Lambie said you could hear the pour soul howling a mile away. She'll be with you as soon as she can.'

'The nerve of it!' Anger choked her. 'I can't believe it! I came first! Didn't you tell her that?' 'You'll have to mind that temper of yours,' old Mairi used to say. '*We* did it properly. We warned her it was due. We worked it out, remember, and it's started when I said. I'm first! Didn't you tell her that?'

'How could I tell her that when she wasn't there at all?'

'You should have gone to the woman's house where she was, told her I'd started, that I was waiting . . .' She suddenly stopped as the vice tightened, felt her face screw up, the cold rush of air through her lips. The wail did not belong to her. It was high, like a female cat in the bushes of the drive at Woodlea. 'Oh, God, oh, God!' she screamed. 'What am I doing here? What have I let myself into?' She felt rushing wetness between her legs, felt Kieran's hand on her, pushing her down. The newspapers rustled and crackled under her. There was a slope on the floor and he rushed and got a cushion, put it under her head, put another one under her hips.

'Raise your legs,' he said. She looked at him through pain-filled eyes.

'Oh, Kieran . . .' She turned her head away, seventeen, shy.

35

'Raise your legs!' His voice was stern. 'Let them fall apart. There's the clean sheet you had ready under you now. We'll have to do without Mrs Lambie. Maybe we're better without her. If you'd seen the state of her place . . .' He had left her, was washing his hands at the basin. She heard the black hiss of the kettle as he poured boiling water from it. And then he was back on the floor beside her, pulling down the sheet he had covered her with, gently. 'Who better than your husband? I can share your pain. Don't bite your lip so hard. You're spoiling your pretty mouth. Howl your head off. The walls are thick . . .' His voice went on softly, calming her.

'Do you remember that sweet little foal Philomel had? A little beauty, pale blonde and a white star on her forehead? And Philomel, so trusting, calm, helping herself, helping me, as if she remembered those rides we'd had over the hills and Sligo Bay gleaming in the distance . . .'

The aftermath of the pains was like the trough of a wave; Kieran's voice had a smoothing, swinging, anaesthetic effect. She drifted back to Woodlea, to Mairi's kitchen; saw the grainy bleached surface of the huge table, heard the slap, slap of her wooden spoon in the batter for the drop scones for tea, saw the drawing-room with its needle-worked chairs and its swagged mantelpiece and its air of not being a lived-in room. Mama gave that air to everywhere she inhabited, or haunted.

Now she was in the panelled dining-room and sitting across from her father. She saw the silver covers on the sideboard behind his head, saw the contrast between his alert face and her mother's drooping one – drooping curls under the muslin cap she wore in the mornings, drooping eyelids, mouth, drooping beringed fingers crumbling her toast. 'I didn't sleep a wink last night. My head . . .'

Heard her father's brisk tones after the cold glance, 'Ready for the meet, Maeve?'

And Crow Wood. The close, dark greenness of their meeting-place, the strength of Kieran's arms. Was it there this baby had been started? There had been that time lying close together when he had . . . and she had not stopped him . . . but it had not been 'altogether'. That was the word she had used to herself. Or the first night in Scotland, when they had slept in the cold attic under Kieran's uncle's roof, on the understanding that it was only for one night? It had been 'altogether' then, again and again and again, the desperation of their loving and the ecstasy and the sureness that she had done the right thing . . .

Kieran's voice came to her. 'I fell in love with you that day you came to see Philomel's foal. Your hair was a thick red plait and it swung over your shoulder as you bent to fondle her. Your eyes were the deepest, darkest blue when you raised them to me, mountain lough blue, and you said in that decided voice of yours, even at fourteen, "We'll call her Philomela, Kieran, and she'll be mine!" '

Tears came into her eyes at the innocent happiness of that day, tears of self-pity and homesickness, for the green fields, the warm stables, for the beauty of her life there compared with the grey grimness here, the meanness and the drudgery of it, even when Kieran had got the job down the pit. 'Only till I get time to look round,' he said each week, his face gaunt and pale already with the lack of light, the long hours in the dark, he who loved the open air so much, who wilted with the lack of it. 'Only till I get time to look around,' he had said each month, then stopped saying it as she became big with child.

And always the unfriendliness of the neighbours compared with the deference she was used to as Major Muldoon's daughter. 'You'd think I had two heads,' she had said to Kieran.

'No, my lovely, it's just that the sight of the one you've got is too much for the ugly bitches – that glorious head of hair and the carriage of you. They're bowled over by your beauty. They've never seen the like of you in a month of Sundays. They're grey women long before they're grey-haired.'

He liked to 'get his wind out' as he said, by calling them down, but he had a milder temperament than hers. She saw him touching his cap to the women as they stood at their cottage doors, laughing with the husbands as they clattered down the Row together. Without her he would be liked and accepted in no time. It was the women who resented her, and they passed on their resentment to their husbands. She could tell by their shamefaced looks when she met them.

Kieran's hands were on her. 'You're doing fine.' He was smiling down at her. 'We shan't need the Royal Embrocation . . .'

'And you won't have to blow a pill down my throat.' She was able to smile back.

'That's my Maeve. Push when I press. The two of us together and you'll have that wee soul lying on the *North British Mail* in two shakes of a lamb's tail.'

'Get your hands off me!' *Groom*, she thought. She was ugly-mouthed in the sudden new onslaught of pain, and then, as she felt the damp cloth on her forehead as he gently wiped it, she turned her lips to meet his hand, 'Oh, my poor love, what am I doing to you?'

'It's what I did to *you*. If I could bear this for you, do anything to share it with you . . .'

'Then stop blaming yourself.' She was clear-headed for

38

a second. 'You always want to take the blame. It's our baby. We made it. We can't go back now, so we'd better get on with it.'

Then it was a whirlwind of pain, of flailing arms, Kieran's anguished face close to hers, his hands on her; once she was aware that they were laughing together, shrieks of laughter, and thought, we've gone mad, crazy, it's this crazy Scotland that's done it to us. We'll have a dead baby, I'll never forgive Kieran, and he'll never forgive himself, it will be the end, the end, the end . . .

Once the pain changed to ecstasy, like a love climax, and she felt she touched God's robe, she who rarely thought of Him, but a new shaft went straight through her, tearing as it went, and all such gentle thoughts, or of Sholton, the people in it, of Woodlea, were obliterated as she was swept out of the quiet trough onto a new, jagged pinnacle of pain. She felt her finger-nails grind against the sinews of Kieran's hand . . . and the pain was gone, like a door shutting.

But it *was* a door shutting. There was a thin mewling in the room; a little parcel of blanket containing something like a kitten was put in her arms and Kieran's lips were on her cheek; then Mrs Lambie's broad Scottish voice was filling the room.

'In the name of God! Scissors, too! and twine! And what's this? Iodine, in a wee blue bottle. My, my, I've never known the like and you a man! Now, get away out of here, Mr McGrath, this instant. It's no' a fit place for you at all. A don't know what the neighbours will think . . .'

They called him Terence, after her brother, although he had the look of Kieran at first. 'A bonny baby,' Mrs Lambie said, examining his limbs professionally, 'and perfect, nothing missing.' And, her face broadening, 'Will you look at the size of his wee toodle! There's no mistakin' he's a laddie all right!'

The neighbours seemed to soften towards her. When she first rolled him in her plaid, passing the other end round her shoulder, under her arm and round the baby again, and ventured out, they came up to her to have a 'wee keek', as they called it. He was a bonny baby, it could not be denied. She was accepted reluctantly, as one who could deliver the goods, who had performed her function in life. She might look different from them, be a bit too colourful for their dreich taste, (she was learning their language), but she could produce a bonny bairn.

It was an outlandish thing for her husband to have helped her with the birthing, but maybe they had been a bit hard on the young couple and they had been feart to ask for help. Aye, all in all, she could be counted as one of them now; and, who could tell? Maybe she would not be so lucky with the next one and then they could come into their own with words of practised consolation. There was nothing quite so satisfying as a good lament round the cottage doors at someone else's misfortune.

But Patrick came quietly, as he lived, a couple of years later, Kate a year after that with no fuss at all. Isobel, three years later, was a difficult birth and a weakly child into the bargain, and the callers with sympathetic nods and shakings of the head quite filled the kitchen with their advice and commiserations.

And filled it again a couple of years later when John arrived. It was as if she had quite lost the art, she thought, because, whereas Isobel, after a shaky start, became a beautiful if fragile little girl, John had a weak chest and tore the heart out of her when he coughed incessantly through the dreary winters. It was then most of all that she longed for the space and lightness of Woodlea.

The cottage was dark and damp, overcrowded now with five children. There was always one between them in the box bed in the kitchen, and one on the makeshift bed on the floor as well. Kieran grew paler, more gaunt, and the colour of her hair dulled and darkened. She was perpetually tired. When she and Kieran made love it was like two different people. The pale-faced, hollow-cheeked man and the thin, tired girl only wanted to sleep.

In 1862, when wee Maeve came, she nearly died. As well as Mrs Lambie in attendance there was the local doctor. She was lucky to be alive. Yet, the wee thing was sturdy, strangely enough, far stronger than her brother, John. There would be no more, the doctor said. When they had all gone she told Kieran, weeping weakly, that he should stick up a notice on their outside door, 'Show Over'.

But Kieran was beyond seeing the joke. He anguished, took the blame on his own shoulders; it made him stoop far more than did the eternal crouching in the pit. Now that he could make love to her without fear, there was no lust left in him, only remorse.

She was the more resilient. It was still there under all the child-bearing, and the penny-pinching and the homesickness. 'Six fine children, Kieran, and you and I still young. Don't forget I need your love as much as you need mine. If it wasn't for that love I'd be back on that boat as quick as my legs could carry me.'

And then she would think, no, I wouldn't. By that time she had given up writing home; her letters had remained unanswered. Her pride, which had made her write cheerfully, belittling the hardships, had kept her from weeping when even the advent of each child was ignored. She was an outcast, disowned like Terence. If she could not make

41

a life for herself here she was finished. Bit by bit she imbued Kieran with her courage, and their new love was of a different kind, more tender; but there was still at times the passion.

3

Maeve McGrath looked up at the clock, the shadow of the pendulum blue on the white-washed wall. Four in the afternoon already. Kieran and Terence would soon be coming in from the pit, and they would want hot water to wash in. The black iron pot was steaming gently on its hook above the fire, its contents ready to be poured into the tin bath in the scullery.

It was Terence's first week down the pit, and he was still bemused by his sudden elevation to a man's status – rising at four in the morning with his father, dressing in the dark, taking his bate and his bottle of cold tea from the kitchen table where Maeve had placed it the night before, clattering down the road in his steel-tipped boots. The first morning she had stood at the door watching them and had waved back when, in a still childish gesture, he had turned round and waved to her.

At fourteen he was as tall as his father, and as handsome, some people said. Secretly Maeve did not think so. Kieran for her was still the young man of twenty-one who had run away with her from Woodlea in far-off Ireland. No wonder their first-born was so head-strong and bursting with life, as if he had been infused with their own early passion.

Standing in her kitchen, dreaming of those days, she felt a surge of regret that Maeve, at three, was the last of the brood. Love such as theirs should have run its proper course; there should still be a child tugging at her breast. But it was only a passing regret. No one in their senses would want to go through that agony again when the afterbirth had broken up in her body and poisoned her blood.

There had been a half-buried acknowledgement of something he had never known in Dr Gray's old eyes. 'But after a while, when you're fully mended, you can resume, er, marital relations.' He had coughed at that and said quickly, 'And how is John's chest these days? Is that liniment I gave you doing any good, do you think?' John, the one who could stir the most tenderness in her because of his uncomplaining temperament and his essential goodness, even as a boy of six. 'I think we're going to have a minister in the family,' she said to Kieran.

But Maeve, the last-born, the Wee Rascal as the rest of the family called her, was a different kettle of fish, spoiled by her brothers and sisters, even by Terence who would lift her and whirl her wildly in his arms, singing like his father, full-throated. She had often said, jokingly, that Kieran and Terence would make a good turn in the penny geggies which came to the village hall in Sholton twice a year; better than their oft-repeated *Maria and the Red Barn Mystery*.

She had never been a mother obsessed by her children. Perhaps the comparatively small difference between her own age and that of her eldest son had made it so. Or perhaps it was because she put Kieran first. You had a husband for ever, children grew up and left you.

Time was getting on, she reminded herself. She must fetch the younger ones. There was the tea to make with two hungry men on her doorstep soon, Terence's face blacker than Kieran's, as if to show he had been down a pit. 'I think you rubbed the coal dust on to impress me,' she had said on his first day. 'Ach, Ma!' He had been sheepish.

Kate had begged after dinner today to take the young ones on a picnic to the Sholton Burn – the Sholtie, as everyone called it. She would take good care of them, she had said, importantly packing a basket with slabs of buttered bread and a bottle of cold tea. Kate was the motherly one of the family, Patrick the quiet one, Isobel the cry-baby, John the delicate one, Maeve . . . the Wee Rascal. She used the name herself (she had a sense of humour even at three), she was roguish, she had dimples in her fat cheeks.

'The devil's in those blue eyes, sure enough,' Kieran would say as she sat on his foot for her nightly ride. 'Off to market, then!' 'Higher, Da, higher!' she would shout. She could wrap her father round her little finger, Maeve often thought.

She swung the pot away from the glowing embers, put a shawl over her red hair and, on an afterthought lifted the clothes rope from its hook on the wall and held it concealed under her apron. She had never used it, but long experience had taught her that a show of strength was useful in dealing with recalcitrance. 'D'you want me to lift down the rope, then?' could be a useful threat. 'You're like Queen Maev herself on the rampage,' Kieran had said to her.

He suffered deeply when the task fell to him to administer punishment. Once, after using the belt on Terence for stealing apples, he had confessed his pain to Maeve. 'It's the shame of it.' He had meant himself. 'Man's inhumanity to man.' She had comforted him, as she had comforted Terence. She was proud of her husband's tenderness, that he could not bear to draw a hen's neck or gut and skin a rabbit. In the hard days when they had first come to Scotland, they would have gone hungry many a time if she had felt the same.

There was his disappointment in his uncle in Sholton, for instance. He and his wife had turned out to be an elderly couple whose children had all left the nest to work in Glasgow. His carting business had been on its last legs. They were sorry, they had said, but this young nephew and his even younger wife would have to fend for themselves. That had been a hard time, sure enough, near to penury, her hands unused to hard work, her knees to getting down on stone floors to scrub them. Only casual labouring for Kieran. He would never know how near she had come to writing to her father and begging his forgiveness, asking for money for her passage home; not to be thought of now with two wages coming in and the children beginning to be off her hands.

She stepped out of the back door between the two rose bushes that Kieran had planted when they had first moved into Colliers' Row. After the heat of the day their smell was overpowering, especially the white one. Even Lady Crawford of the Big House had commented on it when she was taking a short cut through their garden to the Sholton Brae. 'A touch of Eden, don't you think?' she had said in her strange English voice.

Sometimes, when she had got the children off to bed, she and Kieran would sit on the bench at the back door and watch the moths blundering amongst the rose bushes like pale shadows of the butterflies that had been so sprightly in the sun. And they would talk about Ireland: of Woodlea, and of riding out in the early morning of a crisp autumn day, the first smell of frost in their nostrils, the ring of the hooves on the road; of their hiding-place in Crow Wood where they had first known love. Kieran's arm would go round her, his hand would close softly on her round breast under the gingham dress.

They hardly ever talked of her father and mother now.

She kept her sorrow to herself, remembering one of old Mairi's axioms that as you make your bed you must lie on it. She and her brother corresponded regularly – 'both in the same boat now,' Terence had written – and each Christmas a long letter would come from him in New York, along with parcels for the children. He was doing well in his shipping company, 'climbing the ladder,' as he put it. They were not in the same boat as far as money was concerned.

'It was as simple as carrying a suitcase instead of a basket when I stepped off that schooner at the Battery,' he had written. 'They recognized a gentleman right away when they saw one.' Maria, his daughter, was growing up now, and he and Caroline had their eye on a piece of property in the Hudson Valley. He had the Irishman's thirst for land, but apart from that he did not seem to suffer from the nostalgia that Maeve felt for Woodlea and the very smell of it: the stables, the cool drawing-room with the scent from the pot-pourri bowl – almost the only task her mother performed – the warm kitchen with the smell of bread; above all, the smell of fresh air. Here in the Lowlands of Scotland it did not have the same soft green sweetness.

Kieran's mother wrote yearly, a painful, difficult letter it looked with its mis-spellings and corrections – she was 'no great hand at the writing', she said – but she kept them informed about the village and Woodlea. Maeve's parents had withdrawn from society altogether, living in seclusion in 'that great barn of a place'. The horses had been sold, Peters dismissed – 'Good riddance to that black-hearted devil,' Maeve said to that, causing Kieran to smile. He was not a man to bear grudges. Old Mairi had died, and Deirdre and her husband looked after the house and garden. 'Sometimes the Major acted funny.'

Maeve grieved for him more than she did for her mother. They had a lot in common, except Kieran. She had not forgotten that beating, probably never would, and yet in a strange way she forgave him, understood his black rage and his pride in her. Sometimes at night, when Kieran was asleep, she would imagine herself back at Woodlea, sitting at breakfast with him discussing horses, seeing his eyes bright with interest. Her mother, with her eternal headaches, never made him look like that. Now, as a married woman, she understood that excuse, one, thank God, she would think, I've never had to use, nor wanted to.

She stepped lightly down the steep slope of the Sholtie Brae, letting her shawl slip from her head, putting up her hand to loosen her hair. The pins pulled at it cruelly. It was a relief to feel the soft wind cool her scalp. She was in shadow now, walking by the high stone wall that bounded the Sholton Estate. Spring was better, when the foliage was less heavy, when you could put a toe in the crevice of the wall and jump up to look over to see the drifts of bluebells under the trees. Or autumn. The children liked to scuff the fallen leaves with their boots, making golden heaps in front of them as they walked.

Only thirty-one, she thought, and with a dead womb. Half of her mind registered that as too dramatic, but she liked the sound of it. She was full of energy, even the care of six children did not drag her down as it did so many of the other wives in the Row. But she was better bred than they. She did not think it in disparagement, simply as a fact, as she would have compared a thoroughbred with a cart-horse. At this moment she could feel the energy bursting through her skin, she was walking on air; there must be something more in store for her . . .

She could not explain to herself those feelings that

came over her, divorced from the love she felt for Kieran and the children, the feeling that while one part of her life had finished, another was going to begin where she would live more fully, in which she would use the vigour of her energy and youth. There isn't much time, she thought, her spirits dipping as if a shadow had crossed the sun.

But today was beautiful. What wouldn't she give to be on Blackthorn's back at this minute, racing towards the Curlew Mountains, seeing or imagining she saw the glint of the sea in Sligo Bay, the wind combing back her hair, searching under her clothes to cool and stroke her skin. Exhilaration. That was the word. Nothing to do with anyone but herself, a feeling of greater awareness, of being on a different plane from everyday cares and worries, cooking, scrubbing, feeding hens, the pig (Roly Poly, the children called him, while Kieran's name for him was 'The Great Provider' because he said they depended upon him for their bacon). John thought it very sad that bits of each successive Roly Poly should hang from the ceiling on hooks.

She was hearing the children's voices now. Their favourite place for playing was the shallows of the Sholtie. They had set off so proudly, headed by Kate like a mother hen. 'We're going for a picnic!' the Wee Rascal had shouted, jumping about, getting in everybody's way. 'Watch her,' Maeve had cautioned Kate. 'You'll need eyes in the back of your head.'

But she had no real fears. Kate was biddable, and their favourite game was harmless enough: to make for the shallows where the flat boulders abounded, and to colour them laboriously with pieces of soft red sandstone which they dipped in the water.

She did not know how the idea had originated. Perhaps it was in imitation of her when she pipeclayed the front doorstep. There was a peculiar satisfaction in the process for them which eluded her, some kind of joyous reward when they saw the rippling Sholtie surrounded by rose-coloured stone that stood out oddly amongst the heavy green overhang of the trees. There would be a meaning to it somewhere. It would be in books . … if she ever had time to read.

It was a pity she could not go to the evening classes run by the Crawford Ironworks for their workers. She laughed out loud at the thought of that, how the men would look up and snigger. Women represented only one thing to them if they were unmarried, and married women were swiftly 'trachled' with bairns.

If she had taken Sean's warning, the thought came to her, perhaps gone down on her knees to her father, asked his forgiveness, she could have gone to Dublin, studied, travelled, perhaps gone to Trinity. An image rose in her mind of that pale English lad who had come to Woodlea as her tutor, and of how he had introduced her to literature and history, a landscape of the mind, she thought, the phrase coming to her. And she heard again his voice, like Lady Crawford's, 'You might find this interesting, Miss Muldoon.'

If ifs and an's were pot and pans, she thought now. She had known, that night long ago, when she had been waiting at the window of Woodlea, that she was at a crossroads in her life. She had made the choice. Her life had crystallized in that moment of discovery by her father behind the laurels in the drive. Their green, glossy dark-ness, Kieran's arms, and then the dog suddenly there, the noise of its frenzied barking, her father's shouts, the terror in her throat as she saw her future with Kieran shattering, even as the noise seemed to shatter her eardrums . . .

A piercing shriek echoed in her head and for a second she thought it was the memory of her own cry that night, then she realized that it was here and now. There was a babble of voices coming from the direction of the Burn, then Kate's rising above them, high, anguished: 'Come back, wee Maeve, come back! You'll fall in!' She was distraught; fear combined with guilt – she had been day-dreaming as usual – shook her. She lifted her skirts and flew down the steep brae, once almost going headlong over a jutting stone, righting herself, half-sobbing, afraid to think.

Now it was Isobel's voice she heard, keening on the still air, but coming from a different direction than the picnic spot with the flat boulders. 'Shut up!' It was Kate shout-ing, drowning the wailing. In the sudden silence she could imagine Isobel being shaken. And Kate again, her voice loud with terror, 'John, you'll slip . . . !'

'Oh, God.' She was sobbing, repeating the words under her breath as she reached the bank and, scarcely pausing, made for the stepping-stones. She had warned them, *warned* them . . . She pushed through the bushes and almost fell over Isobel who was sitting on the ground weeping, her face buried in her white pinny. She stood panting, her eyes widening with horror.

Kate was teetering on the stepping-stones, one hand to her mouth, the other arm outstretched backwards to Isobel as if to debar her, or quieten her. John was kneeling on the stones in the middle of the burn, bending over to try and grasp the Wee Rascal who was in the water, spluttering, choking, thrashing her arms like a windmill. There was a dip in the bed of the burn there . . .

'Come back, Kate, and let me get to them!' She tried to calm her voice. 'That's right.' She patted the girl's

51

shoulder as she squeezed past her. 'You stay with Isobel.'
She began to cross, swiftly, carefully, her arms outstretched for balance. In one of her hands, she noticed,
was the rope she had been holding under her apron.
'Mammy's coming, John. Hold on to her.' She saw his
startled face turn to her, he slipped, and then he was in
the water, too, struggling beside his sister.

She was beside them in a second, kneeling down,
placing the coil of rope on a flat stone. 'It's all right, John.
Hold on to wee Maeve and catch that branch.' His face
was white, pinched and blue round the nostrils. He
gasped, did not speak.

She stretched and grasped wee Maeve's shoulder; the
child's face, unlike her brother's was as red as a turkey-
cock's, her mouth open. Heaving with all her strength,
she managed to drag her from the water kicking and
screaming. 'Kate!' she shouted. 'Come and hold her!
Good girl. Watch going back. Now, John, it's your turn.'
She was panting with the effort. 'Give me your hand.'

'I can't, Mammy!' he wailed. 'I can't let go. My fingers
have gone stiff . . .'

'The other one, silly. Keep hold of the branch.' He was
shivering violently. They had once had a puppy which
they had rescued from the burn. It had shivered like that,
gone on shivering. She did not want to think of that.

'All right. It's not too deep here, you're all right.' His
small body was floating in the pool between the stepping-
stones where you could look down and see the minnows
swimming – the 'baggies', the children called them. She
had once pointed them out to Maeve when she was a
baby, carrying her easily in a plaid. Was that what had
enticed her here today? 'Just keep a tight grip. Mammy
will get you.'

She lowered herself into the water, and its cold grip

52

was feeling round her thighs, into the places where it could still be tender after wee Maeve's birth.

'I can't, I can't. I can't feel my fingers. They're . . . deid.'

'Yes, you can. Look, I've got a rope.' She lifted it from the stone beside her. 'I'm going to put it round a tree and then you'll have something to hold on to. It'll be easy. John! Oh, John . . . !' In the second she had taken to fling an end round a branch he had released his grip, and his body, like a leaf, was slipping between two large boulders and sailing, like a leaf, away from her.

It's not true, she thought, as she flung herself at him. Her grasping hands missed his clothes and she floundered after him, half swimming, half-walking, bruising her legs against the stones, sometimes floating as her skirts spread like sails. It's not true! It's a shallow burn – there was amazement in her terror – a shallow burn!

It became a nightmare of grasping and clutching, of his body eluding her grasp by inches, by less than inches, of following his progress along the stony bed, of being aware of the quickening and deepening of the water – and knowing why; of sometimes floating, sometimes swimming, sometimes going under in its brown depths. Some of the pebbles were brown and gold, polished, like cornelian stones. There were shoals of minnows all going one way . . .

She could not hear him, did not know if he was calling to her. The combined wailing of Kate, wee Maeve and Isobel was far behind her now. But maybe Kieran would hear the commotion, or Terence, come running down the steep Sholtie Brae, run along the bank and plunge in further down the burn in time to catch John before . . . before . . . she could hardly allow herself to think it . . . before the Falls. That was the terror which had been at

53

the back of her mind as she stumbled and fell through the reaches, her hands and feet torn with the sharp shale. But the stinging was as nothing compared with the thought of the Falls. She felt the summer sun on her head, the almost drowsy warmth of the water. It was a dream, a bad dream, a punishment for thinking about herself, for looking back . . .

She knew they were coming near now. She could tell by the rushing sound of the water, the small wind that lifted her hair. She would go over them after John, rush down their steep watery slope, steeper than the slope of the Sholtie Brae, be dashed to pieces in the boiling pot at the foot. (Would the pot have boiled over in the kitchen by this time? Had she pulled it aside?)

Well, that's what she would want, to go after John. She could never face Kieran and tell him John had drowned because of her carelessness and selfishness, that lad who never harmed a mouse . . . 'Oh no, I couldn't bear it, bear it, bear it . . . !' She heard her own voice in her ears, knew her body suddenly swirled and stopped against arms that grasped and held her, that she was dragged to the bank, lifted out and laid on the grass. Kieran, his face black with coal dust, was looking down at her, eyeballs peeled white against the blackness and seeming to fall out of his head. 'John . . .' she wanted to say, but the name would not come and she had to try again, 'John . . .'

'Terence's gone to get him at the foot. Lie still, mavourneen.' He bent down and put his arms round her for a second, 'My wife, oh, my wife . . .'

She closed her eyes against his eyes, red-rimmed, agonized. 'Get . . . John. Leave me . . .'

It was still a dream when she got slowly to her feet, made her way back along the path to the stepping-stones, found the three girls weeping and gathered them together.

Their white petticoats were stained with the red sandstone and she scolded them, still in a dream. 'When you think of the washing I'll have to do when I get back!' There were other people there now, a tight little knot of people seemingly with one face of puzzlement. It disintegrated, and Mrs Haddow, who lived at the end of the Row, came out of it and put a shawl round her.

'You're shivering. Come away up to my house, Mrs McGrath. And bring the bairns. Ma man is helping yours and Terence.'

'No, thank you all the same, Mrs Haddow,' she said, 'I prefer to wait.' She felt her back straighten as she spoke, her chin go up. She put her arm round Kate who was carrying the Wee Rascal. The child was whimpering, half-asleep from shock, her thumb in her mouth. Isobel pressed into her mother's other side.

'It was the Wee Rascal's fault,' she said. 'Kate told her and told her, but she was that bad. All she kept on saying was "baggies".'

'Hush, Isobel,' Maeve said, feeling ashamed for this weak daughter of hers. She put her arm round her.

She saw Kieran coming towards her with John in his arms, his head downbent. Terence and Mr Haddow were behind them, their clothes black and dripping, their hair plastered on their brows. She knew by their faces that John was dead. She went to meet them. She wanted to take John in her arms, held them out, but Kieran shook his head. She looked at her son's face. It had escaped injury except for a bruise on his temple. He looked peaceful. They said death by drowning could be pleasant.

She met Kieran's eyes, set now in a face washed clean by the burn water. And by tears. They flowed ceaselessly from his eyes. Terence was beside her. She put a hand on his shoulder but he turned away from her, sullen. She understood his reaction. He did not want anything like this to happen in his family. Life was exciting for him just now, down the pit like his father, pennies to jingle in his pocket, village girls . . . she saw it all in his face.

Mrs Haddow had shepherded the girls together like an elderly ewe. 'I'll take the bairns up to my house, Mrs McGrath. This is no sight for them and they just wee things. Oh, my, it's awfy sad for you all the same, such a nice quiet lad, no harm in him . . .' She interrupted the woman's talk.

'What do you mean, it isn't a sight for them, Mrs Haddow?' She raised her chin. Stuck-up Irish bitch, she knew they called her.

'I just meant, you know, wee lassies, they'll never forget, it's no' right . . .'

'I want them to remember!' She heard her voice, loud, shrill, saw the woman start back, draw her shawl round her. 'He's their brother, isn't he?'

Somehow they fell into a little procession like coming out of the kirk on Sunday, and walked up the hill, Kieran in front with his burden.

4

Life had to go on, the Reverend Mr Murdoch said in the
kirk that Sunday, but it would never go on in the same
way. There was a blight on the house because everybody
felt responsible for John's death. Kieran tried to make
Maeve talk about it when they were in bed, but she turned
away from him when he wanted to take her in his arms.
All her sexual impetus had gone with the tragedy, and she
resented his, that he could think of such a thing while she
mourned.

'You'll have to think of us, too,' he said to her. 'Terence
and me feel terrible that we didn't manage to save him;
Kate, poor wee soul, that she let the Wee Rascal stray to
the stepping-stones; and I know you're thinking *you* might
have got there earlier. We could comfort each other.' His
body was hard against her side. She hated men at that
moment. She could not tell him of her real guilt, that she
had been selfishly day-dreaming, what she thought of as
her mental unfaithfulness. It was as if she had been
punished . . .

Even the Wee Rascal seemed subdued. She did not
understand the 'badness' Isobel accused her of, just that
her brother was not there any more. 'Will Johnnie no'
come back?' she asked, looking up with her wide, innocent eyes, her golden curls – 'a wee picture', they'd said
of her at the funeral.

'No, he's gone to heaven,' Isobel told her, 'but if you
hadn't run away . . .'

'Isobel!' Maeve shouted, hearing the sharp, querulous

note in her voice, which was new to her. 'Enough of that!' And to wee Maeve, 'He was drowned in the Burn. We won't see him again. You just have to remember your brother now, how good and kind he was, and how he saved you.'

'Maybe he'll float up again, Mammy? I saw a tin-can floating once . . .'

'No, he's gone for good, gone to God.' She had to say that since Mr Murdoch had said it. 'Now away and look after your dolly. It's crying in its crib.'

The only one who went scot-free of self-recrimination was Patrick who had been at Tweedie's farm playing with Jock, the son. It was as if he took on his younger brother's mantle of tenderness, although he was a big, uncouth boy on the edge of puberty. He helped Maeve with the chores of the cottage, filled the pails at the well, dug potatoes, fed the hens and the pig; and once, when he came home from school and found her sitting gazing out of the window, the floor half-scrubbed, he got down on his knees and finished it.

He was as considerate with Kieran, helping him to plant the kale for the winter soup, taking on his task of cleaning all the boots for Sunday kirk. He put up with Terence's moods which sometimes were as black as his face, poured water for his bath, joked with him, splashed water on him, coaxed him into laughter. He was like John, except that he lacked that special trait, Maeve thought, a kind of spirituality, a consistency of goodness; and she was right, in that as the time passed Patrick's solicitude dwindled and he was back with Jock Tweedie at the farm.

Kieran came home from the pit a few months after the funeral with his face alight. 'They're taking on some men of my age at the Ironworks for labouring. I'm thinking of applying.'

She was worried. It was coming up to the New Year, Ne'erday, they called it here. He would lose his bonus for one thing, and the free coal. 'Is that what you want to do?'

She knew any change from the mine was a good one as far as he was concerned. To go underground was a daily purgatory to him, and he had tried often to get employment on the land. But there had only been seasonal work available, since the farms around were small and mostly run with the help of their own families. He had been forced to take his present job because the babies had been coming one after another, and they had needed a steady wage to support them.

'Oh, yes, if they'll take me,' he said. 'I'm too old at thirty-five for an apprenticeship, but maybe I could get something better later. I'll miss out on the free coal and Ne'erday bonus right enough, but Terence will get his share, and Patrick, if he follows after him. He seems bent on it. The cottage will be all right.' The Crawfords owned the Ironworks as well as the pits, and they had a tied house.

'There wouldn't be a chance for Terence?'

'That's what I was thinking. The two of them, maybe. They like families to work in the same place. They're . . .'

'Paternalistic ?'

'You're the one with the learning, Maeve.' Her heart warmed to him. He also had had to make sacrifices. His feeling for the land was even deeper than hers, the difference between someone who worked on it rather than took pleasure from it. 'If I had my way, I'd rather not see the boys down the pit. Terence is happy enough just now, won't hear a thing against it, though I warned

59

him before he went. He thinks he's a man with the other pit lads. Too much of a man. I found him round the back of the winding-house with a gambling school the other day.'

'He'll not be gambling much with all the money he's left with.'

'I know, but I don't want him to get into bad company. Nor influence Patrick too much.'

In an effort at cheerfulness she said, 'We'll have to get out your best suit when you go for the interview. And I'll iron your white shirt.'

She was pleased for Kieran's sake, but envious. Everybody was finding their own solace except her. She it was who missed John most. He had been for her a companion beyond his years, although sometimes, when grief lifted its weight from her, she saw clearly enough that she was in danger of crediting the child with properties he had never possessed.

Then memories would sweep over her, of how they had sat together on the bench outside the door while he read his books, how she had answered his questions as best as she could, listened to him reciting his poems. He had had an unusual intellect for a child of six, a bright questing spirit. He was to have done all the things she might have done.

She had nursed him through winter ailments, sat at night holding his hand while he coughed interminably. How could she ever forget those apologetic eyes, the sweet smile, the secret jokes they had shared? 'He was too good for this world,' that fool, Mrs Haddow, had said at the funeral. The world *needed* good people like John. *She* had needed him. The loss during those grey autumnal days, when the mist rose in the field outside the cottage windows, was at times unbearable.

* * *

She was hanging out clothes one morning when she saw Lady Crawford coming through the garden in her usual shapeless clothes, the big boots, the hat bashed on top of her head. The gentry could dress as carelessly as they liked, she remembered Kieran saying, forgetting she had been gentry once. Old Mairi had often reproved her for her muddied skirts. 'A fine sight for the drawing-room you are, Miss . . .'

The woman was walking towards her, not waving and then climbing over the stile as she usually did. She had long since given up apologizing for her intrusion. The cottage was the end one and stood at the head of the Sholton Brae. 'It's such a good short cut,' Lady Crawford had said, and Maeve, smiling, had replied, 'Trespassers won't be prosecuted.' Kieran had laughed when she told him and said it was some way to talk to her ladyship.

'Good-morning to you, Mrs McGrath,' she said. 'I see you're busy.'

'Yes, Lady Crawford. They say a woman's work is never done.' The cliché rose to her lips and, ashamed of it, she added, 'I've got to keep myself busy.' That was worse. Now she was asking for sympathy.

Lady Crawford nodded. 'It must be hard to lose a son the way you did. Such a lovable child.'

'Yes, he was that.' She pegged out a pair of Kieran's drawers. Her father had had fine merino ones for wearing under his hunting clothes. Why was she so bitter this morning?

'I can sympathize with you. I never suffered such a tragic accident, but I lost three babies after Alastair, my first-born. And that was that.' She had a face like a squirrel, small with great dark eyes, and it was prematurely lined, surely. She could scarcely be fifty.

'You couldn't have any more?' She stopped with one of

61

Terence's semmits in her hands, recognizing the same sorrow as she had known. Nor did it seem strange to be talking like this to the laird's wife.

'No. I think often of those sad little faces. And the tiny coffins. Such tiny coffins.' She sighed, raising her shoulders. 'One son only and he isn't married yet. I tell him he'll have to hurry up.' There was a quirk at the side of her mouth. 'His father badly wants an heir.'

'I can understand that.' *Her* father did not want a grandson. 'I still have two fine boys, Terence and Patrick.'

'You're fortunate there. I've often seen you coming in with your family at church. More heads turn than mine, I may say. You make a fine couple, you so straight and tall, and your husband . . . he has a noble head. Forgive me, my husband tells me I let my tongue run away with me. Tell me about your family, Mrs McGrath.' Somehow the two women had left the bleaching green and were walking towards the bench outside the door. It was a fine October morning. The mist had lifted and the sun had the late warmth of an Indian summer. 'Yes,' Lady Crawford said, 'one sees everything at church. What a loss the old one was. It had a fine birdcage belfry, but perhaps you aren't interested in architectural details? And it would be before your time, I expect.'

'Yes, we came in 1851.'

'Ah, yes. Not so long after that terrible Potato Famine.' They had reached the bench. 'May I sit down? We should enjoy this beautiful weather while we have it. That's why I set off this morning. I love walking, as no doubt you've noticed.' Again there was that shy quirk of a smile. 'I like to study nature in all its aspects.' People said she sat in the Sholtie woods for hours with spy-glasses, a strange past-time. Someone in her position in Ireland would have been out riding.

'I love the fresh air, too.' Maeve sat down beside her. 'And Kieran even more than me. He's never taken to going down the pit.' He's thinking of applying for a job at the Ironworks . . . no, she would never say that, her pride would not let her. She changed the subject, smiling at the woman. 'This is a rare enough thing for me to do, but wee Maeve is having her morning sleep.'

'The golden-haired one? I've noticed she doesn't like being cooped up in a pew.' Did she notice everything with her bright, inquisitive eyes? 'The eldest boy is down the pit with his father?'

'Yes, and Patrick is dying to join him. They think differently from their father.'

'I can understand his dislike. The feeling of being trapped, a cramping of the spirit as well as the body. I crave the open air. I'm like a bird in a cage when I'm indoors.'

'He was brought up with horses. He was a groom.'

'Really? Which part of Ireland, Mrs McGrath?'

'The West.' She would be no more explicit.

'Did you used to ride, Mrs McGrath?'

'Oh, yes. I've probably lost the touch now, but the joy of it comes back to me on mornings like this, the cub-hunting, the frisky puppies, the smell of frost in the air . . .' She laughed shamefacedly at her enthusiasm.

'I never felt like that. How strange. I prefer to be on the ground. I can stop and stare . . .' her bright eyes were on Maeve. She said slowly, consideringly, 'I have an old hunter eating his head off in the stables. Why don't you take him out? You'd be doing me a favour.'

Her immediate thought was how naïve this woman was. What would Lord Garston Crawford say if his wife told him she had offered her horse to a miner's wife in Colliers' Row? It was as quickly followed by a kind of angry shame. If she accepted, was she expected to mount her ladyship's horse wearing her striped cotton dress and apron, have everyone at the Hall stables laugh at her?

But the anger quickly died. She was a kindly woman, if impractical, strange and unworldly for her position. 'Thank you, Lady Crawford,' she said, 'I appreciate your kindness. But I've left all that behind me.' Their eyes met and held.

'Yes, of course. Forgive me.' Lady Crawford got up. 'I mustn't waste any more of your time. I've enjoyed our little chat.' She did a surprising thing. She put her hand on Maeve's. 'It will pass, you know, your grief will pass.' She withdrew her hand shyly, and said as if to cover her embarrassment, 'What a sweet smell this white rose has! Do you mind if I take one?'

'Let me give you a bunch. They're beginning to fall already. The last rose of summer . . .'

'No, one will do to smell on my walk. We haven't such a finely scented one at the Hall.'

'Kieran planted them for me.'

'"My love is like a red, red rose . . ."' the woman smiled. 'Young love . . . but the white ones smell sweeter.'

'And fall quicker.'

'That is the sadness.' Her small face looked sad, the eyes almost black in its paleness. 'I'll say good morning to you.'

'Good morning, Lady Crawford.'

She stood and watched the woman climb the stile, saw her skirts catch on the post because of a tear in them, saw the flick of the white petticoats with the bedraggled edging, and the black-stockinged leg. An odd creature, Maeve thought, but there was a warmth left in her. What had been between them for a few minutes was what she had missed with John's death, a meeting of minds. A strange thing to think of a boy of six, she mused, but true. She went back to pegging out her clothes, sniffing their clean, frosty smell the way Lady Crawford had sniffed the white rose.

5

Terence dipped his comb in the ewer of water and carefully plastered his hair down on his forehead, patting it with the towel to induce it to lie flat. It had his mother's colour but his father's curliness, that being the bane of Terence's existence. Patrick was sitting on the edge of their bed, lacing up his boots.

'I've never seen anyone make as much fuss about their appearance before going to the kirk. Is it Miss Catherine Murdoch you're wanting to impress? It's no' her father, old Mooly Murdoch, that's for sure.'

Terence dipped the comb into the water again and flicked it in the direction of his brother, causing him to duck. 'It's high time you took an interest in *your* appearance. No wonder you want to go down the pit. It's just to save you washing.'

'I think Da's giving in to that.' Patrick went on with his lacing. 'I'm going on for thirteen now. I can leave school, thank goodness. He's worried. I heard him talking to Ma. He wants to make sure we hang on to the house and get the coal if they take him on at the Ironworks.'

'He hasn't a chance in hell,' Terence said, running his finger between his neck and his stiff white collar. He would far rather be wearing his comfortable woollen pit shirt than this monstrosity. 'He's no' strappin' enough for a labourer, but he's desperate to get out of the pit. The only thing he likes about it is the ponies. Have you seen him with them, stroking them and petting them, and stealing turnips from the garden for them every morning?'

'Aye. There's six in our field just now. He offered it to Dowthie for the blind ones. Hey, Terence!' he raised his head excitedly, 'I jumped on one the other day and went round bareback! Remember we saw Wild Bill last year in the circus? Ma came after me with the clothes-rope.'

'No wonder. You're no' wise. Nor is Da. *I* would have a better chance of getting taken on at the works than he has, but I like best where I am.'

'He'd like best to be working with horses. Poor Da. He has long cracks with Mr Tweedie about his. I think he keeps on hoping he'll offer him a job but he's only got room for Jock. He's leaving school along with me. And then there's the auld uncle that comes in to help at the harvest.'

'What *would* suit our Da,' Terence said, straightening his tie at the mirror . . . yes, there was something about a white collar even if it nearly throttled you, it kind of showed off your face if that damned hair would stay straight instead of springing up into these daft curls like old Tweedie's bull . . . 'What *would* suit our Da would be to work on Crawford's estate, maybe in the stables, or as a gardener. I don't know why he hasn't thought of that.'

'Maybe he has, or there'll be some reason. You never know what your folks are thinking. They're both gey sleekit, come to think of it. I heard Ma once saying it would bring back too many memories. Maybe of Ireland.'

'Well, there's no accounting for what they think, and I'm not all that caring. I've got my own affairs.' He brushed some dandruff off his shoulders with the back of his hand. That hair . . .

'Like gambling?' Patrick said. 'Hey, Terence, leave me be! That's not fair, you're bigger than me.' Terence had flung himself on his brother, knocked him back onto the bed and was sitting astride him, aiming playful slaps at his face. 'Hey, that hurts!'

'It's meant to. I gave you a share, didn't I? Have you been cliping on me?'

'You know I wouldn't do that. Stop it, no, stop it, no . . . Listen!' He struggled. 'It's Joey outside. D'you not hear him? I wouldn't tell a lie. It's Joey!'

'I know your tricks.' Terence went on administering stinging little slaps. 'There's nobody there.'

'You can't hear because you're hitting me. Honest, Terence, I never told on you. It *is* Joey.'

Terence gave his brother's face a final cuff and got off him, stood up straight, smoothed his hair carefully. He knew it was Joey. He could hear the hurdy-gurdy with its one cracked tune, something Italian. He came at this time every week in the hope of trading on the Sunday piety of the people in Colliers' Row. He strode over to their bedroom window and looked out.

'The Wee Rascal's there.' He was laughing now. 'She's got a penny from Ma and she's giving it to the monkey.' Patrick had come over. 'Look at her face, for Christ's sake.'

'If Da heard you swearing . . .' Patrick joined in his brother's laughter. 'Will you look at her dancing! Heel, toe, burl roon'. And Ma's got her decked out in her Sunday best, if you please. She's a wee picture all the same, isn't she? That bonnet on her curls and dressed just like Ma with the buttons and the braid and everything. She's clever, Ma. She made them outfits herself. Will you look at her with her arms spread out! Ma says she's too young for the kirk. It's Da's idea.'

'Patrick! Terence!' It was Kieran's voice. 'We're all ready now and waiting. Come on, lads.'

'I'd rather be sitting at the back of the winding-shed,'

Terence said, giving a last look at himself in the mirror. He would knock that stuck-up bitch, Miss Catherine Murdoch, cold when she saw him.

They filed into church, their father and mother at the head with wee Maeve between them, followed by Kate and Isobel, then the two boys. Last year there had been John as well. God, he thought he had got rid of that. Sometimes at night even yet he would think of that terrible day when he had plunged through the water in time to see John's body swirling over the Falls. He had been like a rag doll, just a flash of the white face like the belly of a fish. Then the heaving panic in his breast as he had struggled back to the bank and raced along it until he came to the place where the water emptied into the Devil's Pool . . . a good name for it.

And there he had been, John, the brother you could never do anything but love, gently swirling round in it, his body nudging against the stones like that old trout under the bridge that nobody could ever catch.

He had stood terrified, knowing he was on his own, that he would have to deal with this himself. Da would be dragging Ma to the bank. He had seen him grab her at the edge of the waterfall and hold her in his arms for a second, looking down at her, forgetting John. Yes, he had thought, it was up to him. He had shut his eyes and said aloud, 'God help me,' and waded in, then stopped, sick to his stomach. This . . . thing was no longer John as he had known him – the bright face, the shy upward glance of admiration, 'You know everything, Terence,' – but a poor, drowned stranger. John, the younger brother, had gone away.

This was where his mind always stuck, like a bogey down the pit, because ahead was darkness and hate, self-hate. He had heard a shout and looked round to see his father coming towards him through the water, stumbling, gesticulating. 'What's stopping you, in the name of God! Lift him out, damn you, lift him out!' This . . . madman who pushed him roughly aside was not the quiet, gentle father he knew. 'He's your own brother! Here, let me . . .'

They seemed to be causing their usual stir amongst the pews. He had already overheard someone whisper, 'Here come the McGraths.' He knew they thought Ma was above herself, that she wore the trousers, that they were all too handsome for their own good. He had heard that whispered, too. Like strange birds, he thought now, remembering how he had surprised a pair of woodpeckers in the darkness of the Sholtie Woods, and the brilliant flash of green as they had darted away.

And true enough, there was no one to beat his mother for looks. Look at the straight back of her and that great pile of dark red hair with the green velvet bonnet on top of it. And the way her skirts spread and swung away from that flat velvet bow low down, and the slimness of her waist.

And Da wasn't bad either with his curls, darker than the Wee Rascal's, but you could see where she took them from. They looked all right on her! He put a hand up and tried to flatten the already springing hair on his forehead. He should have put some sugar in the water. That would have stuck it down.

There was Bessie Haddow giving him the glad eye. She was working now, too, in a spinning factory. One minute she had been a lassie playing about with Kate at jumping ropes, now she was pert, with wicked eyes.

They all got up when Mooly Murdoch tottered down the aisle, then there were the prayers and the mumblings

70

about one thing and another, then an announcement from auld Mooly about the 'demise', he called it, of their well-loved organist, Mr Paterson, pin-leg Paterson was nearer the mark, who had been replaced by a new young man – here he waved a hand in the direction of the organ – who had studied in Glasgow and Edinburgh, and they were more than lucky, indeed privileged, to get him. Mr Scrymsher – what a name – would now lead the choir in the opening hymn, 'Holy, holy, holy, Lord, God Almighty.' The loud chords rang out, filling the church. If that was playing, Terence thought, he would rather have Joey with his barrel organ. He felt the Wee Rascal moving against him. She was sitting between him and Isobel. He gave her a nudge with his elbow to quieten her.

'Early in the morning . . . our song shall rise to thee . . .' the choir sang. They had tried to get him to join. He liked singing, but who'd be seen dead standing up, mouth gawping like a fish, before this lot? The Wee Rascal was pushing and shoving like mad. She had been sitting on the seat, legs doubled up underneath her; now she was half-standing. 'Maeve . . .' he whispered, agonized, trying to drag her down, but she shook him off with her sharp little elbows. What was that daft Isobel on the other side of her mooning about now? She was always in a dream.

To his horror the Wee Rascal had scrambled up now, was standing on the seat. His whole body seemed to freeze as he heard her voice ringing round the church. 'Where's the monkey, Terence?' A man guffawed loudly behind him in the silence, coughed, someone tittered, the new organist whirled round on his seat, eyes nearly jumping out of his head, whirled back again and played some terrible notes, squeaking and grinding. Terence, the blood surging into his face, dragged wee Maeve roughly down by her pointing arm.

Under cover of the choir, 'God . . . in three Per . . . sons,' louder than ever now to drown the wrong notes, he whispered out of the side of his mouth, 'Wait till I get you outside. I'll wring your bluidy neck for you.' 'Blessed Trin . . . ity,' the choir was quieter now, the danger averted.

'You're swearing, Terence. I'll tell . . .'

He clapped his hand over her mouth and whispered again, fiercely, 'I told you, if you don't shut your gob I'll . . . I'll . . .' '*A . . . men*,' the choir sang, heads lowered. Mr Scrymsher, his sanity restored, pulled out all the stops.

'Shall we bow our heads and pray for forgiveness for our sins?' he heard old Mooly saying. His eyes were on their pew. God, that's finished me with Catherine, he thought. He took out the white handkerchief his mother had doled out, 'just for show', and mopped his brow.

It was like Purgatory walking up the aisle when the service was over. Everybody was looking at him. He tried to appear unconcerned as he joined his mother in the porch where she was waiting with his father. 'We'll just get away home, Ma. I'm in a hurry . . .' He met her eyes. Trust Ma to think it was a joke instead of being black affronted.

'Why should we be doing that, Terence?' she said. Her voice was still different from the other wives in the Row. She was always correcting them at the table – 'Speak properly, please, and not spoil the Queen's English.' Her mouth was quirking up at the side. 'I like to speak to my neighbours.'

'I thought we might have a walk . . .'

'But we've got over a mile back to the house! Surely that's a long enough walk for you? Oh, good-day, Mrs Thompson. Are you feeling better now? It's nice to see you out. Yes, she *is* a wee rascal. That's what we call her at home. Still, she's only young . . .' Terence caught Catherine Murdoch's eye and smiled sheepishly, but she turned away with a haughty lift of her head. That wee besom had ruined his chances there. Patrick was at his side.

'What a laugh, Terence! I nearly wet myself when wee Maeve stood up! Did you ever know anything like it?'

'I'm going to kill her,' Terence said, looking around wildly. 'I told her, I'm going to kill her. She'll never stand up on another pew as sure as I'm alive. Where is she?'

'Kate and Isobel are walking back with her. Ma told them to go on. She thought that by the time everybody had spoken to her about it she'd be like a turkey cock with pride.'

'Phew . . .' Terence shook his head. This time his eye met Bessie Haddow's. *She* did not turn away. She came towards him, her skirts swaying from one side to the other. She did it deliberately to show off her ankles. She was laughing at him. He could see it, she was fair bursting trying to keep it in.

'Hello, Terence.' She was beside him, stinking of lavender water. 'How are you this bright Sunday morning?'

'Fine, thank you. How are you?'

'All the better for seeing you. Did you know the Campbells are having a barn dance next Saturday?'

'Yes, I know. I've got an invite.'

'Are you going?'

'I might. I'm thinking about it.' He half-forgot about the Wee Rascal. He liked this kind of talk. It was not what you said but how you said it, and what you put into your eyes. It was a new game. He loved it. It made gambling seem dull. 'That is,' he said, attempting to make his eyes turn in a full circle, 'if *you* go . . .'

'Would that make any difference?' Bessie's eyes seemed to slide along her lower lids.

'I wouldn't know, would I? Not till you went.'

'We'd have to see, wouldn't we?'

'Aye, we'd have to see . . . how the bools ran.' He pursed his lips, screwed them to one side

'Aye, that's right.' She stood looking at him, her eyes softer now. You had to learn how to read girls' eyes. It was a great, new, wonderful game.

'I hear tell you're a fine dancer.'

'I get the name of it. Though I have to have a good partner.'

'So have I.'

'And a good band.'

'The Sholtie Four aren't bad . . . especially that one with the drum.'

'I like the fiddler best.' Her eyes had changed now, sparkling like the first frost on Sholtie Brae. They were brown to match the brown velvet of her bonnet, its cream ribbons were the same as the creaminess of her skin. Had she planned it? Girls spent hours at their mirrors. Even Kate who was sensible was forever primping. 'I know who I'd rather have,' she said. Her mouth was quivering. What was wrong with her, for God's sake? Was it a new ploy?

'Who?' He racked his brains to remember the names of any other bands. They talked about them down the pit.

'Guess?' she said. He was stumped.

'Who?' he asked again, feebly.

'Joey and his monkey.' Her whole face was quivering now, her mouth opened and he saw her white teeth and the pink tip of her tongue which came and went like a baggie under a stone. She was laughing, killing herself with laughing.

'J . . . J . . . Joey?' Curse it, curse it, curse it, he felt

74

the tide of red sweep over his face. He would have liked to dig up one of those gravestones and crawl under it, coorie doon with whoever was there, bones and all. He would have liked to get his hands on the Wee Rascal's neck.

'Don't tell me you're blushing, Terence McGrath.' Bessie's laughter rang out. Several people turned their heads and looked at them.

'Maybe I'll see you at the Campbells', then.' He walked away.

6

Strangely enough, Terence was right about his father. He did not get the job at the Sholton Ironworks, and even more strangely, it could have been blamed partly on Maeve.

He had persuaded her that it would be foolish to wear his suit. 'That's only for a job in the counting house,' he had told her, and by her disappointed face he had seen she was hoping they would see something different in him and offer him a job where he did not have to dirty his hands. If he got a job like that, there might be a chance for the boys . . .

She had ironed the white shirt and had only reluctantly given in to him not wearing a collar. 'You want to look your best, Kieran.' 'I want to look like the job I'm applying for,' he had said, 'not mutton dressed as lamb.'

But standing in the queue outside the foreman's shed he knew even the white shirt was a mistake, in spite of the fact that he was wearing it with his rough working suit. The other men's shirts were thick and striped, fastened at the neck with a stud; his was fine, unstriped, and cold, if you asked him, on this January day. He was glad of this thick semmet, could have done with a woollen cravat crossed on his chest as well, like some of the older men.

'All dressed up and nowhere to go,' Dickie said to him, a great bull of a man bursting with health, with great ham-like hands. He would be engaged on the spot. In fact all the men looked massive. He knew his wiry build and thin nervous hands had never been suited for labouring.

Already at thirty-six he was beginning to feel a chronic tiredness in his limbs when he got up in the morning, caused, he knew, by the perpetual crouching under the pit supports, but, more importantly, by a growing reluctance to go down the pit and take up his shovel day after day. He hated its weight and the coldness of the shaft, its inanimation. His hands on a horse got an immediate response. There was an affinity between him and even those poor blind ponies that ran in his field. When one of them blundered against him and nuzzled in his hand, he felt a happiness he never found down the pit. That was what he was meant for, not working with a hard, intractable element like coal which did not give an inch and had to be wrested painfully from the dark tunnels running with water.

Another man in the queue, Davy Cox, was speaking to him from behind. 'They say the truck's better here than down the pit.' His eye also flicked over the white shirt.

'Is it?' He turned. 'I wasn't thinking of that. It was the house and coal that was bothering me. Anyhow, the owners are going against the law now. Truck's been abolished.'

'What do people like the Crawfords care about the law? They think they're above it with their tokens that they claw back into their store. I've got an ailing wife. We've run into debt a few times.' The man did not look very fit himself, thin, with a cough that brought a flush to his cheeks when it racked him.

'Aye. Anything that puts money into their pockets is fair game.' He was shivering standing there. You would think they would let you go inside at least. They treated you like animals. He thought for a moment of the cosy stables at Woodlea, where the heavy sweaty smell of horses made it a warm womb in winter; even outside your blood ran hot as you exercised them. And the smell of that Irish air . . . was there anything to beat it in the whole wide world?

He and Maeve used to talk about it, but not so often now. She was quieter since John's death; their closeness was fractured. He did not understand why she turned away from him. She was restless in his arms. Maybe if he got this job and worked himself up like Dowthie who took on men at the pit and the works, got her a better house, she would become her bright self again. And then the boys could climb up on his back, maybe go beyond him . . . Standing there in the clinging cold mist of this Lowland country, his heart ached for her. There would never be another woman for him.

'McGrath!' It was Dowthie calling his name. He walked smartly in, stood while the man looked sourly at him. And what was more, they had no manners, the Scots. They were dour and irascible. In Boyle they would have said, 'The top of the morning to you,' at least.

'You're down No 3 Pit, McGrath?' Dowthie said. He looked up and his eye seemed to rest on the white shirt. Kieran had seen the same gleam in the eye of a horse which had decided to be fractious, a sly, sliding gleam.

'Yes, Mr Dowthie. But I've been working with Crawford going on for fifteen years.'

'Are you no' satisfied in the pit?'

'To tell you the truth . . .' He decided to appeal to the man's kindly instincts, if he had any. 'I want to come up. I've had enough of it.'

'There's no' going to be a great difference here. You'd hardly see the light o' day if you're in that heat helping the puddlers.' Someone like Dowthie could not see the difference between an ironworks and being down a pit, never mind the heat.

'I'm prepared to do anything, Mr Dowthie,' and then boldly, 'but I'd expect bigger wages than I've got. Surely all that time is worth something?'

'You'd have to sign a contract like everybody else. Everything's covered in the twenty-one clauses. You're paid for your capabilities, no more, no less.'

'I'd do my best.' He tried to pull himself up, to push out his chest, to look like Dickie.

Dowthie was looking him up and down. 'It's no' an easy job at the furnaces. Hammering an iron ball into a flat bar. They weigh more than a hundredweight. Strength, McGrath. Do you know what a rabble is?'

'It wouldn't take me long to find out.' Kieran spoke jauntily. The man was playing with him. He saw it in the half-closed eyes, the smile that was a sneer.

'It's a long pole with a hook at the end, no' a fight on a Saturday night.' Again his eyes seemed to rest on the white shirt. 'No, it's not everybody who's fit enough to help a puddler. Have you been laid off sick much?'

'Just that bad winter the year before last. But only for two days.'

He and Maeve had had their first fight when he had struggled up on the third morning. 'You're fair murdering yourself going out with a cough hanging on you like that.' She had put her arms round him, trying to pull him back beside her. She had even used her body to persuade him. 'See, dear heart, it's warm beside me. I'll get up soon and give you some warm gruel. You need a day about the house before you go back.'

He had succumbed for a few minutes, feeling her soft breasts between them, her hands on him; then he had pushed her aside roughly and got out of bed. His head

79

had swum. 'You know they'd stop my pay. Leave me be.'

She had lain for a moment longer, then got up, stony-faced, and set about preparing his breakfast. Her slimness in the big white nightgown had made him sick with desire, maybe because of the fever . . .

'I've got ma complement of men for the time being, McGrath.' Dowthie was still looking at him. 'I'm sorry.' There was no sorrow in his eyes, just that gleam. 'You've got good experience, I'll grant you, but no' in the right place. Besides, it's younger men I'm looking for this morning.'

'I'm only thirty-six!' He spoke sharply, for him.

'Take ten years off that and it would have been fine.'

'You haven't got a job for me, then?' He remembered Maeve's unspoken desire. 'In another part of the Works? I'm willing to study at nights, to do anything to get started.'

'No, nothing.' Dowthie hesitated, and Kieran's spirits lifted. Maybe his heart was not all black.

'You've a son ready to start work, haven't you?'

'Aye, Patrick.'

'It's not my line, but they're looking for apprentices. If I were you I'd send him along.'

'He wanted to go down the pit with his brother.'

'*He* wants it, and you don't.' Dowthie shrugged. 'Well, it's up to you and him. Send in the next man.'

He had gone home, taken off his white shirt and folded it, put it into the chest of drawers. It would do for Sunday without washing. Maeve had enough to do.

'You didn't get it.' She was busy in the scullery peeling potatoes. She took a swift glance at his face.

'No, I'm too old.' She looked up again, astonished. A few tendrils of hair had escaped and lay on her forehead, her white forehead, showing through the red hair.

'Too old!' She laughed. 'They should see you in bed!'

'Maeve!' he smiled in spite of his misery. 'What a thing for a married woman to say!'

'It's true, isn't it?' Her face sobered. 'You're disappointed.'

'Aye, disappointed. It would have been good in the mornings, to have walked to the Works, not to have to go down . . . I could have watched the seasons, cut across the field a bit of the way, seen things growing . . .'

She turned towards him and held out her arms. 'You're shivering with just that semmet on. Come here.' He went to her, feeling the ache of tears in his throat.

'Who needs a shirt with a wife like you?' he said against her hair.

7

Nobody could remember it raining on the day of the Sunday School Picnic. So they said, but memories could be conveniently short. However, on this particular morning, the 6th of June, 1866, the sun had shone from a cloudless sky from five o'clock in the morning when Maeve and Kieran had roused the family.

'You feed the hens, Kate and Isobel,' Maeve told them. 'Patrick will see to the pig and sweep out the sheds. Where's Terence?'

'Titivating at the mirror already, maybe squeezing his plooks. He's like a lassie.' Patrick laughed.

'Tell him to get off to the well, then,' said Kieran. 'If he's big enough to start wenching he's big enough to carry a few pails of water for his mother.' He was full of happiness, Maeve thought, because there was no going down the pit today. Instead, as soon as she had prepared breakfast she knew he would be off to Tweedie's farm to get the horses ready.

He had been grooming them for the past week, feeding them up until their coats gleamed like the still water under the Packhorse Bridge. Now there were only the final touches, the final rub to the harness and traces, the checking of the tasselled fringes on the saddles, and to make sure there was fresh straw in the foot of the lorry in which the younger children would travel to the field kindly loaned each year by the laird Lord Garston Crawford – to give him his full title.

If Lady Crawford was retiring in manner, the laird

more than made up for it, Maeve thought, but then if you owned more than half the village, the pits and the ironworks, perhaps you had reason to feel important. People said he had a kindly side to his nature – wasn't he always giving donations to the kirk? – but on the occasions when Maeve had seen him handing out prizes at the miners' school, she had thought he had a hard mouth. And weren't the prize books always religious tracts? John had looked at them – he had been the prize-winner of the family, although so young – and put them aside. Her John . . .

But she was not going to think sad thoughts today. She, like Kieran, was happy to be spending it with their family. There was no work to be done, they would all be together, relaxed and happy. Tonight there would be no tired men trooping into her kitchen, Terence and Kieran bringing with them the stale smell of the pits, Patrick the reek from the ironworks. He had given in to his father's pressure and applied for an apprenticeship, and had started work at Easter, glad to be rid of school.

Today there would not be the apathy of exhaustion, the taciturnity she had to melt with cheerful words and water heated above the fire most of the day, with thick tasty soup made from vegetables she had dug up from the garden. Did they realize the work behind it all, she wondered? Most men did not, although Kieran was more considerate than most.

'Come and get your breakfast, Kieran,' she said fondly. 'I know you're dying to get off to Tweedie's.' They smiled at each other and she thought, the lines on his face have faded today. Sometimes he looked more than his thirty-six years.

She did not sit down with him. There was wee Maeve to dress as she was travelling on the lorry. Lady Crawford had suggested a 'rustic theme' and Maeve, remembering the woman's usual dishevelled appearance, had thought smilingly that she ought to know all about that.

But there was an essential kindness there. Since that talk last autumn, sitting on the bench at the back door, there had been some kind of bond between them. She had never sat down again, but her brief remarks as she scurried through the garden on her strange pursuits were those of a friend and an equal.

Maeve had made a shepherdess dress for the Wee Rascal, sprigged white muslin sprinkled with blue and white flowers, and had given it panniers cut from the lace shawl she had brought from Ireland. There had never been any occasion to wear it here. Kieran had made her a small crook, and they had spent some of their precious savings from Gladstone's Post Office Bank on a toy lamb that she was to carry under her arm.

'Now you must stand nice and steady on the lorry when it's going round the field,' Maeve admonished her. 'The laird and his wife and son will be watching, and we want Mr Tweedie to get the first prize.'

'What if the lorry goes over a rough bit, Mammy, and I fall down?' The child's eyes were bright with excitement, but there was no fear in them. She's a born performer, Maeve thought.

'Well, you get up as fast as you can, that's all. When you get on at the village hall you just see that you're in a corner where you've got something to hold on to.'

'What if Jeanie Laidlaw shoves me? She shoves me every time she sees me. She *runs* at me and shoves me!' Her small face was bursting with anger.

'She's not likely to have much room to run in a lorry. She'll be behaving herself, just as you have to do.'

'Will I wear my tinny on its ribbon on the top? If I

don't wear my tinny I'll not get my milk with my buns.'
Each child had a tin mug which was filled from the churns
donated from the laird's farms, along with a paper poke
of buns, sugar and plain, an apple and an orange, and a
few caramels.

'No, that would spoil the effect. I'll keep it, and then,
after the judging, I'll see that you get it.'

'What's "spoil the effect"?'

'Oh, never mind, Maeve! I've got more to do than
spend all day answering your questions. Sit down on that
stool till I'm ready, and if you dare move I'll take down
the rope!'

She was proud of them as they walked behind the
decorated lorries the two miles to the field behind the
Hall stables. Patrick and Terence had shining pink faces
and gleaming white collars, their suits pressed and
brushed, and Kate and Isobel looked pretty in their white
muslins, Kate with a pink sash to suit her dark hair, Isobel
with a blue one since she was 'blind' fair, the palest of
flaxen, like silk, which hung round the pearly paleness of
her face.

But then she had always been frail. And frail of spirit,
Maeve thought. She was not one for favouritism, but
sometimes she preferred Kate's steadiness and wee
Maeve's occasional 'badness' to the inevitable 'rightness'
of Isobel.

When they reached the field she saw that the estate
workers had as usual put up the bunting and erected a
platform at one end, and tents at the other to house the
tea urns and the non-alcoholic refreshments which the
laird always supplied. It was difficult to explain why, as
time went on, collars would be loosened, and many a man
would walk home less steadier than when he arrived. But

it was the Sunday School Picnic. It only happened once a year, blessed by the Church which was in turn supported by the laird. Some thought if he had added the money to their wages it might have provided a quicker way into God's grace, if that was what he was after.

And if he cut out the truck system, Maeve thought. Kieran seemed to be always talking about it these days, as if his grudge about being underground had centred on it. She had always been careful not to run into debt, but some of the less provident colliers' families spent their tokens on the first day, and then for the rest of the fortnight had scarcely enough to eat.

But he was not in a grudging mood today. She was standing at the edge of the field with the girls – Terence and Patrick had drifted away to join their friends, saying it was 'soft' to be seen with their mother – when she caught sight of him driving the pair of drays pulling Tweedie's lorry.

He was bareheaded, his curls glinting in the sun, he was smiling above his white collar, a man at peace with himself, showing no shyness because he was in his element. The horses were a wonderful sight, she thought, as they came nearer. He must have washed and combed their fetlocks until they looked like Isobel's hair, pale as the moon and as silky; the tassels round their saddles seemed to sway and jump for joy.

'Tweedie's got a fine turnout,' she heard someone say beside her, and the reply, 'Aye, thanks to McGrath.'

Now that the lorry was passing her, Maeve could see its shaky complement of small children dressed as rustic maidens, or as near to that concept as their mothers had been able to achieve. Wee Maeve was easily the best, she thought complacently; her shepherdess dress looked professional compared with the lumpy confections of the rest, even although she spoiled the effect by suddenly catching sight of her, waving her crook and yelling, 'Mammy, Mammy! Have you got my tinny?' She heard the gust of laughter, the comments: 'That wee Maeve McGrath. She's a caution!'

She looked down the field, and saw that the platform party had arrived. A wave of nostalgia swept over her. Long ago she and her father had gone to the village fair together. Her mother usually called off at the last moment, sending down a message by Deirdre where they stood waiting. She had a clear picture of her father standing there, impatiently comparing his gold hunter with the grandfather clock, and his 'Tcha!' of annoyance: 'The mistress has never slept a wink all night, sir.'

Together they had walked round the field, chatting and laughing with anyone they met, occasionally stopping at the stalls. 'Guess the weight of this cake, Miss Maeve'; 'Go on, sir, have a try at shooting down the Aunt Sally'. There had not been the formality which she found here, but then the Muldoons had been small fry compared with the Crawfords, a run-down estate, the only money her father had going into breeding horses.

Nor had the villagers been overawed by them as they seemed to be in Sholton. Was it power and money they admired, or was it that their livelihood depended on a proper recognition of the laird and all he stood for?

She discreetly steered the girls closer to the platform. Lord and Lady Garston Crawford had taken their seats, she in cream silk with her bonnet slightly askew and the ribbons creased under her chin, but looking every inch a lady nevertheless. Or was it because of it? She had known women in the old days who were only happy on the hunting field, just as the laird's wife seemed to find her solace in Sholton Woods.

And there was the Honourable Alastair, their son,

unmarried at thirty-one and supposed to be the most eligible bachelor in the country, looking elegant in his cut-away coat and tall hat. He was escorting a middle-aged couple and a young girl; now he was bowing them to their seats.

There was a sound of 'Whoa!' from the throats of the drivers, the cracking of whips; the lorries drew up in a neat circle and the laird rose to his feet. There was a respectful silence as his voice boomed across the field like the horn the dominie blew each morning to summon the children.

'I bid you all welcome to the Sunday School Picnic once again. Some of you older ones may have been here at the first one held in 1842, the year when I took over the running of the Crawford pits and ironworks on my father's death. I think I can safely say it has become established as an old Sholton custom.' His smile had no warmth, Maeve thought, a benefactory smile.

'The year 1842 was also when women and children were debarred from going underground, and it was on the basis of the old saying that Satan finds mischief for idle hands to do that I instituted the first picnic, from which sprang today's happy event. The Lord must have approved, because the sun has shone on us every year.' He waited for the ripple of laughter. 'I think you will agree with me that both the Sunday School and the picnics have contributed to the moral and social welfare of the small community where we live.' He paused again, and there was some feeble clapping.

'But I can see you don't want a history lesson on this auspicious occasion. Suffice to say that I have at all times endeavoured in my own small way to improve the quality of your lives here. A hard-working, God-fearing man is a happy man, and I think I can safely promise you that there will be plenty of work in Sholton for a long time to come. There is a rising tide of prosperity in this country. Coal and iron are in great demand both here and abroad, and it behoves us all to work towards the rewards which lie ahead of us if we lead sober and industrious lives.' He paused; there was a small clatter of applause that swelled uncertainly and died. It's more money they want, Maeve thought, not preaching.

'But this is a holiday' – he must have detected the restlessness – 'and I know you are all waiting for the judging of the lorries. Without more ado, therefore, I shall ask my son, the Honourable Alastair Garston Crawford, to perform this pleasant task for the first time. I know you will accord him the respect you have always accorded me. He may not have my experience in mining, but he tells me he's a better judge of horse flesh.' He paused again, a faint smile on his face at the ripple of laughter. He's a man who needs acclaim, Maeve thought. His wife grows tired of his need and escapes to the darkness of the woods where the animals and birds demand nothing of her.

'A final word.' The laird's voice boomed again. 'Our field has been the venue of the Sunday School Picnic for many years. It will continue to be so as long as the simple rules laid down are respected. Leave it as you found it, a pleasant, unlittered sward.' A sour note to finish with, she thought. The applause was more because he had at last sat down than in appreciation. The middle-aged couple on the platform were bending forward to congratulate him. The young girl was watching the Honourable Alastair.

Maeve's eyes followed him, too, as he stepped down and began his inspection of the lorries. He would be a good horseman, she thought. He moved easily and had the erectness and suppleness of body which she saw so rarely in the Sholton people. Men here had bowed backs at thirty, were often crippled at forty, sometimes dead by the time they reached fifty.

His physique had not been cramped by working underground. He had not had to crouch for four hours at a time between stoops, the wooden props above often bruising his back. He had not had to put on a jacket which was soaked with the perpetual running damp and walk home at the end of a shift with the wind blowing through it, chilling his bones.

Now he had made his rounds. He had dutifully stopped at each lorry and had a few words with the driver. She had noticed how scrupulous he was in giving the same amount of time to each one, but also how keen and professional his scrutiny had been and how sure his hands were as he ran them over the horses. He mounted the platform, bent to speak to his father for a moment, then faced the crowd.

'I know you must all be tired waiting.' His voice was pleasant, without the haughty harshness of his father's. 'The children are dying for their milk and buns . . . isn't that so?' There was a ragged shout of 'Yes . . . !' 'And fathers and mothers wouldn't say "no" to a cup of tea and refreshments. There's a full programme ahead – the sack race and the relay race and the three-legged race and the competition for the strongest man in Sholton . . . I'm glad I'm not entering for that!' He clenched his fist and bent his arm in a pugilistic pose. Maeve saw the smiles, heard the laughter. He was going down well. 'And then there's the dancing with our old friend Harry Dickon to play the fiddle. So . . .' He looked round smiling, 'I shan't keep you in suspense a moment longer. The winner of the best decorated lorry with the finest pair of horses is . . .' he

90

looked at the piece of paper in his hand, 'Robert Tweedie of Lochburn Farm.'

There was an outburst of clapping. Rab Tweedie had few enemies. The laird's son held up a hand. 'A word before the fun begins. I'd like to congratulate Kieran McGrath on his splendid turnout. I know a little about horses, even my father admits that,' he smiled, 'and I thought those under his care were in fine fettle. I can assure you, he knows more than a little. Thank you.' He sat down to even louder applause. The Honourable Alastair had been a hit.

Maeve set off with the girls at her heels towards Kieran. She met his eyes over the crowd when she was a few yards away, and they smiled at each other. For a second she saw the Kieran she had known fifteen years ago, the handsome lad in the stables who had taken possession of her senses and of her, remembered the trembling delight of those early days at Woodlea.

'Oh, Kieran!' she said, reaching him. She would have liked to throw her arms round his neck. 'Isn't it grand for you? You must be pleased.'

'I'm pleased, yes, but I had good beasts.' He was beaming with delight. 'Rab never skimps when he goes to the horse fair.'

'Will we go and have a cup of tea to celebrate?' She turned to Kate and Isobel. 'Lift the Wee Rascal down and get off for your milk and buns. Here's her tinny. And stand in the queue nicely. No pushing.'

'I'll have to drive the lorry round the back and unharness the horses,' Kieran said. 'Will you be after making your way to the tea tent and I'll meet you there in ten minutes?'

'I'll be after doing that.' They stood smiling at each other for a second, and she wanted to say, 'We've been losing each other this past year, since John. Let it stay like this . . .'

She walked slowly round the field, enjoying the summer sun on her, the swish of her skirts on the grass. She had bought a bolt of faulty muslin going cheap at the market and made a dress for herself as well as those for the girls and, greatly daring, had attempted a bustle. Crinolines were going out. She had trimmed the bustle with tucks and lace insertion to hide the faults in the material, and placed a blue velvet bow low down on the back for emphasis. What will the Sholton women say, she had thought delightedly, putting in the last stitch. She had made a petticoat from the blue silk ball-dress she had brought from Woodlea, which had lain in the back of the drawer ever since, and the gleam of the satin through the muslin pleased her. She had trimmed the bonnet with blue cornflowers, tied it with blue velvet ribbon.

She stopped at a small tent with 'Gypsy Sarah' written across it in spangles, thinking that nothing would get her in there. You made your own future, so how could it be already there in a crystal ball? Some day Kieran would get a fine job and they would move away from Colliers' Row.

When they had first come to Sholton she had thought it would be only a matter of time, but it was now fifteen years. Had she to face the fact that he had not got the necessary ability, or was it a kind of ruthlessness he lacked, like Lord Crawford's? She thought of the laird's hard mouth and the contrast between him and his son. He did not look as if he had the hard driving force of his father. But then he's third generation, she thought. Perhaps success was a matter of energy, too. I have that energy. If I were a man I could . . .

'Are you thinking of having your fortune told, Mrs

McGrath?' A man's voice broke into her thoughts.

She turned, embarrassed, knowing who it was. No one else had a voice with that inflection, that timbre. He was alone. Usually the platform party made a round of the field before they withdrew to the Hall for tea, then returned in time for the presentation of the prizes.

'No, Mr Alastair.' She laughed, trying to hide her astonishment that he should recognize her. 'It's not for me. But how did you know who I was?' She should not have spoken like that, lightly. Mrs Haddow, for instance, would have been horrified.

He laughed, too. 'Simple. My mother pointed you out.'

'Ah, I see.' Had Lady Crawford told him also of Maeve McGrath's familiarity with the gentry? She was sure that was how Mrs Haddow would have described it.

'I expect you'll be feeling very proud of your husband?'

'Yes, very.' She smiled. 'He's also very proud and pleased. I've just spoken to him.'

'My mother tells me you're familiar with horses, too.'

'That was a long time ago.' She was wary.

'In Ireland, was it?' She felt uncomfortable under his scrutiny. He had strange eyes, amber in colour like his mother's, far sighted. He, too, would be at home in the woods. His eyes would match the autumn leaves. He would be first after the fox, erect and handsome in his riding coat. She remembered her own habit, the skirts of which had been shorter than the other women's, 'scandalizing the neighbourhood', Papa had said. She remembered the snug fit of her riding boots, their black gleam.

'Yes, Ireland.' She realized he was waiting, his eyes on her. 'I always walk out to see the first meet of the hunt here. But that's a long time off yet,' she added, thinking, my tongue's running away with me, 'still only June.'

'Still only June,' he repeated. His eyes had not left her. 'Is autumn your favourite time?'

'It used to be.'

'What was it you liked?' She suddenly objected to this cross-questioning, as if she was a child.

'Perhaps because it made the blood tingle,' she said sharply.

'Ah, yes, it made the blood tingle.' Why did he repeat everything she said? Now, momentarily, his eyes left her, and she thought he was looking to see if they were drawing attention to themselves.

'My husband is waiting for me at the tea tent,' she said. 'I'll say good-day to you, sir.'

'Yes, of course. We all have our obligations.' He touched his hat with his cane. 'Good-day to you, Mrs McGrath.' He was smiling as he bowed, then he was gone, walking swiftly towards the Hall party whom she could see slowly making their way along the field, the dark girl holding a frilled lace parasol.

Why had he singled her out, she thought, as she walked towards the tea tent. Was it curiosity? She was flustered and yet intrigued; a small part of her was flattered that in spite of the fifteen years of drudgery – which had been doubly hard for her because she had not been used to it – she could still meet someone like him on equal terms.

At first when she had come to Sholton she had been hurt by the suspicious attitude of her neighbours. As a young girl she had made strenuous efforts to win their confidence, but she had never wholly succeeded. She knew they thought of her as 'different'; also, even more reprehensible, that she it was who made decisions for the family instead of leaving it to Kieran. And she had compounded these faults by having been seen chatting

94

easily to Lady Crawford, instead of twisting her apron in awe. Their opinions did not seem to matter to her nowadays. She recognized the Scots as a dour, hardworking race, even more riddled with class distinction than the Irish.

Her mind went back to the Honourable Alastair. Why should she look for hidden reasons for their conversation? He could have been activated by simple kindness. He would know of John's drowning in the Sholton Burn which also ran through their estate. He was more like his mother than his father, she felt sure. And if they *had* singled her out, she had no false modesty on that score; it was for the same reason as that which had made her neighbours suspicious of her and of her background which she never talked about, but which they knew instinctively differed from theirs.

And yet, she sensed, as well as a similarity, there was an essential difference between Lady Crawford and her son. Her goodness went with unworldliness. The son was not unworldly. She remembered his amber eyes as they glanced quickly around to see if they were being observed. She caught sight of Kieran, his head turning anxiously from side to side, and she went running towards him, as if fleeing from something.

That evening when the children were in bed, she and Kieran walked by the Sholton Burn, not in the direction of the Falls – she still could not bear to go near them – but along the leafy path towards the footbridge where the children sometimes fished for minnows with bent safety pins tied to lengths of string.

There was a full moon, and the air was still warm and balmy as if it had been trapped during the long summer day and was now being exuded from the leaves and the water. One or two courting couples passed them from time to time, and Kieran laughed, his arm round Maeve's waist.

'They take us for the same as themselves.' He pressed her against his side.

'It's nice, though.' She was happy and at peace. 'We can say what we like here. The boys have ears like foxes, and sometimes I hear the girls sniggering in bed.'

Perhaps that was the reason for the restraint which had grown up between them, she thought. Terence and Patrick were practically grown men, the girls weren't far behind and wee Maeve had until recently shared their box bed in the kitchen. Privacy was something you bought with money.

They stood on the footbridge and looked down at the gently purling water gleaming in the moonlight. 'It's been a great day,' Kieran said, 'the sun and fresh air and then the prize. Although the others were just as good.'

'Rubbish – ' she was fondly impatient. 'You know your turnout was the best.'

'The laird's son didn't give anything away when he spoke to me, although I could tell he knew a thing or two about horses.'

'What *did* he say to you?' She was curious.

'Nothing much. Just asked a few questions, then said, "I see you come from Ireland by the way you talk."'

'He didn't ask where you worked?'

'No, I expect it was on the entry form. It's not hard to guess with the men around here, we're all minions of his father, either at the ironworks or the pits.'

'The son spoke to me in the field.' It was better to tell him.

'Did he?' Typically, he wasn't suspicious. 'He's an affable chap, has an easy way with him. Not like the laird.'

'He said I must be proud of you. I think Lady Crawford had pointed me out to him. We're by way of being acquaintances because of her taking the short cut through our garden.' She laughed.

'She's a queer one, right enough, doesn't fit in with his lordship at all. They tell me that other man on the platform was one of his business associates from London with his wife and daughter. Maybe trying to arrange a match between the two young ones. Money marries money.'

'Maybe so.' She wanted to leave the subject of the Garston Crawfords alone. 'Isn't it lovely here? On an evening like this it could be Ireland, the softness of it.'

'Do you still yearn for it?' His voice was tender.

'Our roots are there, but I think not as much as you now.'

'I've learned the hard way not to yearn too much, but, yes, there will never be another place for me. I'll tell you one thing, mavourneen, I'd like to die there.' She glanced at him and thought she saw a shadow cross his face.

'Who's talking about dying? You're a young man yet, years ahead of you, with a fine growing family. They'll be keeping us in clover yet, just you wait and see.'

'*I* wanted to do that for you.' He turned to her, took her in his arms. 'I know it's been far from easy for you, reared gently as you were, but you've never complained, you've stood by me and supported me, you've been my support, my life.'

She was shaken, tried to laugh it off. 'We've stood by each other, so don't talk nonsense. You were always the only one for me. You know that.' She put her head against his shoulder and he swayed her softly. She heard him humming, recognized the tune and the sadness of it. 'Oh the sound of the Kerry Dancers . . .'

'You should have joined the village choir with that fine voice of yours. It's wasted, sure enough, in the scullery when you're sluicing water over yourself in the tin bath.'

'Now what would I be doing in the village choir?' he said, 'when they only sing Scottish songs! "Who'll tak the *keel* row, the *keel* row, the *keel* row," ' he sang, jigging her up and down. They laughed together like children, and then they were silent.

The moon had slipped behind a cloud, and she heard a rustle in the bushes as a small wind sprang up. 'Best to get back,' she said, 'and stop pretending we're courting instead of a staid married couple. If the Wee Rascal wakes up she'll lead them a merry dance.'

'If you say so.'

They left the bridge and walked along the path, his arm still round her waist. This time there were no entwined couples, no sound of a young man's gruff voice or the giggle of a girl. In the silence only the trees moved, and the water.

'The girls have gone running home in case their fathers are waiting with the belt.' She thought of her own father, of the loneliness of Woodlea now with only him and her mother in that big house. What was the point of it all, marriage, children, children leaving you, old age, death?

'But you're an old married wife.' He steered her towards a large oak at the side of the path and pinioned her there, his arms on either side of the trunk. 'Do you remember Crow Wood, Maeve?' His voice had thickened. 'Those stolen times together, and the wonder of it?'

'The terror and the wonder,' she said softly, 'like the beginning of the world, as if we had discovered it. Were we stupid, Kieran, do you think, or just over-young?'

'Or overmuch in love?' His voice was shaking now. 'I still feel the same. When I watched you today at the

98

picnic my heart was nearly bursting with pride. The beauty of you, like a queen.'

'I thought you didn't look too bad yourself. You reminded me of that young Kieran.'

'Maeve, Maeve . . .' They slipped down on the still-warm grass together and he lay on top of her. She could feel his heart thumping.

'This is . . . this is . . .' she wanted to say, 'this is stupid', but his hands were on her and the love words came from him as if they had been pent up for years. She gave herself up to his passion, responding to it. At one time she hushed him to say, 'It's a good thing the boys aren't listening,' but he did not want to be amused. He was her lover again, as strong as he had ever been, but now there was a kind of desperation in his loving.

8

The cottage was a hive of activity this evening. Most of the colliers' wives, Maeve had found, did not set much store by Christmas. Hogmanay was the great night of celebration when they visited each other's homes – first-footed, as they called it – carrying gifts, or even lumps of coal, which were supposed to bring good luck. A dark man had to be first to cross the threshold for the same reason. Kieran had never been in that category, even although his fair curls had now darkened.

With her natural generosity she, too, had kept open house, but her memories were of Woodlea and the Christmas log roaring in the fireplace for the hunt, stirrup cups both there and in the kitchen. Because of that she had always made a point of celebrating the festival in their own home.

Kieran was at the table which Maeve had spread with newspapers, making holly wreaths, wee Maeve was helping by tying ribbons on them with woollen-gloved hands to avoid the prickles. Isobel and Kate were cutting out paper chains from coloured paper. Long ago Mairi had taught Maeve the art which she had passed on to them.

'That's lovely, girls,' she praised them when they brought their work to show her. 'It's a pity we didn't have Terence and Patrick here to put them up for you.'

'I'll do it,' Kieran said, looking up. The firelight seemed to etch deeper lines on his face.

'Will Johnnie come back for Christmas?' wee Maeve asked her. 'He was always here.'

'No, my sweetheart. He'll never come back.' She had asked the same question last Christmas, Maeve thought. She spoke gently. 'But he's far better where he is.'

'How do you know, Mammy? Johnnie liked Christmas best here.'

'I do know. The Good Book tells us.'

'Well, could I have his stocking to hang up for Santa, then I'll get a great big lot?'

'Oh, Maeve, you're bad!' Isobel said. 'Isn't she, Mammy? She's selfish.'

'Just practical.' Maeve met Kieran's eyes. This is married life, she thought, the sharing. I should be content that we have each other, I should banish the restlessness in me, live for them all . . . 'Where have the boys got to?' she asked him, 'the time's getting on.'

'Oh, they'll be back soon. It's like trying to cage young lions with those two.'

'Terence leads Patrick on,' Kate said. Kate's usual quietness made one listen when she spoke.

'What do you mean?' Maeve looked at her.

'Oh, I don't know. I shouldn't have said that.'

'Well, you started, so you might as well go on.'

'Honest, Ma.' The girl looked uncomfortable. 'It's just that they're always talking and laughing in bed.'

'And I saw them talking to Old Beardie once at the head of the Brae,' Isobel said.

'Well, that's not a great crime, is it?' Old Beardie was a tramp who lived mostly by his wits in a broken-down hovel of a place near the Sholtie.

'Davy Cox is coming round tonight to have a word with me,' Kieran said. 'Will I take him into the parlour?'

'It's cold in there. Could he not come into the kitchen?'

'No, he wouldn't talk.'

Kieran had become obsessed by what he believed were

101

the abuses of the truck system. He held that there was coercion on the miners to get credit in the Company stores because of the custom of paying the men fort-nightly, sometimes monthly, so that they ran into debt. He maintained the owners were circumventing the law, and poor managers of their household finances, like the Coxes, were taken advantage of.

'Is he coming to borrow again? Remember we've got a lot to do with our money.' She felt ashamed saying that. She had three wages coming in, the Coxes only one.

'I don't think so. It's a terrible system. It sucks the life-blood out of people like the Coxes.'

'You've warned them. They shouldn't let themselves run into debt.'

'Don't get hard, mavourneen.' He smiled across at her. 'And it so near Christmas.'

'I'm sorry.' She was hurt by his remark. 'Am I hard?'

'No, just downright. I wouldn't have you any other way.'

'Now you're trying to butter me up. Do you hear him, Kate and Isobel, trying to butter me up? I'll go and see Mrs Cox tomorrow and take her some fresh eggs.' The hens were not laying well in the cold weather, so it would be all the less for them. There's your punishment, Maeve McGrath, she thought, for being hard.

'Yes, that's what to do. Cheer her up.' Someone knocked at the door. 'This'll be Davy Cox.' Kieran rose and went into the small lobby. Maeve heard him, the surprise in his voice. 'Will you not come in, Mr Guthrie?' And the reply, 'No, thank ye. I've got a cart outside. I don't want to keep the horse standing.' Kieran came back with a large parcel, a look of puzzlement on his face. 'It was Guthrie, the gamekeeper from the Hall. It's addressed to you, Maeve, not the children.'

102

'Our presents go to the school,' Isobel said, 'something for everybody. Teacher hands them out. I'd like a toy sweetie shop this time, with wee bottles and rosebud sweeties . . .'

'Open it,' Kieran said, 'we're all dying of curiosity.' He handed Maeve the scissors from the table. She cut the string and undid the brown paper. Inside was a riding habit of black broadcloth and a pair of well-polished riding boots. And a letter. The envelope had the Crawford crest on it.

'It's a riding habit,' Kieran said.

'I can see that.' Her voice was sharp with embarrassment. She should have told him about Lady Crawford's offer. It had been on the tip of her tongue many times, but something had stopped her. She put the point of the scissors in the flap of the envelope, drew out the piece of folded writing-paper – how thick and rich-feeling it was – and held it to the lamp to see it.

Dear Mrs McGrath (she read), my son is always telling me I'm scatter-brained. It was stupid of me to suggest you should ride old Walpole without the necessary clothes. If these are any use to you, please have them. And have no fear of disturbing us. The stables are quite a distance from the house and you can come and go as you please. I've told Craig, the groom, to saddle you any time. Your friend, Annabel Garston Crawford.

'What's the meaning of this?' Kieran's voice was stern. She should have told him . . .

'They're Lady Crawford's. A long time ago she asked me if I would like to exercise her hunter. We had got on to talking about riding. I thought no more about it. Well, how could I?' She blustered. 'Riding habits are a thing of the past. And now she's sent me these . . . her cast-offs.' She was confused, guilty. 'What do you think, Kieran?'

103

'It's kindness, there's no doubt about that. But I don't know. It's . . .'

'. . . What other people might say?'

'You should go, Mammy,' Kate said. The girls had gathered round and were fingering the habit, lifting and stroking the fine leather of the boots. 'You've told us of Ireland and how you liked riding on a horse in the mornings . . .'

'Maybe we could come, too.' Isobel's eyes were alight, her pale cheeks flushed. 'I've always wanted to see inside the gates of the Hall. I could tell the girls at school.'

'No, you couldn't,' Maeve said. 'It's not a free-for-all for the whole McGrath family, miss.' She turned again to Kieran. 'If you think I should decline with thanks I'll do it. After all, *her* habit, and *her* boots . . .'

He shook his head. 'No, she doesn't see it that way. She's a lady. She's realized you can't ride without them. It's she who's embarrassed, making the suggestion.'

'You wouldn't mind if I went, then?'

He looked doubtful. 'No, I wouldn't mind. It's not for me to mind . . .'

'Well, we'll see.' She'd leave it now. 'I'll write and thank her, and maybe if the spirit moves me one of these fine winter mornings . . .' she smiled at him, 'but it would have been better if you could have come, too.'

'I'm underground on fine winter mornings.' She heard the bitterness in his voice. There was another knock at the door and he got up quickly, as if glad to leave the subject alone. 'This will be Davy Cox this time,' he said. In a minute he was back with the man, a poor shilpit creature, Maeve thought, his face blue with cold, his woollen cravat grimy and unravelled at the edges. He had his cap between his hands.

'Good-evening to you, Mrs McGrath,' he said, 'a coldrife night.'

'Yes, it is. Come and warm yourself at the fire. Kate, go and make a cup of tea for Mr Cox.'

'A canna stay,' he said, looking around the decorated kitchen. 'My, you've made this place real nice, and what a fire! Enough to set your chilblains loupin'.' He went towards it and held out his hands as if trying to gather the heat into his thin body. 'The wife's ailin'. I think there's anither bairn coming.' He had the air of someone buffeted by fate. His shoulders were bony under the worn jacket.

'Could you talk here, Mr Cox?' she asked him, 'it's warmer.'

'No, it's private.' He turned to look at Kieran. 'A canna stay long.'

'Well, on you go through to the parlour. I'll lift a shovelful of coal for the fire ben there and we'll soon have you warm as toast. Kate!' Maeve raised her voice. 'Take the tea into the parlour, and there's a treacle scone in the bread bin. Butter it for Mr Cox.'

While the men were in the parlour she went through the children's clothes which they had outgrown, wrapping them in the paper that had contained the riding habit. Mrs Cox should have had the barren womb, not me, she thought, going to the scullery to see what she could spare from the larder. Tomorrow she would go and see the woman. I'm like Lady Crawford in relation to her, she thought. Would Mrs Cox have the same mixed feelings about receiving gifts as she had when the riding-habit arrived?

She was busy getting the girls to bed when she heard the door shut behind Davy Cox. 'Now, lie down and be a good girl,' she said to her youngest daughter, 'or Santa Claus won't come down the chimney to see you.'

'Why doesn't he get all black, Mammy?' The child's eyes were bright with tiredness.

'Because he's magic.'

'But why does he have to go down the chimney at all when he's got nice reindeers to bring him right to the door?'

'That wouldn't be as exciting,' Kate said, sitting up in bed plaiting her hair. '*Anybody* walks in the door, like Mr Cox, for instance. It's only Santa that comes down chimneys.'

'I'm going to write him a letter and tell him all the things I want,' Isobel said.

'Will you write for me as well, will you, Isobel?' The Wee Rascal shot up in bed and Maeve pushed her down again.

'What am I going to do with this girl?' She tried to hide a smile.

'I'll write one if you promise not to be bad,' Isobel said.

'Bad' and 'good', Maeve thought, shutting the bedroom door behind them. Isobel was obsessed by it. When she was older she would find out that nothing was wholly bad or wholly good, black or white. It was the infinite shades of grey in between that were the problem, the decisions . . . she heard outside the sound of singing, not strictly in tune. The voices sounded young. Did they also sound familiar? She went bursting into the kitchen where Kieran was warming his hands at the fire.

'That parlour chimney needs cleaning, Maeve. The fire didn't draw. Davy . . .'

'What's that singing?'

'I heard it.' He looked at her, puzzled. 'I don't know.'

'It's coming nearer. It sounds . . . listen!' They stood. It was a clear frosty night, the kind of night when sound carries well. There was no doubting the sound now, a

106

drunken chorus, or a duo – she could only hear two voices – that went wobbling up and down the scale. The words were slurred, impossible as yet to make out.

'The boys aren't in yet.' She looked at Kieran, fearfully.

'No.' He met her eyes. 'I was just going to take a look down the street. It isn't like Patrick.'

'Terence leads him on. And now that he's working . . .'

'They wouldn't serve them at the alehouse . . . ?'

'It sounds . . . like them. Oh, maybe I'm imagining things.'

'Maybe . . .'

Together they made for the door, their hands on the knob at the same time, and opened it. The cold struck their faces. Maeve shivered. She should have thrown her shawl round her shoulders. She looked up and down the Row. There were still lights in the windows, and now she saw larger oblongs of light as doors were opened, the silhouettes of men and women against them. Oh, God, she thought, we're finished now.

Rounding the corner at the end of the houses came Patrick and Terence, arms linked, roaring lustily, 'Gin a body . . . meet a body . . .'

'Go and get them.' Maeve put her hand on Kieran's arm. 'And tell them to keep quiet, for God's sake!' She could hear the deep guffaw of a man at his door, followed by the high, indignant clack-clack of a woman's voice, Mrs Haddow, more than likely. Kieran gave Maeve an agonized look over his shoulder as he set off to meet his sons, half-running.

'Hello, Father!' She heard Terence's bold, tipsy voice. 'It's a fine night, Father, sure it is!'

'Get home at once!' She could guess rather than hear what Kieran was saying. 'You're disturbing the neighbours.'

'Aye, that's right, McGrath!' A miner shouted from his doorway. 'Disturbing the neighbours it is, and them just lads.' And then another. 'Hae ye got yer belt handy, McGrath?'

Maeve watched Kieran walking between the boys, pushing them towards their own cottage, Patrick with his head bowed, Terence leaning back, protesting loudly. Oh, poor, poor Kieran, she thought, it isn't fair . . . Her voice rang out sharply: 'Terence, Patrick! Get in here at once!'

'Do whit your mither tells ye!' she heard someone say, followed by laughter, and then as she and Kieran bundled the boys inside and shut the door, she heard the banging of the others along the Row, like shots in the darkness. In the sudden silence a dog howled, a long, high note.

'Into your room!' Kieran shouted. 'Into your room at once. I've never been so ashamed in all my born days. Your mother and I work our fingers to the bone for you and then you shame us in front of the neighbours!'

'Ach, Father,' Terence said, still bold, 'it was just a tare. We didn't mean to . . .' his face suddenly blanched and he leaned against the wall, speechless.

'How did it happen, Patrick?' Maeve asked her younger son. 'I'm surprised at you being led astray.' He looked miserable. She saw the tears start in his eyes.

'Old Beardie sold Terence a wee bottle of whisky cheap. He thought he'd just try it, just for fun . . . just for Christmas,' he said pathetically.

'You're as daft as he is,' Kieran said, 'and I credited you with more sense.'

'Are you going to belt us, Father? If you are, just get on with it. I feel . . .'

'I feel . . . awful,' Terence said, stirring. His face was like a ghost. He went stumbling down the small passage and out of the back door, followed by his brother.

'Away to your beds!' Maeve shouted, turning to find the three girls standing in their nightgowns. 'Come on, hop it!' She wheeled them round, gave each a smart slap on their bottoms. 'And not another word from you!' They scampered off, giggling.

She and Kieran went into the kitchen, dropped into chairs at the table. 'Are you going to belt them when they come back?' she said.

He looked at her. 'I could kill them for the shame of it, far less belt them.'

'Oh, never mind that! It'll be a nine days' wonder, that's all. The women don't think too highly of me, anyhow. They'll be laughing up their sleeves, pleased . . .' I'll go and ride that hunter, she thought, defiant for a moment, and then sorry for Kieran in his misery. '*Are* you going to belt them?'

'What's the point? They'll be like wet rags when they come back from the privy.'

'They've learned their lesson the hard way.'

'I hope so.' He was disconsolate.

'It's not the end of the world, Kieran.'

'It seems like it.' He looked at her, and she saw the glimmer of humour in his eyes. He was beginning to get over it.

There was a fumbling at the door. The two boys came in, whey-faced, their hair plastered on their foreheads with sweat.

'We're sorry,' Terence said, 'awful sorry.'

'Aye, we're awful sorry,' Patrick said. 'We didn't think.'

'It was just a joke at first,' Terence went on. His brother nodded. 'A caper. There's not much fun down the bluidy pit.'

'Watch your language!' Maeve said. She would have liked to rise and crack their heads together, put her arms round them, laugh, weep.

'Get away out of my sight.' Kieran got up and the boys seemed to fall backwards out of the room. In a second they heard the heavy clump of boots being dropped on the floor, and then silence.

Maeve went and stood beside Kieran, laid her head on his shoulder. 'It could have been worse, my love.'

'Not much.'

'We'll get over it. It's a trifle compared with the other things we've been through together.'

'Yes, you get over everything in time. But the funny thing is that it made me feel my age for the first time. It was like looking at myself.' He put his arms round her and they stood silently before the dying fire. After a second or two she said, 'I've never seen such a sight as you coming up the Row pushing those great lads in front of you. Like a drover with his sheep.'

'And Terence singing "Comin' through the Rye".'

'Head bloody but unbowed.' The words came to her from the past.

'He's a terrible lad to be sure. We're going to have trouble . . .'

'But it was the sight of the three of you, and those gawping folk! As good as the penny geggies. Oh, Kieran . . .'

They were suddenly laughing against each other, moaning in their effort to subdue it.

9

Sholton Hall stables were, as Lady Crawford had said, quite a distance from the Big House, at least a quarter of a mile across the arched stone bridge over the Sholtie. They were imposing, Maeve thought, much more so than theirs at Woodlea, which had lain immediately behind the house.

But the architect seemed to have spent as much thought on the Hall stables as on the house itself, giving them a large archway on which he had carved the family crest, and incorporating a dwelling house on either side with mullioned windows and identical doors set in pillared architraves. The whole building enclosed a square courtyard.

The first time Maeve went was in the spring of 1867. Winter had been too difficult to think of anything but the family. Kieran had been off work with bronchitis, Terence had cut his hand badly using a metal pick – he was now helping the sinkmen – and Patrick was taciturn and hard to deal with. He was working with the puddlers, and the constant changes of temperature from the heat of the furnace to the cold outside seemed to drain his strength. He had been a burly lad when he first started. Now he was taller and thinner than his father.

There had been no repetition of their escapade with Old Beardie's whisky, although sometimes on Sunday Maeve would see Terence hanging round the kirk door waiting for Catherine Murdoch. 'He's obsessed by that lass,' she told Kieran, 'begging for favours like a spaniel grovelling on its belly.' She had never liked the girl, mistrusted her haughty airs and her small mouth. She was the wrong person for Terence, and Maeve felt that it was only his handsomeness that made her even deign to take a sedate walk with him by the Sholtie Burn.

Bessie Haddow would have been a far better choice, a riproaring kind of girl after Maeve's own heart, even if she had the name of being 'fast'. Once Maeve had intercepted a look Bessie had cast in Terence's direction over the bonneted heads at the kirk, and she had been surprised by its sadness. How could a girl be so different from her mother? she had thought.

This morning wee Maeve had gone proudly to school between Kate and Isobel – she was now five – and the house was empty. The old restlessness which had died during the winter was upon her again. She opened the door. The air was fresh. It stung her nostrils. The sky was as blue as it must be in Italy – one of the places she had always wanted to see. You could have travelled, she told herself, you could have studied, if you hadn't come with Kieran to this dreary place with the lowering skies and the people who look at you from under lowering brows.

She had no regrets. Kieran was worth it all, if it were not for the old feeling upon her that time was slipping past. She was thirty-three. Here, women were old at forty. She went inside again, drew the chest from under the box bed, and took out the riding habit. She would just see if it fitted.

In ten minutes she was dressed, and no longer the Maeve McGrath everyone knew in Sholton. This was a woman of thirty-three, certainly, but with all the sophistication that was implied if you did *not* live in Colliers' Row; a woman with a still slim waist and a neat ankle in the riding boots that fitted like gloves. She swept her hair back, tied it with a broad black band the way she had worn it at Woodlea, and looked outside again, fearfully.

The Row was deserted. At this time in the morning the woman of the house was sitting having a cup of tea before she 'got on with things'. Already she had been up for four hours, lighting the fire, cooking the breakfast, getting her men and children off to work and to school. It was the most precious time of her day, a brief interlude when she sat and drew breath with her hands round the hot cup before she began the washing, the scrubbing, the cooking . . . She shut the door quietly behind her and made herself walk, not run, to the end of the Row.

Mr Craig greeted her with little show of surprise. He was that rare thing, a man without curiosity, a bachelor, as Peters had been, but as different from him as night from day.

'Aye, her ladyship told me some time since you might be coming. Old Walpole could do with some exercise. The lads are busy with the hunt the now.'

It had been so simple that she knew it was right: the saddling of the horse, the mounting of him as if it was yesterday, the gentle canter round the paddock to get them used to each other, then round and round the stable buildings for half-an-hour. All her love of riding came back to her, the movement, the feeling of oneness, of being transported to a different world, of elevation both physical and spiritual. She walked old Walpole to his box where she tethered him and rubbed him down, memories crowding in on her of the old days at Woodlea. Craig was at her elbow.

'My, he looks pleased, that yin! I could see you knew what you were about.'

'I learned in Ireland.' She patted Walpole's muzzle.

'Ay, they all ride there, they tell me, some of them

113

bare-back. It's a different world, Ireland.'

'Yes, a different world. Thank you, Mr Craig. He's a grand horse. He just needs some shaping up. They crave discipline, like everybody else.'

'You're off, then?'

'Yes. I have to get on with my work.'

'You'll be back again?'

'I'd like to.'

'If you want to leave your habit here the next time, the other house is empty. The laird has plans to use it as a store.'

'It would certainly be better . . .'

'Then there's no bother, eh?' Had he realized how difficult it was to walk down the Row dressed as she was?

'Then there would be no bother . . . I'm grateful to you.'

'And don't worry about me. I'm a man that keeps himself to himself. I like my own company better than that at the Farmer's Arms.'

'Thank you, Mr Craig,' she said.

It became a drug, an addiction. She had never been more devoted in her household duties: the boys and Kieran were well tended, their clothes washed and ironed, warm water was waiting for them when they came home dirty and tired; the girls were turned out like bandboxes, hair shining, clothes starched; nothing was too much trouble.

She told Kieran what she was doing, but except for a quick, surprised look he seemed uninterested. He was absorbed in meetings at the pit-head about the truck system, and each night he was bent over the petition he was preparing concerning the loopholes which still existed in it. Davy Cox was in and out of the house. She knew that sometimes he did not go away empty-handed.

The summer picnic came and went, but this time the laird's son was not in evidence. Some said he was in Spain looking after the firm's interests there. She saw Lady Crawford from time to time as she cut through the garden, and she always waved or passed the time of day. Once she stopped. 'I haven't been taking my walks so frequently, Mrs McGrath.' She looked ill, her face more wizened than ever. Only the great dark eyes seemed alive.

'I wanted to thank you for the riding habit, Lady Crawford. I wrote. It was most kind of you.'

'I hope it has been of some use.'

'Yes, I've been to the stables a few times.'

'I'm glad. Don't forget you're doing old Walpole a favour. The thanks are on my side.' Watching her climbing over the stile more slowly than before, Maeve thought there was a change in her. Life was so short. She felt a wave of sadness. What was that saying, 'Time's winged chariot . . .'? She had always been aware of her own mortality, and that of others. We're meant to have some enjoyment in this life, she told herself fiercely.

It was autumn again, the brisk mornings that she loved. This particular one caught at her heart, the blueness and the gold . . . 'It's a grand morning,' she said to Kieran at the door. 'Do you feel the nip in the air?'

He was pale through lack of sleep. He had sat up at the kitchen table long after she had been in the box bed, working at his papers. There was to be a big meeting tonight in the Miners' Recreation Hut, and he was speaking at it. He had been gathering evidence all through the summer for his speech, and reading incessantly.

She watched the three of them clattering down the Row in their iron-clad boots, listened to the ringing sound that always seemed to spell frosty mornings. She saw a spark fly as one of their boots struck stone.

He finds it hard because he has no great aptitude for figures, she thought. His art lies in his hands, his intuitive sympathy with horses. He should be outside working in the fresh air. The thought came to her that this obsession with the truck was a way of keeping his mind off his hatred of the pit.

She felt guilty when she set off for the stables at nine o'clock, walking along the road to the cross-roads, avoiding the large gates leading to the Hall and taking the narrower track to the right, which led over the stone bridge. Old Walpole would have the smell of frost in his nostrils, too. He would be champing at the bit to get out, to feel the hard ground under his hooves.

She made her way to the harness room and took down the key of the empty cottage from its nail. She had been told by Mr Craig to take it if he were not there. He had long ago accepted her presence. Today was market day; he would have set off to order fodder or have a talk with his only friend, it seemed, Mr Masters, the vet.

She looked round the small room of the cottage as she laid aside her shawl and woollen dress and put on the riding habit. It was a pity the place was not being used as a home. Many a person would have jumped at it with its pretty garden. She pulled on her boots, let down her hair and tied it back with the ribbon she had brought, went into the cobbled yard and across it to the horse-boxes.

Old Walpole gave a whinny when he saw her. He was a docile beast, not given to great turns of speed, but he enjoyed his gallops. He, too, she had sometimes thought, riding him, had his memories. She led him out, saddled him up, and then they were clattering out of the yard, Walpole throwing up his head playfully, feet stumbling for a second, then responding to Maeve's touch on the reins. She took him into the paddock and round it a few times, feeling the old pleasure steal over her, an innocent enough pleasure, she told herself.

They came across a gap in the hedge and, without consciously thinking, she put the horse to it and immediately they were in a different world, the rolling fields and woods beyond the stables. There's no harm in it, she assured herself. I can keep well away from the Big House, skirt the Brow Farm and go into the woods beyond it. She could see their dark mass above the stone huddle of the farm buildings.

Old Walpole seemed to be enjoying his adventure as much as she was. He galloped along, occasionally tossing his head and friskily weaving between occasional clumps of bushes. He went up the low incline to the right of the farm like a two-year-old, and down the dip on the other side into the wood.

She saw there was a clear ride through it. It had been used before. She slowed down, but did not dismount. It was dark. She had to pick her way carefully, crouching over the back of the horse to avoid the low branches. The wood was also vaster than she had imagined, and she followed the winding track carefully in case she should lose her way. She remembered Crow Wood, a mere copse compared with this, the mounting excitement as she had crept through it at night to meet Kieran. She had been different then, but there was still buried within her the same need for excitement, some kind of challenge, which had not been killed, despite the long hard struggle of her years in Scotland.

Now the trees were thinning out and the ground, instead of being spongy under the horse's hooves, was crackling with the first fallen leaves. Ahead she could see a ruin, some standing walls of rough stone partly covered by moss, a flight of stone steps running round a tower. She remembered hearing that there had once been a monastery hereabouts. Old Walpole was puffing slightly. She would rest him before she started back. She would not wish Mr Craig to think she had overtired him.

She cantered up to the grassy sward that ringed the ruin, reined in the horse and slipped to the ground. 'Good lad,' she said, patting his neck, 'take it easy.'

'Are you on the same track as I am this morning, Mrs McGrath?' She whirled round to see Alastair Crawford leading his horse towards her. He was smiling. His face was deeply tanned, a tan you never got in dreich Scotland.

'Mr Crawford! You startled me!' Her heart was beating rapidly, partly from the ride, more from astonishment. 'I never expected . . .' A thought struck her. 'Oh, I do hope I haven't got in the way of the hunt.'

'No, they aren't out today. I merely came out for some exercise. I've been sitting in trains, it seems, for months on my journeying.' She nodded, remembering having heard he had been in Spain.

'Your mother gave me permission to ride her horse. I've been taking advantage of it. I hope . . .' He interrupted her.

'And the habit fitted well, I see.' Was it he who had suggested his mother send it? The words in the letter came back to her: 'My son is always telling me I'm scatter-brained.'

'Yes, it did. Even the boots.' She stuck out one of them, smiling, confused.

'If you'll allow me to say so, the whole outfit is vastly becoming. But tell me, as a matter of interest . . .' he was still smiling, at least in the amber eyes, '. . . do you walk through the village wearing them?'

'No, I don't.' She spoke sharply, annoyed at his perspicacity. 'I change at the stables. Mr Craig has given me permission to use the other cottage since it's untenanted.'

'Good for Craig. I remember now, the second groom prefers village life. Something to do with an old mother who won't move. So all's well that ends well, Mrs McGrath?'

'If you mean, am I enjoying riding, yes, I am. But only as long as it's convenient to Mr Craig.'

'My dear woman, it's no business of Craig's. It's the wish of my mother.' His smile was teasing. 'Besides, Craig is that rare being, a man without imagination. He takes things as he finds them. He never questions.'

'That's all right, then.' An unexpected shyness came over her. It was strange to be standing on this deserted spot with the laird's son. It would look strange. She had been unwise to leave the paddock.

'Perfectly all right, and everybody's happy. Have you got to know the lie of the land now?' It was as if he could read her thoughts. 'There's nothing like being on the back of a horse to give a new perspective to one's surroundings.'

'As a matter of fact, this is the first day I've left the paddock. I suddenly wanted . . .'

'. . . to try your wings?'

'I'm curious. Unlike Mr Craig.' She smiled at him, at ease now. 'My besetting sin and, worse still, I'm impulsive. I saw a gap in the hedge and took it.'

'Why not? Will you let me appoint myself as your guide? There's glorious country around here. Indeed, I feel it my duty to do so because before long my father will have covered it with ironworks or sunk shafts in it. I believe if he discovered coal under the Hall he'd have no hesitation in pulling it down.'

119

'But only a small number of people can be employed on the land compared with the hundreds in ironworks and mines.'

'Clever as well as beautiful.' His smile was mocking. 'But all the same, you're more like my mother. You and your husband don't fit in here, at least, not in the working part of it. Do you mind me saying that?'

She shrugged. 'Ireland hasn't had an industrial revolution. We're country people, that's true, born and bred. Kieran even more than I am. He has a . . . feeling for nature. He used to have a turn of words as well to describe it.' She laughed. 'I'd say to him he was going to be a poet.' He was looking at her intently as she spoke and she turned away from his amber gaze. His voice was soft.

'Nothing turns out as one expects, does it, Mrs McGrath?' She shook her head, looking down at her boots, Lady Crawford's boots. 'Still, you have each other.'

'Yes. And our family.' She wished he would take his eyes away.

'There are problems . . .' he spoke slowly, '. . . for me, too. Looking at me, the son of a wealthy landowner and industrialist, you wouldn't think so, would you?'

She shrugged again. 'You can't tell by appearances. I've learned that at least. Already one of my sons is learning to hide his true feelings.' She was thinking of Patrick. 'And sometimes husbands don't wish to distress their wives with their worries.' Was she being indiscreet? It was his eyes . . . 'No one is as he appears to be.'

'You're perceptive.' His smile was winning, his eyes merry now. 'But since that is so, don't you also believe that we must make the best of what we have and, if possible, even add some pleasure to it?'

'Of course.' She returned his smile. 'And that's what I'm doing by taking advantage of your mother's kind offer. I forget all my cares when I'm riding.'

'You haven't taken advantage of mine.'

'What was that?'

'To act as your guide. I should hate you to get sucked into a bog, or take a tumble into Jenny's Well.'

'Jenny's Well?' She avoided answering him directly. 'Where's that?'

'I can show it to you. It's named after a woman who drowned in it, or was drowned in it by the kind villagers who were convinced she was a witch. So, what do you say?'

She felt pinned down, confused, was anxious to get back. 'I only come about once a week. It's difficult . . .'

'Next week on the same morning will suit me capitally. I have a million things to do now that I'm back home. You can't turn down my kind offer, Mrs McGrath. Shall we meet here, then, at ten o'clock, in a week's time?'

'Well . . .'

'You told me you were impulsive.' His smile was teasing.

'I am, usually . . .' her mind was whirling. The situation was unreal – she and the laird's son, talking here together. Whatever she had been, she was now a collier's wife. And if she did accept, and they were seen, if people started talking . . . there would be the kind of scandal that would set Mrs Haddow and her kind talking for weeks.

'We'll steer clear of the farms and then no one will be any the wiser, if that's what you're thinking. From afar off it would simply be the laird's son riding out with a companion, no more, no less.' Now he was acknowledging the . . . unseemliness of it, the risk. But then again, she thought, a proper ride, to go racing across the fields neck

121

and neck as she had done long ago. She had always competed with Kieran. It was necessary for complete enjoyment, the striving. But what would he say if it came to his ears? She could not tell him. He would forbid it. He was easily ashamed, 'knew his place'. What was hers?

'All right,' she said. 'It's most kind. And perhaps if you show me the lie of the land once I'll know which paths to avoid, which bogs, even Jenny's Well.' To say it like that, lightly, carelessly, eased her conscience. 'Now I must get back.'

He assisted her to mount Walpole who was nibbling the grass beside her. 'Until next week, then,' he said, 'here at the ruins.'

She nodded, not trusting herself to speak. Of course it was foolish, a far worse caper than Terence and Patrick had ever indulged in. She tapped Walpole and rode away, full of misgiving, at the foot of which there was – she could only describe it so – an unholy kind of excitement.

10

Kieran was in the parlour with Davy Cox, a brushed and spruced Davy Cox, or as far as the poor soul could go in that direction. His scanty hair was plastered on his forehead (he must have sluiced his face at the last minute), and he had changed his usual grey woollen cravat for one only fractionally less worn but of a different colour, a dark maroon.

He himself was clean and well-fed looking in comparison, thanks to Maeve. She had had a piping hot dinner ready for him when he came back from the pit: stovies, which she knew were his favourite, and floury dumplings in the mince, a special treat.

When he remembered that she had never had to do a hand's turn at Woodlea, and how, full of spirit, she had set herself to learn, he could still feel ashamed that he had taken her away from that life. But she had wanted it, too, and even yet her zest for life astonished him. She kept them all on their toes. She was their mainspring.

He had thought this evening she had looked particularly beautiful, her hair gleaming dark red in the firelight, her face glowing as if lit from underneath, her eyes a deeper blue, almost black. They were always darker when she got excited, and he had commented on her appearance.

'What's up tonight, Maeve? You look as if you've robbed a bank.'

'Do I?' She had smiled swiftly round at him. 'Maybe it's the thought of your meeting tonight. I hope Davy Cox doesn't let you down.'

'He'll be in soon. We'll go over what he has to say before we leave, just to make sure.'

She said when the boys were washing in the scullery, 'I took Lady Crawford's horse out today again.'

'What does Craig say when you turn up?' He remembered Peters' sly remarks about her 'haunting the stables', as he had put it. Why did that come back to him?

'Nothing much. He's a man of few words. He accepts me because Lady Crawford has told him to accept me. He doesn't think about it.'

'One thing, he won't talk. He never goes near the Farmers' Arms. A thrawn man, Craig.'

'No, he's not a talker.'

He had watched her dishing up the boys' dinner and thought what a fine woman she was in every way. Far too good for him. She had had so much to offer; he had had nothing except his love. Maybe if he carried this thing through well tonight, she would be proud of him . . .

'Now, just go over what you're going to say, Davy, when you stand up.'

The man looked fearful. Was he going to lose his nerve at the last minute? 'You don't think they'll kick me out, I mean, the bosses?'

'There won't be any of them there. It's not got to that stage yet. Everybody in the hall will sympathize with you. Some of them have been in the same position. Many of them would cheerfully wring Brodie's neck.'

'Aye, I blame him more than the laird. He gave the shop over to Brodie a long time since, they tell me, when the high heid yins got word of how the colliers were being . . . exploited.' He stumbled over the word. 'Is that it, "exploited"?'

'Yes, but you don't have to go into that. I can give them chapter and verse if need be. I've been reading it up.' He did not think Lord Crawford's hands were clean, either. He still allowed the shop to run, didn't he? 'But one thing at a time, Davy. Come on, now, what have you to say about Brodie?'

'Well, I was in debt as usual. The missus has to get decent food, the doctor says, and what with the take-offs, the doctor himsel', tools, coals, rent and God knows what, and these bairns, I was at my wits' end. I don't know what I would have done if you hadn't helped me out.'

'Keep that under your hat. Go on, Davy.'

'I'm no' good with figures, what with this and that being stopped off ma wages. And then I began to jalouse that Brodie's bills were always bigger than I thought they should have been. So I did what you told me. I kept a note of the last lot I bought, wrote it down on a wee piece of paper and then compared it with Brodie's account. There were three items on it I never asked for! I've got them off by heart.' He held up a half-washed hand and marked off the items on his fingers: 'A two pun' bag o' flour . . . I wouldn't have bought that because the wife's given up the baking since she's been poorly. And a dozen eggs. Nor them either. Mrs McGrath's been giving us eggs, so *that*'s a lie. And two straps of liquorice. I think that was the one I minded most, when I can hardly buy food for they wee things, far less straps o' liquorice! God knows when they last had a treat like that.'

'He'd put them in to make the bill look authentic.'

'What's that?'

'True. You've got your list and his account?'

'Aye, they're in my pocket.' He produced two grubby pieces of paper. Brodie would say Davy had altered his, but it was worth a try.

'You have them ready to pass round the hall. Maybe it

125

will make some of the other men think and check up with *their* wives.'

'Then there's the interest Brodie's been charging me. It's far more than the other men in my room in the pit. I checked with them.'

'That's because you're far more in his debt. He'd say that, if challenged.'

'But I'm in debt before I start oot!' The man's voice was despairing. 'Hardly any wages to come to me with all the take-offs. It's a bluidy trap. I tell you, Kieran, sometimes I feel like doin' away wi' maself in the Sholtie . . .' He stopped. 'I'm sorry, I forgot about your wee lad.'

'It's all right, and don't talk such nonsense. You've got your wife to think about.'

'Aye, but she's no' much. A just have to look at her and she falls wi' another yin. We've got nine already and another on the way and I'm just aboot at the end of ma tether.' The man put his head in his hands.

'I'll maybe get a collection going for you tonight,' Kieran said. 'Just you tell them what you've told me. And be ready with your pieces of paper. We'll beat that bugger yet.'

Cox raised his head. 'You've fairly got it in for Brodie, haven't you? I've often wondered, I mean, I can understand myself, plagued with debt as I am, but you're doing fine with a good able wife . . . by God, she's a special one that, far too good for us around here, and that grand family of yours, although your Terence is a bit wild. What is it that gets your goat with Brodie?'

'It's the system. Brodie himself is just a pawn.' He sighed. 'Or, to tell the truth, maybe I'm looking back. He reminds me of a gamekeeper I used to know. I've seen him with animals trapped and dying, beasts that weren't doing anyone any harm except living. He and Peters, a groom, used to go out at nights together.' He looked at the man. 'I haven't been a great success, Davy, although you may think so. I've got the best wife in the world and I'm not a patch on her. I can tell you,' he thumped his fist in his hand, 'I'm going to get that Brodie if it's the last thing I do!' He blew out his breath and laughed. 'Maeve said I had to keep cool, and just listen to me, ranting and raving. Are you ready, then?'

'Aye, I'm ready, but I don't mind telling you I'm not one for standing up before all my cronies. It's no' ma line.'

'You get nothing if you don't stand up.' You're not a fighter, either, he thought, as he went out of the house with the man. You're going against your nature, doing this.

The hall was nearly full, Kieran saw, as he looked around. Most of the men had been pushed out by their wives. It was a pity *they* could not come instead of their husbands. They were the ones who had to make ends meet on the few tokens left to them when all the deductions from their wages had been made.

They don't give women their proper place here, he thought. Maeve and I are different. We've always shared responsibility. But then, *she's* different. He remembered Davy Cox's words, 'She's a special one, that. Far too good for us around here.' Far too good for him.

At first, when they were married, he had not had this sense of not measuring up to her. They had both been young, overwhelmed by their love for each other. He had been the provider while she was bearing the children. She had not grumbled about that, either. 'Big with love,' she had once said when he had laid his head on her swollen belly and said, 'Maeve, I'm sorry.'

But now, at thirty-seven, he felt drained, not the man he had been, while she bloomed. Her breeding days were behind her, there was more money coming into the house, there was time for her to look outside the Row, to go riding . . . no, he would not think of that. It disturbed him too deeply, a fundamental unease that seemed to attack his manhood. She escaped him by doing that, slipped back to her former life when she went to the Hall stables. 'This is something I've missed,' she seemed to be saying, 'which you haven't been able to give me, which you will never be able to give me . . .' he heard Mr Cranston, the gaffer, speaking.

Now there was a man you could admire, a true-bred collier who had been trained to the task of hewing coal since his father had taken him down the pit as a boy, proud of his work and his heritage, passing it on to his own two boys who had followed the Cranston tradition. He looked and listened, thinking the hewn features, the burly torso, the huge hands, told you what he was.

'Everybody in this hall tonight has a grudge against Brodie or we wouldn't be here. Some of you will say the laird's to blame as well, but he did abide by the laws, he handed over the store long before the big strike in . . .' he snapped his fingers, smiled round . . .

'Eighteen hundred and forty-two!' Kieran called out. He had to get used to the sound of his own voice. It rang too loudly in his ears, too strident.

'McGrath's got it right, God knows why, because he wasn't down the pit then like the rest of us.' There was laughter.

'Cutting peat, more likely, ower there, or tattie howkin',' someone said, and again there were several loud guffaws. If they had some fun at this meeting their wives had pushed them out to, so much the better.

128

'Yes, you're near enough.' Kieran got to his feet and his head swum for a second. 'But don't forget, the onlooker sees most of the game. And I've been reading it up. There was a man, Tancred, by name, who wrote a report at the same time as the strike, condemning the truck system, and here we are, more than twenty years later, still suffering from its iniquities.' There was applause as he sat down.

'You come doon, Cranston,' someone shouted, 'and let McGrath take your place!'

Cranston waved amiably. 'I'm no' here to make speeches. It's the Irish, sure enough, who have the gift of the gab.' He spoke sternly. 'What this meeting has been convened for is to examine the complaints which many of you have who turned out tonight, and to submit them to higher authorities.' There was a drumming of boots on the wooden floor, the men began to mutter amongst themselves, the noise swelled. Cranston held up his hand. 'One at a time, men. Stand up, give your name and let's hear it.'

A man in the front row got to his feet. Kieran could not recognize him from where he was sitting, but, then, they all looked the same, flat caps on their heads, woollen cravats showing above the jacket collars. Now that the evenings were getting nippy, the mornings colder, the coughing and spitting would start in the pit – even the ponies, as if infected, would puff and pant as they drew their heavy loads.

They were the only good thing about it. He remembered many night-shifts down there with them, giving them their corn at four in the morning, cleaning out their stables, saying a word to each of them, running his hands over their rough coats to look for bruises, making sure they had no loose shoes. 'You've got a right good way with the ponies,' Cranston had once said to him, 'they never seem to ail when you're about.'

'Danny Maguire,' the man said, 'No 2 Pit.' Now Kieran remembered him, a fellow-countryman but a townsman. He had come over during the Potato Famine as a boy, he had told him, and his mother and three sisters had died during it. 'I was down to skin and bone,' he had said, 'but I was down the pit with my father before we were housed, even, howkin' coal.'

He was still down to skin and bone, Kieran thought, seeing the scrawny neck, the thin shoulders, as if he had never recovered from that terrible time. But he was a good worker. The mine owners liked the Irish. They made few demands and helped to keep the wages down. We're used to being exploited, he thought.

'I'm no' speakin' for myself,' Maguire was saying, 'just about my neighbour, Wally Logan. Some of you will mind him. He was up to the ears in debt because of what Brodie was charging him in interest, a penny on every shilling as you all know.' He was a natural talker.

'Aye, we mind him,' someone said.

'Well, one night the wife and me heard some bumpings and bangings next door, and we thought, the Logans are fighting again, and didnae bother. In the morning their door was open. The whole jing bang o' them had scarpered off in an old cart, bag and baggage. That was what we'd heard. They'd done a moonlight. God knows where they are today.' He sat down, nodded around him, as if gratified to have set the ball rolling.

'I heard tell they were in the workhouse,' someone said. There were mutters, consultations, heads together. A voice emerged.

'I heard tell he cut his throat and the wife went back to

her ain folk with a' the bairns.' There was an awed silence.

'Did anyone else know the Logans?' Cranston looked round the hall. Kieran stood up again. This time he was more confident.

'He worked beside me for a time. He's just one of the many who've been ruined by the system. He tried to get poor relief but he didn't get it because he didn't go to kirk. You can't blame that on Brodie.' He had the courage to stop, to let his words sink in. 'They couldn't go to the kirk in rags, he said. He hadn't a penny coming in when his wages were docked. He was tied to the store, a slave to a system that's still running today when it should have been removed a long time since. If he cut his throat in the end I'm not surprised. We're all victims of this invidious system to a greater or lesser degree. Tancred said he didn't hesitate to condemn the truck system as an evil that poisoned industrial relations.' There was an outburst of clapping as Kieran sat down. Maeve should have heard it. She had rehearsed that last bit with him.

'That's the stuff to give the troops!' someone shouted. 'The Kirk Session's as bad as the store. You've to buy your way to heaven!'

Davy Cox nudged Kieran. 'Will I stand up now?' he asked, emboldened by the excitement that was sweeping through the hall.

'No,' he whispered, 'let them go on for a bit. Their dander's up.'

'Come on, lads,' Cranston said, 'you're here to air your grievances. We want facts, though, not threats. We've got to act democratically now that we have a Union behind us. It worked when we got our representatives to check the weights of a coal hutch, didn't it? Democracy . . .' His voice was drowned in the steady muttering amongst the men. Some were arguing with raised voices. Kieran stood up again. 'Try to win their confidence,' Maeve had said.

'I think Maguire should have pointed out that the Logans left because they'd had a summons to turn out at the Small Debt Court, not the first by any means. He just couldn't face any more of it.' A torrent of assenting voices drowned his last words.

Now their tongues were loosened. One man after another stood up to tell of how his debts had mounted, how the summons had come in, shaming him before his neighbours, the struggle he and his wife had, were still having. Always it was the shame of it that was emphasized and reiterated. Stripped of their pride, Kieran thought, and when that goes there's one last resort, to do away with themselves, like Wally Logan. Had not Davy Cox talked about the Sholtie Burn?

One man got up and complained about the shoddy goods in the store. 'We're not even getting value for our money. That bugger Brodie's making a fortune out of us, one way or the other.' Cranston held up a warning hand. He was laboriously writing down the names and addresses of the men who spoke.

'We'll get nowhere if we use foul language. It's facts, not threats, I told you before.'

'On you go, Davy,' Kieran said, giving the man a nudge. He got shakily to his feet, stood for a second turning his cap in his hands.

'Come on, Davy!' someone shouted, 'we're no' here all night!'

'It was . . . McGrath who brocht me. We had a talk before we came. I'm no' very good at this . . .' There was a burst of laughter, a voice above it, 'You'll be on the stage before long, lad, never fear!'

132

'I'm . . . minded of . . . something he said. He's not a miner bred in the bone like many of us. He's lived on the land . . .'

'Get on wi' it, Davy!' A loud voice came from the back. The man looked round fearfully.

'Say what you've got to say, Davy,' Cranston said kindly.

'Aye, all right, Mr Cranston. It's like this . . .' He stumbled through the recital he had rehearsed with Kieran, his confidence gone, but there was no denying that his experience struck a chord with many in the hall. There were mutters of agreement, whispering between men as they compared notes.

'That's aboot it, then,' he concluded. 'I can understand Wally Logan, the desperation. We're not beasts, we're men. We shouldn't be trapped, or treated like beasts . . . that's it, that's what McGrath said. That's what I was going to say . . . at the beginning . . .' His voice trailed away and he sat down, wiping his brow with his cap. 'God, that was terrible, Kieran,' he said.

'You couldn't have done better. You didn't forget a thing.'

Mr Cranston asked him to stay behind after the meeting. 'I could do with someone like you to help me. You spoke out well. There's a lot of bookwork. Are you willing?'

'More than willing, Mr Cranston,' he said.

'You'll get yourself into disfavour, not only with Brodie, or the owners, but the men. I've experience of that. You never do enough for them or do it right. They'll turn against you, blame you, if it doesn't go the way they want.'

'I'm prepared for that.'

'Good. I'll be round to see you one night. We'll work fine together, you and me.'

He went home walking on air. He had acquitted himself, he had a purpose now, something he believed in. Maeve would be proud of him.

She was waiting for him when he went into the kitchen. The girls were in bed, Patrick and Terence were at the Tweedie's farm, so they had said. He had reservations about that, wondered what capers they would be getting up to. She looked up, smiling from her mending. 'It's you who looks as if you've robbed a bank this time. Sit down and tell me about it.'

Afterwards he was the old Kieran, full of strength and purpose. She sighed once during his lovemaking, a sigh he could not understand. Was it happiness, or regret?

'That should have made triplets at least,' he whispered, when they lay exhausted beside each other. It was a coarse remark, he thought, not like him. It had something to do with tonight's happenings, and his new assurance.

'Yes,' she said, 'but that part of my life's finished.' She sighed again and he took her gently in his arms, satisfied in his body, but not content in his mind.

11

Terence walked sedately beside Catherine Murdoch along
the tow-path by the Sholtie Burn. It had taken him a year
to get to this stage with her, cajoling her when they came
out of the kirk, getting one of the girls to slip her notes
. . . different from Bessie Haddow. He was annoyed at
how his body quickened when he thought of *her*. 'It's a
lovely day, sure enough,' he said, stealing a quick look at
Catherine.

'Yes.' She tilted her parasol. 'It's very pleasant.' She
was wearing a bluey-mauve dress which was the same
colour as the bluebells in Sholton Wood where maybe he
would persuade her to have a stroll. It was too busy here
on a Sunday afternoon.

She tilted her parasol further forward as if she resented
his feasting his eyes on her. But, by God, she was taking,
with her dark curls and little mouth like a rosebud. Bessie
Haddow's mouth was large and she smiled a lot, and her
hair was thick like tow, with no gloss in it . . .

She did not hide behind parasols or need any persuading. He thought of the times in Jock Tweedie's barn –
Patrick and himself, Bessie Haddow and her crony, Lily
Docherty. They pushed each other and rolled about in
the hay, told rude jokes and giggled a lot. Once when he
and Bessie were in a corner together he had taken his
opportunity and landed a good long kiss on that mouth of
hers.

'Terence McGrath!' She had pushed him away, laughing. 'You're terrible!'

'You led me on.'

'It's *you* who're leading that nice young brother of yours astray. Just look at him with Lily there.'

Patrick was a deep one, not as rude as he was, but sometimes Terence suspected him of going further than he did. Maybe it was the puddlers he worked with who taught him a thing or two. They were supposed to be a rough lot, with more money to spend than the colliers.

'How are your parents, Terence?' Catherine said, twirling her parasol so that he caught tantalizing glimpses of her neat little face. It was hot for May. Maybe he could say, 'How about going into the Sholton Woods, Catherine? It would be cooler there . . .'

'They're not so bad, thank you. I don't see very much of them. I'm out a lot at nights, gallivanting.' He laughed, but his laughter seemed to fall flat.

There was a different atmosphere at home now. His father was always having long confabs in the parlour with Mr Cranston, and the kitchen table was spread with his papers as soon as dinner was cleared at night. No wonder he and Patrick were glad to clear out and go to Tweedie's farm.

And his mother was different, too. There was something about her which reminded him of Bessie Haddow, although that one, with her loud laugh, could not hold a candle to her for looks.

'Your father is getting himself talked about,' Catherine said.

'Talked about?' Terence echoed, pretending to be stupid. He knew what she meant, all right. He had heard some of it down the pit, some for, some against. It was the fearful ones who were against him, he had thought. But now his ire rose that his own father should be prejudicing his chances with Catherine. And there was no doubt that his eternal paperwork had spoiled their family evenings. One night he had spoken up, annoyed that his tasty dinner had been whipped away from him before he had scraped his plate.

'What's all the rush, clearing away my dinner before I'm rightly finished? It's a mystery to me what you're up to with these eternal papers!' His father had flushed with anger, and that was another thing, he was much more short-tempered now.

'It wouldn't be such a damn' mystery if you'd show some interest! You work down the pit, too. I gave you the chance to come to the first meeting, but, oh, no, you were away larking at the Tweedie's. The biggest mystery is what you get up to there, if you ask me!'

He had caught his mother's amused look. For once she was not siding with the old man, as if she was no longer involved with him, and that was strange enough. Like two pouter pigeons they usually were, billing and cooing.

'Don't be hard on him, Kieran,' she'd said. 'You're only young once, as you should know.' *She* had looked young enough as she had spoken. Neither Bessie, nor Catherine, come to that, could touch her for looks, he had thought, seeing the creamy skin, the red hair, seeing her as a woman.

'Yes,' Catherine was saying. 'I heard our cook saying something – her nephew works with you down the pit – a terrible tearaway, she says. It was something to do with truck.'

'I don't know him,' Terence said, lying in his teeth. Big Jimmie Lang was one of his best pals. But it had taken all winter and the best part of spring to persuade Catherine to take this walk with him. He was not going to admit to a pal like big Jimmie Lang.

'I don't know what father would say if he could see me

137

with you.' Her rosebud mouth pouted. 'You've got such a dirty job.' If she knew how he had scrubbed at his hands before he came out today until they were red-raw . . . he had a brilliant idea.

'Of course my father is one of the high heid ones now, you know. I expect he'll be going up to Glasgow any day to attend meetings and such like. Maybe we'll all get good jobs out of it, clean ones, a big house . . .' She interrupted him, apparently unimpressed.

'Father thinks it will cause trouble. I heard him discussing it with one of his elders. He's on the Kirk Session, you know, and he says some of the people are so feckless, with no thought for tomorrow, always asking for charity when you get into trouble . . .'

'They may ask for it but they don't get it!' Terence forgot for a moment to be diplomatic. 'My father says it's only the ones who turn out to kirk who get poor relief.'

She turned upon him, her parasol at the back of her bonnet making a further entrancing frame for her little face. 'I hope you're not implying, Terence McGrath, that my father cannot preach? He has letters of commendation from his College because of his fine delivery. *Framed* letters!'

'Oh, I'm not denying that, Catherine,' Terence said, abasing himself. The auld fool made him yawn his head off with his interminable sermons. 'I was fair carried away listening to him this morning.' He had been carried away before he entered the church, but that was because of delicious preoccupations with this afternoon's meeting. And here he was, wasting a golden opportunity talking about their folks! What had their folks got to do with anything, for God's sake?

'I should never have come with you this afternoon at all!' Her voice was petulant. 'It was against my better judgement. Papa always has a sleep in the afternoon before the evening service – Sundays wear him out – but you talked me into it.'

'Because I'm daft about you, Catherine.' He decided to put his cards on the table. 'Honest, I've never seen anyone so beautiful in all my life. Those dark curls of yours, and the way you dress, and so neat on your little feet. You sort of . . . flit, rather than walk. My heart fair turns over when I see you coming down the aisle. I think of you morning, noon and night.'

'Do you, Terence?' Her face softened. 'But you know lots of girls. I've seen you talking and laughing with them outside the church.'

'Just while I'm hanging about in the hopes of clapping my eyes on you. Phew!' He fanned his face. 'What a day! A bobby-dazzler! I'm fair sweatin' . . . I mean, perspiring with the heat of it. We get the full force of the sun here, and it's that crowded on Sundays . . .' There was only the occasional couple strolling past them.

'There's safety in numbers,' she said, twirling her parasol.

'I hope you're not implying that you're not safe with me.' He put on his pout. ('I know that pout of yours, Terence,' his mother sometimes said, 'you can't get round me with it, but it'll break some young girl's heart.') 'It's just, with that complexion of yours, you ought to watch it.'

'Yes, dear Mama had the same delicate skin.' She sighed. Terence remembered the late Mrs Murdoch chiefly for her pasty face and how she'd scuttled into her pew like a frightened rabbit. 'I actually saw one of your friends without gloves this morning, that Haddow girl. Pale hands are the sign of a lady. I use glycerine and rosewater for mine.'

139

'You can tell that. What do you say if we go into the Bluebell Wood? It will be lovely and cool there.'

Catherine shivered. 'But it's dark. I wouldn't feel . . . safe.'

'I'll take care of you. I'll guard you from the wild animals, from the birds of prey, anything . . .' He was disgusted at himself for talking so soft, but, never mind, if it worked . . .

'I must admit I love the Sholton Woods at bluebell time,' she said, looking pensive, 'I wouldn't mind gathering a bunch.'

'That would give the game away,' he laughed at her, 'going back with a bunch after walking out with me.'

She turned an astonished face on him. 'You don't think I said I was going with you! I wouldn't *think* of telling! No, you're my best friend, Mary Grant, for today, and don't you forget it!' She had a silvery little laugh. It came out of the small mouth like a peal of fairy bells, he thought.

It was the smell rather than the colour that knocked him over, such a drift of sweetness that he stopped and took great gulps of it. There was nothing like that down the pit, just foul odours, a mixture of everything, paraffin, horse dung, and that smell every miner knew but could never put a name to, the smell of being hundreds of feet under the ground in the bowels of the earth – and everybody knew what bowels were like. 'You'd think Auld Nick himself had farted down here,' one of the older men had once said to him as they made their way down the shaft, and that described it. His eyes closed for a second at the thought of repeating a remark like that to Catherine. He could imagine her little ears which were like pink pearls turning white with the shock.

'What a beautiful colour! They exactly match my dress, don't you think, Terence?' She held out her skirt, pointing a dainty strapped shoe.

'Oh, aye!' He got down on his knees and picked a few stems, held them against the hem of her blue voile. 'Would you like me to gather you a big bunch?'

'Yes, oh, yes, I'll help you!' She put down her parasol and together they knelt on the mossy ground, breaking off the pale stems, pulling some of the bulbs out by the root, taking handfuls at a time until Catherine had an armful. The sweetness, as if released, was all around them. 'I'll put them in water as soon as I get home.'

'And will you think of me when you look at them?' They were standing now, facing each other.

'I might.' The flowers covered her bosom, her chin was sunk in them, their colour matching her eyes.

'I always thought your eyes were green,' he said. 'The bluebells make them look blue.'

'They're greeny-blue.' She fluttered her eyelashes. 'They're supposed to be one of my best features. It depends what I wear.'

'I can't make them out,' Terence said, peering. Now he was brushing lightly against the flowers. The movement, or the heat, released their scent even more. It rose between them like an aphrodisiac.

'They'll be blue just now, because of the flowers.' Her eyelashes batted.

'I can't see. It's the darkness in here. I think my eyes are going bad.'

'Oh, Terence McGrath!' She laughed. 'You're teasing me! You'll be telling me next you're as blind as a pit pony.'

'Well, so I am.' He moved a fraction closer. 'I have to

141

get right near to look.' He put his hands on her shoulders, greatly daring.

'You're crushing my flowers.'

'I'm sorry, Catherine. I'm that clumsy. But being near you, I don't know what it is, a kind of mist comes over my eyes . . . it's the same when I think of you. I seem to drift away into dreamland . . .' Could he risk it?

His face was only two inches away from hers. She had not pushed him away. In fact her eyes had gone soft, as if she was . . . waiting. He took the plunge and kissed her lightly on the side of her mouth.

'Terence!' She drew back immediately. 'You're very wicked! If I had known what you were intending to do . . . I thought you only wanted to look at my eyes.'

'I couldn't resist it.' He remembered to pout.

'Well, please don't let it happen again or I'll regret I ever said I'd meet you.'

'I'll be careful,' he said, and cunningly, 'Will we walk on? I wouldn't like you to get into trouble on account of me.'

'Yes, perhaps we'd better.' She lifted her parasol and held it tilted back so that he could still see her face. There was a little smile round her lips, he noticed, and her cheeks were pink.

The sun was warm on his head as they regained the towpath, and the scent from Catherine's flowers seemed to be wafted to him in warm waves. I have never been so happy,he thought. This is different from the rough and tumble in Tweedie's barn, this is elegant, pure, and yet exciting. What would she be like if he kissed her longer the next time, maybe put his arms round her. He would keep his body away from hers . . . he suddenly thought of the smallness of Bessie's breasts against him when they

142

had kissed, and his surprise at their smallness. Catherine's looked more rounded, firm . . .

He heard voices, bursts of laughter, and round the corner came Jock Tweedie and Patrick, with Bessie and Lily. He cursed his luck, took a long breath, preparing himself.

'Aren't they noisy?' Catherine said, 'those people . . .'

'Yes,' and then, with well-simulated surprise, 'It's our Patrick! He gets in with right bad company sometimes. Da's always telling him.'

The four young people drew near. Terence caught Bessie's eye, and immediately her laughter rang out. 'Terence! Fancy meeting you!' She had no manners.

Now they were abreast. He saw Jock nudge Patrick. 'Out for a walk, Terence?' his brother said with a solemn face. You never knew if he was joking or not.

'It looks like it, doesn't it?' he said, glaring fiercely to silence him. Catherine bowed, turning her head away immediately and quickening her steps. He made up after her, hearing the tittering behind him.

'You should watch your young brother,' she said when they were scarcely out of earshot, 'and the company he keeps. He's at an impressionable age.'

'Yes, I'm always telling him.'

He could not get Bessie Haddow's eyes out of his mind for the next half-mile. 'It looks like it, doesn't it?' he had said, glaring at the four of them, and his eyes had met Bessie's. The laughter had died out of hers. They had been heavy with a kind of knowledge, a kind of sadness. I owe nothing to her, he told himself, but the memory would not go away.

12

Maeve sat beside Kate as they trundled to Glasgow along the new railway line further down the Sholton where it broadened out. 'Your father was telling me the train used to go over the old Sholton Viaduct,' she said, 'but it became unsafe with all the iron and steel.' Kate looked at her with a nervous smile.

'Well, thank goodness we're not going over it. I'm shaky enough at the thought of the interview. What do you think they'll think of me?'

'Just the same as Mr Liddell. Didn't he tell you that when the gentleman came to see him at the school he said he wanted a trustworthy girl, neat, of good character, and one who would be kind to children? And didn't Mr Liddell pick you out?'

'Yes, but . . .'

'No "yes buts". You're made for the job with the Murray-Hyslops. Don't forget that's their name. Mr and Mrs Murray-Hyslop, with a hyphen.'

'No, I won't forget. I'm glad you're coming with me, Ma. You can speak for me.'

'I have no intention of speaking for you. I'm just coming to see if the Murray-Hyslops are good enough for *you*. I wouldn't let my daughter go just anywhere, but I must admit it sounds right for you. They live in a fine town house in one of the best parts of Glasgow, Mr Liddell tells me. He's in the export business, and sometimes he and his wife go abroad. They wanted a country girl, so you fit the bill, and one whose parents weren't too far away so that she could go home occasionally. Yes, I think they'll do us.' Maeve nodded, a smile quirking at her lips.

'Oh, Ma, you're funny!' Kate laughed at her, her anxiety appeased. Her daughter looked just right, Maeve thought with satisfaction, in her neat blue dress which she'd made for her, with the lace collar, and her neat little black boots. A lovely girl, my pride and joy, she thought fondly.

'So don't worry about being away from home, Kate. If ever you weren't happy you'd just have to let me know and I'd be there in two shakes of a lamb's tail.'

Kate laughed. 'Isobel and wee Maeve were funny as well. Isobel said it would be a treat to have only two in the bed if it wasn't that the Wee Rascal kicks so much . . .'

'Don't call her the Wee Rascal, Kate. She's six now.'

'All right, but she's still a wee rascal all the same. "Will they be in their beds all the time, Kate?" she said to me. She'd heard us talking. "Why should they be in their beds?" I asked. "Well, it's a children's nurse you're going to be, isn't it?" she says. Can you beat it?'

'Yes, she's bright, that wee one.'

'I told her. "It's different from a real nurse," I said. "It's just to take care of them and take them for walks in the park and that." "You won't have to bandage up their legs, then?" she said. She makes you laugh, doesn't she, with that bright wee face of hers. I'll miss her . . . "No," I said, "I told you. They're not ill!" Do you know what she said then, Ma?' Maeve shook her head, smiling. '"When I grow up I'm going to be a real nurse! *My* lot will be in bed all the time and I can bandage them up and give them spoonfuls of cough linctus whether they like it or not!"'

'She wants to get her own back on Dr Gray. She made awful faces when I gave her the bottle he left last winter.'

'Oh, dear,' Kate sighed, looking out of the window. 'I'm beginning to get shaky again.'

'Read your book. It will take your mind off things. And just remember to speak out when spoken to. There's nothing worse than someone who doesn't lift her head and speak out. You've got nothing to be ashamed of.'

Maeve looked out at the countryside as the train ran through the farmland on either side of the tracks. Here and there were the giant winding wheels of the coal workings. The cows grazed round them as they would round a clump of trees. In the distance she could see the tall chimneys and cluttered buildings of the blast furnaces. People like the Crawfords did not give a thought to how they ruined and scarred the countryside with these huge workings which could become blazing volcanoes in the darkness, and how the whole length of the canal was obliterated by the perpetual steam from the waste water from the blast-engines. As well as the air being foul beneath the ground, it was contaminated above. She thought of the greenness and cleanness of the land around Boyle, of its untouched, untarnished quality.

But then there was no living for people. Did they not all leave and come to places like this, as she and Kieran had done? Dirt bred wealth, although the workers shared precious little of it. The rich, like the Crawfords, took the lion's share. She had thought sometimes, when she was riding with the son, that while he was enjoying the best of the morning, there were hundreds of men toiling under the ground to enable him to do so, Kieran included. Did she not condone it, she had thought, ashamed, by her own participation?

She and Alastair Crawford had rode together all winter

146

and into spring, a regular weekly occurrence which had become for her the bright spot of the week. It would not be that for him – his life held far more variety than hers – but nevertheless he was always waiting for her at the ruined monastery when she saddled Walpole and rode over the fields towards it.

There was no excuse now for showing her the lie of the land. She knew it as well as he did. She could have found her own way long ago, had pointed that out to him, but he had smiled at her, unabashed. 'You don't grudge me my pleasures, do you?' He had a mocking way with him that charmed her.

At first on their rides together she had been wary of him, wary of his questions, of his smile, of his amber eyes on her. 'You can't keep your secret any longer, Mrs McGrath. You've never so much as dug a potato out of the ground in that green isle you're so fond of. You're a born horsewoman. You've been in the saddle since your first fat pony!'

She had stalled at first, been cajoled a little, had let fall a few snippets of information, that, yes, she had always ridden, that yes, they had had a bit of land, nothing much compared with this. If she was building up a picture of him, he was bound to be doing the same about her.

He told her of Spain – not the beautiful middle or the south, but the Asturias where most of the mining was done; of his schooling in England, of the lush countryside of Wiltshire – 'Oh, you'd enjoy the hunting there!'; of his year in Paris – the Seine, the Champs Elysée, Versailles with its mirrors, the stained glass of Chartres. They were all magical names to her, feeding her with images of places she had wanted to see, which she might have seen if she had not run away with . . . she would not finish the thought.

147

'How does a woman of your beauty and spirit land up in a rotten little hole like Sholton? You're like a strange exotic bird amongst a crowd of barnyard fowls.'

She laughed aloud at that. 'You can't win me over with flattery like that!' Immediately she realized her mistake.

'Who said anything about winning you over?' And then, as if seeing her chagrin, he changed the subject. She saw his mother in him, his consideration. 'From what I know of your husband he isn't at all suited to going down the pit. He's as much a misfit as you are. I remember him with that turnout at the Sunday School Picnic. He should have Craig's job.'

'He could certainly do it as well as Mr Craig,' she said.

'So why didn't he look around?'

'It's easy to say that. When we came here we were very young. It was a case of the first job offered to get a roof over our heads.'

'Yes, I do see that,' he said. 'Bribery and corruption. We need the men just as the men need the work. But mining is wrong for him.'

'He knows it but he's never been able to take time off to look around, as you call it. And we had a tied house, children to bring up. A man loses his . . . zest after nearly twenty years. He knows he's caught, trapped. He can do nothing about it, hasn't the energy, is fearful . . .' She knew she was talking too much but could not stop her tongue from running on. 'But you're right about Kieran. He understands horses. He can be inside their heads, anticipating their every move, cajoling them, working with them, getting them to trust him. There was a horse . . . once, which followed him around like a dog.' She knew she had better stop. 'No, compared with Kieran, Mr Craig is only . . . competent.' The last word seemed to fall into silence. She felt his eyes on her.

'Would you like me to sack Craig and take on your husband in his place? I could do it, you know.' His chin had gone up, he smiled. 'I'm the laird's son,' his look said. She was angry at him, at herself.

'No, I wouldn't!' She struck her boot. 'What an idea! Kieran is a man of principle.'

'So I've been hearing.' The tone of his voice changed. She looked up to find his eyes flat, cold. 'I'll give you a word of advice, Mrs McGrath. Persuade him to give up the course he's pursuing concerning truck. He's going to get on the wrong side of my father and that would be unwise, take it from me. He won't tolerate anyone who stirs up discontent amongst his workers.'

She felt her temper rising. 'If your father's hands are clean, why should he worry?' she wanted to say, but stopped herself. 'Even when there are injustices?' She spoke as coldly as he had done.

'Is your husband so sure about that?'

'What do you mean?' She held her head high.

'The Irish labour under a sense of injustice, isn't that so?' She shrugged. 'It's endemic, and who can blame them?' His voice changed. 'I could make a good guess at your husband's background.' She looked at him, and saw the glimmer of humour in his eyes, mollifying her. 'I know my Irish history. You must tell me if my guess is right. Wasn't his father a one time tenant farmer whose land had been lost to his employer's antecedents?'

She didn't answer for a second, surprised at his astuteness. She remembered Joseph McGrath's taciturnity, and also a remark of her father's: 'McGrath's got a chip on his shoulder, don't you know? Thinks we usurped him, if you please. By God, he bears a long grudge. The talk came over it at the last meet. They've got to be put in their place . . .' Why had it never occurred to her that Kieran

149

might share his father's views? 'Your knowledge of Irish history does you credit,' she said.

He laughed outright at that and spurred his horse. His words came to her, blown by the wind, 'You're a rare bird, I'll give you that. Come on, I'll race you to that copse!'

I shouldn't continue to meet him, she had thought that same morning, when she was walking home. The hunting season's long over, we'll be seen . . . Of course he's intrigued by me, a woman who doesn't fit her niche. I'm a challenge to his curiosity, someone to amuse him when he's forced to spend time in this dull country. His friends are predictable, even perhaps the dark-haired girl at the Sunday School Picnic the year before last . . .

'Ma,' Kate was touching her elbow. 'How long now?' She recognized the outskirts of Glasgow, could smell it through the lowered window. The Lord preserve her from living in a filthy place like that. But up on the hill at Blythswood Square, Kate would be all right.

'About ten minutes. Then we'll take a cab to the house. We don't want to arrive looking hot and untidy. It would put us at a disadvantage.'

Kate sighed. 'I wish I was on my way back.' She bent her head again to her book.

'You'll be all right, my pet. They'll jump at the chance of getting a fine girl like you . . .' Her thoughts went back again to those morning rides.

She told herself it was her love of riding which had taken her to the ruined monastery a few days ago. But she knew also she was giving in to the feeling of dangerous excitement which had kept her on tenterhooks all week. Her heart had lifted with sheer pleasure when she saw him from afar off. What a seat he had, so elegant, so right against his background, so different from . . . she stopped herself.

It was as if their altercation of the previous week had put them on a different footing. They greeted each other laughingly, patted each other's horses, commented on the weather which was stormy, somehow suited to her mood.

'A grand day for a gallop,' he said. 'Look at that sky with the clouds racing across it. Let's race them!'

They set off, keeping neck and neck, she trying, at first unsuccessfully, to get ahead. She had never managed it with Kieran. It was in his hands, the secret, she would tell him, horses do more for you than anyone else.

But she and this man were equally matched. If she just gave it that extra effort, tried to get her thoughts to the horse as Kieran did, she could manage it. Walpole was responding, forgetting his years, she was gaining, gaining . . . the next moment she was lying on the ground, stunned. She was aware of Alastair Crawford bending over her, saw him at first through a mist.

'Are you all right, Maeve?' He'd said 'Maeve' . . .

'Yes, I'm all right . . . Walpole must have stumbled.' She lay still, trying to focus on him, feeling her head swim with the effort of talking. It was not the first tumble she had taken. She had just to lie still for a moment.

'Your hair has come loose.' She felt his hands on it, her head cleared and her eyes met his, very close, looked into their amber depths. 'Beautiful . . .' She could hardly hear him. 'You need love, you need . . .'

'Help me up.' She would pretend she had not heard him. Perhaps she had been imagining the words or . . . hoping for them?

She stood still while he fetched Walpole who was grazing nearby, unhurt. He, like her, had known how to fall even with no warning. 'There's an art . . .' she tried to steady her voice, 'in falling. I think . . . Walpole and I have mastered it.'

'You're not doing any more riding today, however experienced you are.' How deep his eyes were, bent on her, somehow at odds with what he was saying.

'Of course I am.' She was light-hearted, or trying to appear so. She smiled. 'Haven't you heard that when you take a tumble you must get on your horse right away?'

'Yes, I've heard that.' He watched her while she gathered up her hair, retied the ribbon. 'You're plucky. I have to add that to your list of attributes.'

'You're not keeping a list, are you?' She was amazed at her pretended insouciance. But she was mounted now, safe . . .

'I don't have to.' He was beside her, on his own horse. 'I know them off by heart. Shall we ride back to the monastery?' She stole a glance at his face. He was looking straight ahead, his mouth stern.

He took her hand when she left him. 'You're sure you're all right?'

Now he was too near again. 'Don't I look it?' I'm speaking like a young girl, she thought.

He shook his head, as if amazed at her. 'You look . . . ah, but if I told you how you look you'd draw away again. Next week, then?'

'I don't know if I'll come, if I *can* come.' She spoke quickly. 'Maeve', he had called her . . .

'But you must. I may be going abroad soon. Time is short. We have to catch it by the forelock.'

The words rang a bell in her own mind. Had she not felt that often, the awareness of mortality? Could it be, she had thought, that the greater one's feeling for life, the more one was aware of death? Was that why she was meeting him? Or was there something else?

'I . . .' She shook her head. It would be foolish.

152

'Don't decide. Not at this moment. I'll be there, waiting.' He turned his horse and left her abruptly, only touching his hat briefly with his gloved hand.

That night she had turned to Kieran and put her arms round him. She needed the assurance of his love. 'Kieran,' she said. She pressed herself against him. 'I get tired waiting for you to come to bed. We never . . .'

'I know. It's my fault. I'm dead beat when I crawl in beside you.'

'Maybe I could . . .' She had never had to do this before.

He responded, groaning, 'Maeve . . .' Alastair Crawford had said that. Kieran's body grew hard against hers, and then as suddenly he was limp, silently, lying down on his back beside her. She got up on her elbow and bent over him. He was asleep. Her frustration was so great that she could have shaken him awake. She had needed him, needed a man. She was honest enough to admit it to herself . . .

Kate was speaking to her, drawing her back. 'Bessie Haddow says her mother and Mrs Brodie have become great cronies.'

'Does she?'

'Yes. Bessie can't stand Mrs Brodie. She says she stirs up trouble. Sometimes I think Bessie doesn't like her mother too much, either. She's different from her, isn't she, Ma, much nicer?'

'Yes, and to tell you the truth, I don't like either of those women . . . but keep it under your hat.' She would not tell Kate about her encounter.

She had been walking down the Row the morning after her tumble, on her way to the store, when Mrs Brodie

153

had planted herself in front of her, arms crossed on her chest.

'I want to have a word with you, Mrs McGrath, if you please.' The woman's look was menacing. And she's ugly into the bargain, Maeve thought, with her bad skin and that nose, thick, large-nostrilled, like a pig's at a trough.

'Yes, Mrs Brodie?' she said, icily calm.

'Will you tell your husband to stop spreading lies about my man?'

She spoke loftily, knowing how irritating that would be. 'I never interfere in my husband's affairs.'

The woman mimicked her. 'I never interfere . . . Lady High and Mighty! Who do you think you are? That's a lie forbye. Everybody knows you put him up to it. Kieran McGrath's a mild enough man on his own. It's you that's at the root of it with your high and mighty ideas, you dirty Irish bitch! You aren't even a good Catholic like the other poor sods that came over with you. Pushing your way into our kirk! Your son daring to walk out with the minister's daughter! You don't suit us, Mrs Holier-Than-Thou with your secret goings-on, slipping away somewhere or other when your husband's back's turned!'

'Are you attacking me or my husband, Mrs Brodie?' She thought for a second that the woman was going to lunge forward and claw her eyes out.

'The two o' ye! You for your airs, him for stirring up trouble for my man. I'll see that you pay for it, I'll show you . . .' She'd walked away with the woman's insults ringing in her ears.

'Here we are at the station,' she said to Kate.

She had to admit she was impressed by the house, the flight of steps with their ironwork railings, the hall cosily panelled in dark oak, and the drawing-room which they

154

were shown into by the smart maid in her black and white uniform. Deirdre at Woodlea had always looked as if she had rushed into hers at the last minute, which she generally had; this one as if she had stood in front of the mirror as she dressed, making sure that each detail was right, from the little cap perched on top of her head, her long, well-ironed streamers, to her well-polished slippers peeping beneath her skirt.

'Mrs McGrath and Miss Kate McGrath, Ma'am,' she said to the woman sitting at the fire, a roaring beauty of a fire since it was drizzling outside – no shortage of coal there.

'Come and sit down, please,' Mrs Murray-Hyslop said, rising and holding out her hand to greet them. At least she's a lady, Maeve thought, not trumped up.

It was the ceiling that she chiefly noticed. She had forgotten how ceilings made a room after so many years under their Sholton one, cluttered as it was with a pulley for drying clothes in wet weather, the hams that had been cured by Donaldson, the butcher, to see them through the year, the flypapers in summer. There were always flies in summer because of the row of privies at the foot of the gardens. She and Kieran were very particular about theirs. It was the other people who were not.

This, she thought, admiring the plasterwork cornices, the rose in the centre from which hung a crystal chandelier, is the kind of ceiling Alastair Crawford will sit under, talking to his mother. This is my kind of place . . .

'You're Irish, then?' Mrs Murray-Hyslop said. 'But not Catholic, I hope? I understood from Mr Liddell . . .'

'No,' Maeve said, 'we've never been that. And all our family have been brought up as Protestants here.'

'I'm glad of that. We worship at the St Vincent Street church. I should like your daughter, if I decide to engage her, to accompany my children there, at least the ones who are old enough.' And in due course the one that's inside you at the moment, Maeve thought.

'She's well able to do that,' she said. 'We're regular attenders.'

'Now, we must let your daughter speak for herself. Kate, isn't it?'

'Yes, Mrs Murray-Hyslop.'

'Are you fond of children?'

Kate smiled. 'You have to be in our family. I've got two sisters and two brothers. And there was John who got drowned in the Sholtie.'

'Oh, how sad for you!' Mrs Murray-Hyslop looked at Maeve. 'When was that?'

'Three years ago.' She did not want sympathy. It was Kate they were here for.

'I have a little boy of three years, and two girls.' Mrs Murray-Hyslop turned to Kate again. 'They're called George, Emily and Victoria. The girls are six and eight respectively.'

Kate forgot her shyness as Maeve had known she would. 'I like dressing girls and looking after them. And a wee boy as well. Our Wee Rascal's six now.' She laughed, 'Though Ma said on the train I haven't to call her that now. She's a tearaway and no mistake. I don't expect your two will be bad like her.'

'She's not bad,' Maeve said to Mrs Murray-Hyslop, smiling, 'just full of life.'

'That sounds like my Emily. Victoria's the quiet one. I have very good reports of you from your schoolmaster, Kate. I would expect you to behave properly if you came to live with us, not to have followers, to do what you are asked to do politely. On our part we would try to make your time with us happy and productive. Tell me, would

156

you miss being away from home? I should like a girl who would settle down well.'

Kate pursed her lips. 'Oh, I'd miss it, but Ma says if I didn't like it here I would just have to let her know and she'd have me home in two shakes of a lamb's tail.' Mrs Murray-Hyslop looked startled for a moment then smiled.

'Well, now we know where we are, don't we? Tell me, are you good with the needle?'

'Ma's taught me. She makes all our clothes and I help her now, although I'll never be as good as her, and I can turn sheets and mend shirts and darn . . .' Mrs Murray-Hyslop held up her hand.

'You've satisfied me on that score.' She looked at Maeve. 'If you're willing to let your daughter come to us, Mrs McGrath, we should like to have her. We are a happy family, like your own, and we should try to guard her for you as long as she was under our care.'

Unaccountably, Maeve felt tears come to her eyes. I'm losing my eldest daughter, she thought, a milestone for a mother. She blew her nose at her own sentimentality. But it was not just that. The bleakness of her life struck her for a second; Kate lost to her, Kieran as good as lost with his constant tiredness and preoccupation with his papers, and recently, because of that woman Brodie, the terrible feeling of isolation which had come over her, of alienation. She was swamped for a second in misery, then as suddenly realized there was silence in the room. Mrs Murray-Hyslop was waiting.

'I'm very willing,' she said, smiling. 'I can't think of anywhere I'd rather see Kate go to.'

The woman nodded, pleased, then turned to Kate. 'And what about you, my dear?'

Kate looked at her mother. For a second Maeve saw in her eyes a greater understanding than her years. She's nearly a grown woman now, she thought, far steadier than I am. 'I'll miss Ma,' Kate said, 'and Pa, and my brothers and sisters, but it'll be nice to look after your ones, and dressing them, and that. Do you think . . .' she hesitated, '. . . I could see them before we go?'

'Of course you can. I'll ring for Grace to take you upstairs. I'm going to need more help soon . . .' she lowered her eyes at Maeve who nodded understandingly. 'And while you're gone your mother and I can discuss wages and other matters.'

She's curious about me, Maeve thought. I make her uneasy, because I'm not ill at ease. She looked around the room surreptitiously while they waited for the servant to return. This is my kind of place, she thought again, where I belong, and again the rare feeling of depression swept over her, of self-pity. She had tried so hard all these years, reared a family, stood by Kieran. Now they were leaving her, Kate, the boys, intent on their own affairs, Kieran on his. She was losing a friend as well as a daughter in Kate. Only now did she appreciate it.

But self-pity was never something she had indulged in, she told herself. Defiance was much better. What was the point in being miserable? She had to make her own life. Life was so short . . . she knew where her thoughts were leading her.

'And now, Mrs McGrath.' Mrs Murray-Hyslop was smiling at her with her soft, well-cared-for face on top of her soft, well-cared-for body, now swollen with child. 'We can have a nice little chat. Grace is bringing in tea. Do you agree to ten pounds a year for Kate's wages?'

It was more than they had paid Deirdre or old Mairi, more than Kieran had earned seventeen years ago. A lot had changed. She, for one, was seventeen years older. Life was rushing by.

13

She went reluctantly to meet Alastair Crawford, and yet
with a feeling of inevitability. The defiance she had felt
after her encounter with Mrs Brodie had gone, also the
sensation in Mrs Murray-Hyslop's drawing-room of it
being her rightful place. It was she who had created a new
dimension in her life from the time she had accepted Lady
Crawford's riding habit. For a time the meetings with her
son had been harmless, simply pleasurable, but she had
known they were subtly changing – a touch of the hand, a
weighted word, particularly a sideways look from those
strange eyes.

She had been surprised, and yet not surprised, at their
depth when he had bent over her after her fall; river eyes,
she thought now, remembering, like the clear amber pools
between the large stones in the Sholtie, those stones
which the children had been colouring when John . . . the
thought of that terrible day should have made her turn
back, remember that she was a married woman with
children still depending on her. But Alastair Crawford's
words in her mind dismissed them, swept them away as if
they did not exist, nor Kieran, nor Colliers' Row . . .
'Maeve,' he had said, and then, 'Don't decide. I'll be
there, waiting . . .'

She saw him afar off against the grey ruins, not moving,
his horse turned in her direction. She checked Walpole
and went even more slowly, pretending to be interested
in looking around. She was mad to have come. Apart
from anything else it was a wild, angry kind of day, as if

making up for a winter and spring of clear skies that had been a joy to be out in. It was a squally day, unfitted for riding. God, or whoever was up there, was showing how unpredictable he was. Like my heart, she thought.

When Kieran had set off at four this morning, he had said, looking up at the sky, 'Maybe for once I'll be glad to be down the pit.' It was a cantankerous, miserable day, out of humour with itself. A sudden wind whipped at her skirts and a squall of icy rain hit them both, making Walpole shy. She spurred him on, forgetting her disinclination to reach the ruins. She was soaked when she reached their shelter, so fierce and vicious had been the downpour. He helped her to dismount, leading her into a sheltered curve of the tower where there was sufficient roof to keep the rain off.

'Summer, they call it,' he said, laughing. 'Do you remember those lovely winter days when the sky was as blue as . . . there's no word to describe the blue of a blue sky.'

'Nor the tiny piece that shows when the clouds are breaking.' It was all right. There was no embarrassment. 'Our old . . .' she corrected herself, '. . . an old friend of ours used to say that if there was as much blue as the tail of a man's shirt it was going to be fine.'

He smiled, looking out. 'Not a sign. Someone up there is busy emptying buckets. Let's shelter here and wait. It's foolish to get soaked.' He produced a large white handkerchief. 'Wipe your habit as best as you can. I should hate you to catch cold.'

'It's all right.'

'Do as I say! First a fall, then pneumonia. It wouldn't do at all.' He was mock-serious. 'Look, I have a supply of handkerchiefs. I'll wipe your boots.' He got down on his knees and began to rub them.

160

She saw the dark top of his head, and thought how intimate that was, to see how his thick hair grew in a swirl from the crown, and the thread or two of grey in its rich blackness. She used the handkerchief on her habit, noting the close weave of the gaberdine, the fineness of the silk of the handkerchief, and compared them in her mind with Kieran's working garb – the thick, striped cotton shirt, the rough woollen serge of his jacket – the kind of clothes to be found in the Company store, cheap, badly-made. Only in the rich Glasgow shops would it be possible to buy a habit like this, silk handkerchiefs. Why am I noticing differences now, she thought, when I've lived as Kieran's wife for seventeen years and never complained? Is it that my love for him, and with it my forbearance, is wearing thin?

Alastair Crawford had got to his feet and was standing facing her. 'You look cold. Let me shelter you from the "cauld blast".' He smiled at his pronunciation. 'Do you know that poem?'

'It's Burns, isn't it?' She tried to speak lightly.

'It is. Not many know the second verse. Would you like me to say it to you?'

'If you wish.' He was too close to her. She could see only him.

He recited without a trace of self-consciousness, his eyes bent on her.

> 'Or were I in the wildest waste,
> Sae black and bare, sae black and bare,
> The desert were a paradise,
> If thou were there, if thou were there.'

There was a silence. She was forced to meet his eyes. They were not amber now, with his back to the light, they were dark, full . . . 'Do you like it?'

'Yes, it's beautiful.'

'Well, perhaps. Heartfelt, romantic, passionate, triumphant, even. Burns never did things by halves. He would promise the kingdom of Heaven to any woman without turning a hair. Perhaps to the lady he loved it *was* the kingdom of Heaven. What do you think, Maeve?'

'I think you shouldn't be so familiar, Mr Crawford.'

He laughed. 'Come, now. It would only be familiar if I were speaking to a little servant maid. You and I are equals. Besides, we've established our friendship. We've rode together all winter, spring and summer. Doesn't that entitle me to call you Maeve?'

She shook her head. 'There's Kieran . . .'

'But there's always been Kieran since the first day you came here. You knew that, didn't you?' There was no space between them now. She became skittish with shame and embarrassment, moving her head.

'I can't see if there's a scrap of blue in the sky.'

'Maeve . . .' He ignored her remark. 'You came today. Of your own volition. I'd hoped so much that you would. I've been very circumspect, but I can't disguise it. I've become unaccountably fond of you.'

He was so very close. She caught a gleam of amber in the dark eyes. A fish hiding in the dark shadows of the Sholtie Burn might be touched also by the sun's rays piercing the water. His hands were on her shoulders. His mouth met hers, and immediately something fierce sprang up inside her, like in the early days of Kieran's loving. Again he brushed her mouth, and his hands moved on the small of her back, pressing her against him. She felt herself become faint with the strength of her feeling, and wrenched herself free. 'This is ridiculous, stupid . . .'

'You wanted it.'

'No, no, I only want . . .' she turned her head from

162

side to side. 'I only want . . . I can't understand myself
. . . I must go home . . .'

'Gently.' He put his hands on her shoulders again. 'You
want to be loved. It's there. I can feel it. You wouldn't
have come if you hadn't . . .'

'That was a mistake . . .'

'But you still came. Your heart told you to. Now, calm
yourself. We'll talk.'

'I'm perfectly calm.'

'Then it must be my heart which is beating so rapidly.
You know,' he touched her cheek, 'I could make your life
. . . different for you. You shouldn't be in that miserable
Row amongst those women. I'll send Craig to Inverness
to our estate there and give your husband his job. It
would make things easier for you. For us. Let me arrange
it.' The arrogance, she thought . . . 'Let me show you
how much I want you.' He drew her into his arms again,
and any criticism of him went. She was ashamed at the
wildness in her, how it responded to his kiss. She was
afraid, not of him but of herself. When he released her
she put trembling hands to her hair which had slipped out
of its pins.

'I must be mad . . .'

'No, not mad, beautiful. And you have such beautiful
hair. I long to see it around your face, the dark red against
the paleness, one lock perhaps raised,' he lifted a tress,
'to show your small ear. We could make . . . opportunities
if you were near, Maeve, Maeve . . .' His face darkened.

She pulled away from him roughly, swept up her hair
on top of her head, secured it inexpertly with shaking
fingers. I'm being seduced in thought, as surely as in deed
. . . She began unaccountably to shiver because of her
emotion. 'I think I must have a fever, otherwise I wouldn't
allow you to . . .'

'Why do you deny your own feelings?'

'I'm going home!' She was beside herself. 'Look, there's a scrap of blue now.' With the capriciousness of the day the sun suddenly sent a long trembling beam down from the clouds.

'We're on the stage!' He laughed. 'No one can see us here, don't worry. I've no intention of distressing you, forcing myself on you, but think carefully. You're a sophisticated woman, a misfit in the society you inhabit. I can give you pleasure, excitement, which I know you long for, I can give your husband security in a job he's fitted for. I'm not a blackguard, Maeve, truly.' His smile was disarming. 'If you could bring yourself to call me Alastair, I assure you you'd feel better about the whole thing. Won't you try? We have an affinity. You must feel it. There are all kinds of ways I can help you. I could influence my father, make sure your husband's case is well represented . . .'

Sanity returned to her like a douche of cold water. 'Are there any more bribes?' she said.

'Bribes!' He shook his head at her, fondly, despairingly. 'Where do you get such ideas?' He sighed hugely. 'You speak like a . . . minion.'

'Then perhaps I am one.' She walked towards Walpole and he followed her.

'Maeve . . .'

'If you would hold the horse while I mount . . .' She felt safer on Walpole's back, looking down at him.

'See, I'm not restraining you.' He smiled up at her, his hand on the bridle. 'Don't make any grand denouncements or pronouncements about being besmirched, insulted, and the like. You're like a statue sitting there.' His voice softened, the amber eyes were full. 'Does it help to say I love you?'

The words seemed to sear her brain. Only Kieran had ever said that to her. She ought to be affronted, humiliated, all the words he'd used, but she was none of them. She was taken aback, moved unaccountably. She felt a great surge of emotion sweep through her. 'And I . . .' She felt her body begin to curve towards him for a second, then by a tremendous force of will she stopped herself, shook his hand free of the bridle and touched Walpole with her whip. The old horse made its way obediently down the mound on which the ruins stood. When she reached level ground she kept her eyes firmly fixed on the scrap of blue sky as if it were a talisman. They were dry, tearless. She did not look back.

Neil Duff, the lad who helped Mr Craig, was in the stables when she went inside after rubbing Walpole down. She composed her face, nodded briefly at him. She did not like him. He had a sly way of looking at her. 'Mr Craig's in bed with his rheumatism,' he said. He was polishing a harness and he did not stop as he spoke. 'I'm in charge.'

'I'm sorry to hear about Mr Craig.' She led Walpole to his stall.

'Did you enjoy your ride?' Duff stopped polishing. His look was insolent.

'Very much. Excuse me, I'm in a hurry.'

Her mind was whirling as she walked home. Had Duff any suspicions about her, had he seen them? He could not have, she consoled herself, the ruins were too far away. She dismissed him from her mind, turned her thoughts to Alastair Crawford, Alastair . . . she would think of him like that now. Had he overpowered her in any way it would have been simple. She would have known how to deal with the situation. Or would she? She remembered the desire that had swept through her at the

165

first touch of his mouth, as fierce and new as the first time Kieran had kissed her.

But he had brought reason into it, or was it bribery as she had said to him? Anyhow, a touch of mockery and good-humour, always his charm. And he had said that he loved her. Ah, that shook you to the core, she thought now. Supposing she accepted what he said to be true, accepted his offer of a job and a house for Kieran, would it be worth it, a life of deceit, of illicit pleasure? Because that was what it would become. Marriage was impossible, had never been mentioned.

Did she love him, or was it infatuation? Was she starved of love because Kieran had grown too tired and too distracted with other things? Would she be doing Kieran a service by getting him a job where he would be happy? Could she then cheat, tell Alastair she did not want anything to do with him? Foolish, foolish, she chided herself. A bargain was a bargain, and he was the laird's son. There would be the same ruthlessness in him. They could just as easily be turned out of the house and be worse off than when Kieran worked down the pit. And you know in any case, she told herself, that Kieran would rather die down the pit than have any bargains with the Crawford family.

She was passing the tall gates of the Hall, and she looked at the crest of the family picked out in gold paint on the fretted ironwork, the outspread wings of the eagle, some words in Latin beneath it. A symbol of power, she thought, as her eyes went to the great house at the end of the drive. She would never be accepted there. The most she could hope for were furtive meetings without Kieran's knowledge. In spite of her own background she would always be the wife of Kieran McGrath, a poor Irish collier. She was tarred with the same stick.

Her heart turned against herself in disgust at the self-denigration in the words. Had she not longed to be with Kieran, encouraged him, run away with him, given up everything willingly for him? Was it proving now not to have been love, but rebellion, and that her true place would have been behind those gates with Alastair Crawford, or even – her mind went back long ago – with James Tynan whom she had scorned but who had had a larger estate than theirs on the other side of the Boyle?

Now she was at the far end of the Row. The cottages ran away from her on either side in their parallel lines, mean hovels, she thought dispassionately, with their sparse accommodation, their lack of privacy. Now her life, stretching behind her, astonished her. Had she really put up with that kind of existence for nearly twenty years, borne children there, swept and scrubbed and cooked, carried water and coal like a servant, dug in the ground, emptied the privy when Kieran had been sick and the boys too young to help?

I buried that girl, Maeve Muldoon, she thought. Now, too late, she's coming back to question, to regret . . . she remembered her father saying that people like the McGraths had to be kept in their place. And had old Mairi been right when she had cautioned her so often about stepping out of her class? 'Take a cat of your own kind . . .'

'And where do you think you're going, *Mrs* McGrath?' The woman, Mrs Brodie, had materialized, it seemed, in front of her, with her ugly piggish face, her strident voice. She was shaken out of her thoughts so abruptly that she stammered.

'I'm going . . . home.' And then, realizing the effrontery of it, 'Will you step out of my way, if you please?'

'Step out of my way, if you please,' the woman mimicked. She could not bear how she spoke, evidently. 'What I'd like to know,' she took a step nearer Maeve, 'is where you've *been*?'

'Aye, it's where you've been. That's what we want to know.' There were two other women there now, Mrs Haddow, and that poor silly creature, Beenie Drummond. 'Aye, it's where you've *been*,' this one said, her great face flaming, '*that*'s what we want to know.' Had she been brought along as a chorus? Maeve stared at her coldly, saw the woman falter and turn stupidly to her companions. 'Isn't it, Ailie? Isn't it, Tibby?' She seemed to be begging for support. 'Isn't *that* what we want to know?'

Mrs Brodie nodded. 'Aye, and we've a good idea.' She smiled. It was not a pleasant smile. It seemed to curl her top lip so that it touched her flat nose, revealing strong yellow teeth.

'I don't know what you're talking about,' Maeve said. 'Let me pass.' She was annoyed to find that her heart was beating rapidly. There was something evil, something vindictive in the confident stance of the three women, as if they had plotted and planned . . .

Mrs Brodie thrust her face forward, nearly touching Maeve's. 'You're no' taking a step till you tell us what you've been up to. We don't like folks here who have secret ploys with the gentry while their men are causing trouble at the other end. We don't like folks polluting the Row, taking away its good name!'

'You don't *like*!' Maeve shouted, her temper suddenly flaring. 'Whatever I do, or my husband, is our own affair!'

'But no' where it concerns *us*, Mrs McGrath.' Mrs Haddow's voice was softer than Mrs Brodie's, but if anything more menacing in its sleekit softness. 'Aye, *we*'ve always played the game, done right, not gone gallivanting about the country hobnobbing with the high heid yins, helped you when your poor wee lad was drowned in the Sholtie . . . though some think you should have taken better care of him . . .'

'You bitch!' Maeve's head swam for a second. 'You lying bitch! To say such a thing about my John, my lovely boy . . . there isn't a day I don't grieve for him . . .'

'Mind your language. I'm no' used to it. And is gallivanting and riding wi' the gentry and who knows what else being sacred to his memory, then? Answer me that!' Mrs Haddow's chin was raised like the Reverend's, her sanctimonious look was the same. Neil Duff, Maeve thought, I might have known, that sly upward look, 'Did you enjoy your ride . . . ?'

'Aye, answer that!' the poor, silly Beenie said, but now she did not look so poor or so silly. Her face was even redder with excitement, her small eyes glittered, her bare arms with the sleeves rolled up above her elbows were like hams, her great bosom swelled.

'We're waiting.' Mrs Brodie spoke. The three women were ranged against Maeve in a tight row, preventing her from passing. Their eyes were cold, malevolent.

'We're waitin' . . .'

'We're waitin' . . .'

Maeve's temper left her at the sheer incredibility of the situation, and with it her fear. They were deranged, the three of them. But there was Neil Duff. He had seen her before today at the Hall stables. Maybe he had followed her when he was exercising the horses. Her feeling of despair, of everything having gone wrong because of her own stupidity, was great. It made her push against them, her hands waving wildly. 'You can't stop me! Get out of my way!' She tried to force her way between Beenie Drummond and Mrs Haddow, and as she did so she felt a stinging blow on the side of her face. She knew there had been a flailing red arm, a great red hand, before the pain made her stagger. She heard Beenie Drummond's heavy breathing, smelled her.

'Who do you think you're shoving? The cheek of it!' Mrs Brodie's piercing voice assaulted her ears. 'Pushing and shoving when we're only asking a few civil questions!' Her face came close, her arms hidden. Maeve felt a vicious blow in her stomach, making her curve round the pain. And as she did so she felt fingers digging into her shoulders, cruelly. She knew they were Mrs Haddow's, pushing her back. She lost her footing and fell heavily, striking her head. Through her misery she felt the thud of boots on her ribs. She moaned aloud for help, but the doors of the cottages remained firmly shut. They're all in it, she thought, half-conscious. They're peering from behind their lace curtains, enjoying it, there isn't one friend . . .

The pit hooter sounded. She was aware of it dimly through her pain, and of the silence that followed it. The women had gone. The men would be changing shifts. They would be coming down the Row any minute. And what about the others who were at home? Had they stood beside their wives at those curtained windows and watched her being punched and kicked? Damn them to hell, she thought, every one of them, damn them to hell. She had to keep thinking fiercely like that in case she should moan aloud again in her agony. She got up slowly.

Her blouse was torn off her shoulders, she could see the livid marks of fingers there, her ribs and belly ached. One eye was stiff and already closing. I would like to die, she thought as she walked slowly along the Row, die, die . . . When she got to her cottage she went round the back to the door which was always open and sat down outside it on the bench.

The roses were heavy with scent. Long, long ago, when they were young, she and Kieran had sat here, content. He had planted them for her, a white and a red. She had told Lady Crawford that and she had asked for a white one to take with her. If you could see me now, she thought, you strange soul. You started it all in your innocence. You were . . . she searched for the word . . . an arbiter of fate.

Terence would be going out soon on the next shift, Kieran would be coming home. The girls would be running back from school before long and telling her all that Mr Liddell had said that day and who had got the tawse. She imagined wee Maeve's bright face, Isobel sanctimonious in the background. 'She should become a lady missionary,' she had once said to Kieran. She put her head in her hands and wept as if her heart would break. After a long time she got up and went indoors.

14

Terence pulled aside the curtains of the box bed. 'Ma,' he
looked aggrieved. 'My bate . . . in the name of God,
what's happened to you!' His face changed to an expression of concern. 'Have you been in a fight?'

She tried to smile. Her face was stiff and swollen where
that henchwoman, Beenie, had caught her with her great
fist. 'Don't be daft, Terence. No, I took a tumble . . . on
Lady Crawford's horse.' Lying in a bundle of pain and
misery for the last few hours, she had decided on this
story.

'Does it hurt?' His young face was handsome in its
puzzled distress. No wonder Catherine Murdoch had
stepped down from her throne to walk out with him.

'It's mostly my eye.' She would say nothing about her
ribs and her stomach. The vicious downward punch Mrs
Brodie had aimed there seemed to have searched out the
tender parts that had lain dormant since Maeve's birth. 'I
thought I'd get up.' She tried to rise but her head swam
and she fell back on the pillows.

'You shouldn't be out riding that horse at your age . . .'
She would have laughed if her ribs had not ached so
much.

'What age do you think I am, you silly lad? Because
you're at the height of your powers doesn't mean I'm an
old hag. I'm only thirty-four!'

'That nearly makes you an auld granny!' His handsome
smile lit his face. 'Don't you bother, Ma. You tell me
where the corned beef is and I'll make my own bate. The

kettle's on the hob. I can soon make a bottle of tea. Would you like a cup?'

'Oh, would you, son?' Tears started in her eyes at what seemed to her his immense kindness. 'Once I get a hot cup I'll be able to get up and get the dinner ready for your father and the girls.'

'Maybe you should give it up . . . I've a feeling Pa doesn't like it that much . . . the going to the Hall stables. It isn't . . .'

'It isn't what?' she said sharply, and was rewarded by a vicious stab of pain piercing her head where that Amazon had hit her. 'What were you going to say? Have you lost your tongue?'

'It isn't . . . fitting.' He looked defiant and ashamed at the same time. 'I've never heard of the mothers of any of the other lads riding a horse. It's . . . it's . . .'

'Don't you like your mother to be different?' She spoke quietly, because it was necessary not to move her head on the pillow.

'Well . . . it might attract attention. It's as bad as you . . . being in the circus! And people, I mean . . .'

'And Catherine Murdoch might get to hear about it? Is that it?' She turned her head away from him. 'Away and make your bate. If it's any comfort to you, I won't be going to the Hall stables for a while . . . if ever.'

The hot tea seemed to ease her pain. Her spirits revived. When Terence had gone clattering out of the house like the Prussian Army on the march, she gingerly got out of bed. There was no point in lying there feeling sorry for herself. She would only stiffen up more.

She walked to the scullery, scooped some water into the tin basin and carefully bathed her face, found some yellow ointment on the shelf and patted it carefully round her eye. The skin had not been broken, thank goodness,

173

and she was sure there were no bones cracked in her ribs since she could walk fairly easily. Kieran and Terence often complained about feeling bruised and sore. She combed her hair back as well as she could. She could not face the bother of taking it down and putting it up again.

If only Kate were here. She had loved combing and brushing it. They had spent many pleasant sessions in the firelit kitchen, a clean towel spread round her shoulders. 'Oh, Ma, what wouldn't I give to have hair the colour of yours instead of this black stuff of mine. How have I got this colour when Pa's fair and you're red?'

'Your grandfather in Ireland is dark,' she had said.

'*Your* father?'

'Yes, Grandfather Muldoon.'

'You never talk about them. Is the other grandfather alive as well?'

'Yes, his wife writes sometimes. She'd say if my parents . . . weren't. When you leave a country, you leave your connections behind you. At least we did . . . Now don't ask me any more questions. Get on with my hair.' It had been a sensuous delight, the long, soothing strokes. Kate's loving kindness came through in everything she did.

Kieran came in when she was sitting at the fire, resting after her efforts. 'I passed Isobel and wee Maeve playing peevor in the school yard. They won't be long behind me.' He put his arm round her shoulders as he came over to stand beside her to warm his hands. 'What weather for summer-time . . .' He turned to her, smiling, and then his face changed. 'My God! What have you been doing to yourself?'

'I fell . . . out riding.' She mumbled the words, ashamed now of her lie, longing to throw herself into his arms and be comforted. But she had been in another

174

man's arms not so long ago . . . she felt isolated by her guilt.

His face had reddened with anger. 'That's terrible! It's time you stopped it. It's not . . .'

'. . . fitting? That's what Terence thinks. That's what the whole place seems to think.'

'What do you mean?'

'You've never liked me going. You know that. But I was counting on your sympathy rather than a lecture.'

He got down on his knees instantly. 'You're right. I'm not thinking, my love. I remember the pain and the stiffness when the same thing happened to me. It was that chestnut mare your father bought, Marcella. She threw me the first day.'

'But she became your willing slave afterwards.'

'Yes. "My fine girl", I used to say to her.' His voice became tender as he looked at her. 'You shouldn't be up, mavourneen.'

'Did *you* take to your bed when you had a tumble?'

'Peters would have shot me.' He laughed. 'But you're not so young now.'

'That's what Terence said, too. You both make me feel like a decrepit old carthorse ready for the knackers.' The tears rolled down her face in her weakness, and he took her in his arms and rocked her against him.

'I'm not watching my tongue. I didn't think . . .' That's the trouble, she thought. He doesn't think nowadays, nor see. Marriage has become like a comfortable old shoe to him. Alastair Crawford doesn't pigeonhole me, a hard-working wife whose sole duty is to look after her children and her husband. He opened doors to me, or took me back through the one I'd left . . .

'Don't pet me,' she said, trying to smile. 'It just makes the tears come. I should be on my feet getting on with the

175

dinner. There's a pot of broth from yesterday – it'll be all the richer – and I was going to peel the potatoes.'

'You sit still if you won't go to bed and I'll do them after I've had a wash. And make the girls run about for you when they come in. Isobel isn't nearly as good as Kate was about the house. She's full of opinions instead of getting on with it.'

'Yes, I miss Kate. And she won't be coming this week. The children have whooping cough, she said in her letter. Mrs Murray-Hyslop is afraid of her spreading the infection.'

'Aye. Well, Kate will manage. She always does.

Patrick gave her a long, steady look when they were all seated round the table. Wee Maeve had set the knives and forks the wrong way round, and they had all been laughing at that. Except Isobel who, revelling in the authority which had been so suddenly thrust upon her, was dishing out the vegetables and the meat which she had fished out of the broth pot. 'That was a hell of a fall, all the same,' he said. She had told him the same story. Patrick's different, she had thought as she stumbled through it. He's deep. He uses his wits.

'No worse nor better than many one takes when riding.'

His eyes did not leave her. 'Is it only your face? You seem to be pretty stiff walking about.'

'I'm putting that on for sympathy,' she said.

'Was it the horse that kicked you, did you say?' His knife and fork were poised over his plate. She met his eyes, looked away. Had he heard something on his way home from the ironworks? Brodie had a few cronies there. He had worked as a storeman in the blast furnace shed before he got his present job as storeman at the pits.

'It feels like it,' she said. 'Why, is it all round the village already?' If I told Patrick the real story, she thought, he'd get up without a word and go to see Big Cochran, the policeman.

He gave her a look as he started to eat. 'I would be the last one to hear gossip.'

'You'd better stay away from the Hall stables,' Kieran said, looking troubled. 'There's enough bad feeling as there is with me taking up this truck business. Brodie would murder me if he got his hands on me, not to mention that targe of a wife of his.'

'I'm not likely to go singing and dancing to the Hall for the next week or so,' she said. She had to bend over her plate to hide the easy tears that had sprung to her eyes. It was not pain that caused them. She saw a door closing which would have led to places of pleasure and delight.

She lay now, like a stricken animal, she thought, for the next day or so, having cautioned the girls not to talk about her to their friends at school. She did not stay in bed, but she did not go out of the house. There was a dull resentment mixed with the pain.

Kieran brought in the food. Patrick and Terence took on the job of digging up the potatoes and pulling the vegetables they needed. Isobel and wee Maeve prepared them.

Their kindness and attention cured her, in spirit also, more quickly than any amount of lying in bed would have done.

Her good physique helped. She had never ailed in her life except that time after wee Maeve's birth. She saw the bruise at the side of her face disappearing, her eye opening, the lustre coming back to her hair. The stiffness eased and with it some of the misery. She took advantage of her unusual leisure, and wrote to Kate.

177

My dear daughter, I've fallen and hurt myself, and so I'm like Lady Crawford herself with five willing servants at my beck and call.

You would laugh if you saw wee Maeve peeling the vegetables. She starts off with a fine big tumshie, and by the time she's taken the skin off and half the flesh with it, she's left with something the size of a pea.

Isobel makes grand soup, kale and broth, and can even wring the neck of a chicken for it, and Patrick and Terence clean out the fire in the morning, feed the hens and bring in the coal and water. Your father is the organizer and does the buying.

I don't know why I didn't think of this long ago. It's high time men took a fair share in the house. I've a feeling that if I live long enough I'll see that happen. Anyhow, the boys are getting good training for that day when it comes.

Your father is still working hard with Mr Cranston, and hardly a night passes that he isn't at his house or he's here. Davy Cox is their prize exhibit, like a poor silly bull being led round the ring. But they seem to be on Brodie's trail. As well as proving that he'd cheated with Davy's bill, they now think he's been slumping. A lot of the wives here, and particularly poor Bella Cox, don't have the gumption to check their slips. I'm behind your father one hundred per cent, if it weren't for the fact that he seems to see more of Bob Cranston than he does of me.

Terence is still like a moon calf over Catherine Murdoch, a nice enough girl, I suppose, but I could think of someone who would be far better suited to him, a girl who is as different from her mother as night from day, and believe me, I say that with feeling . . . (She drew a stroke with her pen, stopping herself.)

Patrick is Patrick, keeps his own counsel, and sometimes I wonder if he'll step in where Terence could so easily have been. I see him at the corner of the Row having long confabs with, well, you know who I mean, Bessie Haddow – or listening to her would be nearer the mark . . . (How much did Bessie know, she thought, staring into space. Was she, too, keeping quiet?)

We were very sorry you couldn't come to see us last week because of the children's illnesses, but we're hoping you'll be able to visit us soon. Wee Maeve keeps asking if you'll bring them with you. She wants to know if little George is a wee rascal like she used to be.

178

We think of you often, my dear daughter, remember you in our prayers, and hope you are happy in your new employment. Our loss is their gain. Your loving mother.

At other times she would sit thinking about Alastair Crawford and that morning, only a few days ago but already like another world, when he had kissed her. What would he think if he knew she had been assaulted by three of her neighbours because of him? Kieran, like Patrick, would have reported it, he would have suffered with her, ached from the blows even more than he had done already. But he was her husband . . .

Why should the laird's son get himself implicated in a common village fight? It was well known that women were worse than men, like spitting cats. Besides, their venom had not been directed against him. He was sacrosanct. She was the culprit. Not for their reason, that she had got 'above herself', but for the fact that she had allowed herself to get involved, that she had gone willingly to meet him, fearing, yet hoping . . . it had been like the excitement of walking on ice, a tremulous kind of excitement. She remembered once running across the village pond before it was sure that the ice was holding, and the children's terrified, admiring faces. 'Oh, Ma!' wee Maeve had shouted, clapping her hands.

That's the sum of it, she would think. I'm a mother of five children, I should have stayed at home, stuck to my duties, had a cup of tea and a gossip with my neighbours if I wanted a change. But I craved something different, pleasure, excitement, I wanted to go back through that door . . .

So what are you going to do now, she would ask herself, sitting hour after hour in the quiet kitchen when the sun slanted through the small window. She longed for the fresh air, the routine pleasure of her rides. Did she still long for Alastair Crawford? Kieran, rushing home from the pit to get cleaned up for his meetings, would say she was pale and that she should get out more. 'Take a walk down the Row and have a blether with your neighbours,' he advised. He looked at her oddly when she smiled.

15

Kieran had set off as usual a few mornings later. Maeve's natural resilience had returned, and she had gone to the door to see him off. She had watched him clattering down the Row, greeting other miners as they emerged from their houses, their bate tins on their belts, their ropes slung round their shoulders.

Let her come out, she had thought, meaning Mrs Haddow. There was less chance of seeing Mrs Brodie since they did not have a tied house here. She had breathed the crisp morning air, drawing strength from it. As for Beenie Drummond, she hadn't the courage to appear on her own. She would stay inside like a great scared rabbit in her hole. I can face them now, she thought, I can face the world again.

She had cleaned the house all morning, had seen Patrick and then the girls off, warning them to be quiet since Terence was still sleeping. Now, as a symbol perhaps, she poured some water into a basin, climbed on a stool at the small window of the kitchen and began to wash it. She would make it sparkling clean so that she could look out, so that anyone who liked could look in.

The view was peaceful, the quiet morning fields, the glitter of gold on the grass from the still-hidden sun, in the distance the shaft where Kieran was working today. She felt benevolent towards the intrusion of the winding-gear at the pit-head. The ironworks where Patrick worked was even uglier with its blast furnaces and chimneys. They had to be endured. Both places gave them a good living, and what did it matter if the Crawfords made their millions out of it? The grandfather had been clever enough to see the land's possibilities. The country benefited as well.

She realized the stool was shuddering gently beneath her. That was the first premonition, the knowledge that the shuddering was not caused by her, nor by the unevenness of the stone flags, but that the ground under the floor was moving, heaving, like a beast stirring in the darkness. A surge of fear went whipping through her, and at the same time she saw a sudden flash dart from the shaft like lightning, turning the trees to an unearthly blue.

She staggered, righted herself, her hand up to shield her eyes from the glare, and then, as she lowered it, a great tumbling waterfall of stones erupted from the shaft and turned the sky around it dust-dark. The windows of the cottage shook and rattled, the walls of the room seemed to bulge then recede, and her ears were filled with a rolling, rumbling noise that sounded like thunder, except that there was a steady reverberation as if a hundred cannons had been fired. As she stared, petrified, a great column of smoke rose from the near shaft, obscuring her view. But there was no doubt now. The loud wailing from the pit siren flooded her mind with its message. She jumped off the stool and made for the scullery door. Kieran . . . her mind was full of him. She would go the back way. It was quicker . . .

'Ma!' Terence's voice halted her. She turned to see him in the middle of the kitchen in his nightshirt, his long legs pale beneath it as if they, too, had paled like his face. 'It's the pit!' Now he was struggling into his trousers which had been over his arm, the braces dangling. 'Oh, God! There's a full shift! Da's there . . .' He lifted his dazed face to her as his hands fumbled with the buttons. 'Don't *you* go!' His hair stood in spikes from his sleep.

'What are you saying!' She knew she screamed at him as she snatched a shawl from its hook. 'Your shoes . . .'

'Bugger my shoes.' He raced for the back door, elbowing her aside. 'Maybe he didn't go down . . .'

But she knew he would be down. His very reluctance to work underground always made him first in the cage.

The night-shift men were there when they arrived, some of them half-dressed, but soon a crowd gathered, mostly women, some of them with small children whom they could not leave on their own. Then the fire-carts came and the ambulances, and soon there was something to do at least, to fill and pass buckets along the line.

Somewhere in the background she heard Patrick talking to Terence. He must have run from the ironworks with the rescue team. One shaft was blocked with rubble, he was saying, but the other was partially cleared. Those in the way of the fire-blast would not stand a . . . she knew they had realized she was there and were silent. Suddenly they're men, she thought. This morning they were just lads. She wanted to say something to show her ability to support them but the words would not come. A man's bitter voice filled the silence. 'The roof was beginning to sag. We've been warning them and warning them about the stoops, but they don't listen . . .'

She turned away from them, sick at heart, and saw the laird and his son hurrying across the field, one burly, one slim. She thought 'son', not 'Alastair'. That was behind her now. She was a miner's wife. Ever to have imagined anything else must have been a kind of madness. She met Alastair Crawford's eyes for a second as he went past her, but he was wrapped in his authority and his desire to assure these grieving women that all would be well, that his and his father's hands were clean, that they would see to it that their husbands and sons would come out unharmed. His face seemed to shine with his noble endeavour. She saw it all in one brief glance, saw that he hardly recognized her.

She went back to helping the firemen, passing buckets endlessly. She seemed to have been doing it all her life. Patrick was at her elbow. 'Where's Terence?' he asked.

'I don't know. He disappeared . . .'

The old man beside her heard. 'He's gone down, Mrs McGrath. They wanted as much help as they could get.'

'I'm going, too.' Patrick's face was set. She put her hand on his arm. She did not feel like herself, piteous, pleading.

'Don't go. There's your father and Terence already. Don't . . .'

'We're ready, Patrick.' It was Jock Tweedie now. How had all these young boys suddenly become men while she had reverted to this weak, wailing creature? This man, who had been the freckled, careless farm-boy she had known for so long, actually smiled, a pitying man's smile. 'They're in need of some young blood, they're saying.' She turned away, defeated, went on helping.

If Kieran comes out alive, she promised, if I get the three of them back unharmed, I'll devote my life to them, I'll cosset them and wait on them, I'll never cross the door. I'll banish Alastair Crawford from my mind, I'll stamp on my rebelliousness like a fire, like that burning hell down below. She made herself imagine it all in detail as if for her own good: the agony of crushed limbs, the fighting for breath, the weight of the earth bearing them down, the desire for death.

I knew, didn't I, the imaginary conversation went on in her head, that wives were supposed to cleave to their

184

husbands, that there could be no doubts and longings and bitter periods of regret. If I was too young to know it when I left Ireland with Kieran, I've been given time.

I should have known that there would come a testing time when marriage would seem like a prison. 'Oh, I'll make it a warm and loving one, God,' she knew she was muttering the words now, 'if only You will let them come back alive.' She was ashamed of herself. She must look crazed. She handed her bucket to someone and made herself walk over to the shaft where a crowd was gathering thickly, peering, exclaiming, sobbing. An old man leaning heavily on his stick turned to let her come near, shaking his head. She saw tears in the furrows of his cheeks.

All the bodies they were bringing up were dead. She knew that by the wailing that came from the women, but even more pitifully from the thin cries of the babies which some of them carried in their shawls, as if their grief was communicated. The lack of life in the still forms being laid out reminded her of John's limp body in Kieran's arms as he had staggered out of the water. They were calling out names. She wanted to listen and not to listen.

She made herself think of the pit ponies that Kieran had cared for with such love. He had often spoken about their patience, their obedience. Had they stood quietly, heads bowed, while the earth was heaving and cracking above them, until they were bearing its weight on their backs, until their poor legs buckled and they were forced to the ground under it, until they died? Men could at least shout or talk to each other, but then again, didn't that make their terror greater because of being able to express it, to see and appreciate another man's terror? Hadn't she heard somewhere that they sang together, hymns like 'Rock of Ages' . . . ? That would please old Murdoch.

'The last time,' the old man's voice was quavering in

her ear, 'some of them were sticking against the coal wall. With the force, ye see . . . they had to be scraped off.'

They had stopped calling names. No one had come near her. She saw some rescuers emerge, black-faced, weary: one had blood from a cut on his brow running through the blackness. They looked barely alive themselves, staggering and overpowered by the choke damp. One of them fell on his knees with weakness, and a woman rushed towards him, sobbing, bearing him to the ground with her strength. Neither Terence nor Patrick was with them.

She could not bear to watch any more. She began to walk about the field, unseeing. The diffusion of her anxiety in different directions nearly crazed her. It was after three now – someone must have told her – Isobel and Maeve would be out of school, alone in the house. Would they keep the fire going, would they be frightened out of their minds, should she run back and reassure them?

But then there was Kieran down there, perhaps under her feet at this very moment, dead or dying, pinned by the debris, Terence crawling along the partially-cleared shaft towards him, a shaft which might collapse at any moment, and Patrick in even more danger because of his ignorance of the pit workings, but doing what he was told, willingly, devoting his mind and his strength to it in his quiet way.

I'll go mad, she thought, drawing her shawl round her because she was shivering in the middle of August. The image of men, the bodies of men, sticking against a pillar, of being torn from it, leaving their clothes, more than their clothes, pursued her. She made herself stop her ceaseless roaming and join the first group she came across. She had not looked to see who composed it, saw now that one of the women was Mrs Haddow, dishevelled, her face collapsed and running with tears. Bessie had her arm round her. She looked up and saw Maeve. The girl's face was white, making her hair look a sickly yellow, her eyes were black-ringed. 'It's my father,' she said, 'he's been brought up.'

'Is he . . . ?' She could not say the word. Bessie nodded, cast her eyes at her mother.

'Aye, he's deid!' The woman raised her head, her shawl slipping back on to her shoulders. 'Say it, Bessie! Don't mind me. He's . . . deid!' Her voice swung up sickeningly.

'Oh, Mrs Haddow.' Maeve stepped forward to put her hand on the woman's arm. 'I'm sorry . . .'

She reared back from Maeve's touch like an animal. 'And yours will be all right, I suppose?' Her primping neatness had gone, her meek voice, her mincing, mealy-mouthed manners. 'The Deil looks after his own, sure enough! You'll still have *two* men at your beck and call.' Her mouth was ugly.

'Ma!' Bessie looked at her mother, ashamed, then turned to Maeve. 'She doesn't know what she's saying, Mrs McGrath. She's fair demented with the shock.'

'It's all right, Bessie. I know . . .' She walked away, sick in her heart, began again her aimless circling round the field, stopping here and there when she came across someone she could comfort, a baby she could hold. She caught sight of Mr Murdoch talking to some men and went and stood beside them, listening shamelessly. She felt like a ghost, unseen, the voices came to her like a dirge.

'Aye, Reverend, it's a bad job.'

'But what's Crawford saying to it, tell me that?'

'He's cleared off with his son. They wouldn't hang around to be blamed, that's for sure.'

'They'll have ridden off to see their lawyers, trust them.'

'Now, now, Mr Gray, Mr Duthie, Mr Bissett, remember your minister is within hearing,' Mr Murdoch's bleat interrupted.

'Maist o' them's deid they're bringing up.' They were not listening to him.

'They didn't stand a chance.'

'They'll have to bring up the rescuers soon. They'll not want to add to the total.'

'Aye, the total casualities.' The broad-vowelled, mispronounced word rang in her mind.

'It's a fair handful of lawyers they'll be needing, the Crawfords.'

She had to speak, to make herself flesh, it seemed to her. 'Mr Murdoch, is there anything I can do? Do you think I could go to the Infirmary, or anything . . .'

He looked around and she thought she saw a slight look of disapproval round his mouth as he recognized her. 'Ah, Mrs McGrath, isn't it? Blankets, hot soup, hot tea. There are many things our womenfolk have been setting their hands to . . .'

'I've done all that.' He wearied her. 'I've emptied the house, torn up sheets . . .'

'Ah, well, then,' he paused, coughed. 'And who have you . . . er . . . down?'

'My husband. Now Terence and Patrick.' It sounded boastful to her. 'They've gone to try and find him.'

'A worrying time for you.' She heard the practised sympathy in his voice, saw the lift of his chin for the pulpit-like delivery. 'You can but watch and pray, Mrs McGrath. If you care to join the other women, I'm conducting a small service of intercession in the manse to keep our spirits up. Catherine will be dispensing tea . . .'

'Thank you, yes, perhaps . . .' She drifted away, a ghost again, skirting the shaft because to go near there could not be borne. She suddenly thought of Isobel and wee Maeve and found herself running back to the house to see if they were all right. She was herself once again as she burst into the house, saw the frightened faces, put on an air of brisk cheerfulness. 'Keep the fire bright, now, I've stoked it, and refilled the pot. They'll need a good warm bath when they come up. Mind what I'm telling you. And be good!' She ran back to the field again.

The smoke pall was lifting now. A sickly sun was sliding through the clouds and the smell was that of autumn wood smoke, only more acrid. The fine day had been defeated by the explosion, a smirr of rain beaded the dusty grass.

Everybody looked wan and exhausted, the ambulance men were leaning wearily against their closed carts, one was bandaging the arm of a miner sitting on the ground. His hair was scorched and grizzled like brown ash on his head. He looked dazed.

And then she saw them, Terence and Patrick, emerging from the shaft, blinking, turning their heads this way and that on their necks like pit ponies. Two stretchers were being carried out, only two. On each of them there was a body covered with jackets.

'Patrick! Terence!' She ran towards them calling, and saw them look up. The skin round their eyes was white where they had knuckled the coal dust out of them. 'Your father? What about your father?' She was weeping, shouting, like the other women crowding round.

The boys looked at each other as if ashamed of her, or afraid to tell her.

'Your *father*!' she screamed.

'There he is, Ma.' Terence nodded his head at one of

the stretchers, meekly, it seemed, as if there was nothing to say. It was more than fatigue, surely . . .

She knelt down where they had laid Kieran on the ground, pulled the jacket away. How had she doubted that they would bring him up? His face was black and yet it seemed pale. How could that be? she wondered, taking an edge of her shawl and gently wiping it. His eyes were closed. He was not breathing.

She looked up at the two boys. Patrick had outstripped Terence in height. She had never noticed that before. 'He's dead, then?' She could not hear her voice, thought that she had better say it again. 'He's not . . . breathing.' She was patient. They were tired. It was as big a shock for them as it was for her. She had to remember how young they were.

'Away with you, Ma.' It was Patrick, gruff-sounding. She heard his father in his voice. 'He's breathing all right. *He*'s the lucky one.' She looked round and saw a woman prostrate over the other stretcher, moaning like an animal. Some men were trying to lift her away, gently. She went to help them.

16

Kieran hovered between life and death in the Infirmary for the first two or three weeks, like so many of his fellow-workers. It was not the broken bones, but the dreadful crushing injuries which caused many of them to die after having been brought out alive.

He caught pneumonia, his chest always having been his weak spot, and there was one occasion when Maeve and the two boys spent the whole night in the Infirmary waiting for the crisis. Kate had been given leave by the sympathetic Murray-Hyslops, and had come to look after the girls at home.

But slowly he recovered. There were still the remnants of the sturdy Irish lad in him despite the punishing years he had spent down the pits, and one brisk October day he was brought home by a triumphant Terence and Patrick, sitting up in one of Jock Tweedie's carts, and installed in the box bed in the kitchen.

His fractured leg was slow in mending because of his weakened condition. Maeve borrowed a truckle bed from the store in the church hall – Lord Crawford had been assiduous in trying to meet all the needs of the stricken families – and there every night she lay down when the family had gone to bed and only the firelight flickered on the walls.

She no longer worried about the time Terence and Patrick came in. After the pit disaster it would have seemed ridiculous, it seemed to her, to treat them as boys. She and Kieran would talk quietly to each other like friends who had been parted for a long time and who had to rebuild their relationship.

'The laird's son did more visiting in the Infirmary than his father,' he said once. 'We had one or two chats. Though I can't deny Lord Crawford has been generous. There is to be a lump sum in compensation as well as a payment from the Union.'

'I would have expected that,' she said. And then, 'What else did he say?'

'Who? Lord Crawford?'

'No . . .' she hesitated, 'the son, Alastair, isn't it?' She was ashamed at her pretence.

'We talked about horses mainly. He said he remembered the Sunday School Picnic when I had the best turnout. We got on very well.'

'Did you talk about my going riding?' She had to ask that.

'No, it was never mentioned.'

'Or if there would be . . . anything else for you if you couldn't go down the pit . . . for a time?'

'Where?'

'Maybe . . . at the Hall?'

'No. I don't know where you got that idea. There's Craig in the stables, and two young lads. All he said was that he and his father intended to do everything they could in recompense. His mother had taken the disaster badly, he told me.'

'Yes, I had a letter from her. I think she wrote to all the wives. Quite short, and a bit spidery in the writing.'

'He said she hasn't been well for some time.'

'That would account for it. She hasn't been going through the garden lately. I've missed her.' She thought sometimes of the shy woman with eyes like the creatures in the woods she liked to walk in. What would she have

192

thought of her son, she wondered, had she known about those morning meetings at the ruined monastery? Mothers never knew their sons completely, not that side of them.

'Lying in that Infirmary bed, Maeve,' his voice came softly to her, 'I would think that maybe the pit paid me back for hating it. Terence has never minded going down and he got off scot free. Maybe it's taught me a lesson to . . . put up with things.'

'You've always had enough to put up with without needing to be taught lessons,' she said.

She still bore the pit a grudge. She tried not to let it spread to the Crawfords, but the feeling was strong. She did not want Kieran to go back. But should Alastair Crawford ever offer him a job as a groom at the Hall she would have to tell him to refuse it. There had to be a clean cut.

She would lie awake wishing that there was something of her own in existence that would prevent Kieran ever having to go underground again, something that would spring out of her own abundant energy, safely channelling it. Then there would be no straying of her mind when Kieran was asleep, no reliving those mornings with the laird's son. 'Alastair . . .' she would whisper the name. 'I never used it. I never will . . .'

She would imagine the wind on her face, lifting her hair as she rode neck and neck with him. That moment when she had been thrown and had opened her eyes to find him bending over her with that strange amber gaze . . . 'Beautiful . . . you need love . . .' She would move her head on the pillow as the long, slow thrills went through her body, hear his voice in her head, 'Let me show you how much I want you . . .' She would surrender to the great waves of feeling, then rebuke herself, straighten her loose limbs, tell herself she was a wicked woman. 'Does it help to say I love you?' His voice had been gentle when he said that.

But in the morning she would be bright and efficient as she folded the truckle bed and stowed it away, got the breakfast ready, saw the girls off to school, and when the house was quiet, washed Kieran, brought him a chamber pot. She would not hear of him walking down the garden to the privy on his crutches.

'This is your throne,' she would say, laughing at his embarrassment, 'you're the king.' She would bow and retreat from the box bed. She wanted to restore his spirits as well as his strength, give him some of her abundant energy.

And, like a king, he had visitors. Kate came each week, bringing her charges as Madam needed quietness. 'She's expecting . . .' she whispered to Maeve.

Wee Maeve particularly was captivated by the children, exclaimed over their sailor hats, George's sailor suit, the white pleated skirts of the girls with the sailor collars on their blouses, their neat buttoned boots with the shiny toecaps.

'How do you manage to keep your dresses clean?' she asked Emily and Victoria.

'Nurse changes us twice each day,' Emily said. She was at first haughty. 'And then, of course, we always wear brown holland in the nursery.'

'But do you never go out and play peevor, or stot your ball or anything?' Wee Maeve was sympathetic. 'We stot ours against the wall at school. It's great fun.'

'We play in the Park when Nurse takes us there,' Emily said. 'Once my ball ran away and I ran after it and I fell and my dress was very dirty, wasn't it, Nurse?' She looked at Kate, her eyes bright with mischief.

194

Maeve sat with little George on her knees, marvelling at the composure of Kate. It's discipline, of course, that makes the difference, she thought. These three children are regimented by carefully-thought-out rules and traditions from the minute they get up to the minute they go to bed. They early learn to accept them. She thought of her own childhood in the nursery at Woodlea with Terence, her brother, and how often the discipline there had been disrupted by the abrupt departure of the young girls who took care of them. She had realized why when she grew older; it had been a combination of her mother's moanings and her father's irascible temper.

The only time she had enjoyed discipline was when Richard, the young English tutor, had been engaged. He had shown her wider horizons, fired her imagination. And then Kieran had come along . . .

But the Murray-Hyslops were different from her parents. They were solid and responsible and they would have solid and responsible children. Emily might give them some trouble, but a rich suitor would be found for her, and because of the earlier discipline, all would be well. She was proud that Kate, her dearest daughter, was a part of this discipline.

She put George in the box bed with Kieran while she made tea. He had earlier teased her about the preparations she was making, seed cake, scones and home-made jam, sponge fingers, and a well-ironed tablecloth on the kitchen table. 'Are we trying to impress the Murray-Hyslops?' he had said.

'No. We have standards here, too. I want them to know that.' She had changed her dress, worn a black satin tea-apron, burnished her red hair.

Kate's visits did Kieran a lot of good. She sat and listened to him in a way that Maeve realized she herself rarely did. There were always a hundred things to do and she had not the temperament to stay still for long. Or the time. But she noticed that Kate had the time although she must have been up at dawn to get her charges ready, to help Cook with their breakfasts, to clean out the nursery, to iron the children's clothes, to perform necessary tasks for Mrs Murray-Hyslop.

'She's getting a bit weary now, Ma, and then the master is often in America. He says maybe if the business grows much more he may have to decide to live there.'

'Would that mean you'd be out of a job?'

'Well, Mrs Murray-Hyslop has discussed it with me. She talks to me often. She once asked me if I would like to go with them.'

'And what did you say?'

'That although I'd miss you all I'd quite like it since I'd never seen America.'

'We'd miss *you*. But I think I would have said the same.'

'Well, you could come and see me.'

'There's that . . .' She was wistful. Still, it might be a door opening.

When they had gone wee Maeve and Isobel were discerning. Isobel liked the girls because they were biddable and not 'bad', wee Maeve because she had bloomed in their admiration of the 'stories' she told them.

'You mean lies,' Isobel said. 'You make up great big lies.'

'They aren't lies. They're stories. That's different.'

She said to Maeve when she was going to bed, surprising her, 'Do you ever think of John, Ma?'

'Yes, often.' She had stopped brushing the girl's hair. 'I'll never forget him.'

'I miss him. That George minded me of him, a right

196

little man in spite of his sailor suit. I think of John often in bed at night.' Her face crumpled and Maeve took her in her arms.

'What is it, my love?' The girl shook her head, hiding against her mother's shoulder. 'You can tell me. Don't keep it to yourself.'

'Isobel will belt me.'

'Isobel will do nothing of the kind. Whisper it in my ear.'

She put her arms round Maeve's neck. Her voice was broken with her sobs. 'Isobel said it was my fault he got drowned. That I shouldn't have run away from Kate.'

'Rubbish!' She put the girl from her to look at her. 'Don't you ever think like that! You might as well say your father got caught in the explosion because I let him go down the pit. Things happen. We don't know before or they never would. I'll speak to Isobel.'

'No, don't.'

'All right. But never think like that, Maeve. Just think of how much you loved John and how you have lots to look forward to in your life, things that would make him proud of you.'

'I'd like to be a nurse,' she said, 'not like Kate. Where they're in bed all the time.'

Maeve laughed and kissed her. 'We'll see. Now off to bed with you.'

'Did you hear that?' She went over to Kieran on the box bed.

'Some of it.' He looked tired. Perhaps the house had been too full and noisy for him today.

'She thinks she's to blame for John.'

He nodded, his face sad. 'I know about regret.'

'What regret?'

197

'The old one, the only one.' He turned his head on the pillows.

'Come on, dear love, tell me.' She stroked his face. How thin he was.

His voice was low. 'Not providing for you in the way you were used to. Now, with this,' he put his hand on his leg under the blankets, 'it seems further away than ever. I'm not going to be up to much when I get out of here.'

'Did you ever hear such rubbish?' She was close to tears. They made her speak brashly. 'And you getting up for half a day already! You'll be making room for me beside you in there before long.'

His eyes smiled at her. She saw the old loving Kieran. 'Maybe that's the tonic I'm needing.'

Another visitor was Bob Cranston, the gaffer. Inevitably, after queries about Kieran's progress, the conversation turned to the truck system. 'We can't come up to England though it hurts me as a true Scotsman to say it, hurts me to the quick.' He had a habit of slapping his thigh. 'Too much of looking after our spiritual welfare, Bible classes and the like on the part of the bosses, while at the same time Brodie's selling whisky in the store. Whisky and religion. That will be our downfall.'

Maeve had grown interested in these discussions. When Kieran had been asleep and she still unwilling to leave the house in case he should need her, she had read the papers he was working on, and had grasped quickly the reason for the truck's existence. Had it not been started as an emergency system because the pit workings were in unpopulated areas? She put this to Bob Cranston.

'Aye, you're right there, Mrs McGrath. Before your time Sholton was a rural parish. We were all farmers or labourers on farms. My, it was a bonny place before the

198

Crawfords got their hands on it, digging for coal and iron ore, setting up blast furnaces and the like. My father was a farm labourer before he was tempted by the money they paid.'

'Yes, it's the money that tempts you down there,' Kieran said.

'Nothing else. The coal was raised by a gin then, worked by farm horses. He died when I was fourteen, worn out. I had been down for two years. Coal was in my blood and coal dust in my lungs, more likely. I've been seeing the light in more ways than one for some time now, the drawbacks. Like the truck system for instance.'

'Didn't the Government realize what was going on when it started?' Maeve asked.

'Give them their due, they did when complaints reached them that the men were never seeing their wages, that it was all pawned to the store. That was a long time ago . . .' He scratched his head.

'It was its abuse that the Act of 1831 was getting at,' Maeve said, 'but it didn't put a stop to it.'

'You've a smart wife there, Kieran.'

'Don't I know it?' He looked pale sitting at the fire with a shawl round his shoulders. I mustn't make an invalid of him, Maeve thought, I must spur him on, make him believe in himself.

Bob Cranston went on. 'The holes in the net were too wide. Give the Crawfords their due, they got rid of the store and handed it over to a contractor. Even that might not have been too bad if Brodie hadn't been made storeman. Talk about out of the frying pan into the fire! Power corrupts in the hands of a weak man.'

'You sound like the Reverend Mr Murdoch himself,' Kieran laughed.

'Scratch a Scotsman and you'll find a philosopher. But you're an Irishman.'

'Scratch an Irishman and you'll find a pessimist, I sometimes think.'

'Now, now, lad.' Bob Cranston's tone was kindly. 'That's because you're not yourself, but with this good wife of yours you'll be back to normal in no time. I need you to help me. We're going to use Davy Cox's case of fraud as an example. You're with me, aren't you?'

'Yes, that's something I can do sitting here. It's the writing. I've got a damaged right wrist.'

'Well, there's Mrs McGrath twiddling her thumbs. She could be your amanuensis. What do you say?' He turned to Maeve. 'We don't want this law made a fool of in the shape of a slippery customer like Brodie, do we?'

'Indeed we don't. I can see it from the wife's point of view. Her money's spent before she gets it. It's a scandal.'

'That's the way to talk!' He clapped his thigh. 'We'll get the papers interested, maybe the Glasgow ones. I might as well tell you, I've decided to come out of the pit now. I've done my stint. My two sons are on compensation, not as severely hurt as you, Kieran, but enough to decide to come in with me. We're going back to the land. I've bought a farm in Crannoch with the money we've got between us, and we're going to run it as a family concern. But we'll fight with you, never fear.'

Kieran looked wistful. 'Coming up, are you? By God, you're wise. It would be horses for me if I had the money.' He shrugged. 'Still, as long as you support me. What we've got to fight for is abolition of the long-pay system, for a start. That's what makes the colliers and their wives debt slaves as well as wage slaves, and become Brodie's victims into the bargain.'

200

'Are you sure the Crawfords get nothing out of it?' Maeve asked.

Kieran looked at Bob. 'No, they handed it over to a contractor. That's right, isn't it?'

'Now you've got a point there, Mrs McGrath.' Cranston's look was admiring. 'It's worth looking into.'

I could do it, Maeve thought. I don't mean truck. That was a moral issue, and it would be rectified in time. There are other people fighting for it beside us, people with far more power. But I could start some kind of business, something profitable, something which would fulfil a need. Kieran could be in it, and the boys, just as Bob Cranston and his family are doing. Terence and Patrick are too good for the hard labouring *they* are doing. What was it Kieran had said to Bob a moment ago? 'It would be horses for me if I had the money . . .' Something to do with horses . . .

'It's a vicious circle,' he was saying. 'The wages pass from the pay office to the truck store and back again.' Kieran, she thought, will always put moral issues first, and that's to his credit. 'The prices are high and the quality's poor. You've said that often, Maeve, haven't you? And on top of it the whisky's there for the buying. That's even more immoral.'

'Especially if they throw in a Bible as well!' she said. Cranston laughed but Kieran did not join in, still fired by his sense of injustice. 'And what about blacklisting and intimidation of men who give their custom elsewhere?'

'Have *you* ever been threatened by Brodie?' Bob Cranston's eyes were on her. He knows about the women assaulting me, she thought.

'No, never by Brodie.' They exchanged looks. Maybe he thought she was showing an interest in the truck system as a means of getting back at Mrs Brodie. But that was behind her. There was something ahead of her, exciting, just out of reach. She had only to keep on thinking . . .

'Some are for it,' Cranston was talking to the two of them now, 'because they think if the store closes down they'll lose their allowance of free coal, but they're few and far between. Are you ready to start the fight again, Kieran?'

'I'm ready.'

'Good lad. And so are my sons. They've been going up to Glasgow to meetings – some schoolmaster who's agitating for the stoppage of truck. He's firing them. They're all for banding together, forming some kind of committee. They've pledged themselves to this man when he's ready. All I ask of you is that you keep the ball rolling while we're getting the farm in order, seeing there's a place for the young wives and their families.'

'And I'll help Kieran,' Maeve said, 'but not for good. I might as well tell you, Mr Cranston, I have other plans.'

'Will you listen to that?' Kieran looked at Bob. 'It's the first I've heard about them.'

'You'll be told in good time.' She smiled at the two men. There was a glimmer, less than a glimmer in her mind, like the flash of the trout under the stones in the Sholtie Burn. But if you were patient, you would see it again, and some day . . .

She got up and went to the drawer in the kitchen table where she kept her precious notepaper for writing to Kate.

'Right.' She sat down, lifted her pen and looked at Kieran and Bob Cranston. 'Reasons for complete abolition of the truck system. Number one. You start, Mr Cranston.'

'Maybe we should have a tot of Brodie's whisky to oil the wheels before we do.' Kieran looked across at her, his eyes smiling.

17

A new relationship seemed to spring up between Maeve and Kieran that winter. Perhaps most of the feeling that they were drifting apart had been caused by the lack of time they had been able to spend together. Now on these quiet afternoons when they worked on the papers concerning the truck, Kieran dictating, she writing busily, they drew close.

The kitchen became like an office at times. Bob Cranston called in to report progress, bringing stamps and notepaper because he knew how every penny counted with them now, and in the evenings his two sons, Arthur and James, would arrive, full of their plans about the farm and the meetings they were attending in Glasgow. Their youthful virility seemed to bring a gust of the keen winter air with them.

Maeve would be fired with their enthusiasm, be swept into it, and at the same time reflect that this was all training for her, these discussions, plans, even the endless writing at the kitchen table. That it was an apprenticeship. She would find herself repeating Kieran's remark, pondering on it, 'Something to do with horses . . .'

The truckle bed was given back to the church hall. The pins were out of Kieran's leg, and she climbed behind him into the box bed once more. Their coming together was tender, tentative at first; they had to relearn each other's bodies, she had to remember his damaged wrist, his still weak leg. 'We've both got our tender parts now,' she said to him, laughing.

But when he penetrated her, and she remembered the old joy, she knew that this new joy was finer, perhaps not so youthfully exuberant, but deeper. 'My wife,' Kieran said, 'Oh, my wife . . .'

There was the family to take care of, and she and the girls were busy making Christmas presents from a box of old pieces of cloth and discarded pieces of wool. Money grew scarcer because she would not allow Kieran's compensation to be used. 'We can manage,' she told him, 'we'll need the money.'

'For your plan?' he said, smiling at her.

'Yes, for my plan. I'll see we don't go short. I can manage.'

But it was difficult. Patrick gave her all his money, but Terence demanded new boots and shirts from time to time, some pomade for his hair 'because it was so curly', he said shamefacedly. He was like a peacock parading his feathers for the benefit chiefly of Catherine Murdoch.

'Precious little,' Patrick said when Maeve asked him what was going on between them. 'Sometimes she lets him escort her from the Bible Class, that's about all. She plays fast and loose with him, and he gets back on her by playing fast and loose with Bessie Haddow.'

'It's frustration that makes him act like that,' she said. 'You've never been in love, Patrick, or you'd understand.'

'Haven't I?' She thought she saw his face flush as he turned away. They had grown up fast because of the pit explosion, she reminded herself. They were both men now.

One evening when the boys were at the Tweedie's farm, Bessie came to see them. The first snow of the winter was on her strong yellow hair. She had run the short distance from her own house with only a shawl round her shoulders.

'Come in, Bessie,' Maeve welcomed her, 'Kieran will be glad to see you.'

'I've heard how ill he's been from Patrick and Terence. I didn't want to disturb you, and . . .' They were in the back scullery. Maeve shut the door so that the girls or Kieran would not overhear them.

'Yes?' she said. The girl looked drawn.

'I didn't want my mother to know I was coming. She's been . . . hard to deal with since my father was killed. I've had to remind myself what a blow it was to her, and then . . .' the words came with a rush, 'I know about her and the other two attacking you, Mrs McGrath. I was that ashamed I couldn't look you in the eye. But I had to come . . .'

'I'm glad you did.' She put her hand on the girl's arm. 'I've put that . . . episode behind me a long time ago. It seemed trivial after what happened, your father dead, Kieran and so many others injured.'

'I've grieved for you, thought of you often.'

She was touched. 'You've a big heart, Bessie, to say that with all your troubles. Now put it out of your mind and come away in and see my man. A bright face is just the tonic he needs.'

'Well, Mr McGrath,' Bessie said as they went into the kitchen, 'you're a fraud and no mistake. Here I've come as an angel of mercy and there you are sitting smoking your pipe as jecoe as ever.'

'Bessie!' He rose stiffly. 'Yes, I'm fine now. Just about jumping over the moon like that old cow. But I'll be all the better for seeing a bobby-dazzler like you.'

'Do you hear him, Mrs McGrath? Isobel? Maeve?' Her smile was rich, it encompassed all of them. The two girls had jumped up, their eyes shining at the interruption. 'By Jove, you've got a father here chock full of the fatal Irish charm! It'll be the death of me.' Maeve thought the girl's eyes darkened for a second.

'Have *I* got it, Bessie?' Wee Maeve asked. 'What you said?'

'Brimming over with it. You'll break someone's heart before long and get married and have ten children, all with that commodity.'

'I'm not getting married. I'm going to be a nurse.'

'Are you now? Ah, well, you could do worse things.'

'Will you take a cup of tea, Bessie?' Maeve asked her.

'No, thank you, I can't stay long. To tell you the truth, I get afraid for my mother at times . . . and of her.' She looked away and said quickly as if to change the subject, 'And where are the two boyos tonight?'

'They're off to Jock Tweedie's place,' Kieran said. 'There's a powerful attraction there. I only hope it's innocent.'

'It was when I used to go with Lily. Just childhood capers. We used to make slides in the hay-loft, see who could jump the furthest. Terence always won. He'd tackle anything . . .' her voice faltered, 'aye, anything. Talk about fatal Irish charm!' Her eyes met Maeve's, and she saw in them such misery that she was taken aback. He's breaking this girl's heart, she thought. Catherine Murdoch can't hold a candle to her. And then she was listening to Bessie teasing Kieran and laughing so heartily that she wondered if she had imagined the look.

'Oh, we had great times. One night Mr Tweedie came into the barn and nearly went off his head when he saw what a mess we'd made of his hay-loft, but before long he was laughing, too, and had asked us into the farm for a bite of supper. Yes, we had fine times. It was a pity . . .' she shook her head. 'I'll have to go. My mother gets worried if she's left alone. It's good to see you looking so well, Mr McGrath. I'm right glad.' She looked around, smiling brightly. 'Well, ta-ta everybody, I'm off.'

'That girl's having a hard time of it,' Kieran said when Maeve came back to the kitchen.

'Yes, I wouldn't be surprised if our Terence was the cause of some of it. Come on, girls, it's time for bed.'

On New Year's Eve Alastair Crawford called to see them. Isobel and wee Maeve were at a party in the church hall given by the laird, and Patrick and Terence had been roped in to help by Mr Murdoch, or perhaps by his daughter, judging by Terence's lengthy preparations before the mirror in the scullery. Maeve was taken aback when she opened the door and saw the tall, elegant figure there, the carriage in the background.

'Good evening, Mrs McGrath,' he said formally. And then with a smile, 'I can't doff my hat, I'm afraid, because of this.' He was carrying a large parcel in front of him. And as she still hesitated, 'May I come in?'

'Certainly.' She stood aside, unable to speak.

Kieran rose from his chair, surprised, but welcoming. She thought, still in a daze, what natural good manners he had. 'Good evening, sir. Terrible weather to be coming out. Will you take a seat?'

'Thank you.' He sat on the chair Kieran offered and put his parcel on the table beside him. 'Just a few gifts from my father and mother to help with the festivities.'

'There's no need,' Maeve said, 'we have enough.'

'I've been delivering them to all the miners who are still not back at work. You were the last.' She felt rebuffed.

'You're very kind,' Kieran said. 'Thank you.'

He waved this aside. 'No, please, don't thank me. It's we who are grateful to you and the others who so nearly

207

lost their lives on our behalf. And to many who did. Are you well now?'

'Yes, I'm almost recovered. I have to pay one more visit to the Infirmary after the New Year and then I think they'll release me to start work.'

'Well done. It's been a hard time for you. And for you, too, Mrs McGrath.' He looked up at Maeve where she was standing.

'No harder than any of the other colliers' wives have to put up with.' She was shaken by his sudden appearance, by his elegance, by his complete inappropriateness in her kitchen.

She saw now how shabby it was. The smoked ceiling – she had not been able to give it its usual coat of whitewash because of Kieran's illness – the worn cushions on the chairs, which she had hoped to replace before Christmas, the rag rug at the fireplace with Tansy, their cat, now very pregnant, sleeping on it . . . not at all in keeping with the Honourable Alastair Crawford. And then she chided herself. I'm glad he's seeing me in this setting, the one I chose deliberately. 'May I offer you some refreshment, sir?' she said.

'No, thank you. I've just risen from dinner.' He turned to Kieran, smiling. 'And how do you employ your time, Mr McGrath? With difficulty, I imagine, for such a practical man as you.'

'I'm doing clerical work for Mr Cranston, the gaffer. Maeve helps me, does the biggest part of it.' He covered his damaged wrist with his other hand. He was still embarrassed by its deformity. It had set badly, and the surgeon had told him he was lucky to have kept the hand at all.

'You have a talented wife.' He was not going to enquire about the clerical work, she thought.

208

'Yes, I know that.' She felt proud of Kieran. He was acting with a dignity equal to that of Alastair Crawford. Perhaps it was true that the land Woodlea stood on had once belonged to the McGraths.

'You'll be sorry to hear that my mother is far from well,' he said, addressing Maeve.

'That grieves me. I've missed her taking her usual short cut through the garden here. We became . . . acquainted. I hope it isn't lasting.'

'The doctors fear so. She's been further upset by the pit explosion, and has often asked about you.' He hesitated. 'I wonder if you would come and see her?'

'Well . . .' she looked at Kieran, surprised, then back again. 'I'd like to, of course, if it would please her.'

'It would please her very much. I told her I was coming to see you this evening, and she suggested you might drive back with me.'

'Drive back with you?' She found herself echoing his words, felt her knees tremble. She looked at Kieran again.

'If it would help her ladyship, Maeve, get yourself ready.'

'Perhaps you would like to accompany us?' Alastair Crawford asked him.

'No.' Kieran shook his head. 'This is a matter between two ladies. On you go, Maeve.'

When she came back the two men were deep in conversation. 'I'll let you know, sir,' she heard Kieran say.

'I'm ready.' She spoke to the laird's son, her chin held high. Combing her hair and putting a fine merino shawl round her shoulders, she had felt a kind of grudge against him. His unexpected visit had shaken her just when she and Kieran had reached a new plane of understanding. 'A new chapter,' she had said to him only last night in his arms. She did not want to be disturbed . . .

He spread a rug over her knees as the carriage rolled the short distance to the Hall. 'Your husband tells me that the work you do together is in connection with truck.' His voice was level.

'That is so.' She would remain calm. Better to talk about truck than anything more personal.

'I want to tell you, as I told your husband, that Crawford's have quite divorced themselves from any dealings in that direction.' Did he suspect that she was getting at him through truck? She waited. 'If there are faults they lie with the contractor or the man he employs there. We have washed our hands of the whole business. My father is too proud of his good name, and you must know as well as I do how the firm looks after its employees.' Provided they go to the kirk, she could have said. She thought of the hard-mouthed laird.

'Do you accept rent?'

'You're clever, Maeve.' His voice was coldly admiring. 'Yes, as it happens, there is no alternative, but it's paid into the Miners' Welfare Fund immediately.' A smile crossed his face. 'My father was all for the Church getting it, but I prefer to deal with the present rather than the future.' He paused, looked at her. 'I hope that will convince you that we aren't the ogres some people think we are.'

Her enthusiasm for helping Bob Cranston seemed to run out of her as she listened to Alastair Crawford explaining the details. She had known they would keep their hands clean. It was a moral issue, as she had always been convinced, and should be taken up by people who could raise it in Parliament, like the headmaster Mr Cranston had spoken about. 'You've taken the wind out of my sails,' she said, 'I must admit it. I always suspected who the real culprit was. If the system were completely abolished, there would be no more Brodies. Do you think that will ever happen?'

'I more than think so. I know so. He's making a noose to hang himself with. It's only a matter of time. Leave it with those who have direct access to the powers that be, and apply your intellect to something which will directly benefit you, and perhaps give you pleasure . . . your intellect and enthusiasm. You have both.'

'You flatter me.' She turned to smile at him, relieved at their talk, and somehow light in heart. He was right. There was something ahead for her. She felt the movement of the high-stepping horses, the carriage wheels rolling smoothly under her. There was a significance . . .

'Maeve . . .'

'Please don't call me that.'

'I think of you as Maeve.' His voice was low, hurried. 'I must tell you. You are still in my thoughts. Perhaps I thought, we had reached some sort of . . . understanding.' He paused, spoke more slowly. 'I offered your husband a position as head groom. Craig has expressed a wish to go to our other estate. Believe me, I didn't press him. But it does seem . . . fortuitous.'

'What did Kieran say?'

'He accepted. I could see the idea pleased him. He's willing to start after the New Year.'

'I see.' Her mind was in a turmoil. She had been too slow.

'You don't sound pleased.' He turned to her. 'Maeve, we could begin again . . . these morning rides . . . I need your company, your presence. You've been in my heart for so long.'

'You mustn't speak like that,' she said quietly. She

211

looked out of the window. They had rolled through the gates. Now they were going up the long drive to the house. 'I have other plans, you see . . .' It's not easy, she thought, to will oneself to continue to strive. I could accept this, live for the present, deceive Kieran. She remembered the morning when this man had kissed her, the longing for him night after night lying in bed beside Kieran. There would be excitement – she had always liked to live dangerously. But your plan, she heard the voice inside her head, what about your plan?

'Here we are,' Alastair Crawford said. He took the rug from her knees, and the touch of his fingers made her blood race. 'Think of what I've said,' he spoke hurriedly, 'and tell me before you go.' He led her up the flight of steps and into the large hall with its stone fireplace and the skin rug in front of it. No pregnant Tansy here, she thought, seeing the wolfhound rise lazily to greet them. She had to combat the sense of familiarity of other days. It would be so easy . . .

She was shocked at Lady Crawford's appearance. She was sitting propped up on her pillows, shrunken, it seemed, to half her size. Her eyes looked bigger than ever in the small face. She held out her thin hands.

'Mrs McGrath! How good of you to come and see me. Sit down there where I can look at you.'

'Thank you.' She saw the elderly nurse go through the adjoining door as if she had been instructed to leave them alone. 'And how are you keeping, your ladyship?' she asked.

'I'm not keeping at all. Indeed, I think I'm slowly disintegrating.' Her mouth quirked. 'I lie here thinking. I have such thoughts. I remember coming through your garden when I was bound for those walks I loved . . . I long for the feel of those woods, the rustling stillness . . .'

'You'll see them again.'

She looked at Maeve with her big eyes, slowly shaking her head. 'And I think of how one day we sat on that bench of yours, and talked.'

'I remember. And you asked for a white rose because you said they smelled sweeter.'

'But you said they fell quicker. You were right. I kept it between the pages of a favourite book, and one day it crumbled in my fingers.'

'You must come and get a fresh one. Next summer.'

'Ah, next summer . . . tell me, how is your husband?'

'He's almost well now. He's had a long illness.'

'Will he be going back to the pit?'

'I don't know.' How penetrating her eyes were.

'Alastair, my son, told me he intended to offer him the head groom's job. Would that appeal to him?'

'I believe so. I only heard of it driving here.'

'Does it appeal to you?' She met those eyes again, as if drawn to them, like her son's, but darker and deeper. Was she trying to say something? 'We know our sons, don't we? I mean, not the details, because they can employ subterfuge, but deep down we feel them rather than know them. The bond is closer than with daughters, I imagine.'

'In a way. The girls are important to me as well, especially Kate. But Terence . . . he has a lot of me in him, I think. He wants to go his own way although I can see it's the wrong way. He won't be advised, not that I've tried.' She smiled. 'That would be useless with Terence.'

'Do you think we learn as we grow older?'

'I think so, I hope so. In time we must learn . . . to put away childish things, not to give in to one's feelings if instinctively we know they're wrong.'

213

The eyes seemed to envelop her in their depths. 'Will you take some advice from me since I'm older than you?'

'If you wish.'

'If you love your husband . . . don't let him accept this post.' The words seemed to fall into a silence. 'Does that . . .' her voice was hesitant, '. . . sound strange advice, coming from me?'

'I don't know.' There was so much more in the woman's eyes than in her voice: the knowledge of those rides with her son, the morning they'd sheltered from the squall, even the nights she'd spent in bed longing for him, imagining him . . . She heard the tired voice.

'I always thought that "Gather ye rosebuds while ye may" was false advice. Maeve . . . I know that is your name. Let me use it.' Her hand moved across the bed-cover, and Maeve took it in hers. There was a fluttering pulse in the thin wrist. 'They wither so soon, like the white rose.' Her eyes closed. Maeve softly stroked her hand. How quiet it was, the enclosed quietness of a sick-room, shut off from the world. The hand moved under her own. 'You have such promise in you. I don't want to know why that is, nor what went before. I just know there is a great deal of . . . spirit in you which has to be expressed, but wisely. When you are near death – no, don't start, I've been accepting it for a long time – you recognize qualities in people which the casual eye doesn't see. Don't . . . dissipate your promise. Ask yourself, rather, why . . . my son . . . who is eminently suited for marriage, still shies away from it. There is a lack of . . . responsibility in him which makes him, I must use the word, unreliable. He has broken one heart I know of. You may remember a charming girl with us one year at the Picnic. I shouldn't like him to break another, someone

214

whom I admire . . . and . . . like . . .' her voice trailed away.

'Rest,' Maeve said, stroking her hand.

'I seem to be talking too much.' There was the quirk at her mouth. 'Suddenly I'm tired, so tired . . .'

'It's my fault. Lady Crawford . . .'

'Say "Annabel". It doesn't matter now.'

'Annabel, I'm so sad to see you like this. So pale. Believe me, I've thought of you often, thought of the . . . feeling,' she would have liked to say 'affinity', 'which lay between us . . .' She saw Lady Crawford's lips move. She had to bend forward to hear.

'Do you know, Maeve, you couldn't have said . . . anything . . . which would have pleased me better. But promise me, will you think of what I said, think . . .'

'Yes, I will.'

'If you but knew it, you are so lucky . . . with a husband who . . . loves you. The Crawfords are . . . different. I have never known a . . . steadfast love . . .' Her head fell on one side. She looked deathly pale. Maeve ran to the communicating door.

'Nurse!' She knocked. 'Nurse! Come quickly!' The woman appeared, brushed past Maeve and went to Lady Crawford's bedside. Maeve saw her take the limp wrist, then look over her shoulder.

'She's all right, but very weak. Anything tires her. She's talked such a lot about you coming.' She said grudgingly, straightening her patient's head on the pillow, straightening the bedcovers as if they were one and the same thing, 'You seem to have taken her fancy.'

He was waiting in the hall, playing with the wolfhound which lolled on its back. He jumped up when he saw her. 'How did you find her?'

'I'm distressed. I hadn't realized . . .' She felt tears come to her eyes.

'She'll be happy to have seen you. Let me drive you home. We can talk.'

'Would you mind if I refused?' All her defiance seemed to have left her, and her uncertainty, to be replaced by a kind of remote gentleness. She grieved for this man, Lady Crawford's son, because he would soon lose his mother, that he should be always searching . . . 'I wish to be alone.'

'Certainly, if you wish it that way.' He spoke quietly. 'I'll tell the coachman.' It was as if his mother's influence was on him

'I'll say good-bye,' she said. She held out her hand.

'How final you sound, Maeve. But I know you're upset. You don't mean it, of course.' He smiled; he had the same quirk at his mouth as his mother's, she noticed, the same fine features, the amber eyes. He touched me with fire, she thought.

'Oh, but I do,' she said. 'It's over,' her mouth quirked too, 'before it had properly begun.' She watched the charm drain out of his face. He looked . . . lonely.

She sat in the carriage, listening to the clip-clop of the horses' hooves on the frosty drive, and then the change in the sound as they swung into the road with its occasional bumps which shook her about in the padded interior.

So much to think about, and yet not to think of logically, just to feel, to absorb, and later to act. She seemed at the moment to be in a world of sensation; grief for her friend – she thought of Lady Crawford like that – and a sadness for her son. I could have gone either way, she thought, but Kieran is my husband, and . . . steadfast. That was the word Annabel had used. It felt right to think 'Annabel'.

The ringing hooves were a steady background to her thoughts. She knew when the coachman helped her down from the carriage that they would give her the answer she was searching for.

18

The New Year passed quietly, partly because they had little money to celebrate with, but principally because Kieran caught a cold that settled on his chest again. When he paid his visit to the Infirmary the surgeon told him he was on no account to go back to work meantime, either in the pit or anywhere else. Maeve wrote a letter for him to Alastair Crawford. He was too weak.

Regarding your kind offer to employ me as head groom, unfortunately I've suffered a severe bronchitis since last I saw you, and I have strict orders from Mr Campbell at the Infirmary not to engage in any employment for the time being. Rather than keep you waiting on my behalf I feel you should make other arrangements for filling the post.

He looked wistful when Maeve read it out to him.

'Maybe we shouldn't have bolted the stable door so firmly, mavourneen.' He laughed feebly at his joke.

'Well, it's up to him if he wishes to keep it open for you. Somehow I don't think he will.' She was sure Alastair Crawford would see it as a final rebuff. 'Meantime we've got the truck affairs to occupy ourselves with and keep our minds from going rusty, and we're managing fine with the money from the boys.'

'And there's your great plan?' He teased her.

'I'll show you,' she said. 'In a year you'll be wondering why you ever worried about a thing.'

There was no reply to the letter. She heard from Terence that the laird's son had set off for Spain again.

* * *

Towards the end of January, when Kieran had recovered but was still confined indoors, she went into the girl's bedroom one Sunday afternoon and began to dress herself. She had washed herself all over at the kitchen fire last night when the rest of the family had retired. Kieran had watched her standing naked in the tin bath.

'You've a figure like a young girl,' he said, 'straight limbs, a rosiness. You don't age, Maeve, there's something . . . indestructible about you, as if you could go out and fight battles . . . as if you could lie in bed with a lover and drive him out of his mind.'

She laughed, pleased. 'You haven't lost your poetic touch. Long ago I always admired it.'

'It's the Irish in me.' He tried to explain, stumbling over the words. 'I feel . . . so strongly . . . the beauty of things, of you, of nature. It's a great rush of feeling which, would you believe it, brings tears to my eyes, makes me want to put it into words.'

'You can write me a poem tomorrow, then,' she said, 'when I leave you for an hour or two.' But she would not be drawn further.

First of all the clean white cotton drawers and chemise trimmed with lace, then the tightly-laced corset to further emphasize her slim waist, the flannel petticoat underneath the flounced cotton one because she had to be warm as well as smart, the small saddle cushion at her back tied on with tapes, the 'dress improver', then lastly the bottle-green velvet gown trimmed with black braid at the sleeves and a row of buttons marching down the tightly-fitted bodice. The gown was a present from Terence in far-off America. A long letter had come with the big parcel.

I read about the terrible explosion in your part of the world and trust neither your husband nor sons were harmed in it, and that no news is good news in that quarter.

219

But in case things have been difficult for you, Maria and Caroline have taken great pleasure in choosing dresses for all the female members of the family, including yourself, and warm clothes for the male members, a little American in cut, but none the worse for that.

Business is booming, and I have now attained my dearest wish, to have a property of my own. It is sited on the banks of the River Hudson, approximately sixty miles from New York and with a fine area of land surrounding it. Maria is delighted that there is a nearby ferry-boat to cross the river if need be, and that at last we can have our own stables. I think we shall be very happy here.

When she had written to thank him for the gifts she had told him that there was the possibility of Mrs Murray-Hyslop moving to America because of the expansion of his export business, and that his wife had spoken of Kate accompanying them.

And although I know America is a vast continent (she had written), if it came about that we were visiting Kate it might mean that we could see you and your family at last. I have come to believe that families should cleave together, that roots are important although we both turned our backs on them. I should like to talk to you about that, to get to know each other again as adults, not wilful children.

Kieran's mother says Mama and Papa are failing. I grieve deeply about this and should have liked to visit them, but they have never replied to any of my letters, and have evidently no wish to see me. Have you, too, been rebuffed, and because of that, do you have a lingering sadness running through your life like a thread? They didn't suit each other, or love each other, and I now see how important a happy marriage is, and how an unhappy one hurts more than the two people concerned . . .

She was nearly ready, except for the jet beads which went so well against the green velvet, and a last burnish to her red hair before pinning on top of it the little black toque. Shawl, reticule. She went back to the kitchen and twirled in front of Kieran. 'What do you think?'

'Maeve!' His eyes were full of loving admiration. 'Terence's present! Is it the Hall you're off to? Is there a summons from Lady Crawford?'

'No, I think the poor soul is too far gone to see anyone, so the rumour goes. I'm going to see your cousin, Duncan McGrath.'

'Duncan! But I thought all the sons were in Glasgow? That's what their father told us when we first came.'

'You aren't so well up in the local gossip as I am. Two of them, Grant and Denis, are still there, working in Dixon's, but Duncan, the eldest, came back to try to resurrect the business when his father died. I don't think he had much luck with that, and he's working in the blast furnace beside Patrick.'

'I've never heard Patrick talk about him.'

'He knows him all the same. He's my informant. But Duncan's twice his age, and taciturn into the bargain. Unmarried.'

'Well, well! Is this a family visit, then?'

'In a way.' She pulled on her gloves. 'I was just saying to Terence in my Christmas letter that roots were important. No, don't smile. When we make our fortune we'll go and see my parents if it's not too late . . .'

'In spite of their treatment of you?'

'I don't blame them any more. I can put myself in their place, and in your father's. We'll make it up to them. And we'll go and see Terence, Maria and Caroline in America. Oh, Kieran, the world's opening out in front of me as I speak. There's so much to do and see. I feel bursting with excitement at the thought of it.'

'If you could see yourself . . .' He came towards her. 'Your eyes are so deeply blue. You look beautiful.' He took her in his arms. 'I wish I could go with you.'

'You know what Mr Campbell said. I want you well. I need you to be well.'

His kiss had the strength of a lover's in it. If he could be like this all the time, she thought, responding, I could forget Alastair Crawford . . .

Duncan McGrath's house proclaimed itself as a bachelor's establishment from the outside at least – the dirty curtains half-drawn, the doorstep unwashed – but it had a fine solid front and the width between the windows on each side of the door indicated that the rooms were large.

He did not know her at first, and she had obviously disturbed him from his Sunday afternoon rest at the fire. His shirt was unbuttoned at the neck, his braces hung over his trousers, his chin was unshaven. He glowered at her, half-afraid.

'Have I startled you, Duncan?' she asked him. 'It's Maeve McGrath, your cousin by marriage.'

'Maeve McGrath!' He stumbled over the words, 'Kieran's . . . ?'

'Yes, Kieran's wife. I'd heard that you had come back from Glasgow, and I've been meaning to come and see you, but the time flashes past with a family.'

'Aye, that's true . . . I expect.' He said hesitantly, 'Will you come in, er . . .'

'Maeve.'

'Maeve. I was just having my Sunday . . . sit-down.'

The interior was no better than the exterior. The kitchen was in disorder, the fireplace full of ash, the bed unmade, the table littered with half-eaten food, there was a sour smell, whether from Duncan or the room itself she could not be sure. He unceremoniously knocked off a cat

222

with some kittens from the one comfortable chair and asked her to sit down.

'Oh, the poor things!' She lifted one of the mewling kittens on to her lap. 'What a wee beauty!'

'You're welcome to it. That cat goes on having them night and day with scarcely a rest. They're due for drowning.'

She winced. 'I'd better not tell my youngest daughter. She'd be clamouring for the whole lot of them. She's a great little nurse.'

'Have you a big family?'

'Not as big as it might have been, but, yes, I have five. My son John was drowned in the Sholtie.' She still had to make herself say it. 'That was before you came back to Sholton, I think.'

'Yes, it must have been. I'm out of touch with it, and I doubt if I'll ever *be* in touch. I don't like village life much. Glasgow suits me better. Folks aren't so nosey there.'

She swallowed that. 'Why did you come back, Duncan, if you don't mind me asking?' She put down the kitten beside its mother, smiled sweetly at her cousin by marriage. He wriggled in his chair.

'It's a long story. I was in Dixon's Blazes, earning good money with my two brothers, and I had a row with the foreman. I daresay I'm difficult to deal with, thrawn,' he looked at her apologetically, 'so I walked out in a stumor. That's my way. I regret it later. We had word that the old carter who worked with my father and who was living here, had died, so my brothers, that's Grant and Denis, thought it would be a good idea if I came here and saw to the property, any roads, see if anything could be made of it.'

'I see. It's a nice house.' She looked around. It was in a terrible state, but at least there was room to move – she

223

had noticed several doors leading off the corridor – and it was a palace compared to their cramped cottage in the Row. It could soon be whitewashed, scrubbed out and disinfected, the windows opened, cushions and curtains made. It was a solid, family house.

'It's far too big for a single man, and I'm not likely to get married.'

'Oh, I don't know.' She smiled at him. 'You're a fine, handsome fellow.'

'No, Maeve.' She thought his answering smile was wistful. 'I'm not one for the married state.'

'I hear you're at the Ironworks?'

'Aye. I've got no liking for carting, and the business was so far gone that it was a waste of time trying to build it up again. I like a pay packet with no responsibility. Crawford's will do me till I get back to Dixon's.'

'Have you stables?' she said casually.

'Fine stables off the yard. There's only one old horse there. I can't think to send him to the knackers. Old Hughie, the carter, treated him like a brother.' He laughed, 'At times you couldn't tell one from the other.'

'Would you like to show me the outside, Duncan? I've always had a great interest in stables.'

He nodded. 'Aye, I heard from my father your folks were in the way of being gentry.' His glance was curious.

'It's so long ago I've forgotten.'

He rose. 'Come on, then, though you're hardly dressed for stables.' He glanced at her again, and she thought back to Alastair Crawford's remark that she was like an exotic bird amongst barnyard fowls. She would show them. 'But it's dry, at least. When it rains it's like a bog.'

It was just as well it was not raining because the yard at the back was as dirty as the house, and littered with the remnants of broken carts, wheels on their own, pieces of

224

machinery she could not recognize propped against the stone wall of the bothies. The contents of a hay-loft had spread half across the yard. It only needed a few puddles to make it impossible to cross it.

Duncan apologized. 'Mind that dress of yours. I always mean to clean this up on Sundays, but I never get round to it. I haven't the heart.'

'I don't think your heart's in Sholton,' she said, avoiding a rusty plough.

'No, that's the truth o' it. Glasgow suits me better. I can wander the streets at night, see a bit of life, and I can count on one of the brothers' wives giving me a good Sunday dinner. I'm no' any great shakes at the cooking.'

'We could provide that for you, Duncan.' Kate had generously left a half-crown saved from her wages last week. 'We would be pleased if you'd join our family. You ought to get to know us better.'

'That's real kind of you, Maeve. It's the first offer I've had.'

The stables were roomy, but again uncared for. The one old horse in its stall turned slowly round when it saw them, casting a long-lashed eye in the direction of Duncan, possibly in the hope of some food.

'Dobbin, old Hughie called him,' Duncan said, whacking the horse's broad back. 'There's room for half-a-dozen at least here. Maybe it's a pity that my father let the place run down, but he always said they were a vagrant lot, carters, travelling from port to docks, never in the same place for long. Mind you, they had long hours, five in the morning till eight at night.'

'And only sixteen shillings a week's pay.'

'Aye, it's no' much compared with what they pay at Crawford's. That's why you can't get any men around here.'

225

'Still, if they were paid more, and if these bothies were made into nice wee cottages for them . . .'

'But you have to tout for the work to be able to pay them a decent wage.'

'Yes, you can't have one without the other. I can see your point, Duncan; it's all too great an effort for you when you can earn good money at Crawford's or back in Glasgow. There are plenty of blast furnaces around there.'

'I could go back to Dixon's now. The foreman's left I had the trouble with. I had a good reputation. Started as a furnace filler and worked my way up to be a puddler. Aye, I'd like to go back there fine.'

'And the house is really too big for you,' Maeve said. They were standing in the yard again. Dusk was falling, but she could just make out a fine piece of ground stretching beyond it, possibly a field and a garden where vegetables could be grown.

'Everything's too big,' Duncan agreed, nodding. 'More than half an acre of garden, and two fields for the horses or for a bit of corn, the stables and a house with three bedrooms and a loft as well. No, I do my best but I'll be glad to be rid of the whole thing.'

'I'll not go back inside with you,' Maeve said. 'It's been a grand pleasure to make your acquaintance. You were just a lad when Kieran and I came to see your father. Now, I'm going to ask a favour of you. Would you come and have your dinner with us next Sunday? It's high time we got to know each other again.'

'Well,' he hesitated, 'I'm not a great one for visiting . . .'

'You'll be a great one for my steak and kidney pudding when you taste it. Best steak,' she said, remembering Kate's half-crown, 'though I shouldn't be boasting. I'll

226

not take "no" for an answer. Twelve o'clock next Sunday, or as soon as the kirk service is over.'

'Oh, I've no patience wi' the kirk, but I must admit I'm very partial to a steak and kidney pudding.'

She walked home, well pleased with her visit.

It took nearly a week of family discussions to talk Kieran and the boys into her way of thinking. Strangely enough, Patrick was the most enthusiastic, Terence the least. The thought of working with horses appealed to Kieran, as she had known it would. Patrick was more far-sighted.

'There would be all kinds of labour problems which we'd know from the inside.'

'Yes. I realize that.' She had determined there would be no bludgeoning. 'But your father and I have had a fair amount of experience dealing with truck, corresponding with societies and the like. And another thing, we could take a leaf out of Crawford's book. They've always done well by their workers in pay and accommodation. That's one of the secrets. Look after your employees. Make them happy. And, think of it. We would be our own masters. It would be up to us to build up a good business, all pulling together. There's a great future ahead. We could move with the times since we'd be in the moving business. How's that for a slogan, boys? I can't think why Duncan's father didn't go on with it, or his boys grab at the chance. I suppose they aren't enterprising, but you never get rich on a paypacket, as the three of you well know.' She tried to curb her enthusiasm. She knew how contrary families could be. 'But, think. Goods have to be transported from ironworks and pits, to the railways. There's going to be constant traffic in Glasgow. Cast your mind back to that Sunday School Picnic when you won the prize, Kieran, for Mr Tweedie. I can remember well what the laird said that day, if you can't. "There's a rising tide of prosperity in this country. Coal and iron are in great demand." Well, it's all to be shifted, hasn't it? Even you must realize that, Terence, if you'd take your eyes off Catherine Murdoch for five minutes.' He grinned sheepishly.

'As long as I have a shilling or two to jingle in my pocket, Ma,' he said.

'But you might have to provide for a home and a family one day. Wouldn't you like to do your best for them? Think of it, you could have a fine house of your own, not like the Hall, though there's no harm in setting your sights high, but maybe like the manse. And there's clothes . . .'

Kieran was with her. As he said, he had nothing to lose. Anything which got him out of going down the pit again and at the same time enabled him to work with horses, sounded like Paradise. He remembered horse fairs in Ireland he had attended, remembered he had been congratulated on having a good eye.

'Though there was that job at the Hall, Maeve . . .' He was a reluctant flier.

'We turned that down when you were ill,' she reminded him. 'Besides, wouldn't it be better to be your own boss? You'd be at the beck and call of anyone at the Big House.'

By Saturday they were all with her and beginning to worry about the same question that had been on her mind since she had seen Duncan McGrath. Supposing he would not sell? On Sunday she excelled herself. It was the best steak and kidney pudding she had ever produced, made with good rump steak, thanks to Kate. It steamed so richly in its bowl that its aroma filled the house; there was a fresh cloth on the kitchen table, the fire was burning brightly, the whole family were washed, brushed and shining-faced to greet this new cousin who had suddenly come into their lives. Wee Maeve could play her part, too, might even tip the balance, Maeve thought, brushing her golden curls.

'Has he got any girls like me, Ma?'

'No, my pet. He isn't married.'

'But has he got any little girls?'

'Don't be daft,' Isobel said with a simper. She was at the age now, Maeve thought, when she would need a quiet talking to if she had not jaloused already how things went. Twelve already. Nearly a young woman.

For the first half-hour Duncan McGrath had little to say. He had evidently cut his chin during a rare Sunday shave, and he had to keep mopping at the bead of blood that formed on it. 'Devil take it,' he said, 'I'm not accustomed to being entertained on a Sunday.' He looked as if he would rather have been back in his dirty kitchen.

But he relaxed in the steam of the steak and kidney pudding when Maeve lifted it out of its pot, and even more with the tot of whisky which Kieran put in his hand when he had ensconced him in his own chair.

'Maeve tells me your place is a bit big for you,' he began. He had been well coached.

'Aye, it is that. I haven't a capable wife like yours, Kieran.'

'You must find Sholton dull after Glasgow. I'd like fine to live there with those busy streets and everything. Somewhere to go at nights.' There was no need to lie so blatantly, Maeve thought, nodding her head in agreement.

'The metropolis,' she said. 'Once you've tasted the joy of living in a city, nothing is quite the same. I remember when I went to Dublin as a girl . . .'

'You would have heard I was injured in the pit explosion?'

'Yes, I heard of that. You haven't got back to work yet?'

'No, nor likely to for a time. I've been looking around for something to do. I was wondering, Duncan, if you would like me to help you about your place? I could tidy up the stables, look after the horse, maybe do a little carting if anyone needed a few sticks of furniture moved . . .'

Duncan looked at him, amazement in his face. 'The place is a ruin! And old Dobbin is hardly capable of pulling a wheel barrow. Well, you saw it, Maeve.'

'Maybe so.' Kieran nodded. 'But you'd be doing me a favour. It would give me something to do, get me out from under Maeve's feet. And if, I'm only saying if, you went back to work at Dixon's – I'm sure you're greatly missed there – we might be able to come to some arrangement. I've got a bit of money laid by from the compensation.'

'You mean, buy the place?'

'Well, give you a down payment.'

Duncan McGrath stroked his chin, obviously remembered the cut and stopped quickly. 'You fair surprise me, Kieran. It's a good enough house, but ramshackle, a ruin. It would want money spent on it . . .'

'I've got two good sons who are handymen into the bargain.' Maeve looked at the two boys. They were poker-faced. 'It's only a suggestion. You would have to discuss it with your brothers.'

'Well, I . . . I . . .' He sipped at his whisky, looked round their kitchen. 'It's a small place this for the seven of you, sure enough.'

'We've managed fine,' Maeve said. 'I'd be sad to leave it. But if you did move to Glasgow . . .' She waited. She looked at Terence and Patrick. Terence had a half-smile on his face, the smile of one who would rather be anywhere else, but Patrick was sitting forward, intently watching his second cousin.

'Is the place owned by the three of you?' he asked. The bluntness of it, Maeve thought.

Duncan looked at him. He's going to be annoyed, she thought, in spite of the whisky, he's thrawn . . . 'No, it's mine. I'm the eldest.' He looked around them. 'I don't want you to get the impression that it's a millstone round my neck. Property's property, whatever the state it's in, though the goodwill's gone many a year ago.'

'You're right,' Maeve said. 'It was left to you. But should you ever part with it, maybe your father would be pleased to think someone in the family was taking an interest in it, carrying on his name.' She cast a pious glance at the ceiling.

'Aye, maybe he would.' He gave her a long look. 'But we can't ask him, can we?' He sipped his whisky again, looking worried.

'Perhaps you could discuss it with Grant and Denis,' Kieran said. 'We wouldn't want them to think we were poking our noses in where we weren't wanted.'

'No, it's mine.' He looked at his glass, stubborn, beset with problems he could not cope with. Wee Maeve was at his side. 'Ma says you've got lovely wee kittens and maybe I would get one, Duncan?' He turned to look at her and Maeve held her breath. 'Could I, cousin Duncan?' Sarah Bernhardt could not have done better.

'You can have the whole jing bang if you like, lass.' He straightened. 'To tell you the truth, there's nobody I'd like better to have the run of the place. You're the first who've shown me any kindness in this hole. I tell you what, I'll take a turn up to Glasgow next week and see if

I can land a job at Dixon's. If I do, we can have a talk about price.'

'That's fair enough,' Kieran said, his face wonderfully calm, 'we'll leave it there. Now, how about another dram?'

'No, I thank you. I'm feeling right sleepy after that dinner. I'll get on my way.'

'We're very grateful to you, Duncan,' Maeve said. 'I don't think you'll regret it.'

He got up, said to Kieran, 'You can thank your wife,' and then, shyly, 'By Jove, she was a sight for sore eyes in that green velvet gown . . .'

'He's a sad soul,' she said to Kieran later that night. 'Lonely.'

'You don't think we tricked him?'

'No.' She shook her head. 'It's a fair deal. As long as you don't think I've tricked *you*, got you into something you'll regret.'

He shook his head. 'I trust you. You've got a good head.' He put his arms round her. 'And a better body. It's a pity Duncan McGrath can't see what's under the green velvet gown.'

She laughed, turned to him. 'Maybe I could get something off the price if . . .' He drew her close. His mouth silenced hers. No, she had no regrets. She had done the right thing. Kieran would work at her side always, see to the buying of horses when they had the money; Patrick would be the business head, Terence the man they would send to the bank when they wanted a loan. He could charm the birds off the tree. It would be hard going. At first there would only be the two of them. The boys would have to hold on to their jobs so that they would all have enough to eat.

232

But it would be worth it. It would be their own. There would be worry, hardship, disagreements but never boredom. It would fulfil her, let her see that Alastair Crawford had only been an escape from that boredom.

And I'll be behind the lot of them, she thought, the power behind the throne, a woman's true place.

BOOK TWO

The Far-off Side
1869–1880

1

It took four years of hard labour before the boys could give up their jobs. They all slaved – that was the only word for it – working at nights and at weekends on Duncan McGrath's house and stables, hoarding such money as they had until they could add to their horses, touting for business, building up connections with pits and blast furnaces in the district, the railways, making themselves always available at all times of the day and night, sometimes even for funerals.

Maeve it was who put on the bottle-green velvet and called on the heads of the various factories with the cards they had had printed, asking for business. At first she had been fearful, then she began to enjoy the stimulation of other minds, pitting her wits against hard-headed businessmen. The one place she could not bring herself to go was the Sholton Ironworks, in case she should see Alastair Crawford.

But it was a new, exciting world. She said jokingly one night that she was sorry they had not called their firm The New World Carting Company, because that was what they were advancing towards.

They moved into the house in 1870, a year after their first payment. Duncan McGrath had been generous. When he left to go back to his old job he also left them the sticks of furniture, but as Maeve said, all his mess as well. This was women's work. She, Isobel, wee Maeve, and Kate on her days off, scoured the place, fumigated it, whitewashed and painted it, dug and planted the garden, scraped the windows of their accumulated dirt, put up new curtains.

The boys, meantime, were replastering, rebuilding, refurbishing the stables and the bothies. Their first commission was to move a miner's family with their goods and chattels to another house. Old Dobbin pulled the cart which Kieran had rewheeled and repainted. The miner gave him what he could afford, five shillings, but they accepted it gratefully. They were in business, and as Maeve said that first night in the new home, 'Our business is moving.' Maybe some day they would have that slogan painted on their smart new lorries.

Business came steadily, and Kieran when they were slack began to haunt the horse fairs. The day he led home a companion to Dobbin, a sprightly bay, (sprightly in temperament although not in age), was a red-letter one. Maeve made a cloth dumpling studded with currants and raisins to celebrate, and put a farthing in it for the lucky one who found it to wish by. Wee Maeve got it.

'I wish we'll stay here for ever,' she said, 'and that when I grow up I'll be a nurse.'

In 1873, the day after Terence came up from the pit for the last time, he got married to Catherine Murdoch. He had never lost his obsession for her and she had finally given in. She had always said she would not think of marriage until he could wear a white collar and not have permanent black rims to his nails. Maeve felt it was her son's good looks which had won her over. At twenty-two he was the most handsome man for miles around, and could have the pick of any of the local girls for the asking, including Bessie Haddow.

She had never grown to like Catherine. There was something small-minded about the girl and she thought the marriage was a mistake. But she had little time to

238

dwell on her family's personal problems. Suddenly, it seemed, business began to increase.

'If we'd planned it,' she said to Kieran and Patrick one night, 'we couldn't have started at a better time. Millions of tons of coal are being mined in Scotland along with the black-band ironstone and it's all got to be transported.' They had agreed, and also to renting a small house in Crannoch for Terence and Catherine because of the new steel works being built there. It would be known as the Crannoch branch.

The Cranstons' farm was nearby. They were well-known and respected in the community, and they put a lot of work in Terence's way. The sons in their spare time were still active in the Trade Union meetings in Glasgow, determined on the complete abolition of truck. They were the new breed, Maeve thought, men who, although they worked the land, took an interest in the country's development. They had won Davy Cox's case for him and Brodie had been sacked. It's a good thing we're no longer living in the Row, she thought. Tibby Brodie would have waylaid me again and torn my hair out.

At the beginning of 1874 the four of them, Kieran, Maeve, Terence and Patrick, met in the office which she had converted from one of the rooms in the house. They had made a good profit the previous year. Duncan McGrath, who never pressed them, could have another payment. Their two carters, Wylie and Dick, who had proved their worth, could each be offered a bothy rent free. They would also have an increase in their wages.

'Look after your employees and they'll look after you,' she reminded the others. 'Maybe we'll move out of this house, turn it entirely over to offices . . .'

'Oh, Ma,' Terence said, 'what next?' He was sprawled

in his chair. He looked somehow shrunken. Marriage was not agreeing with him.

'Dreams become reality,' she retorted, 'but not without hard work. I notice you're last on the job in the mornings.' She put it down to Catherine. She was taking the spunk out of him.

And that year Kate set off for America with the Murray-Hyslops, and the whole family drove to the Broomielaw in Glasgow to see her off.

They went in one of the carts, swept and cleaned by the girls and driven by Patrick, although Catherine demurred and said it was not the kind of thing for a minister's daughter. 'Next year you'll have a carriage of your own, Catherine, never fear,' Maeve told her. Her very dislike of the girl made her patient.

But standing on the windy dockside and looking around her family she was proud of them. Kieran at forty-four was still handsome, although beginning to put on a little weight, 'a belly for a gold chain,' he said, patting it. That would come next year as well, Maeve promised him. Patrick, not as handsome as his brother, had, nevertheless, a quiet dark face full of character, an air of composure. He's like a rock, Maeve thought, you can't shake him.

Isobel, seventeen, was now keeping the firm's books in the office. 'If it's to be a family firm, let it be that,' Maeve had said, and bought her a desk and a wooden filing cabinet. She was an asset with her lint-white hair, her narrow, pretty features. She could win over the men who called for quotations, but more important, she had a sharp, quick mind. She reminded Maeve of her own father. He had died two years ago, and her mother shortly after him. She had left Woodlea to a nephew, Mrs

McGrath had written, the son of Aunt Maud Daly in Dublin.

She had been surprised how much she minded that, but even more so, she had grieved deeply for her parents. The feeling of guilt and regret that she had never gone back could still rise up and choke her.

Maeve, at twelve, was nearly as tall as Isobel, but a different make, round, laughing, bouncy like her curls. She adored Terence. And Terence, she thought, looking at him, so handsome, still dashing, with such a flair for wearing his clothes – she had once said laughingly that he would rather have a fancy waistcoat than a good plate of broth. But why should a handsome young man of twenty-two look so worried unless he was not happily married?

It was not hard to find the cause of that worry, she thought, glancing at the thin, peevish face of Catherine who was hanging on his arm, at her tight mouth. Was she trying to save wear and tear on her teeth? She would be a shrew in bed. You could tell by her clothes if nothing else: dull, brown, plain, never a bright colour nor a bit of dash about her like her young husband.

And there was her father who had joined them on the quayside. He had been attending some Holy Willies' Convention in Glasgow – that was how Maeve thought of it – and had decided Kate could not go to America without his blessing. His attitude to the McGrath family had gradually improved in direct relation to their advancement in business, there was no doubt about that. Maybe he's beginning to angle for a substantial contribution from us to the kirk, Maeve thought, like the Crawfords . . .

The Crawfords . . . She had little time to think about them now, or of their son. When she looked back on those morning rides it seemed like two other people. She remembered Lady Crawford's words that night in the Morris wall-papered bedroom. 'You have such promise in you . . . don't dissipate your promise.' She had taken her advice, although she would never know it. She had been dead for three years.

Patrick, who still had cronies in the blast furnace, had told her that since the death of his wife the laird had the reputation of being more tight-fisted than ever, except where the kirk was concerned. Perhaps the Sunday School Picnic had been her idea, although her husband had taken the credit.

'We should be keeping an eye on the amount of pig-iron Crawford's are importing from Spain,' Patrick had told her at the same time. 'I hear tell the laird's son is always there. One of these days they'll give up mining it at Sholton. The Cranston lads were right to move out to the farm when they did.'

But changes from iron to steel did not affect the carting business. Whatever they consisted of, goods had to be moved, back and forth, back and forth. Transport was the life blood of the nation. She and Patrick shared hopes and ideals they rarely talked about. Horses would not last for ever. They would be replaced by lorries driven by engines – look at the change from the sailing-ship which had taken her brother Terence to America a quarter of a century ago, to this sleek ocean greyhound which was going to take Kate away from them.

My bonny Kate, she thought, seeing the Murray-Hyslops' carriage arrive, Mr Murray-Hyslop step out, assist his wife, then Kate, carrying the youngest, Ernest, followed by Emily, Victoria and George, now a school-boy. She saw her daughter's bright face, her admonishments to George as she set down little Ernest, the two girls gathering round her, laughing and talking . . . what lovely girls they had become . . . Mrs Murray-Hyslop beckoning her, faint, faded, as if the last thing she wanted to do was to set off for America this morning, or any other morning. The woman had changed from the brisk, practical one who had interviewed them more than six years ago. Perhaps there had been trouble with the last child. Maeve remembered Kate saying there had been visits from the doctor.

'They'll forgive us if we join them,' she said, 'this is our last time with her,' and went towards the little party followed by her own brood. 'Good-day, Mrs Murray-Hyslop, sir,' and then laughingly to Kate, 'Oh, Kate, I thought you were going to miss the boat!'

'No, no! Mr Murray-Hyslop would never let that happen. But there was a lot to do.' She looked up smilingly at the tall man by her side.

'It was the other way round, I assure you, Mrs McGrath,' he said, doffing his hat. 'Kate keeps us all in order.'

'That's true,' his wife smiled tremulously at Maeve, 'and yet she still had time to bring me an early cup of tea and assist me to dress. We'd paid off the maids, you see.'

'It's a great upheaval for you,' Maeve said, 'but so exciting. Imagine, the New World!'

'Yes, I suppose so. But I loved our house in Blythswood Square. The Old World suited me.' She looked around. 'Such a bustle already.' And to Kate, 'Are the children . . . ?'

'They're all here, Madam,' Kate said. 'They've promised me not to stray. And see, I have little Ernest by the hand.'

Mr Murray-Hyslop drew Maeve aside, leaving Kieran speaking to his wife. 'I'm glad to get the chance of having a word with you, Mrs McGrath, and to tell you that we shall take good care of your treasure, our treasure, dear Kate.'

'I'm glad to hear you say so.' She liked the severe features bent upon her, redeemed by the hint of humour

243

in his eyes, and his straight back. Alastair Crawford had had such a one . . .

'I hope you'll forgive us for begging her to accompany us, but for the last few years my wife has developed a delicate constitution, and she has come to rely so much on Kate's good sense and help.'

'I understand, and sympathize. Don't worry. My husband and I have talked it over with her. Besides,' she brightened, 'it's a wonderful opportunity to see the world. I would have done the same in her position.'

He smiled at her. 'Kate has a lot of you in her. Now, why don't you take the opportunity as well once we're settled in Wanapeake? You would always be welcome in our home.'

'Thank you.' She looked at him. He was sincere. She knew that. 'Kieran and I have talked about visiting America. It isn't possible just now, our business demands all our attention, but we've promised ourselves we shall go sometime. I have a brother there, perhaps Kate has mentioned it. He's in a shipping company.'

'Yes, she did, although I didn't realize he was in shipping. We ought to have a lot in common. Does he live in New York?'

'He used to, but now he has moved to a small town on the Hudson River called Wallace Point. I believe he sometimes sails up the river to it.'

'How very strange! Wanapeake is also on the Hudson. But, of course, it's a huge river, like the sea . . .'

'My dear . . .' His wife had placed her hand on his arm. 'The baggage . . .'

'Yes, of course, I'm forgetting my duties. And Mrs McGrath will want to speak to Kate. I've been telling her they would be welcome to visit us.'

'Yes, indeed.' Mrs Murray-Hyslop smiled at Maeve. 'I should think we would have a lot in common.' The woman looked worn. Had she had the same experience with her last child as she had had? My constitution was better than hers, she thought.

The family were crowded around Kate. Isobel was already wiping her eyes, but her young sister was too excited to feel sorrow. She was chattering in her usual style. 'Could we see where you're going to sleep, Kate? Could you ask the Captain?'

'No, Maeve,' Kieran said. They had already decided it would be too heart-rending to walk off the boat and leave Kate. Better the other way round. 'I'm not going to let my daughter remember me with a face ruined with tears,' Maeve had said to him. 'We'll see her off from the dockside, smile and wave, keep on smiling.' She had got her weeping over and done with in Kieran's arms.

'Kate, my love,' she said, 'when you get to your destination you must search your map to see if you can find Wallace Point, your Uncle Terence's address. It's on the Hudson, too.'

'Wouldn't it be lovely if they were near enough to visit!' The girl's fine dark eyes glowed. 'I've always longed to meet my cousin, Maria. We are the same age.'

'I'd like to meet my cousin, Maria,' Isobel said. She had put away her handkerchief on Maeve's instructions.

'Well, so you shall, Isobel. Mr Murray-Hyslop has said that any of you are welcome. Oh, Mother, isn't it exciting? And you and Father will come, too! You are all invited.'

'I don't believe you could keep us away,' Kieran said. He looked as if he was finding it more difficult to keep from weeping than Isobel. 'I can't seem to imagine you not at Blythswood Square any more, not coming to see us.'

'We'll write, though,' Patrick said, 'and tell you when

we buy our carriage, and when Mother gets her first maid.'

'*I* could do with a maid,' Catherine said. 'That house at Crannoch is so awkward and ugly, and my hands are being ruined, Father was saying. I miss my piano.'

'You shall have one, my love, very soon,' Terence muttered, looking abashed.

'Mother says walking is good for the figure,' wee Maeve said, 'and scrubbing.'

'Well, it hasn't done much for *yours*,' Catherine, clinging to Terence's arm, looked down her nose at her sister-in-law. '*Wee* Maeve! It should be big Maeve.'

'She's a fine lass.' Kieran looked miserable. 'Puppy fat . . .'

I won't say anything, Maeve thought. It's trivial compared with Kate going away. She looked at her family glancing in different directions as if a blight had been put on the parting. The moment's come, she thought, quicker than it should have done because of Catherine, when words run out, when I look at Kate and find my eyes filling with tears against all my promises to myself.

'You'll write, Kate,' she said feebly, and looked at Patrick. He was the stalwart one. She knew if she appealed to Kieran he would burst into tears, and Terence was no support nowadays.

Patrick spoke like Mr Liddell, the dominie. 'You must keep your eyes open, Kate. You're our ambassador. McGraths will become known in America some day as well as Scotland, mark my words. You must tell us what it's like at the Battery when you arrive at New York, what kind of carts and horses they use for moving the goods and luggage, what it's like at the Fort.'

'What's the Fort?' Kate's face brightened.

'Castle Garden. Where you'll be cleared for entry into

the New World. Because we'll be coming soon, don't forget, and we'll want to be prepared.'

'There you are, Kate. There are your orders.' Kieran cleared his throat.

'I'll do that, Patrick. I'll keep my eyes and ears open. Have you got any of your business cards in your pocket? I could distribute them on the quayside.' Her eyes danced, teasing him.

He took her seriously, opened his jacket, brought out an envelope. 'I thought of that. Give them to anyone you speak to who might be interested, especially Uncle Terence, if you ever manage to see him.'

'But she will,' Maeve said, the threat of tears making her voice rough. 'Oh, Kate, it brings you nearer in a way, to know that there's a part of our family already in America . . .' Mr Murray-Hyslop's tall figure loomed.

'Kate. It's time to go. My wife will need you.' He shook hands briskly all round, said when he came to Kieran and Maeve, 'Have no fears, I'll take care of her.' He turned away as if afraid to show his feelings.

Maeve put her arms round Kate. It had come. She must not disgrace herself. The tears were streaming down Kate's face. 'Don't cry. You'll only make me start. God go with you, my dearest daughter.' Mr Murdoch would be proud of me, she thought wryly, stepping aside to let Kieran take her place. Then it was Isobel, wee Maeve, Terence, Catherine, Patrick, and lastly the Reverend himself, murmuring some kind of benediction while Kate stood with her head bent.

From then on it was a jumble of blurred figures before Maeve's streaming eyes. . .the tears refused to be held back; Ernest in his white suit in Kate's arms, the girls clinging to her, George clinging to the girls, Mr Murray-Hyslop assisting his wife, all going towards the gangway, the bridge, Maeve thought, between the Old and the New.

The worst time was the waiting until the ship left the quay, all of them silent except Catherine who complained of the cold, Maeve comparing the feeling of desolation in her heart with what she had experienced at the pit disaster. But she chided herself. That had been a tragedy, a matter of life and death. This was life, adventure, living to the full.

Their tears dried as they saw the great ship preparing to leave the dock-side. They smiled and waved as it drew away, looking at each other to make sure everyone was smiling and waving. Besides, some friends of the Murray-Hyslops had joined them and they did not want to disgrace Kate. They were the McGrath Carting Company, weren't they, with cards to prove it. Maeve bit her lip in a smile at the thought of Kate distributing them in far-off New York.

She looked small and far away on the high deck, the children around her smaller still. Little Ernest was a speck of white. Mrs Murray-Hyslop was nowhere to be seen, but the tall figure of her husband stood behind his little group, bare-headed.

2

It was six weeks before Kate's letter arrived, and Maeve invited Terence and Catherine for supper that evening so that they would hear it.

They were all gathered in the parlour, the biggest room in the house, which she had furnished with a judicious mixture of the sticks of furniture Duncan McGrath had left – they turned out to be of sturdy oak when the grime had been washed off and the wood polished with beeswax and turpentine – and some of the contents of a wealthy widow's house outside Sholton. She had called upon Kieran to move her to her daughter's house, and she had been so impressed by his sympathetic help that she had given him a fine desk, some chairs with cushioned bottoms and a set of velvet curtains which her daughter did not want.

'You've got this place looking very nice,' Catherine said. 'I don't know how you find the time.'

'I make it,' Maeve said crisply. 'Besides, I've worked twice as hard these last weeks so that I wouldn't think of Kate too much.'

'I miss her.' Terence smiled at his mother. 'There was something about Kate. She was like a breath of fresh air blowing into the house. And she always had time to listen to you.'

'Well, we're all waiting, Mother.' His wife looked at him disparagingly. 'Oh, thank you, Isobel.' She took the proffered cup of tea. 'And when are *you* coming to visit us at Crannoch? Or are you too busy as well?'

'Soon, Catherine. Maevy and I will take a walk over

one night.' Wee Maeve had become Maevy since Catherine's remark about her size. Maeve did not know who had instigated it amongst her family. She suspected Patrick.

'Let me know first. I like to get the best china out. Only the best is good enough for the McGraths.'

What sours the girl? Maeve wondered, feeling a reluctant pity for her. Was marriage a disappointment? Had Terence in his youthful exuberance, and because of his long frustration, surprised her and even made her feel ashamed? Her mother had died when she was young, and what did that old father of hers know about two people in bed? Though he must have known something . . . Should she have attempted to advise her, or should Kieran have spoken to Terence? Well, it was too late now.

'Are you all ready? This isn't a letter. It's like one of Mr Dickens' novels.' She lifted the bulky wad on her lap. 'Kate is as generous with her writing paper as with everything else.'

'Oh, get started, Ma,' Maevy said. 'You're just tantalizing us. I know you've read wee snippets all day. And don't smile like that!'

'Like what?' she smiled. 'Here goes, then.' She began to read.

'Dear Father, Mother, and all of you . . .' She looked up at Kieran. His eyes were soft with loving pride.

'We've been settled in our home at Wanapeake for almost a month now, and believe me, there hasn't been a minute to write to you before this. Unfortunately Mrs Murray-Hyslop hasn't been well since we arrived – she was in her cabin most of the way to America – and I've had to take on the job of putting the new house in order as far as I can.

'It was bought furnished from the last owners, but they had taken carpets and curtains with them, and pulled out fittings from the wall and removed urns and statues from the garden – but it's a grand place all the same. It's called Wolf House. I'm sure they run wild in the forests here, such forests you would never believe. They put the Sholton Woods to shame with their giant oaks.

'Unlike many of the houses round here it isn't made of wood – clapboard, they call it – but of brick, and the windows are all painted white with white shutters. It has what Mr Murray-Hyslop calls a French style roof, that is, it's built up square like a loaf and there are four rooms set in it, and that's where I am with the children. Emily and Victoria share a room, George being the elder son has a small one of his own, and Ernest sleeps in mine. That leaves a room for the nursery.

'It has a beautiful front door painted white with a round arch and steps with railings on either side, and these railings run round the porch as well. We all sat there one sunny afternoon so that the children could admire the colours of the trees, the Fall, they call it here, but it's too cold most of the time. It's already been snowing and this is just November.

'Do you remember those winter days when we skated on Sholton pond and held hot potatoes in our gloves? It would take a bushelful to warm our hands here, and I've had to go to the town store and buy plenty of warm jerseys and scarves for the children because we hadn't nearly enough. Oh, but it's cold, a piercing, biting kind of coldness!

'There are altogether eight bedrooms in the house and an annexe of two bedrooms and a kitchen for the cook and two housemaids, four public rooms which include a fine study for Mr Murray-Hyslop on the ground floor, and yet he says it is small by Wanapeake standards . . .'

Maeve looked up and met Catherine's envious eyes.

'I could do with one of their bedrooms,' she said, 'there's hardly room to swing a cat at Crannoch. Terence says . . .'

'Do you think their servants will be black?' Maevy interrupted. 'Remember those pictures we used to stick in our books at Sunday School? The people all had black faces.'

'That was the Holy Land, daftie,' Isobel said.

'Where's the Holy Land? Is it near America?'

'Well, it's far across the sea,' Isobel said, judiciously.

'Kate says something about black people.' Maeve looked down at the letter and began to read again.

'It's a great mixture of people here, polyglot, Mr Murray-Hyslop calls it, Irish, Dutch, Italian. The Italians came to work in a quarry nearby, and all our marble fireplaces came from it. But it's very strongly Dutch. When the Dutch settlers in New Amsterdam – that's what New York was called then – made a lot of money, they came to this part of the Hudson because they could sail here easily, and they built beautiful houses on its banks. Mr and Mrs Murray-Hyslop have already had invitations from some of those grand people. If Isobel comes to stay perhaps she'll marry a millionaire. That would suit her, wouldn't it?'

Isobel made a prune mouth.

'Look at her blushing,' Terence said, laughing.

'Well, why shouldn't she set her cap high?' His wife raised her chin at him. 'I would if I had to do it again.' What a tongue, Maeve thought. Poor Terence. He hasn't the right way of her at all.

'There's more than money in the world,' Kieran said, stung. 'There's happiness, and doing your best with what's nearest your hand . . .'

'How about getting on with Kate's letter?' Patrick smiled across at Maeve. Father is the moralist, his smile seemed to be saying. Maeve bent her head.

'One of their friends is a black man, a famous judge, if you please, but Mr Murray-Hyslop says it doesn't matter what colour people's skins are as long as their hearts are in the right place.' (Catherine sniffed.)

'He says if he could have engaged black people to work for us in the house he would have done so, but they don't seem to come here. Our cook is an Italian lady called Mrs Vanaressi, one housemaid is Polish, Irma, and the other is Swedish, called Ingrid. Oh, it's all so different and exciting, and do you know, Mr Murray-Hyslop says the stage coach from New York to Albany used to pass our door!

'He's well-satisfied with life here, he says. There will be great opportunities for George and Ernest when they grow older. The rail roads will be expanding, steam-ships will grow bigger and faster, horses will be done away with, and when I said, "What about our carting?" he said, "A good business always moves with the times."

'And yet he's interested in the past. One day he took us in the carriage to see the Treaty Oak where – now I'm going to copy this out from George's schoolbook – "Aepjen, Chief Sachem of the Mohegans signed a treaty of peace with the Dutch on behalf of the Kitchewanc Indians who had a Fort near here in 1609". Can you imagine it, real live Indians lived here once!

'Do you remember the Wild West Circus when it came to Sholton and the boys riding bareback on the pit ponies? The trees are so tall here, crowding in at the back of the house, that you could imagine Chief Sachem himself creeping through any minute with his bow and arrow and his row of scalps on his belt!'

'Oh, isn't she lucky!' Maevy sighed. 'We've got nothing like that in Sholton Woods. You're lucky if you see a rabbit.'

'If you've eyes to see there's plenty,' Maeve said, thinking of Lady Crawford. But those great dark eyes were closed for ever now. And, smiling at the boys, '*Now* it's coming out about riding bareback on the ponies! You're lucky you're too big for me to take the rope down.' She shook her head at them, her boys. If they were only as carefree now as they had been then . . .

'The children go to a pretty little one-roomed school near here made of clapboard with a porch and a fancy wooden decoration on the roof – it looks like the Sholton Railway Station. But Mr Murray-Hyslop has the intention of sending Emily and Victoria to a girls' Academy which Uncle Terence told him about . . .'

Maeve raised her head to see the surprised faces, lowered it again.

253

'I can hear you all gasp, but you'll never believe it, Wallace Point where Uncle Terence lives is on the other side of the river from us! Mr Murray-Hyslop looked it up on the map and said I must write immediately which I did, and in no time at all there was a kind letter from Aunt Caroline saying what a beautiful surprise mine had been and they could scarcely believe that I was so near and I had to come for tea right away with my employers and get to know them . . .'

Maeve looked up. 'What do you think of that?'

'It must have been meant!' Isobel said.

'There's a daughter, isn't there?' Catherine was aloof.

Patrick was leaning forward. 'Go on, Mother. We're all . . . stunned.'

'So was I.' She looked down at the page.

'Well, Mr Murray-Hyslop said to prevent me rowing across right away, he was teasing since the Hudson is far too wide, he'd take his wife and myself on the ferry the very next day to pay a visit. Well . . .'

Maeve could see Kate in her mind's eye, her glowing face, enjoying the surprise as she wrote . . .

'Well, Uncle Terence has the look of you, Mother, but not nearly so . . .'

'Go on, say it, or I will.' Kieran smiled at her.

'Don't be daft.' She kept her head down.

'"Lovely", Kate says. "Not nearly so lovely".' Kieran looked proudly round the family. 'You can go on now, mavourneen, but don't pretend you're not pleased that I let the cat out of the bag.'

Maeve read, swallowing her smile. Lovely at forty, well, that was saying something . . .

'He has the same red hair and a straight back, you once called it a rider's back. He's got a healthy country face and he's hearty and jolly as if he was acting the part of an Irish gentleman . . .'

She stopped, looked up. 'And he is an Irish gentleman, my brother.'

'So that makes you an Irish lady,' Isobel said.

'Yes, when I get the time. Where was I?'

'. . . and his wife obviously worships him. "Yes, Terence," she says, "You know best, Terence," in her strange American voice.'

'Just like Ma with our father,' Patrick said. He sought his brother's eyes, as if trying to coax a laugh from him. Terence smiled wanly.

'Maria is dark like me, a dashing girl, very fond of riding, she's another one with a back like a ramrod, and she's outspoken in her manner. She rules the roost, I can tell you . . .'

'Just like Ma again,' Patrick said, smiling.

'Will you stop making a fool of your mother?' Kieran smiled, too. 'And where would you be without her, eh? Tell me that?' His glance at Maeve was fond.

'Their house is beautiful, bigger than ours, with what is called a columned portico. There is a central staircase leading from the hall, and it divides at the top. Maria took me up it to her bedroom, and the view from it over the Hudson is beautiful. And can you imagine? She pointed out to me Wolf House standing on its hill amongst the trees on the other side! I shan't feel so lonely now when I look across the river at them. Oh, it's a grand river indeed. I long to sail on it right up to Albany which Mr Murray-Hyslop says is a fine city. Perhaps I shall some day.

'Mrs Murray-Hyslop was very impressed by Uncle Terence's house. "I feel I should be in your place and you in mine, Kate," she said when we were coming home. I told her that was nonsense and there was nothing I liked better than being with her and the children. I've grown very fond of her. Sometimes she has such a sad look on her face, especially after the doctor has called.

'We have a nice jolly one, Dr Rudebaeker – the names here

take a bit of getting used to. He asked the children if they knew the story of Rip Van Winkle, and little Ernest said, "No, only 'Wee Willie Winkie' which Kate has taught us." I remember learning it at your knee, Mother. It makes me sad to think of that and you so far away . . .'

'She's written out the verse,' Maeve said, keeping her head down to hide the quick rush of tears. She recited.

'Wee Willie Winkie runs through the town,
Upstairs and downstairs in his night gown,
Tirlin' at the window, cryin' at the lock,
"Are the weans in their bed, for it's now ten o'clock".'

'I remember that,' Isobel said.

'So do I. At the fireside in the old house.' Maevy looked at her sister, her eyes soft.

'I remember it as well,' Terence said, 'the old days. And the songs you and me used to sing together, Father. Somehow we got out of the habit.'

'Because you were always courting Catherine, most likely.'

Terence blushed. 'Aye, maybe. Do you never sing now?'

'Sometimes your mother and I have a sing-song together now that we have a room to ourselves. But it's the Irish ones we sing, to remind us. When I was trapped down the pit we all had a go to keep our spirits up. When the singing stopped, we knew the singer was . . . past it. That was terrible, sure enough, to hear the voice faltering, and then going . . .' His own voice faltered.

'What was yours?' asked Patrick.

'Oh, I had a repertoire. "Come on, Kieran," they'd say, "Give us one from the owld country." But it was a strange thing, it was the sad songs that came out when I searched my mind, and me wanting to cheer them up.

256

"The Kerry Dancers", for instance. It brought back my home in Boyle to me, the young days, and the village dances where the fiddler always played it when we were having a sit-down and a rest. That song, and the smell of paraffin from the lamps, and the kind of quietness that fell on us . . .'

'We're not going to get sad,' said Maeve. 'This is our home now where our children are, and we've got a new one in America as well. Where Kate and Terence are. We're spreading ourselves, the McGraths. That's how it should be.' She took up the letter again.

'The reason why the doctor was asking about Rip Van Winkle is that the man who wrote it, called Washington Irving, lived near us. Mr Murray-Hyslop told me a lot about him, and that he once visited Sir Walter Scott. You can see how learned I'm becoming under Mr Murray-Hyslop's influence.

'Sometimes at dinner he tells us all kinds of interesting things, about painters in Paris called "Impressionists". He wants Emily and Victoria to go to school there for a year to learn the language. I said they'd have to learn American first and we all had a good laugh.

'I've written this letter backside foremost which used to be one of Terence's expressions. I trust Catherine has made a gentleman of him by this time, but I've not forgotten that Patrick wanted to know about the voyage and what it was like when we got to New York.

'Well, our ship, *The Scotia*, put both Wolf House and Springhill, which is the name of Uncle Terence's house, completely in the shade. It was like a palace. Great staterooms, staircases, boudoirs for the ladies and a smoking room like a house on the deck for the gentlemen.

'The food was almost too rich and plentiful. You should have seen the great platters of ham the stewards brought in, and once a sucking pig with an orange in its mouth which quite turned my stomach because it made me think of Old Roly Poly which the butcher took away every Christmas and how I covered my face with the sheets and wept for it. (When I was very small I thought it was the same Roly Poly every year!)'

'So did I,' Maevy said.

Maeve looked at Terence. The sadness in his face was not just for Old Roly Poly. She bent her head.

'But I'm afraid many of the passengers didn't sample the dishes very often because a lot of them got seasick. I was attending to Mrs Murray-Hyslop a good part of the time and to little Ernest who was poorly, but in the evenings everyone seemed to rally, and we had some fine times. A gentleman played a grand piano in the lounge, and Emily, Victoria and I took part in the Lancers. The young officers squired us. On the last night before arriving in New York we had a concert. The girls sang a duet, Mr Murray-Hyslop a boating song, and even I was persuaded to get up. And do you know the only song that came to mind? "The Kerry Dancers", the song Father and Terence used to sing . . .'

Maeve heard the rustling amongst the listeners. She kept her head down, her heart full.

'I would rather have sung something jolly but out it came and, funnily enough, when I was singing it I forget where I was and instead thought of far-away Ireland which I'd never seen but where my roots are – you've said that often, Mother – a green misty impression I have of it, like a magic land somehow. And I thought, here am I being transported to a different part of the world entirely and yet I've never seen where you and Father came from. Mr Murray-Hyslop said I'd brought tears to many people's eyes because I'd sung it with love. Maybe so.

'Well, Patrick, you wanted to hear all about New York and not of your sister having the cheek to stand up in an ocean greyhound and sing an Irish song, so here it is as far as I can remember.

'You may be sure when the great day arrived we were all up fine and early. I had the younger children dressed and ready and then went to help Mrs Murray-Hyslop who looked a good deal better. "It's because the die's cast, Kate," she said, "and oh, it'll be good to get my feet on dry land again." She never complains, but you can see she is far from well. Maybe America will make a new woman of her.

'We dropped anchor and waited a long time while the immigration inspectors came on board from a cutter and examined all the people who'd been taken ill on the voyage. Some might be carrying contagious diseases, and these had to be taken off and if they were serious the poor souls were sent back to where they came from. I think they were mostly steerage passengers. Mr Murray-Hyslop took the girls and myself down below so that we could see how they had to live in comparison with us. They had a great room which served for everything. The sleeping berths were made of canvas and could be folded away, and even the table could be lowered from the ceiling and stowed away after meals. But the night we went down they were dancing and singing and having as good a time as they had above, so maybe it wasn't so bad. Anyhow his pity for them didn't go to the extent of having us travel steerage!'

'That's our practical Kate,' Maeve said, looking up and smiling.

'However, we were all discovered to be free of anything infectious, thank goodness – I'd been beginning to wonder if Ernest had picked up something – and then the captain steered us into New York Harbour.

'How can I describe the wonderful place it is with its tall narrow towers rising out from the island of Manhattan, as it's called – the strangest thing I've ever seen and as far removed from Glasgow with its solid sonsy buildings as you are ever likely to see in a month of Sundays.

'And then it was as you said, Patrick, being examined by doctors and cleared at Castle Garden, which was a lengthy business. But fortunately when it was over, Mr Murray-Hyslop's American friend who has invited him to become a partner in their firm, was waiting with his carriage, and he whisked us through the New York streets to a hotel near the Battery where we were to rest until we caught the train next morning from Grand Central Station. This was built by a famous man called Cornelius Vanderbilt who helped to build the railroad also. "A go-getter", Mr Murray-Hyslop calls him. I believe our laird, even, would be pretty small fry beside him.

'Even in the short ride in the carriage, the part of New York we drove through seemed to be teeming with people all sitting out on the steps of their houses, the children dodging in and out amongst the carts and carriages, everyone jostling everyone else. I've never seen such crowds in my life. I imagine the Gorbals on a Saturday night would be like a Sunday-school picnic compared to those crowds of people, all half-dressed and poor-looking in spite of the cold. Mr Murray-Hyslop says that on the lower East Side, as it's called, the housing conditions are so dreadful that they prefer the streets to their miserable homes. They're mostly immigrants who were led to believe that the streets of New York were paved with gold.

'I said it was terrible to think of the difference between the rich and the poor, the luxury on that big ship and then this, but he said at least in America people had a chance to get on by their own efforts, whereas in Britain they were divided by the class system. When I said it was high time we got rid of that he said he'd make a good socialist of me yet!

'Oh, and the horses, Patrick and Terence and Father, big ones, little ones, fat ones, thin ones, donkeys, mules, anything that can pull a cart, and even people. Everything's moving in New York, that's for sure.

'I've filled pages and pages between-times, and now I hear little Ernest being a nuisance with George who is a serious boy and likes to read, so I'd better stop. Today I've been given an assistant, if you please, a young American girl with hair the colour of wee Maeve's, but I don't know if it's curly or not for she does it in tight plaits wrapped round and round her head. Mr Murray-Hyslop would like me to become a kind of companion to his wife, I think, or at least divide my time between her and the children, because he is obliged to be away a lot on business, and he fears for her being lonely in this new land.

'And I am, too, at times, although I don't say so to anybody because I feel I have to keep a cheerful face. But often at nights when I'm in bed I think of you all together in Sholton. I dwell on each one of you, Isobel, wee Maeve, Patrick, Terence, Catherine now, and especially you, my dear father and mother. I think of you all busy working away in the McGrath Carting Company – the streets of New York are littered with the cards you gave me, Patrick – and I long to be arriving with the children from Blythswood Square and to see Mother's bright face and Father's sweet smile and hear the welcome I always got. "Oh, here's Kate! Come away in." And that is what sustains me, that back home in Scotland I have a loving family whom I love so deeply. Please write all of you, and I'll keep writing so that we have a life-line between us. Your loving daughter, Kate.'

3

'What's up with you?' Catherine said. 'You know Father will think it's queer if you don't go to the manse for dinner. We always go.' She was preparing herself for church in their small bedroom at Crannoch, pinning her mother's cameo brooch on the white collar of her severe navy-blue brocade. She never seemed to wear what Terence called in his mind 'floating dresses', always stiff materials which seemed too old for her. Once, when he had tried to convey this to her, she had said, 'Where would I get the money for them, pray? My dresses have to last. It's all right for your mother. She sees that they get the lion's share of the profits. French silk for her!'

'That's not true,' he had said. She was constantly making comparisons. 'It's fair shares for all. Besides, I've told you and *told* you, we're doing well. You can have the money for any kind of gown you like.'

'And I've told you and *told* you I'm not spending money on fine clothes like her. When she goes to the kirk with Maevy and Isobel it's like a fashion show. What I want is somewhere decent to live. I can't abide this hole.'

He looked at her now as she prinked. Everything had to be just so with Catherine, never anything out of place. Even her husband. 'God Almighty,' he had said last night, throwing himself away from her. The cold air on his thighs told him she had got out of bed. He had found her wrapped up in a plaid in a chair in the kitchen, weeping.

'I'm not sharing a bed with blasphemers! Go away. Leave me . . .'

'Catherine.' He'd knelt at her feet, abashed himself. 'I'm a man, with a man's passions. You're my wife. You've to show your love to me. There's nothing wrong in it.'

'You're a beast, Terence McGrath.' She had looked up at him with streaming eyes. 'I always knew it. It's the Irish in you in spite of the airs and graces that precious mother of yours puts on. If you ask me, I think it's all Irish blarney about her having lived in style over there.'

'Leave my mother out of it.'

'You never could see anything wrong with her, could you? Even when the whole village was talking about her and her goings-on with the Honourable Alastair. She was the laughing stock . . .' She was mad as well as spiteful. He had not heard any talk.

'I told you, shut your mouth about my mother.' He felt hate for the first time in his life. 'Don't ever talk about my mother like that again or I'll kill you!'

Now she turned from the mirror to face him, trim, neat. She had a fine, slim figure. If only she did not draw her hair so tightly away from her face it could look lovely. It had a rich dark colour, he had often thought when he had seen it loose at night.

'Come on, Terry.' She was the only one who ever called him that. He felt like a stranger to himself. 'We always go to Father's on Sunday. It looks right, us walking back with him.' She came to him and put her arms round his neck.

He looked down at her, sick at heart. 'Have you forgotten last night? You're trying to make me think it didn't happen, that's what you always do, mixing me up . . .'

'Cathy was cross.' She pouted. 'It's when you get big and rough and demanding that Cathy gets cross. Why aren't you gentle and say nice things to me, things I can

262

write down?' She had a leatherbound diary which she kept assiduously.

'You drove me mad,' he said. 'When I married you I'd waited six years. I could never see past you. I thought of you day and night. I thought when we got married it would be like heaven on earth.'

She threw back her head and laughed. 'Heaven on earth! It's more like Sodom and Gomorrah!' He saw her small white teeth, the pink gums, the dart of the pink tongue. He hit her across the face with the back of his hand. Her mouth seemed to collapse. He saw her eyes widen, watched the red weals of his fingers come up on her white skin. He tried to take her in his arms but she struggled against him. Her eyes were wild.

'Don't touch me, you Irish . . . filth!' One hand went to her cheek to cover the mark. 'Now we know where we stand! Because I won't wallow in bed with you like a couple of pigs you're going to lift your hand to me, is that it, beat me into submission?'

'Cathy!' He was appalled at himself. 'I didn't know what I was doing. You try me too far.'

'I try *you*!' She turned to the table where her white gloves lay, lifted them, began to smooth them on. He noticed, thankfully, that her hands were steady. It had only been a slap, for God's sake. 'And what do you think it's been like for me living in this . . . *hovel* since I married you?'

He laughed, and that was a mistake. 'You keep saying that. It's a fine wee house, a palace compared with what I was brought up in, maybe not you at the manse. But I was going to tell you last night. The profits are the best they've ever been. We're getting work all over the place, from Glasgow, from the other side of it out by Paisley, the Clydeside. We've had to build new stables. Mother and Father have decided to move. They've bought the old Naismith house.'

She looked at him. One hand stayed curved round the other. 'They're going to live in Braidholme! Colonel Naismith's place!'

'Yes, they've always had an eye on it. It's got a lot of land. They'll keep a horse or two . . .'

'A horse or two . . .' She sounded dazed. 'And what are they going to do with the one they're in? Give it to Patrick? Or one of the carters from the bothies?'

'They're giving it to us. That's what I was going to tell you. You're always saying you haven't any room here, though there's plenty for the two of us. You'd be back in Sholton, near the Reverend.' He'd never been able to call him 'Father'. 'And there's a fine garden mother's made. We'll put one of the carters, Tam Simpson, in here to manage this end. He's a sensible chap.'

'Am I hearing properly?' She lifted her Bible and held it between her gloved hands. 'Do you mean to say I'm being offered their left-overs?'

'It isn't exactly left-overs. It's a grand roomy house and it's been greatly improved. It would be ours. We've paid my cousin Duncan long ago and the deeds would be in our name.'

She put up her hand to her reddened cheek and he went to her. 'Cathy, I shouldn't have struck you. I'm ashamed. But it isn't so bad, is it, just a wee slap? Put some of your rice powder on it. Don't go this morning. Stay and talk it out with me. We could plan about the house, when we could move in, and that. Mother says we can have a lump sum to get the kind of furniture we'd like. It's her idea. She knew you weren't happy.'

Her voice was flat, as if she was considering what he had said. 'Your mother's idea, you say. And isn't everything your mother's idea from start to finish? Now she's decided to throw that old place of hers to me like a bone to a dog. Her left-overs! *They* should have stayed there. They're getting old. *We* should have moved into Braidholme. You're the eldest son!'

He stared at her. 'There's no pleasing you, is there?'

'You've never had the least idea what would please me.' She shook her head. 'The whole thing's a terrible mistake.' She turned to the mirror, lifted her little hat and pinned it carefully with a long pin, funereal-looking black jet with a round top, one of her mother's. She turned back again. 'I'm going to church. People can think what they like about my face. Your Irish temper is well-known down in that terrible place where you go drinking with the carters. They'll pity me, the minister's daughter, knocked about by her husband. Well, I can do with pity. I'm not coming back here till you go down on your bended knees and beg me, till you tell that mother of yours that she can give her house to Patrick or whoever else she likes but not to us!'

'It's not for ever, Cathy. We can look around from there, get the kind of house you'd like. We could buy a carriage so that we could view properties . . .'

'I'm not going to that house. When you see eye to eye with me, come and tell me.' She walked past him. He heard the door shut. Not slam. It would have been better if she had slammed it.

The day had become like a millstone round his neck. At Sholton he could have dug in the garden, looked after the horses, but here there was nothing to do. Catherine had never made it a home. The Sunday quietness seemed to suffocate him. He thought of going out for a walk but the Crannoch people would stare and wonder why he was not at the kirk with his wife, the minister's daughter.

He thought of going to the Cranstons, but the idea of

breaking into that family gathering at their dinner table could not be borne. Generally he enjoyed talking to the sons, especially Arthur, but he might not be there. He had become so involved with the Commission of Inquiry into truck that he had taken a house in Glasgow. He even wrote articles for the *North British Daily Mail*.

You can only become involved in things like that if you're happily married, he thought. If I had a quiet mind I could enjoy those wordy tussles the Cranston lads have with the Chief Inspector of Factories and the like. Father did once and Mother helped him when he was ill, because they were at peace with one another. He knew she still visited Davy Cox's widow and was for ever giving to the children. He had died in the cholera epidemic of 1872 at Sholton. You had to be supported by your wife to be at peace with yourself. And by your children, if you had any.

He, unlike Catherine, longed for a child, for children. He wanted them climbing on his knee, taking his hand, looking up to him. He knew he had a feeling for children and animals, like his father, he thought now. By God, *he* was lucky with a wife like Mother. And she would be good in bed. A blush came to his cheeks at the sacrilege.

What would she think of him striking Catherine? He had an overwhelming desire to go to Sholton, to put his head on her lap. He had never done that in his life, but the thought was there. She gave the same comfort as if he had, but in a feminine rather than a motherly fashion. A bobby-dazzler, she was.

He went to the cupboard in the kitchen, took out the whisky bottle, poured himself a stiff drink and swallowed it in a gulp. Then another. That would do instead of dinner. He had never been any good at cooking, like Patrick. He was a queer one, Patrick, not married yet. At one time he thought he had fallen for Bessie Haddow, but she had been in Glasgow for a long time now, working in a shop or some kind of thing.

The afternoon ticked slowly past. He sat at the window staring out at the sun on the fields, and thought of Catherine. The first time he had kissed her had been when the bluebells were out in Sholton Wood, nearly ten years ago. He remembered their sweetness in his senses, and the effort he had made not to frighten her, so sweet herself, so unattainable. She was still that.

Should he walk to the manse now? The Reverend would be resting bloated after his dinner of roast beef, preparatory to setting forth again for the evening service. Catherine would be going through the drawers and cupboards as she generally did. She liked to check up on Grace, the housekeeper, a thrawn body, who could not be coaxed into a smile at all.

If you're going, he told himself, you'll have to go now. She'll soon be going into the kitchen to tell Grace to make a cup of tea to waken her father, then she'll be tidying herself, making everyone else tidy themselves, so that they can go forth to the Lord . . . He found himself tittering. Too much whisky on an empty stomach.

What was it she had said? 'I'm not going to that house. When you see eye to eye with me, come and tell me. On your bended knees . . .' He tittered again. It was a long way to Sholton on his bended knees. He chided himself. It was nothing to laugh about. If he went, if he said, 'I agree with you, we'll tell my mother to stuff her house up her . . .' 'None of that talk, Terence.' He spoke aloud. If he did all that, what would it mean?

He shut his eyes, saw himself in ten years going through the same rigmarole every Sunday wherever they lived (last night and this morning had just been worse than usual), driving to the kirk in their carriage, stuffing himself afterwards with Grace's lumpy cooking, sitting in that cold parlour and listening to the Reverend snoring with the occasional fart, listening to Catherine rummaging through Grace's drawers – 'No, don't laugh, this is serious . . .' Was that his own voice in his ears? Drinking a cup of tea, walking to the kirk again, not listening to the usual dreary drone, driving home to a loveless bed.

The only difference would be that they would be driving, not walking. There would be no children. That was another thing he had liked to imagine, them spilling out of the carriage. He remembered the first time Kate had been driven from Blythswood Square, and how her three charges had tumbled out, laughing, in their white clothes. The Murray-Hyslops would be another happy marriage.

He thought he slept at the window. When he opened his eyes the sun was still on the fields but the trees on the horizon had gone dark against a pinkness. He glanced at the clock on the wall. Half-past five. It was too late to stop Catherine going to the evening service now. Besides, he had not made up his mind. 'When you see eye to eye with me, come and tell me.'

He got up and poured water into the basin in the scullery – it had been made nice for her with water piped in and fine cupboards – dipped his face and head in it then went to the mirror and combed his springing wet curls.

He would go and have tea at Sholton – they never went to the kirk in the evening, saying that once was enough of Terence's father-in-law. He imagined the twinkle in their eyes raised to him, his whole loving family. They would be sitting down soon to that great spread Mother always put on for Sundays with samples of Isobel's and Maevy's baking. They had given up asking him to bring Catherine. She had refused too often.

He dressed himself carefully in his Sunday suit, took his walking stick with the silver knob, and set off. He would not tell them anything to begin with, but later, perhaps, he would see . . . He looked down at his flowered waistcoat as he strode along. He had always liked walking, and perhaps because he had had so much to do with horses he did not long for a carriage the way Catherine did. Maybe he should have thought of that. He caught a whiff of his own breath. And maybe he should have chewed a peppermint or two to get rid of the smell of whisky. His mother would be sure to spot it.

Bessie Haddow was there when he went into the kitchen at Sholton, or as his mother liked it to be called now, the dining-room. The scullery had been transformed with a fine new Carron range. They were all sitting round the table and there was a scraping of chairs as his father and mother got up, smiling. They always welcomed you – he remembered Kate commenting on it in her first letter – with a kind of old-fashioned formality which he supposed was more Irish than Scottish where a good-natured grunt was as much as you could expect.

'Well, Terence, what a surprise! But all the better for that.'

'Hello, Father, hello, Mother. I thought I'd walk over. It was a fine evening.'

'We're pleased to see you, son, very pleased.' Maeve put an arm round him. 'Patrick, bring another chair for Terence. Where's Catherine?'

'She's at the manse.' It was too soon for explanations. He sat down beside Bessie. 'You're a stranger to these parts. I thought you'd forgotten us.' She looked thinner, and her hair was done differently, in a low chignon. There were wisps on her forehead, yellow against the dark of her brows. He had never noticed before how dark they were, nor the fine set of her eyes, a rich nut-brown like

269

the hazels you found in the woods. She looked smart, a city smartness.

'Could I ever forget a boyo like you?' She smiled at him. The old smile was the same. 'I wouldn't be coming back to Sholton at all if it wasn't for the hope of seeing you. And how's married life agreeing with you?'

'Fine. Are you married yourself?'

'Me! No, I'm not *that* daft. I've a fine job in a hardware's shop in Bridgeton, Grieve's. If you're ever passing come in and see me and I'll sell you nails and a hammer at cost price.'

'Oh, those days are past.' He stuck out his chest. 'We're going to be gentry soon. Haven't you heard of the new family home?'

'No.' She looked at Maeve. 'Are you moving then, Mrs McGrath?'

'Yes.' He admired his mother because she did not look apologetic. She *was* a lady. She would grace Braidholme. 'To the Naismith's old place. It's been too big for the Colonel for a long time. Kieran has been helping him with the horses. He'll move into the cottage at the gates where we can keep an eye on him.' Keep an eye on Colonel Naismith, Terence thought delightedly. Not so long ago one bark from the old gentleman would have made *him* stand to attention. 'It suits Kieran and me, and the girls, and Patrick.' She smiled at her younger son. 'Till he goes off and gets married.'

'Are you likely to do that, Patrick?' Bessie looked at him.

'There's only one girl I ever fancied and she wouldn't look at me.'

'Well, he's kept it bloody quiet till now, that's all I can say.' Terence winked at Maeve. 'Sorry, Mother. I know it's Sunday.'

'Well, just remember it, and help yourself to some

270

ham.' Her eyes were on him. She had always been too quick, the brains behind them all, well, maybe her and Patrick. He and Father were the cart-horses.

'What news is there of Kate?' Bessie asked. 'I don't hear much now that my mother's . . . moved away.'

'No, you won't. How is she?'

'The same.' Her face was set, the smile gone.

'Mrs Murray-Hyslop died two years ago. She had cancer, poor soul. Kate nursed her till the end.'

'Kate would. Is she staying on?'

'Yes, there are still the two younger boys to take care of, though I think George is going off to a boarding school this year, and the two girls are to spend a year in Paris. I don't think Mr Murray-Hyslop could do without Kate.' Terence saw the look that passed between the two women. How alike they were in many ways. 'But Kate's got the run of my brother's house. They live across the Hudson River from them. She and Maria, my niece, are great friends.'

'Well, I never! You should be out visiting them, you and Mr McGrath.'

'Well, it's not for want of being invited. Kate was home last year, you know. It was during your . . . trouble with your mother. Mr Murray-Hyslop gave her a present of the fare. We tried to get in touch with you. I wish you'd seen her.'

'What is she like?'

'Well . . .' she looked round the table, caught Kieran's eye. 'I don't want to boast . . .'

'She's dying to,' Kieran said, 'but I'll do it for her. She's a beautiful young woman, beautifully dressed, with a hint of America in her voice, and she has an American beau, a friend of Maria's. But she's still the same Kate. By God, she's blossomed out there. She said she felt she

271

couldn't settle here, although Mr Murray-Hyslop had said she was free to do that, if she wished.'

'I'm going next year,' Isobel said. 'Mother and Father are giving me a present of the fare for my twenty-first birthday. And Maevy's going to try and keep the books while I'm away.'

'I've been doing it for the past two years! I'm quite capable. Don't listen to her, Bessie. And I can use the new typing machine for the accounts. I've been practising. We've got an office in Sholton now. There are four in it, a clerk, a salesman . . .'

Terence sat watching his two sisters as they talked.

Isobel had their mother's elegance but not her fine figure. She was too thin. Maeve was more rounded. The golden curls were now tied back by a sedate bow. Yet it would be Isobel who would drive the men mad when she got out there. She had something . . . she was damned choosy in Sholton. He had heard talk. By God, he thought, I wish I could go, too, clear out, away from Catherine, spread my wings. I should have been sensible like Patrick, not tied myself down too quickly. 'We'll have to build a boat of our own,' he said, 'for all the McGraths who want to go to America, like that Cunard liner, the *City of Berlin*. It seems a hell of a place, and yes, Mother, I know it's Sunday.' He grinned at her.

'You see what I have to put up with, Bessie,' Maeve said.

His mother took him aside in the scullery when he was carrying in some plates. 'What's wrong with Catherine? Why isn't she with you?'

'I told you.' He was sullen. 'She's at the manse.'

'Are you calling for her there?'

'I don't think I'd be very welcome. I told her about coming to live here and she scorned the idea. So I hit

272

her.' He felt the same guilty defiance as the small boy who had confessed to misdemeanours in the past.

'You enjoyed saying that, didn't you?' Her glance was cool. 'Did you hurt her?'

'No, it was just a slap, but I know I shouldn't have done it. And I shouldn't have told you. But it's been a terrible day. I sat thinking about it all afternoon. She gave me an ultimatum. I can't take any more. I need to think.'

'You've been drinking, Terence. I warned you about that.'

'Just one dram.'

'It must have been a big one. I know you have problems. I wish I could help you with them. But don't solve them by going to the bottle. It never was the right way.'

'Don't lecture me.'

'All right. I've said my say.' She turned to the sink, ran the tap.

'Where's Susan?'

'I always give her Sunday off as you well know. Take this towel. Terence, Catherine's your wife. You'll have to sit down and talk to her. She's had a bad time.'

'*Her* a bad time! She's been brought up in the lap of luxury compared with me.'

'Don't make the mistake of confusing money with happiness. Can you imagine anything worse than a young girl being brought up by old Murdoch?'

'Maybe not, but don't preach at me, Mother. I told you.' Her words did not touch him. She should try living with someone who spurned you, looked down on you, treated you like dirt. She had never known unhappiness with Father. They had been faithful and loving to each other . . . or had they? He remembered Catherine's words. Had he the courage to ask her . . . now?

'All right. You go into the parlour and have a chat with everybody. The girls love to get you on your own. You're their favourite.' She touched his cheek with a soapy finger. 'Maybe you're mine, too.'

'Away with you,' he said. blushing. He went back into the parlour.

4

He and Bessie were walking along the tow path towards Crannoch. He had left with her, saying that he would probably call at the manse for Catherine, but when they got near the gates he said, 'I'm not going in for her.'

'Catherine?' She looked at him.

'She might be back home. She wouldn't wait as long as this.'

'Suit yourself.' Her glance was mocking. 'Did you have a bit of a tiff with her?'

'How did you know that?' They were past the gates now. The die was cast.

'You're not like Patrick, Terence. Everything is written on your face. Well, you can see me home to the Cranstons' instead. It will be your good deed for the day.'

'Are you staying with them?'

'Yes, it's handy for the Asylum. You knew my mother was there?' He nodded. 'I'll go up to Glasgow with Arthur and his wife tomorrow morning. He's staying for the weekend to tell them about the latest developments on truck. That's the way to put your worries on one side. Work for the good of the community.'

'I know that. Some day . . . when I'm landed gentry.' He laughed, sobered. 'How is your mother getting on at the . . . place?'

'Fine, I think, from her point of view. She's violent, so violent sometimes that when I go to see her I'm not allowed in. And, believe it or not, I walk up that long drive hoping they'll say, "The doctor thinks the patient shouldn't be disturbed." It's the terrible feeling I get of despair and guilt because I didn't *like* her – fancy saying that about your own mother.' She said brightly as a couple passed them, 'Good evening, Lizzie, John . . .' And then to Terence, 'It'll be all round the village now that we've been seen on the towpath.'

'*Her* tongue's always wagging about something or other. Go on about your mother, Bessie.' It stopped him thinking about Catherine, about her anger when he failed to turn up.

'You see, I knew all the time before she went to Crannoch Asylum that she wasn't the nice, quiet body everybody thought her to be. The violence is the real Ailie Haddow. When she attacked your mother in the Row that time that was the real person . . .'

'Here, Bessie!' He was suddenly listening intently. 'I'm learning a bit too much today; Catherine this morning, and now you. Did your mother actually attack *my* mother?' He felt as if he was taking leave of his senses.

'Yes, she and the Brodie woman and that daft Beenie Drummond.'

'What in God's name for?'

'You're an innocent, Terence McGrath. For going to the Hall and riding with the laird's son, for "carrying-on", as they called it.'

'My God! The old bitches! Do you believe that rubbish?'

'If you want me to pretend your mother's the Virgin Mary herself I can't. She's a beautiful woman, different from the rest of them, including my mother. She's got spirit and fire. I wouldn't say she wouldn't be tempted. The pit explosion came after they battered her. Maybe that put a stop to the "carrying-on" with your father so ill.'

'My God! My own mother!' He clutched his head and he felt her glance.

'Don't strike poses with me, Terence McGrath. You of all people should understand. You've got a good bit of your mother in you. Anyone can see that.'

'Well, if I have it's faint for want of exercise.' He looked at her and suddenly they were laughing. He saw her open mouth, the white teeth, and felt a sudden lust for her, walking along the towpath on a Sunday afternoon with the quiet Sholtie on one side and the fields and woods on the other. He took a deep breath, blew it out, felt his body quieten again. 'You haven't your sorrows to seek with your mother either, Bessie.'

She shrugged. 'It's mostly self-pity. That's why I visited your mother and father today. They're so wholesome, so normal. They just ask after her and leave it at that. But I have the feeling that they understand, know how it feels, all that locking of doors, and then that long corridor they call the day-room. It's the terrible self-centredness of them, the feeling that there's glass between them and me, each in their own little world of misery, and suspicion. No love, and precious little love amongst the attendants. They're more like jailers than nurses. Sometimes she doesn't recognize me, and worse, I don't recognize her. Remember those farm cats we used to see at Tweedie's barn, half-wild? You didn't know which way they were going to jump? She's jumped at me a few times. That's why my brothers cleared off to Canada. They couldn't stand it. My God, I'm letting my hair down with you. It's the fatal McGrath charm.' She laughed shortly.

'I hope you've got a man back in Glasgow to cheer you up.'

She shook her head. 'No, there's only one man I was ever interested in and he was never interested in me.'

He frowned. 'He must have been blind.' She couldn't mean him, could she? 'You could do with someone.

Whatever my worries are, I've always got a good family to fall back on.'

'You're lucky. Your father's the salt of the earth, and your mother, well, she's so full of life, and love. It wraps round you like a plaid. Maybe some of it spilled over in the direction of the laird's son for a time, so what? Don't grieve about that. I know how much you admire her. She'd be . . . curious, love the excitement of it, and I've never believed that if you're married to a good man you should be blind to all the rest, like a horse with blinkers. It keeps you on your toes, gives you new eyes, like seeing freshly all this . . .' she swept her arm around her – 'that burn, douce and silky like my best moiré gown, and those long shadows of the trees across it, like the black braid trimming.' She laughed. 'Hark at me! If you love, you love life. You aren't defeated by it. You have . . . courage to live it to the full.'

'You sound like Rabbie Burns himself. You're like her in many ways, full of surprises. Do you smell that smell?' He stopped, put a hand on her arm.

'Yes, it's from the Bluebell Wood. It's just behind the trees there. Dark, secret . . .' She had changed. She was not the same Bessie.

'Could we go and have a look at it? Have you the time?'

Her glance was cool. Her eyes seemed to slide under the lids. 'Bob Cranston isn't my keeper. I'm twenty-three and master of my fate. Come on.' She laughed as she climbed the stile. 'And no keekin' up my skirts, Terence McGrath!'

'Away with you. It's the bluebells I'm after.' He felt light-hearted for the first time that day. This was what life should be like with Catherine. 'Courage', Bessie had said, 'to live life to the full . . .'

'I think all that courage and love you were talking about

278

is flowing into the business. Seven years since we started and we've got more work than we can handle, livery stables that are the envy of all the other carters . . .'

'That's thanks to your father.'

'Yes, you're right there, but she's behind it all. She takes a back seat because women aren't supposed to have brains. Father and I are the team, yoked together, steady plodders, she's the one with the ideas. And Patrick. Aye, Patrick's different.'

'Deep. And yet I feel at ease with Patrick, always have. There's strength there.' The path narrowed. She had to walk in front, turn her head to speak to him. 'You've done well, I'll hand you that. The McGrath Carting Company. A household name in Glasgow, not to mention in England, America and the world.'

'You're pulling my leg.'

'As sure as God made me I'm not.'

'Do you know what I think?' It felt like a momentous thought. He wanted to share it with her.

'How do I know what you think when I can't see your bonny face?'

'We're at the Wood now. The path's widening.'

'So it is.' She came beside him and linked her arm through his in a friendly gesture that touched him. 'What do you think, Terence McGrath, senior partner of the McGrath Carting Company with branches throughout the world?'

'So there will be.' He thought of America, of Kate, of his Uncle Terence. 'I think the really clever thing about women is that they hide that they're clever.'

She squeezed his arm, laughing. 'It's taken you a long time to learn that.'

'I'm a slow learner.' He breathed in deeply. 'Do you *smell* those bluebells?' Long ago he had kissed Catherine there and had floated on air, full of young-lad romantic notions, believed that young, sweet, pure feeling was love. Bessie's arm through his was suddenly different, as intimate in the quiet gloom as bodies being pressed together, not side by side as they were now. And with the image he felt a dark surging turbulence in him which made that pure feeling he had had for Catherine seem puny, bloodless, like the married life they had been living, like . . . skimmed milk. He laughed.

'What's tickling you?' She turned to face him, released his arm. He thought her face was white in the dusk of the wood, and yet there was a pearly gleam on the cheeks that entranced him. Her lips were parted, her teeth gleamed like her cheeks.

'I've not been . . . living, Bessie. It's come to me. I've made a bloody hash of things. I've been barking up the wrong tree for years. I thought Catherine held the answer, that she could give me love, happiness . . .' Her eyes were dark. He could not see their expression.

'More people than you have to live with their mistakes.'

'Oh, I'll thole it all right, I'm tied to the manse, to all that false stuff that trips from the old man's lips every Sunday. But just once if I could . . .'

'It's too late.'

'Sit down.' He put his hand on her arm. 'There's no hurry. We're old friends.'

She looked at him steadily. How dark her eyes were, he thought. 'Well, for a wee while.' She spread a light shawl she was carrying on the grass. When she sat down her skirts ballooned and seemed to release a waft of sweetness, or perhaps it was the bluebells.

'You said . . .' he chewed at a blade of grass, '. . . that there was only one man you'd ever been interested in. I wondered . . .'

'What I said has nothing to do with how I behave. You're a married man.'

Now he became cunning because of the flame in him. 'The handsomest lad in the district . . .' 'Could get any lass he wanted . . .' 'Terence's pout, his mother used to say . . .' He felt his lips take the shape. *She* had had her fling, followed her instincts . . . 'Bessie . . .' he stroked her hair, felt its yellowness, its vitality, 'be kind to me.'

'Don't,' she said, shrugging away from him.

'She's never let me . . .'

'Don't come whining to me about your wife. You made your bed so you can lie on it.'

He took his hand from her hair, and with the action seemed to put away childish things, tricks. The flame was steady, burning brightly, but no longer consuming him. Now there was certainty. This woman beside him should have been his partner. They would have had a marriage worth something, she had all the generosity of his mother. He felt himself grow up, become the Terence McGrath he was meant to be. How long had it taken him, for God's sake? Some people were born mature, like Patrick, other people like himself never really learned except by trial and error. Surely a feeling such as this should transcend marriage, should be welcomed because it was fulfilling, made you into a better man. He felt sorrow for Catherine, not hate. It was because she had never known any true feelings with her father that she had turned out the way she had. It was too late for her. But not too late for him . . . Bessie had turned to him. He had been aware of small movements, a rustle. His hand strayed, a life of its own, and touched flesh, strayed again . . . 'You've got your blouse off,' he said.

'Aye,' there was a smile in her voice. 'It's a warm day. I felt like it.' They laughed together as he took her strongly in his arms. Just once, to see what it could be, to see what he could have been.

He found out there was more growing up to be done.

Because it was not a question of what *he* wanted, but what *they* wanted. Sometimes she wanted more, sometimes less. When it was more, she was possessive, fierce, demanding, when it was less she was tender and supplicating, asking for a respite. But at the final coming together they were evenly matched, and the flame burned strongly and truthfully for them for a long time before it died.

He left her at the Cranstons' house. 'Will you regret it, Bessie?' he said.

'No.' She shook her head. She was very white. 'I always wanted it.'

'Will I see you again?'

'What's the use? You're married.'

'I love you. Oh, God, Bessie, I love you. If only I'd known sooner.'

'I tried to tell you often, but you wouldn't listen.'

'I didn't know.'

'You didn't see.'

'I could meet you in Glasgow.'

'No, don't start that kind of thing, for God's sake. I'll maybe let you know when I'm coming to visit my mother. Maybe . . .'

She went into the lit house. He could hear the voices. The laughter. They would all be round the lamp on the table going at it hammer and tongs; the wives would be sitting quietly knitting, proud of their husbands but not understanding this fire in their bellies which made them work for what they thought was right.

When he reached his own house it was empty and dark.

5

Kate, Emily and Victoria and their father were rolling along in their carriage en route for Springhill. The two girls were going to say good-bye as they were leaving for Paris the following morning.

'If you can take your mind off the excitement of leaving home,' Mr Murray-Hyslop said, 'I beg you girls to look at the foliage. I've seldom seen a more beautiful Fall.'

Kate had been thinking the same thing. Of all the seasons in this new country she still liked autumn best, the one which had greeted them when they had first arrived. In the summer the heavy greenery surrounding them could be claustrophobic, but as Mr Murray-Hyslop pointed out, the cool shade provided was welcome.

He has a sanguine temperament, she thought now, looking at the gold of the cottonwoods, the vivid scarlet of the maples against the china blue of the sky; he always sees the best in everything. Even when his wife died he had soon taken up the reins again, saying to her that the family depended upon him for support. 'And I depend on yours, Kate,' he had said, 'but only if you wish to stay.' 'What made you think I wouldn't wish to?' she had said. 'I love you all dearly, almost as dearly as my own family.' Hadn't he insisted she should go home for a holiday?

He has the same gift as my mother, she thought, he creates happiness around him. I knew that when I was at Sholton.

'Oh, Victoria,' Emily said, 'do look at all those leaves! They remind me of our bronze velvet gowns. But I have a *dreadful* feeling they'll look unsmart in Paris.'

'It's beautiful material.'

'I know, but Maria was telling me they wear the bodices lower, and the bustle is more . . . pronounced.'

'Well, we showed the Harper's magazine to Deborah and Kate.' Victoria sounded doubtful.

'We copied them faithfully, I assure you,' said Kate, smiling across at her employer. 'What else could we do with two young ladies breathing down our necks all the time?'

'I'm sure the gowns are delightful,' their father said. 'In any case, I don't intend to have my daughters parading about half-naked in Paris, nor with small sofas strapped to their waists for the sake of fashion.'

'Oh, Papa,' Emily wailed, 'we want to be *mondaine*! We don't want them to think that because we come from America we are squaws!'

Kate burst out laughing. 'Now that would really cause a sensation! Feathers in your hair and leather jerkins.' She quoted, her eyes sparkling . . .

> 'From the forests and the prairies,
> From the great lakes of the Northland,
> From the land of the Ojibways,
> From the land of the Dacotahs . . .'

James Murray-Hyslop joined in the laughter. 'Have you been reading him, Kate?'

'Yes, when I'm allowed to put down my needle for a moment.'

'You and Father,' Emily said, 'you have a wicked sense of humour. You're always laughing at us. It isn't fair.'

'We're only teasing, my pet.' Kate looked at the flushed face, the pout. 'You must learn to take it. There will be all those delicious Frenchmen who are past masters at it, with their *je ne sais quoi* this and that.'

'I hope Miss Arbuthnot will keep a close eye on the

two of you,' their father said. 'I'm all for international relations, but not quite ready for French sons-in-law.'

'So long as they find happiness.' Kate looked out of the window, saw the wide blue expanse of the Hudson. 'Goodness, we've arrived. Oh, I wish Ernest had been with us. He does enjoy the ferry-boat.'

'He's better at school,' her employer said. 'Think how hard he and George will have to work when they're married to two beautiful young ladies like our Emily and Victoria.'

'Did you write down George's address?' Kate asked Victoria as they walked along the landing stage.

'Yes. He wants us to send him lots of letters so that he'll be able to show off the French stamps to the other boys in Albany. They're always trying to beat each other at something.'

'I'm glad we didn't go to a boarding school,' said Emily. 'Miss Arbuthnot's Academy is bad enough, goodness knows.' James Murray-Hyslop shot an amused glance at Kate as he helped them aboard.

He's like a boy at times, she thought, feeling tender towards him. She told herself it was because of the day, its mellowness, the hint of sadness behind the gold and the blue. She sat quietly as the girls settled beside her in a flurry of petticoats. Their father had excused himself, saying he would take a walk round the deck. She watched his tall, erect figure as he disappeared behind the wheel-house. He must be only a few years younger than Father, and yet at times he could look absurdly young and insouciant for a man with four children.

Her aunt and uncle were sitting in deck chairs on the lawn which stretched in a pleasant sward towards the river, here and there broken by groves of trees and shrubs. They rose to greet them as the little party appeared.

285

Uncle Terence looks more American than Mr Murray-Hyslop, Kate thought. Is it that the Irish assimilate more easily than the Scots or the English, or is it because he has an American wife? Goodness, she thought, I'm introspective today. She hurried the last few steps towards them.

Her uncle turned towards James Murray-Hyslop after greeting her and the girls. 'I've been looking forward to your coming all day, my dear fellow.' He shook him vigorously by the hand. 'It's petticoat territory here, I can tell you. Nobody listens to me.' He did not look unduly cast down by his situation, Kate thought. He had the same positive approach to life that Mother had, more ebullient, perhaps, a slight extravagance in his gestures, but the resemblance was there in the height and the colouring. It must have been their temperaments, that feeling of them being all of a piece, which had made them both leave Ireland and carve their own lives, far away from it.

'I suffer from the same situation,' his guest smiled, 'only in greater measure. Not a word I say is listened to. Now you know why I'm packing two of them off to Paris.'

'Oh, don't listen to Father, Mr McGrath!' Emily said. 'He's been teasing us all the way here. Perhaps *you*'ll take us seriously, Mrs McGrath, because I assure you Kate's just as bad.'

'Indeed I shall, and I'm dying to hear about your wardrobe. There's nothing I like better than talking about clothes. They're very important to me.' She looked down at her pale mauve muslin with its frills and little bows, what Kate thought of as a 'fluffy' dress; but then Aunt Caroline herself was fluffy, with her pale gold hair in ringlets that were too young for her. Sometimes, though, there was a fleeting sadness in her eyes, and from the first visit Kate had noticed Uncle Terence's tender concern for her. She had chided herself. Never judge by appearances . . .

'Where's Maria, Aunt?' she asked.

'She's in her room. Go up and talk to her. She was riding all morning and she's changing. Come and sit down on this seat beside me, dear girls.'

'And you, James,' Uncle Terence said, 'will accompany me in a walk round the garden, if you will. I want to hear, as an expatriate like myself, what you think about this new invention which enables one to speak over the air. Do you realize, Kate, if I had this contraption installed, I could telephone to your mother and father?'

'Oh, Uncle, I was reading about it, and Mr Murray-Hyslop and myself have discussed it! It hardly seems possible.'

'It's possible, and probable. This is a great country, Kate, young, vigorous. There's no doubt it's going to lead the world. Why else do you think it attracts splendid types like myself and this gentleman here.' His laugh was full-throated. 'Come along, then, James, and you run upstairs, Kate, and tell that girl to put in an appearance. She rides herself stupid . . . but sure, I was the same myself at her age. It's in the blood.'

Kate went into the great square hall with its tiled black and white marble floor, and made towards the staircase. The river light, a whiter, clearer, more luminous light than at Wolf House, streamed through the tall windows. 'When I get married,' Maria had said, laughing, 'I'll sweep down here into the arms of my lover. It's a perfect setting. And Emily and Victoria shall be my bridesmaids, and you, too, Kate, although I think you'll be married before me.' She had the same mischievous glance as her father.

She found her cousin sitting in her petticoat at her desk. She laughed and put her arm round the letter she was writing. 'Caught in the act! My secret is out!'

'You're writing to a beau. I know it!'

'I am, Kate McGrath, and what of it? Didn't your own mother go a step further and run away with hers?'

Kate nodded. 'So you say. It's strange. She never talks about it. Does your father?'

'About Ireland, yes, but rarely about his parents. But then he isn't a backward-looking man.'

'Nor is Mother. Her eyes are on the future at the moment especially, with the business.'

'Ah, sure, it's all a long time ago their Irish past, and they're both good at keeping a close tongue in their heads.' She pointed to the letter, bubbling with laughter. ' "Run away with me, my dearest Maria," this spalpeen says, "or I'll kill myself." ' She spoke with her father's Irish brogue to tease. 'Sure and it runs in the family, the romantic urge. You'll be doing the same thing yourself one of these days.'

'No, I'm far too sensible.'

'Maybe I am, too. I still prefer horses.' She got up from the desk, lifted a black and white striped gown from the bed and slipped it over her head. 'Do it up at the back, there's a good girl.'

'Stand still, then. Why do girls always wriggle when they're being done up?'

'Goodness only knows. Maybe it's the constriction we fight against. Or at least we did at Vassar. I wonder Mr Murray-Hyslop didn't send his daughters there.'

'He prefers European culture, or maybe he knows more about it. There. Finished.'

'Thank you, cousin.' Maria whirled round, her eyes sparkling, her face glowing above the white collar with its neat black bow. 'When did you arrive?'

'Just this minute. Your mother's giving the girls last-minute advice on their gowns, and I hope telling them a few other things as well, because I don't feel quite competent in that direction.' She sat down on the bed.

'You mean men and that sort of thing?'

Kate laughed. 'Yes, men and that sort of thing. I haven't much experience of men.'

'But there was that Winthrop boy who was crazy about you. I know he bored me to tears talking about you when you were in Scotland.'

'He bored *me* to tears when I was here. No, that's unfair. He was gentle, and attentive, but he seemed so . . . immature.'

'That all depends, doesn't it?' She tapped Kate on the shoulder and went to the window where she stood, looking out. 'You know,' she said, 'my mother didn't give me any advice, either. She would have been too embarrassed. She's shy. Sometimes I feel like *her* mother. Luckily I went to a progressive college. But I don't think the girls would have much advice from Miss Arbuthnot. She's the kind who'll make them undress under their nightgowns.'

Kate laughed. 'I'm sure you're right. I've tried . . .'

'One thing about being interested in horses, you . . . accept.' She peered. 'There's the ferry-boat again. How pretty it looks with its white sails. Nature's there, in front of you all the time with animals. They're not inhibited like us, they don't wear clothes . . .'

'I *have* noticed.' Kate smiled. 'And I've assimilated a fair amount, some of it even from "that Winthrop boy".'

'Did he . . . ?' Maria turned round, her eyes sparkling.

'No, I told you he was gentle, but he seemed to think he was in love with me.' She shrugged. 'Anyhow, it's in the past. Still, at times like these, with Emily and Victoria setting off, I feel Mr Murray-Hyslop misses his wife all the more.'

'I rather think he relies on you to take her place.' Maria

seemed to be intently scanning the broad expanse of the Hudson.

'Oh, I'd never do that!' Kate felt her cheeks flush unaccountably. These Fall days could be rather humid. 'I've tried my best to keep the children happy . . . I don't know if I succeed. Sometimes he looks so sad . . . and why, may I ask, Maria, have you stopped looking for ferry-boats and turned to look at me?'

'You're such an honest girl, Kate, that's why. There's no subterfuge in you at all. I know you don't want an answer but you shall have one all the same. You've taken charge of that house since Mrs Murray-Hyslop died, and even before, in a way that is a credit to you. No, don't blush, we all think so, Mother, Father and me. In a way you're better with the children than she was because you're nearer their age and they love you as a friend as well as respect you. I can't speak for Mr Murray-Hyslop, of course, but he'd be a fool if he weren't grateful.'

'Oh, anything I do, Maria, I don't do for his thanks! It's because I want to.'

'You're clear-cut, Kate. I think you must be like your mother from what Father has told me, and you. Let's change the subject which I see is making you as red as a beetroot. How are they all in Scotland?'

'Well,' Kate took a deep inward breath, hoping it would draw the colour from her cheeks, 'they've moved into their new home. It's called Braidholme, and they like it very much. Mother says it's the kind of house she's always wanted, long, low, a rambling farmhouse which has been added to over many years, beamed ceilings, white-washed, an old garden with a sundial, a courtyard behind with plenty of loose-boxes. I suppose you could call it a country gentleman's residence, plenty of land, eight bed-rooms, a servants' wing, a garden room which she says they had at Woodlea, the family home in Ireland.'

'Sometimes I wonder if it existed.'

'Oh, it existed all right. You just have to watch my father's face when he talks about it, and the sadness in it, as much for the past, I imagine, as for anything else. Mother's different. Her face lights up, certainly, but I've a feeling if she ever went back to Ireland, to live, I mean, it would be to please my father. They're a fond couple. That look that passes between them, which I've seen often, that's true love.'

'I'd like well to meet them.'

'Why don't you go back with Isobel when she comes next spring? Mother would love to see you, and so would the boys, Isobel, and my youngest sister, Maevy they call her now . . . I used to call her the Wee Rascal. Oh, Maria, I'd like fine for you to meet my family!'

'You miss them, don't you?'

'Yes, I miss them.'

'I wondered, after Mrs Murray-Hyslop died, if you would decide to go back for good?'

'No, you see, Maria, I couldn't have left them in the lurch. But maybe when Ernest goes to boarding school beside his brother there won't be the same need for me.'

'Maybe not.'

'Why are you looking at me? You've done that once or twice since I came upstairs.' Kate got up from the bed, bent her head while she smoothed her dress. It would hide the blush.

'Because you are my favourite cousin since I haven't met the rest of them. And I love to tease you.' What a character Maria was. She had no need to go to Paris to become *mondaine*, as Emily put it. 'Shall we go down and have tea? I've got to give Emily and Victoria the satisfaction of thinking I'm dying of envy.'

They laughed as they went out of the room, arm in arm, and walked down the wide staircase. They passed the long window, the blue, sparkling river filling its frame, a glimmer of red in the distance, the Fall foliage, the white dots of sails. 'Who would want to leave all that?' Maria said.

'Who indeed?' But autumn, she had not learned to think of it as the Fall, had a touch of melancholy in it. Or was it in herself?

The girls and their father had departed early that morning in a flurry of tearful farewells, too early, fortunately, for the rest of the servants to be up. We should have had a regular crying match then, Kate thought to herself to excuse the fact that the tears were still in her own throat. She sat in the kitchen drinking tea until Mrs Vanaressi bustled in.

'What a sad face this morning, Kate.' Cook, Kate thought, had the enviable attribute of having a face which never showed any emotion. Indeed, Mr Murray-Hyslop had once said that he thought it had been carved out of the same marble as their mantelpieces. 'Is it because your little birds have flown their nest?'

'Yes, Mrs Vanaressi. The house is going to seem so quiet.'

'They are not dead, remember, unlike Mr Vanaressi.' She knelt down to rake the ashes, speaking above the noise. 'It will get you used to them going for good. Both my daughters were married at their ages and I haven't seen them since they went back to Italy with their husbands when the quarry closed.'

'You must miss them so badly. Don't you ever want to go back there?'

Mrs Vanaressi straightened herself. 'Clinker, clinker, all the time. No, this country gave my husband a good living and now it gives me one. Everyone must stand on their own feet. Besides, I have my three sons in New

York. When they make a lot of money they have promised to take me on a visit. Meantime I work for Mr Murray-Hyslop.' She went to the meat safe. 'Left-overs. I make a pie, or a risotto?' She turned to Kate.

'Whatever you wish. Part of your family is as far away as mine.'

'That is the way of the world and home is where the heart is. You have heard that saying, Kate?'

'Yes, yes, indeed.' She bestirred herself and got up. 'I'll go to the store for you, but first I must get Ernest up and off to school, and after I come back I've decided to turn out the linen cupboards today, and there are all the clothes Emily and Victoria left which must be sorted out and packed away. Oh, there are a million things to do.'

'So, so.' Mrs Vanaressi was assembling the tools of her trade on the big kitchen table. She looked pointedly at Kate. She left.

She exhausted herself all day with the doing of the tasks she had set herself. After dinner she hearkened to Ernest with his homework, then sat in the kitchen and talked with Ingrid, Irma and Deborah, which meant listening chiefly to the attributes of Deborah's beau. Fortunately she was leaving soon to be married. For a long time Kate had thought there were too many women in the house, now even more so, as far as servants were concerned, with the girls gone. Later she wrote a letter to George telling him about his sisters' departure and that his racoon, Joseph, which had been left in her charge, was doing well. She then retired to bed.

But it was impossible to sleep. She could not understand the strange feeling of loss that had come over her. It was so stupid, she told herself. The girls had only gone for a year, Mr Murray-Hyslop for a day and a night. For the first time in her life she began to question seriously the necessity for her being here at all in this New World to which she had set off so confidently three years ago.

There were Uncle Terence, Aunt Caroline and Maria, of course, but wasn't her place with her own family back in Scotland? But you were restless when you *were* back, she reminded herself. But the girls would marry, the boys would be away at school, then university, Mr Murray-Hyslop might marry . . . the thought sent a physical pain through her, so strong, so swift, that she had to rise and walk about her bedroom until its intensity wore off.

She sat at the window and looked through the trees towards the road, the old coach road. The carriage had stood on it this morning, waiting, taking the three of them out of her life, leaving her bereft . . . 'Kate McGrath,' she found herself saying to herself as she pulled on a loose robe, 'you will go downstairs and fetch that book of Mr Longfellow's and select a poem in it that will calm you. There must be at least one in it appropriate to the occasion since he has written so many . . .'

She went downstairs quietly, through the dark hall and into Mr Murray-Hyslop's study, lit the lamp on the desk. It illuminated one of the prints of the French painter Cezanne which he had asked her to admire. Yes, she thought, glancing at it, quite different from Landseer's dogs . . . how kind he always was to her, how he had enriched her life. Perhaps she would sit here for a time and read. Had he not expressly requested her to use the room at any time when he was away. 'It gives me pleasure,' he had said, 'to think of your quiet head bent over your book. You leave an aura there for me to come back to that removes my loneliness.'

Yes, she was grateful to him, a good and kind employer. He had introduced her to the joys of reading, had selected books for her. Often at the table they had discussed their merits or demerits. He had asked for her opinion. 'Kate has a receptive mind,' he had said once. 'Look how she gets to the root of the discussion. You can't fool our Kate . . .'

She found the book, opened it and began to riffle through the pages. What an energetic man Mr Longfellow was! Every idea that had struck him had been put into words, and between these pages. Mother used to say Father was a poet, she remembered, that he had had a poetic way of speaking when he was young. You could see that when he sang, how he savoured the words of the song as well as the music, how his eyes grew soft. I love him, she thought, my quiet father, just as I love my mother who sustains us. She had a clear image of her mother's bright face, the fine eyes, the deep blue of them, the red hair. An Irish beauty, she thought, remembering a quotation she had read recently, 'Age cannot wither her, nor custom stale her infinite variety . . .'

I wish I could see her at this moment, she thought, ask her why I have this strange feeling inside me of desolation and hope, of excitement and desperation, and running through them a kind of melancholy so that everything I look at seems so inexpressibly beautiful, and yet so transient . . . 'Oh, I need my mother to tell me . . .'

She was speaking aloud again, so that it covered the noise; it had been there for a second or two, in the hall, and she jumped up from her seat, alarmed. Not a man in the house, she thought, except Ernest who would be fast asleep dreaming about the Russians – they had had a long talk about them tonight, and the Turks – but she had locked the door soundly, hadn't she? Only someone who had a key could come in. She went to the door, opened it inch by inch. Mr Murray-Hyslop was hanging up his cloak in the hall. He turned and saw her.

'Kate!' he said. 'What on earth . . . ?'

'Oh, dear.' He was so pale. 'You look so tired.'

295

'Do I?' He passed his hand over his brow. 'Yes, perhaps it was stupid – I've travelled all day and all night – in all kinds of conveyances – but one should not ignore one's impulses . . .'

'No . . .' She must hide her pleasure, the feeling of happiness that made her want to smile and keep on smiling. 'Perhaps not. Come and sit down in your study and I'll fetch you something warm to drink.'

'Later, Kate.' He waved his hand. He followed her into the study but did not sit down. 'And what, may I ask, are you doing at this time of night, or is it morning?' He took out his watch and consulted it. 'Yes, two A.M., it says here.'

'I couldn't sleep.' She smiled. 'I had hopes that Mr Longfellow could do something for me.'

'Poetry never lulled anyone to sleep. Have you been all right? What have you been doing?'

'Everything under the sun. Did you get the girls away safely?'

'Yes. They sent their love.'

They were standing facing each other. A new feeling of unease came over her with him. Perhaps it was because she was undressed under her robe, her hair loose. She touched it. 'Forgive me. I didn't expect you so late. My hair . . .'

'It's lovely like that. I've known you for so long but I've never seen it anything but closely confined, tidy Miss Kate.'

'I was stupid. I kept so busy that I exhausted myself and then couldn't sleep. It's losing the girls, you see. I never thought I'd miss them so much. I knew it was going to happen. I'm sensible, you know that, I'd warned myself how I would feel, but all my warnings didn't prepare me for this feeling of . . .' She'd felt them lurking in her eyes,

296

roll down her cheeks, had no way of hiding them, those *stupid* tears . . .

'Ah, Kate, come here.' He held out his arms and she went into them, naturally, the way Ernest used to do when he had fallen down.

'I've had the same . . . feeling all day.' She wept against his shoulder.

'So have I.' He stroked her hair. 'When I saw Emma and Victoria into the capable hands of Miss Arbuthnot I was desolated, too, and I had only one thought in my mind, to get home.' His voice was soft. 'That therein lay my happiness, the only cure for my desolation.' I'm dreaming, she thought, I'll wake up and find that I'm in my bed upstairs. 'You have made a home for me, for the children, since my wife died . . .'

'Oh, oh . . . this is . . . !' She tried to push him away, met his eyes. He looked haggard in the light.

'You don't have to struggle, Kate.' He released her. 'You can leave me if you wish.'

She looked at him and her heart seemed to fill and run over with love, as the tears had spilled out of her eyes a short time ago. 'You said . . . this was . . . where your happiness lay. You mean . . . Ernest?'

He laughed. 'Ernest, of course, but you, Kate, you. When we visited your uncle yesterday, do you remember I walked round the garden with him?'

'Yes, I do.'

'We didn't talk about Edison Bell after all. We talked about Miss Kate McGrath. I told him I loved you, and did he think I could ask you to marry me. And he said, "Go ahead and try. She'll give you a straight answer at least." So, what's it to be, Kate?'

She felt her heart dissolve with happiness, a physical sensation, all the desolation and doubt melt away. 'So *that*'s what it's been,' she said.

'What?'

'Love. The love for the girls I recognized. But I didn't realize it was mixed up with . . .' She laughed, swallowed . . . 'I can't believe I'm saying this, love for *you*.'

'Oh, Kate!' He took her in his arms again, and kissed her. And kissed her. 'Men and that sort of thing,' Maria had said yesterday. Was it only yesterday? 'My mother didn't give me any advice . . .' But you didn't need any advice if your heart was full of love. You showed it. There was no need for subterfuge.

'I didn't dare hope.' Mr Murray-Hyslop had released her to let them draw breath. She must think of him as James now. One couldn't possibly marry someone and go on calling him Mr Murray-Hyslop. 'Shall we make it soon, Christmas?' She nodded. Her heart was too full for words. 'I want to hold you while I tell you this.' His arms were comfortable now. They were at peace with each other. Content to wait. Until Christmas. 'What I felt for my dear wife was different. Don't ever confuse the love I had for her and what I feel for you. It was a young man's love, partly arranged by parents who were friends and threw us together, but we were happy and I grieved deeply when she died. But I feel I've been waiting for you all my life.'

'If I can . . . fill her place, that'll be enough.' She heard the roughness of tears in her voice and disengaged herself. 'And now this is becoming altogether too much like the bioscopes they used to show in the village hall in Sholton. Mother and Terence used to imitate them at home to make us laugh. You are to rest here, and I'll go and make you a warm drink, and . . .'

'And I can see you are going to run my life for me, sweet Kate. And make me laugh.' He took her hand. 'What I never had with Agnes was your light-heartedness. I think you and I are going to have . . . fun.' She bit her lip, smiling at him, then hurried out of the room.

My goodness, she thought, standing at the range in the kitchen waiting for the kettle to boil, what will Mother say when she hears? I hope it won't be too much of a surprise. If only we had one of Mr Bell's telephones . . .

6

Maeve put down Kate's letter which she had been reading aloud to Kieran. Isobel and Maevy had set off already for the Sholton office, but she and Kieran had stayed behind at Braidholme because there was a horse dealer coming to see them that morning. ' "I know this will be a great surprise to you . . ." ' she quoted. She shook her head delightedly, ' "Surprise," the poor lamb says, and her letters brimming over with Mr Murray-Hyslop this and Mr Murray-Hyslop that for the past few years . . .'

'And the wistful face of her sometimes when she was home visiting us . . .'

'All the same, it's grand news, isn't it?'

'Grand news it is if she's happy.'

'You don't think he's too old for her, Kieran? Forty-two and twenty-three?'

He shook his head. 'I don't think so. Kate needs a mature man. She says he's writing, too. He'll make a good case for himself.'

'And four children.'

'A ready-made family whom Kate loves. And if I know her she'll soon be adding to it.'

'He seemed a nice enough man that time we saw him on the Broomielaw.'

'Indeed he did, and your brother Terence says nothing but good about him in his letters. They are friends. He would have told you if he'd had any objections.'

'Yes, oh, yes. Kate to be married . . . yes, it's right for her and so is he. I feel it's been . . . ordained. What do

300

you think, Kieran? Shall we go to the wedding at Christmas?'

'She wants us to come. I'd dearly like to go to cast a quick eye over him.'

'It would be too late for that.'

'Too true. I'll have to think about it. There's this new business venture ahead. I'll be very busy in Glasgow around that time. This man who's coming today has been looking out for new horses. And there will be carters to be hired . . .'

'Yes, there's a hundred things to do and we're sitting here over breakfast at ten o'clock. I tell you what. There's the monthly meeting today. We'll put it on the agenda and see what the rest think.'

He smiled at her. 'Yes, you might as well put it through the proper channels, but I know you . . .'

'What do you know, Kieran McGrath?' She got up from the table, stood behind him and put her hands on his shoulders. She rested her cheek against his.

'That nothing except a volcanic eruption or the outbreak of war will keep you away from Kate's wedding.'

She kissed his cheek. 'Yes, you're right. And you'll come, too?'

'Just try and stop me.'

They were happily busy all morning in the stables, showing the horse dealer their own stock, discussing the relative merits of Shires and Clydesdales with him, *vis à vis* Cleveland Bays, conducting him round the grounds of Braidholme.

'You have a fine little place here,' he told them at an early lunch which had been set for them in the dining-room. Maeve had furnished it with a long refectory table so that all the family could be gathered round it, a fine Scottish dresser and plenty of small tables for photographs and pots of flowers, today great sheaves of tawny chrysan-

themums grown in the green-houses. Some fine prints of
Irish racehorses which Kieran had acquired in a Glasgow
saleroom were on the walls. 'Yes, it's in good heart. Put
your money in property always. You can't go wrong.'
Places had been set for them at one end of the long table.
Susan brought in a platter of cold roast beef, a jug of beer
for the two men, curtseyed and left.

'I always thought we'd buy a fine Georgian residence,'
Maeve told him . . . Woodlea could have been called that
. . . 'but Kieran and I fell in love with this place. It's a
working farm as well as a home. Two for the price of
one.' She smiled at him.

Mr Rintoul helped himself to a generous plateful of
roast beef, added some baked potatoes and pickle. 'Aye,
you're a fine business woman, Mrs McGrath, I'll hand
you that, but you remember,' he waved his fork at her,
'property! Your money's better in it than in the bank. By
Jove, this is a rare piece of meat. Don't tell me you bred
this yourself, too?'

'No, we stick to pigs and horses,' Kieran said, laughing,
'we're true Irish.'

They were all seated round the table when Maeve and
Kieran went into the committee room. When they'd
moved from Duncan McGrath's house to the offices in
Sholton, a former lawyer's house in the main street,
Maeve had insisted on the dining-room being reserved for
the monthly meetings, and any other discussions with
clients. The fine, high-ceilinged room gave the right
impression. She had had 'The McGrath Carting Company' picked out in large gold letters on the lower halves
of the windows.

Patrick, Terence, Isobel and Maevy were already there,
the senior clerk and their accountant. Johnson, the clerk,
had proved himself so valuable that the family had

302

discussed in private the possibility of making him a partner. The hint which had been dropped had made Tom Johnson more assiduous than ever. He had a head for figures; at thirty-five he was as dry as dust and as interesting, Maeve thought, but his shrewd business sense was a great asset. He would be rewarded in due course.

Kieran took the chair as usual. 'Well, it's nice to see all those bright shining morning faces around me, although it's two o'clock in the afternoon. But don't think we haven't been busy. We've been trying to get the better of Mr Rintoul this morning, and believe me there's no tighter-fisted creature than a horse-dealer . . .'

He still surprised Maeve by his ease at their meetings. Maybe the truck business had given him a taste for public speaking. Every Irishman is a bit of a performer, she thought, watching him, happy with words.

'We've tentatively arranged to add four Clydesdales and two Shires to our count. There are some steep streets in Glasgow and we need plenty of beef between the shafts. I've particulars and prices of them here.' He put a paper on the table. 'We think we know a good horse when we see one, but if any of you see any defect, speak out. That's what you're here for.'

Maeve watched the smiling faces. Only Terence would make some comment later. Patrick had never been interested in livestock, looking forward to the day when they got rid of them and relied on mechanical means of transport. She knew it would come. The state of the streets in Glasgow with all those horse droppings was a sufficient enough reason, but in the country, what better thing was there than a horse, a living, breathing animal, beautiful to look at? Even the sturdy Clydesdales with their feathery fetlocks and their patient, good-humoured faces.

Terence held out his hand for the paper, and when it

was passed to him he scanned it, but not with his usual close attention. He's unhappy, she thought again, watching him. It's Catherine. Is there anything worse than two beings forced to live closely, who can't get on? At least Patrick hasn't that problem. Her eyes fell on him for reassurance, and surprised a look of preoccupation which was unusual enough to make her look again. He was paler than usual. His eyes were dark-ringed.

'Patrick,' it was Kieran speaking, 'you were going to present your findings of suitable properties in Glasgow for our new branch.' His father's voice seemed to alert him. He became the calm, business-like younger son again.

'Yes, I've looked into that. There are three properties, one in Stobhill, one in Bridgeton and one in the Gallowgate. I think the Gallowgate one has the most advantages because of the room for expansion. There's a junk yard behind it that we could buy out at any time. The old man is trading at a loss when he sobers up sufficiently to trade at all. Bob has the figures.'

Bob Carter, their accountant (they had teased him at the beginning, saying it was only his name which had got him the job), produced a sheaf of typed sheets from his case and put it on the table. 'Anybody can leaf through these,' he said, and then smiling in the girls' direction, 'even Miss Maeve and Miss Isobel.'

'What do you mean, *even* Miss Maeve and Miss Isobel?' Maeve demanded. 'There are no prejudices in this firm. Everybody, regardless of their sex, is as good as the next man, or woman, as the case may be.'

'You're ahead of your time, Mrs McGrath,' Bob Carter laughed, 'but I'll say this, if they're half as good as you, they'll do.'

'And don't flatter me either because I'm a woman. That's prejudice, too.'

He threw up his hands in mock horror. 'Well, there are the figures, copied by *Miss* Isobel and checked by *Miss* Maeve.' He bowed across to them. 'I think Patrick's choice is the right one in the right place, nearest the centre of the town. It's cheaper than the others because of the mess the old dealer has made around it, but that's to its advantage. If we buy him out and tidy the place up we'll have a fine stables, and sheds for the carts. Location is the key word every time in connection with property. There's even a little house the man lived in that could be made habitable for a night watchman.'

'Fine,' Kieran said. 'It's a question of outlay this morning, the new horses, the new Glasgow premises. But property's property. You never lose money on it.' You heard Rintoul saying that, Maeve thought, smiling, but it was true. There might come a day when the business would dwindle, but good property was worth its weight in gold. 'Are we all agreed?' Kieran asked. She smiled across at Isobel and Maevy with their raised hands. That's how she wanted them to be, to know what went on outside their kitchens when they were married. They were both lovely girls. Kate had started the ball rolling . . .

'Carried unanimously,' she said, looking at Kieran. He nodded.

'And now we come to the next question, still a matter of property.' He looked at Terence. 'What about the house we've vacated, Duncan McGrath's?' They still called it that. 'Has Catherine given it more thought?'

Terence looked miserable. 'It's no good. She's taken against the house. It's not . . . what she had . . . thought of . . .' Maeve interrupted.

'There's no need to apologize for her, Terence. Every woman is entitled to her own opinion about where she wants to live. But there's the possibility of getting an architect to have a look at it, enlarge it, draw plans to her liking. Bearing in mind what we've been talking about, the site's valuable if nothing else.'

'I've suggested all that.' He shook his head, looked down at the table. There was an awkward pause. Maeve saw Maevy and Isobel exchange glances. They had little time for Catherine. What a pity one of them isn't getting married, she thought, and then it would be occupied. She'd been married for three years at Isobel's age, had Terence, was carrying Patrick . . . She saw Patrick on his feet again. How tense and pale he was! Surely he wasn't taking this business about Catherine too much to heart? He'd never expressed any opinion about his sister-in-law, but then, that was his way . . .

'I think I have a solution about the house,' he said. 'Catherine is obviously against it. If the firm goes on as it's doing and we have a thriving business in Glasgow, we might buy a town house for them there.'

'That doesn't solve the question of Duncan McGrath's,' his father said. 'These offices here suit us. We don't want to move back . . .'

'*I* would be willing to occupy it.' He paused, looked round the table. 'That is, my wife and I. I'm marrying Bessie Haddow.' He stood, chin up, face stern, as if waiting for some reaction. Maevy was the first to speak, forgetting her business decorum.

'Oh, Patrick,' she said, 'you sly devil! You never let on to a soul. We thought you were doing *business* in Glasgow!'

'So I was.' Everyone laughed.

'Well, congratulations!' Bob Carter got up, holding out his hand.

'Yes, we're very pleased, Patrick. Aren't we, Kieran?' Maeve met his eyes, saw the puzzlement in them.

'Downright pleased.' He nodded. 'The whole family is.'

'I like Bessie,' Isobel said.

'She's a favourite with all of us.' Maeve smiled across at her younger son. 'And you couldn't have thought of a better solution for the house.'

'Quite so.' Tom Johnson got to his feet, assiduous as always in the performance of his duties. 'On behalf of the firm, Patrick, I would like formally to congratulate you and wish you and your future wife every happiness.'

'Thank you.'

'Terence looks as if he's been struck by lightning,' Isobel said.

He cast a glance at his sister. Maeve saw that his face had flushed a dark red.

'Aren't you going to congratulate me?' Patrick said.

'Yes . . . yes . . . by all means.' He looked at his brother, then round the table, as if trapped. He half-rose. 'It's . . . hot in here.'

'Where are you going?' Maeve said.

'Nowhere. I thought I'd get some air . . .'

'Pass Terence a glass of water, Tom. Since family matters are intruding, I might as well tell you that we have an announcement to make.' She nodded at Kieran and he got to his feet again, smiling.

'It looks as if we're losing our family all at once. We had a letter from Kate this morning and she's marrying her employer, Mr Murray-Hyslop.'

'Oh! Kate and Mr Murray-Hyslop!' Isobel sounded ecstatic. 'How truly romantic!' Perhaps young women at the monthly meeting were not such a good idea after all.

'They've asked us to the wedding,' Kieran went on. 'We wanted to put it to you, if we could absent ourselves for the occasion, bearing in mind that there's a lot to be done here. But she's our eldest daughter.' He smiled round the table.

'It would mean being away over Christmas,' Maeve said.

Patrick looked across at her. 'That's when Bessie and I have chosen to be married.'

She was astonished. This was November. 'Maybe you could . . .'

'No.' His face was set. 'It can't be altered.'

'It looks as if . . .' Kieran was plainly as astonished as she was, '. . . as if family business is taking up too much time altogether. Could we have our financial report, Bob?'

Maeve applied herself to listening to Bob Carter. She and Kieran would have to have a talk later. Would he be thinking what she was thinking? But, no, the notion was too outlandish. Patrick was far too sensible. Only fools got girls into trouble.

She looked at her two sons. Terence's head was bowed. His pencil turned slowly in his hand, methodically, as if he was giving all his attention to Bob; Patrick's face was inscrutable. It will be like prising open an oyster shell to get anything from him, she thought, and yet at the foot of her puzzlement she was pleased. Bessie was a girl she would be glad to have in her family.

At dinner that night Kieran agreed with her that it would be better to have a talk with Patrick alone. 'You're better at it than I am, especially with the boys.'

'I used to think so,' she said, 'but not any longer. Terence is wrapped in his own misery, and Patrick has shut himself away from me recently. I thought it was affairs in connection with the new branch in Glasgow that were taking him up there. Now we know.'

He had not come into dinner that evening, but when she went into the sitting-room later – Kieran had gone for a last look round the stables – she found him sitting there. He got up when he saw her.

'Just toasting myself,' he said. 'I had a cold train ride from Glasgow.'

'Seeing Bessie?'

He nodded. 'Telling her you were all glad about the news.' His mouth quirked, scarcely a smile.

'So we are.' She sat down beside him on the sofa. 'But surprised at the quickness of it. I thought she would want time to get her trousseau ready. The girls would have loved to help her. They've got a sewing meeting tonight at their old teacher's house, learning tatting. Do business girls tat?' She wanted to make him smile.

'She's pregnant,' he said. 'Does that save you a lot of quizzing?'

'Mind your tongue!' The flush seemed to be inside her body, as if drawing the colour from her face. She waited, tried to calm herself. 'When is it due?'

'At the beginning of March.'

'So why did you wait till November before you started making arrangements to marry? It's not like you . . .'

'Look, Mother,' he turned to her, 'there are some things you'd better not concern yourself with. What I do is my own concern and no one else's.'

The ache spread through her. To be spoken to like that . . . but it had to happen sometime. Maybe she needed it. She got up and walked over the soft rose-coloured carpet, looked out through the mullioned windows to the dark garden. She had told Susan there was no need to draw the curtains. The moonlight shone on the sundial backed by the dark clump of trees which grew at the crest of the hill. At the foot of it was the Sholtie. Next year, she had decided, they would have a summer house built there so that they could see the burn . . . next year I'll be a grandmother. Meantime I'm a mother who has been put in her place.

She turned and looked into the room, at Patrick sitting gazing at the fire, waiting. She had thought it was such a pleasing room, not much furniture, their book-cases, a

309

china cabinet for the few pieces she had collected – she no longer mourned the loss of the fine stuff at Woodlea to her mother's side; now it was just a room with her younger son in it, waiting for her to speak. He hadn't a temper, Patrick, but his words could wound.

She went and sat down beside him. 'I counted up to a hundred,' she said. 'Whatever you say. Would you like to have the wedding here? It's a lovely house for a wedding, made for it. It would christen it, in a way.'

'But I thought you were going to America?'

'Oh, no, not now.' She bent forward and kissed his cheek, smiled at how his hand went up to wipe away the trace of it. 'I'm very fond of Bessie,' she said, 'I'd want to see that . . . everything . . . was all right.'

He caught her hand awkwardly. 'Mother . . .' he shook his head at her, 'she's the only one . . . who ever measured up to you.'

They talked late in bed that night. Her mind was clear, and yet Kieran had an Irish kind of intuition, a sensibility which transcended her way of thinking. She wanted to hear him talk.

'I said we'd have the wedding here.'

'So we're not going to America?'

'No.'

'I think you're right. We're more needed here.'

'There's never been anyone else for Patrick but Bessie, but why didn't he go after her sooner?'

'You know the answer, mavourneen. Because there was never anyone else for Bessie but Terence. And remember, she went to work in Glasgow after he got married.'

'Wasn't that because of her house being broken up when her mother went into the Asylum?'

310

'You're a contrary woman. You know it would have been a sight handier if she'd stayed in Sholton. No, she couldn't abide the place when Terence married Catherine.'

'But what made her change her mind and agree to marry Patrick? And do you see him as a seducer?'

'Didn't you ask him?'

'In a way, but he put me in my place.'

'There you are, then. Accept it, Maeve. He's a man.'

'I'll have to.' She was glad of his arm around her. 'Things have been happening when I wasn't looking. I've been absorbed in getting this house in order, absorbed in the business. I knew, of course, Terence's marriage wasn't going well . . .'

'Is it Terence we're on to now?'

'It is. Remember that Sunday he came to the other house? There had been a row and he'd been drinking. That would be . . .'

'Towards the end of May.' He was always right about dates. He checked them by the birth of foals, by the first primrose, the first bluebell, the first frost . . .

'And he left with Bessie.'

'So he did.'

'And we know Catherine stayed at the manse for a week before she went back.' She waited for him to speak. 'Why don't you answer?'

He spoke slowly, as if to himself. 'What you can't hope to understand because you're a woman is the strength of the urge in a man. It's different for a woman.'

'How can you know that?' She thought of Alastair Crawford, now laird since his father had died and seen about Sholton more than before. It meant nothing now, but she could remember the strength of her urge all right, how she had lain awake, her mind and her heart full of him, feeling strong desire for another man as she lay beside her husband. And what about her desire for Kieran so many years ago, still strong. Terence was her son. He, more than the others, had a vitality like hers, a zest for life; or had, before it had been damped down by Catherine, but not put out.

'Kieran . . .'

'Don't put it into words. Just wait . . .'

He took her in his arms, and perhaps because their conversation had triggered off desire in them, they made love together, laughing at their own enthusiasm, one of those rare bursts of love that come without warning and are treasured all the more because of that.

'It must be all those weddings in the air,' Kieran said when they lay quiet again. His arm was round her, her head was on his shoulder. She was at peace. There was nothing like it for settling the senses, she thought.

'I'll write to Kate tomorrow and tell her.'

'Just that we can't come to her wedding.'

'Yes. That Patrick comes first.'

'She'll wonder why.'

'I'll tell her later. I'll tell her when I go in the spring with Isobel. Will you come with us then?'

'We'll see. I'd thought I might have a look at Ireland in the summer.' He spoke casually. 'Visit my folks, look at a horse or two at the same time.'

'You still long to be back there, don't you?'

'Ach, just to clap my eyes on it, to smell it, to feel its softness on my cheek.'

'To feel its softness on his cheek'. Yes, he had a way with words. 'We'll go soon. We'll go to Woodlea and Sligo Bay and the Curragh, and compare the Shannon with the Sholtie. We'll go and see the cousin who's living at Woodlea now, since Terence and I were passed by. You remind me of many things, Kieran. I shouldn't have to be reminded.'

'Sure your head's full of worries for us all.' She felt his lips on her cheek.

'So is yours, but you remember.' His head moved against hers in a kind of denial.

'The place won't let me forget it, and that's the truth of it.' His love of Ireland was in his voice, in its nuances. He carried it with him wherever he was.

'We'll go, once . . .'

'Don't commit yourself. It won't go away. Now, let's get to sleep.'

Once the child arrives . . . whose child? Once she had been to visit Kate and her new husband . . . You could go through your whole life, making promises.

7

Mercifully, the planning of the new branch in Glasgow kept them all busy and, as well, Maeve had the preparations for the wedding to see to, not to mention the girls' dresses and her own. She did not want to have time to think.

Bessie had called to see her, not a noticeably pregnant Bessie because of her voluminous skirts. The new fullness of her figure suited her. There was a soft bloom on her features; her hair seemed to have lost its strident yellowness and taken on a darker tint.

'I'm glad you came, Bessie,' Maeve said when they were sitting in the drawing-room having tea. It was a cold, miserable day in late November. The room was cosy with its great log fire; the silver candlesticks on the mantelpiece were bronzed by the reflection of its flames. 'I wanted to ask you about the wedding arrangements.'

'I thought it would be to give me a telling-off.' She bit her lip.

'About being pregnant? No, I've been told it's none of my business. A timely reminder. As long as you're happy, the two of you.'

'Sholton tongues will wag. And think what young Mrs McGrath will say.' Her smile was mocking.

'It's of no account. Besides, Catherine is far too busy just now. She's at the manse most of the time. The Reverend's ailing. A liver complaint. He isn't expected to get better.'

'That's sad enough. Patrick's seen the young minister. He'll see that the knot's tied all right.'

'Yes, he's a nice young man, Mr Craigie. I've asked him to stay on after the ceremony. I wondered if you had a list of people you'd like to be asked?'

She shook her head. 'We want it to be as quiet as possible. My brothers are in Canada and my mother wouldn't know what it's all about.'

'How is she?'

'Worse in her mind, better in her body. As if her mind fed on it.'

'What about Lily Docherty?'

'I'd like to ask her but she's got small children, and she lives in Glasgow now.'

'Well, you give me her address anyhow. There will just be the family, Tom and Mary Johnson and Bob and Agnes Carter. They come every year. If you asked anyone outside that, you'd have to invite the whole village. Oh, and Kieran has asked the carters to look in after the ceremony and drink your health. They're always keen enough to wet their whistles.'

'That's all right. Though Patrick isn't as popular with them as . . .' she paused, '. . . Terence.'

'Maybe not, but they're part of the firm.' She looked at the girl and longed to take her in her arms. That one in the Asylum, poor soul, wasn't any use to her. Every girl needed a mother when she was getting married.

'How is Terence these days?' Bessie's voice was light, too light.

'Working and drinking in equal proportions. With Catherine at the manse so much he has nobody to stop him. His father had a strong word with him the other day. I'm hoping it will have some effect.' Their eyes met. She saw the suffering in Bessie's, remembered Patrick. 'Look, Mother, there are some things you'd better not concern yourself with . . .' It was a bitter lesson to learn. She sighed. 'And have you decided on your dress, Bessie?'

'Yes, grey silk,' she smiled like Patrick, close-mouthed, 'with plenty of stuff in it.'

'That's fashionable. The girls were thinking of golden brown velvet. Would that suit you?'

'Anything suits me.' She got up. 'I'll have to go, Mrs McGrath. They don't let you in after three o'clock, and I have to get back to Glasgow tonight.'

'You're welcome to stay here, Bessie. Stay until the wedding for that matter.'

'No, thanks. I've my own wee place in Glasgow. I'm better there.'

'But it will be lonely, and you'll have given up your job . . .'

'I have things to do. I'm grateful to you, Mrs McGrath, for the offer, and all you're doing for Patrick and me. If I'm rude to you I don't mean to be. Patrick said to me you'd be all right, you'd . . . support me. I want to say . . . how grateful we both are.'

'As long as you're happy, that's the main thing.'

'Oh, we'll be happy. I'm determined on it. And don't think Patrick was . . . slow in coming forward. He only knew a month ago.'

Maeve got up and put her arms round her. 'You don't have to tell me anything.' She smiled at her. 'And think of calling me "Mother" if it comes easily to your lips.' She saw the girl's eyes flood with tears. 'Now, on you go, and don't keep your mother waiting.'

'That's the last thing *she*'ll be doing.' They smiled at each other.

The drawing-room was at the back of the house and so she could not watch Bessie going down the drive, nor wave to her. Maybe it was as well. Her eyes were full of tears, too.

* * *

316

The girls had decorated the room with tinsel and red ribbons, the table in the dining-room was groaning with food to which Susan, Maeve, Isobel and Maevy had all contributed their own particular expertise. Isobel was responsible for the wedding-cake. She was as deft in the kitchen as she was in the office. She had iced it in a professional manner and decorated it with silver baubles, placed it on a silver mat. It occupied pride of place amongst the jellied tongues, the roast pork, the mince pies and Scotch bun which was always a great favourite with the carters, to be washed down with their seasonal dram.

And the fact that it was a festive time lent an air of extra celebration that was sorely needed, she thought. Bessie was pale, Patrick stern, Kieran falsely cheerful, and Terence half-drunk when he arrived, exuberant, going around whacking the men on the back, pressing food and drink on everyone. When the young minister was performing the ceremony he was nowhere to be seen, and she thought he might have gone outside to be sick. When he came back he was ashen, but quieter.

Mr Craigie was a decided attribute, not like the old Reverend who had always made a wedding seem more like a funeral, but full of fun and good-heartedness which had its influence as the whisky flowed. Isobel and Maevy, drinking blackcurrant wine, seemed to be impressed, too. 'He's a blessing in disguise,' Maeve whispered to Kieran, watching the girls laughing with him.

The other person who seemed to give the proceedings some semblance of normality was, strangely enough, Catherine. She was wearing a cream dress which set off her dark hair and made her if anything more bridal than the bride, and she appeared to be in her element helping Maeve at the table, talking graciously to the carters, even sharing a joke with them.

The house became her, or perhaps Catherine became the house. Perhaps the girl recognized her own setting better than anyone else. That could well be a town house in Glasgow where there would be concerts – she was a fine pianist – balls in the Assembly Halls, fine folks to visit in her carriage. Perhaps she had always felt like a fish out of water in Sholton, which had lost a lot of its rusticity when it became a mining village.

She said to Kieran, 'I've never seen Catherine so cheerful, although her father's at death's door.'

'Maybe that's why,' he said.

'Now, that's not Christian, but I'll let you off, Kieran McGrath, because you're the handsomest man in the room.'

'You just want me to say you're the handsomest woman.'

'No, that goes to Bessie. It . . . becomes her. She'll make a good mother. I hope a good wife.' Tom Johnson was at their side.

'Mr McGrath, Mrs McGrath.' He bowed, like a stork in his frock coat. 'They're cutting the cake now. We're waiting.'

'Some authority and a good dram inside him and there's no stopping our Tom,' she whispered to Kieran as they joined the crowd round the table. She had decided there would be no formal meal.

Patrick and Bessie stood together before the cake, sharing the holding of the knife. There was a lot of laughter and admonitions from the carters to 'keep a straight eye'.

'Oh, maybe I've made the icing too hard!' Isobel said in an anguished voice. There was a cheer as the first slice was cut.

'Before we taste this wonderful concoction or confection of Isobel's,' Kieran's voice was strong, 'I'd like you

318

to join me in wishing the happy couple long life and happiness.' He held up his glass.

'Long life and happiness!' everyone repeated. Maeve saw Catherine beside Terence, sipping daintily at her wine. Her eyes were bright. She was smiling around the room. Had she guessed that Bessie was pregnant? And had she always been secretly jealous of her? But she wouldn't know . . . ?

'Speech! Speech!' Bob Carter shouted. 'Come on, Patrick. You're not getting off as lightly as that!'

Patrick smiled, his arm round Bessie. 'I'll make it short because I'm a man of few words, as you all know.' There was laughter. 'I'd like to thank you all for coming to see Bessie and me married, I'd like to thank my mother for putting on such a fine show for us, and my father, and my sisters, and to say that I think I have the best wife in the land.'

'And we'll all drink to that!' young Mr Craigie said, flanked by Isobel and Maevy. He poured his wine down his throat with gusto. 'Now, who's going to give a toast to the charming young bridesmaids?' He looked around, his face beaming. 'Mr Terence?' Maeve saw the sudden flood of colour darken his face, the quick turning away. 'Come on, now, you're the eldest son.' Already young Mr Craigie had a hint of Presbyterian authority in his voice.

'We want Mr Terence,' the carters were chanting. Kieran had been free with the whisky. 'We want Mr Terence!'

'Come on, Terry.' It was Catherine's clear voice above the rough shouts of the men. Maeve saw his hand go to the table as if to steady himself. His eyes had a glazed look. He's drunk, she thought. If he spoils this wedding for them I'll kill him . . .

His voice when it came was quiet, controlled. 'Our thanks to Isobel and Maevy who have helped to make this

day go so well. They're a grand credit to the McGraths.'
He turned slowly to Patrick and Bessie, raised his glass,
swayed, righted himself. 'To Bessie, who never looked
better, and to Patrick . . .' he was very white, '. . . who
has all the luck in the world.'

She said to Kieran, 'Get the carriage out now and take
Bessie and Patrick to Sholton.' He nodded. 'And after
that it's Terence and Catherine.'

The house was tidied up, the girls had gone to bed, not
without singing the praises of the young minister.

'And Bessie looked lovely,' Maevy said.

'I thought her dress looked a bit bunchy round the
waist.' Isobel was the astute one. They would have to be
told soon. And to hold their heads high against the gossip.

Kieran came back and they sat at the dying embers of
the fire, reluctant to go to bed. 'I suddenly feel older.'
She looked at him. His face was grey with fatigue, the
flesh slack.

'Weddings do that to parents. Milestones along the
way.'

She was no longer so young herself. Forty-four. That's
nonsense she thought immediately. You've been up since
five. All you need is a good sleep. 'What was Terence
like?'

'Nearly paralytic. Something's got to be done about
him. The strange thing is I don't think Catherine noticed.
She seemed . . .'

'Triumphant?'

He looked at her. 'Yes, that's the word.'

8

It was a fact, Maeve reflected, that as you got older, time went more quickly. She compared it to a snowball at the top of a hill, difficult to set rolling, but once it got going it was away, nothing could stop it.

Perhaps it was the hard winter that had made her think of such an analogy, but the severity of the weather had had one good effect: people kept to their houses. The sudden wedding and Bessie's evident pregnancy did not create the furore it might have done in Sholton on the fine days when people stood at their doors and gossiped. Or perhaps it was just that at Braidholme, set back from the road and the village, she was unaware of it.

It had been a busy and eventful winter – business meetings in Glasgow, endless conferences with solicitors and accountants, endless journeyings. She worried about their effect on Kieran. He had a recurrence of his old bronchitic complaint, and she insisted on him being at home while she took over the reins.

'I'll be miserable,' he said. 'I'm no good at being idle.'

'You've got the horses, and you can take charge of my project.'

'What project?' he asked, smiling. 'I thought we had enough projects to keep us going for many a year. We've worn a road between Braidholme and the Gallowgate.'

'Those are for the firm. This is for us. I've decided to have a summer-house built at the end of the garden. You can help me to choose the best place for it, where we can get a view of the Sholtie.'

'That's a good idea. Trust you to think of it. I've often

thought it was a pity we could not see the burn.'

'There,' she teased him, 'you like the idea! I thought it would be a pleasant place to sit in the evenings when I get back from America. We'll have steps cut in the bank so that you can do a bit of fishing in the pool down there, become a real laird of your policies.'

He laughed at that, but seemed pleased. 'The country gentleman is it you want me to be?'

'Only when you're tired of the McGrath Carting Company.' She sobered. 'This summer-house is a kind of memorial to John, Kieran. It's thirteen years since he drowned in the Sholtie. I've made my peace with it now. I can look at it without bitterness.' She smiled. 'Besides, a summer-house, think of it! We'll make it revolve as well so that we can follow the sun. Our grandchildren will love it. I always wanted a garden house at Woodlea to play in with my dolls. Mother thought it was nonsense, if she thought of it at all; Father stuck me on a pony at five and that was that.'

'Gone are the days . . .' She saw the Irish softness in his eyes.

The bad weather did not keep the young minister away from Braidholme, either. It became a habit for him to come every Sunday evening for supper and, as Kieran said, the primping that went on upstairs in the girls' bedrooms was nobody's business.

But it soon became evident that Isobel was the reason. Maeve, watching her become less brittle, luminous-eyed, was pleased. She had always been a bit of a holy Willie. To be a minister's wife would suit her down to the ground . . . as long as she was not bowled over by some rich young man when they went to visit Kate. 'That would be quite a tussle between God and Mammon,' Kieran said, smiling, 'but have you noticed Maevy?'

'Noticed her? She's quieter, yes, but she's growing up. She's losing her boisterousness.'

'She's in love with John Craigie.'

'Ah, she's only a child.' And then, 'Do you think so?' She was shaken. Had she allowed her preoccupation with the Company to prevent her noticing? Besides, Maevy had never given her any trouble . . .

The following Sunday, when John Craigie came for supper, she knew Kieran was right. In affairs of the heart he was always right. When he had gone away (it was Isobel who had seen him off and taken an unconscionable time in doing it), she asked Maevy to stay downstairs. 'I want to have a talk with you,' she said.

'What's this great secret that doesn't include me?' Isobel had returned, looking flushed and happy.

'It's only to tell Maevy what to do when we're away.' Maeve was bland. 'On you go and get your beauty sleep.'

'All right, Mother.' She was radiant. There was no doubt about it.

'Put on a few logs, Maevy,' she said when Isobel had gone. 'That's right. We hardly ever get a chance to talk. It's been such a busy winter, the new venture in Glasgow, your father not so well at times, keeping an eye on Terence . . .'

'I don't think he's drinking so much, Mother.' She had returned to the sofa, was sitting with her hands clasped. She looked pale, older. Nothing makes anyone grow up more quickly than unrequited love, Maeve thought. I've never known that.

'No, I think you're right. Strangely enough, I'm sure it's Catherine we have to thank. She's a different girl since her father died . . .'

'And since Bessie married Patrick.' Their eyes met.

'Maybe so. And maybe the thought of leaving the district. I've had a talk with her and told her that when the Glasgow end is established she and Terence can think of a house there.'

'That will suit Catherine. She never liked it here, thought it was beneath her. She has important connections on her mother's side, she once told me.'

'No doubt. Maybe they'll have a family, too, and that would settle Terence better than anything else. He could put his love into children, work for them.'

'Second best.'

'You're thrawn tonight. Second-best's better than nothing. What's wrong, Maevy?' She saw the girl's eyes widen. Had she not done the same thing herself many times in an effort to keep back the tears? Sure, experience was the great thing.

'Mother . . . I think I'll go and be a nurse.'

'You've always said that.' She was surprised. 'But you're not old enough, my pet.'

'I soon will be.'

'Well, if your heart's in it, your father and I wouldn't stand in your way. But if it's because of . . .'

'No. I made up my mind years ago . . . when Isobel said I'd caused John's death by running along the stepping-stones.'

She wanted to laugh, or weep. 'Oh, what nonsense! You were just a wee thing, Isobel not a great deal older. She didn't mean it.'

'It stuck, just the same.'

'Maevy, you'll have to have a better reason than that.'

'I have.'

She looked at the girl's bent head, got up and sat down beside her on the sofa, put an arm round her shoulders. 'Sometimes first love isn't the best love.'

'It was with you.'

'Maybe so.' There had been Alastair Crawford. Who was to say which would have been better? 'Meantime, if you want to exercise your nursing talents, why don't you go and sit with Bessie sometimes, rub her back for her? It's getting near her time, and it's a miserable enough time for a woman, whatever all those romantic books say, hardly able to waddle about, feeling your body's been taken over by an invader . . .'

'Oh, Mother!' Maevy laughed. 'That woman, Ouida, wouldn't like that sort of talk.'

'Half of them are probably spinsters who've never known a man, far less had a baby!'

'You're the limit!' Maevy wiped her eyes. They were not tears of laughter. Maeve felt her own heart twist, felt in it the sorrow this young daughter of hers was feeling, the longing . . . 'I'll do that. Patrick's away a lot, but I don't think she's miserable. Haven't you noticed the serene look on her face? I never thought Bessie was beautiful – though she could attract men with that yellow hair and her loud manner and everything – but now she's different.'

'So is Patrick. Not so stern. You know that face he puts on!' They laughed together. 'He's got what he wants,' however he got it, she thought, 'because he knew what he wanted all along. Oh, I know you're thinking it doesn't always work out that way, but give it time. Now, my lovely, will you do something for me?'

'Yes, Mother.' The girl's head was on Maeve's shoulder, her voice was rough. 'My ears are pinned back.'

'You're being cheeky, too.' And gallant. 'Isobel and I will be going away soon. You're going to be in my place. Men think they run everything but we know better. Women are behind them all the time. You'll have to keep an eye on Susan and see that she looks after the house, but don't let her do the dusting. She'd be clumsy with my china pieces. And that new gardener. See what he's up to from time to time. I don't trust him to do the planting properly. And you'll have to keep an eye on the office and not let Tom Johnson get above himself.' They both laughed. 'And see that your father doesn't overtire himself. He's not as strong as I am. Men never are. And keep an eye on Bessie and see she doesn't do too much . . .'

'I'm going to need an awful lot of eyes.'

'None of your lip.' She squeezed Maevy's shoulders. 'I was nearly married at your age. It doesn't do anyone any harm to have to face up to responsibility early. You're my namesake. When you're twenty-one you'll become a partner if you want. It will be a great enterprise by that time, mark my words, the McGrath Carting Company. Once the boys get over to America I wouldn't be surprised if they didn't spread their wings even further.' She laughed. 'Maybe I'm letting myself go a bit but you have to aim high. And about being a nurse . . . don't make up your mind about anything when you're feeling down. It never is the right decision . . .' She held the girl while she wept her heart out, wished she could bear the hurt for her. After a long time, she said, 'Now, you get off to bed. There's a busy day ahead of us tomorrow.'

Maevy got up. Her eyes were red from weeping. One golden curl was black with tears. 'You're our backbone, Mother,' she said, 'I don't know what we'd do without you.'

'Away with you and your soft talk. You're just like your father.' When the girl had gone she felt her own eyes widen, and she looked down at her hands the way Maevy had done.

It became a race between leaving for America and the arrival of the baby. It's birth-date passed and still it did not come. Kate's letters were brimming over with happiness about the joys of marriage and at the thought of her mother and Isobel coming.

'I'll tell you this, Kieran,' Maeve said, 'I'll cancel the whole thing if the baby isn't here before we go.'

'You wouldn't.'

'I would. I wonder if there's something wrong. Her ankles are swelling . . .'

'I never remember you making such a fuss when yours were coming.'

'That was different.'

But a fortnight before they were due to leave, Elizabeth Maeve slipped into the world with comparatively little fuss. The first they knew about it was when an unshaven and slightly incoherent Patrick arrived at Braidholme with the news that Bessie had a little daughter and they were both well.

Kieran took him into the dining-room and gave him a stiff whisky. They were standing, glasses in hand, smiling at each other with moist eyes, when Maeve joined them. She had had to slip upstairs and have a good cry herself.

A fortnight later Bessie was up and about when she and Isobel went to say good-bye. They were due to set off the following morning, returning in a month's time. 'It's long enough for me to be away,' Maeve had said to Kieran, 'but maybe Kate will persuade Isobel to stay on longer.'

'Being a mother suits you, Bessie,' she said. They were sitting in front of a bright fire in the parlour. The little maid had just brought in the tea-tray.

'So Patrick tells me.' She looked up smiling, the baby in her arms. The fire seemed to glow on her face, make her dark eyes shine. I'll remember her like this when I'm away, Maeve thought, the happiness in her face, the peace, and that beautiful grandchild of mine . . . she bent down to kiss the baby's head.

'She's got your dark eyes. And yet she's going to be . . . fair.' She thought, red.

'Patrick thinks she's going to be a mixture of you and

327

me, the best of both worlds, he says.' She laughed. The laugh turned into a cough.

'Don't tell me you've been out already. There was a snell wind yesterday although we're into April.'

'No, Patrick wouldn't hear of it. He's as fussy as an old hen. I think I've caught a bit of a cold from Mrs Robinson. She still comes in to do the necessary down below.' She smiled apologetically at Isobel. 'I shouldn't be mentioning things like that in front of a young girl.'

'Rubbish. She's twenty-one nearly. I'd had several visits from the midwife by the time I was her age.'

'Oh, Mother!' Isobel looked embarrassed.

'All right, I'll spare your blushes. But you take care of yourself, Bessie. And ask Maevy to look in.'

'I can scarcely keep her away. She's here every night to see Elizabeth and nurse her. And she's promised to stay with me when Patrick's up in Glasgow.'

'I feel I shouldn't be going away with all that new business to attend to.'

'Don't you worry about them. Maevy and I will see that they're all right. You be sure to enjoy yourselves.'

'We can hardly believe we're going even yet,' Isobel said. 'Think of it, crossing the Atlantic to America! Kate says it's like a holiday on the ship. There's a band playing at nights, and dancing!'

'You make the most of it, then. I wouldn't be surprised if you don't come back.' She smiled at the girl's enthusiasm. 'Just think of all the wonderful sights to see, and meeting your new cousin, and an aunt and uncle you've never seen, and Kate married now.'

'Yes, but I'll come back with Mother. A month's long enough to be away.'

'She means from the McGrath Carting Company, of course,' Maeve said, exchanging a smiling glance with Bessie.

'I thought she did. I wonder why she's blushing? Anyhow, you take care of Elizabeth's granny, Isobel.' She looked at Maeve. 'Have you got used to the idea?'

'Being a granny? I still feel too young for it, but if I have to be a grandmother, my lovely, there's no one I'd rather have as a grandchild than this wee lamb.'

The girl's eyes were soft. The bloom on her was worth seeing, a fulfilled woman with a child and a man who adored her, never mind if . . . And what about Terence? Ah, don't think of that, she told herself.

9

Mr Murray-Hyslop was waiting at the Battery to greet
them when they had been cleared; mercifully, from Kate's
letters they knew what to expect, and the necessary
procedures seemed to have been expedited. But then,
wasn't Mr Murray-Hyslop a man of some importance in
the export business? She must really learn to call him
James.

And indeed, she would have known him anywhere, not
only from that meeting at the Broomielaw four years ago,
or if her memory had deserted her which it had not,
certainly by Kate's glowing description in her letters, a
tall handsome man with a humorous mouth and an air of
being at peace with the world. Yes, he would make a
good husband for Kate.

He was accompanied by a man as tall as he, more
burly, more florid in complexion, perhaps a bit more
dashing in his checked suit and the tilt of his pork-pie hat
which was whipped off as they came forward, to reveal
unmistakably red hair. She caught Isobel's arm. It
couldn't be, yes, it was . . .

'It's Terence! It's Terence, my brother! Oh, Isobel, it's
your uncle!' She ran the few steps and was in his arms,
weeping and exclaiming, 'Oh, Terence! My mind was
ready for Mr Murray-Hyslop, I mean, James, but not
you, oh, I would have known you anywhere . . . it was
the tilt of your hat!'

'My little sister, Maeve!' He released her to look at her,
and she saw the tears running down his cheeks as they
were down hers. He produced a handkerchief and unas-

hamedly wiped his eyes, and she did the same, never taking their glance from each other, both weeping and laughing at the same time.

'Kate had warned me . . .' he shook his head, mopping and smiling, 'but I never expected this . . . beauty!'

'Away with you,' she said, 'I'm still that hobbledehoy of a sister who rode bareback if she got the chance, who looked up to her big brother, who cried her heart out when he went away . . .'

He sighed, shook his head. 'We'll tire the night out by the going over of it. Now, here's someone else waiting his turn. Did you ever see such a dream of delight, James, as this?'

She turned and saw that Isobel had been welcomed by James who was standing smilingly waiting to greet her. He took her hand but she put her arms round him. 'You're my dear son. We'll have none of this formality. And I must learn to call you James. It's too ridiculous, but I still think of you as Mr Murray-Hyslop!'

'Kate had a little trouble, too, at the beginning,' he said, 'but she soon learned.' His eyes were twinkling. There were no tears in his, but then, why should there be? She had only met him once, never been parted from him for . . .

'How many years is it, Terence?' She turned back to her brother who was standing with his arm round a smiling, blushing Isobel.

'Just a minute.' He stroked his whiskers. 'I'm still getting my breath back from meeting this beauty, standing here as neat as ninepence. Is it the Scottish air or something, James, that breeds such beauties?'

'I've got another sister at home,' Isobel said, laughing delightedly. She's loving it, Maeve thought, looking at the pretty, lively face. Already she's saying to herself, 'Oh, this is the life . . .'

331

'Don't!' Terence said holding up his hand in mock amazement. 'Don't tell me there's another one. I couldn't stand the strain. And in answer to your question, Maeve, I came here in eighteen forty-eight. Thirty years ago. Who would have thought that this fellow would come to live near us, and what's more, that he would marry your lovely Kate.'

'Will you listen to the Irish blarney!' Maeve said, laughing at Isobel and James.

'Sure to God it's the truth I'm saying. Wait till my wife and daughter clap eyes on you both. Maria is all of a dither waiting to greet you, not to mention my dear Caroline who's been choosing dresses for the last week in case she won't be smart enough for you. She's going to have a hard time. It's never a Scottish village you're from, it's Paris and nowhere else.'

'This is too heavy a brew altogether. You'll turn Isobel's head.' Privately she thought Isobel looked enchanting in her faye. Maevy had said the fitted back was like the skeleton of a fish and the flounces like little waves. And her own costume, with its asymmetrical row of buttons and the skirt lifted over a striped silk petticoat, did her justice at least. Kieran had said more than that when she had tried it on for his benefit.

'The choosing of dresses, and the baking and the cooking and the refurbishing that has gone on for the last month!' James said. 'I've never known so many feminine consultations as have taken place. Terence and I have had to take a back seat. And the discussions about whose house you will go to first, and the programmes planned, and the . . . and the . . .' He pretended to wipe his brow, laughing.

'I'm dying to meet everybody,' Isobel said, 'just dying . . .'

'Then we'd better not keep them waiting a minute

more,' Terence gave his arm to Maeve, 'or they'll be setting off themselves to hurry us on. You escort Isobel, James.'

'Can you really believe this, Terence,' she said to him as they walked to the carriage.

He shook his head. 'It's like one of those stories old Mairi used to tell us when we were sitting round the kitchen table. I had a rush of Ireland to my head, sure enough, when I saw you and Isobel standing there.'

'Did you really know me right away?'

'Indeed I did. Your red hair, and your carriage. Like Father's. Poor Father . . . yes, I saw my little sister right away inside the finery.' He said softly, 'I saw Ireland.'

She nodded. 'That's what brought those silly tears to my eyes. You were my childhood, Woodlea, Father and Mother, our youth.' She felt her throat thickening, cleared it. There would be plenty of time to talk later. 'Do we stay with you or Kate?'

'Kate it is to begin with. And when she can spare you, we want you at Springhill. Caroline is intent on giving a big party for Isobel's birthday. But long before, you and I will get into a corner the two of us and talk about Ireland till the cows come home.'

'Kieran longs to be back across the sea. More than I do now. But now, for the first time, maybe, I understand his wish. He said to me once he longed to feel its softness on his cheek.' She spoke softly, and Terence repeated the words.

To feel its softness on his cheek. Ah, sure, he was a sensitive lad as I remember him, sensitive hands. Your Kieran has hit the nail on the head there. Now, here we are, and in no time we'll be at our wonderful Railway Station and then we'll be boarding the train for Wanapeake.'

Isobel chatted to her uncle on the journey as if she had

known him all her life, and as if she had quite forgotten John Craigie, Maeve thought, watching her glowing face. And she herself felt a quiet happiness as she got to know her new son-in-law. No worries here, thank goodness, a mature man but no stuffed shirt. 'I'm glad I'm able to thank you personally at last,' he said with his wry smile, 'for giving me Kate.'

Kate gave them a rapturous welcome when the carriage deposited them at the steps of Wolf House. She was standing at the top with her two stepsons, but when Isobel and Maeve were being helped out she ran down and threw herself into her mother's arms.

'Oh, Mother, I thought you were never coming. I've been at the window for ages! I was sure the train had fallen into the Hudson! Oh, how beautiful you look, and Isobel!' She disengaged herself and threw her arms round her sister. 'But I didn't realize you'd become the beauty of the family, Isobel. Oh, James, don't they both look ravishing, oh, James, my mother, and my sister, here in America at last!'

'I should let them get further than the foot of the steps, my dearest, if I were you,' he said, 'they've had a long and tiring journey.'

'Yes, oh, yes, and Uncle Terence, I'm forgetting you, come in, come in. Fancy you seeing your own sister after all these years!' She kept an arm round Maeve and Isobel as they went up the steps together, the men following. George and Ernest stood shyly at the top in their best suits and stiff white collars, hair slicked on their soap-shining brows. Maeve thought they looked healthy boys. Ernest was the one who would demand more attention. It was often the case with the youngest. 'This is your grandmother and your aunt, George, Ernest.' Kate stopped in front of them. 'Come all the way from Scotland to see you.'

The boys each held out a hand, bowing politely, but Maeve bent and kissed them. 'I promise I won't do that every time,' she said to them, smiling, 'but it's a special occasion.'

'Did you enjoy being on the ship?' George said. 'Papa says it is a most interesting experience.'

'It was,' Maeve said. 'I was astonished at its size and its accoutrements. And you should have seen how spick and span the crew kept it.'

'Were you sick?' Ernest asked.

'No, we weren't sick at all,' Isobel answered. 'We were very lucky. It was as smooth as a mill-pond. The only noise was from the ship's engines, especially in the bow.'

'Move aside, boys,' James said from the rear. 'I'm sure your grandmother and your aunt will give you an hour-by-hour description later.'

It was a gracious house, Maeve thought, differently furnished from Braidholme, the pieces heavier and bulkier-looking, but it was beautifully warm and welcoming, with a huge fire in the hall and pipes on the walls, which were warm to the touch.

The servants were lined up to welcome them, and she could see Kate's attention to detail in their spruce uniforms, their starched aprons and long starched streamers from their caps. Much grander altogether than Braidholme, she decided, which still retained its farmlike quality, but then the young were always further ahead of their elders. When Catherine got her house in Glasgow, she would set the pace, no doubt.

'I'm only sorry my daughters aren't here to greet you as well,' James said when he had led them into the warm drawing-room with its plump sofas and profusion of

335

hanging plants, as if there wasn't enough foliage outside. 'They're in Paris for a year, presumably studying under the care of the redoubtable Miss Arbuthnot. I rather fancy they'll manage to have some pleasure as well.'

'Oh, how lucky they are,' Isobel said, 'I've never been abroad. I mean . . . *that* kind of abroad.' She laughed at James like a woman, Maeve thought, not a niece.

'Don't forget,' he smiled at her, 'you've just accomplished a much longer journey than Victoria and Emily. Why do we think of only Europe as "abroad"? It is they who will be envious of you.'

'Then they must come and see us in Scotland,' Maeve said, 'whenever they can be spared.'

'I can see the Anchor Shipping Line is going to go from strength to strength when the McGraths and the Murray-Hyslops start going backwards and forwards across the Atlantic.' James turned laughingly to Terence.

'Yes, and once we get there it's only a hop, skip and a jump to the Green Isle, sure enough.'

'Terence's brogue is becoming thicker by the minute since his sister arrived. Have you noticed?' James looked round the company with great good humour. And to George and Ernest, 'Are you anxious to travel, boys?'

'Yes, sir,' George said. 'One of my chums has been to Canada and says he's seen a grizzly bear. I ought to brag a bit about Scotland.'

'I ought to brag a bit, too.' Ernest looked admiringly at his brother. 'What kind of wild animals are there in Scotland?' He turned to his aunt.

Isobel considered. 'Rabbits, hares, rats by the river, that's about all. And my brothers used to keep ferrets. But in the Highlands of Scotland you can see deer with great antlers. I've only seen them on pictures, standing on a crag.'

One of the maids came in with a loaded tea-tray

followed by another carrying a mahogany cakestand.

'You can see Kate is determined you shan't die of hunger while you're here,' James said. 'Cook's face has been permanently red bending down to the oven for yet another batch of something or other.'

'It's a lovely spread,' said Maeve. She looked round them all. 'Oh, I'm so happy to be here!'

She and Isobel quickly settled down at Wolf House. Kate insisted they should rest quietly there for a day or two to get their strength back, but Maeve suspected it was so that she could have them to herself before the 'jollifications' began at Springhill.

'It's a partying house,' Kate explained to them. 'You'll find out when you go there. Aunt Caroline loves social gatherings, and while Maria isn't fond of the same kind of life, she's such an outgoing, jolly person that she approves of keeping open house. Her mother's been planning to show you off to the whole of the Hudson Valley from the first minute she heard you were coming.'

So, in the late afternoon, when they had walked outside in the fresh spring air to admire the grounds, or driven into the small town to get the lie of the land so that Maeve could report to Kieran, the three of them would gather round the fire with the tea-tray in front of them and talk and talk.

Kate was avid for descriptions of Glasgow and Sholton, wanting to know if they had changed. She was keen to hear, also, about the firm and their new venture in the city, about Braidholme and, of course, about the new baby.

'I can see now why you didn't want to come to my wedding, Mother,' she said, 'with the birth so imminent. Were you shocked at the baby arriving so soon?'

'No, not shocked. You could say, surprised. I left the

shock to the Sholton folks. Truth to tell, it didn't cause as big a commotion as I'd thought, or maybe I just didn't notice. That's the great advantage of being a business woman. You don't even hear the tittle tattle.'

'I got a few sideways looks when I went into the shops,' Isobel said.

'Did it affect you, Isobel?' Kate looked at her sister.

'No, not by that time. I made sure I'd come to terms with it before I sallied forth. What does it matter?' Her narrow, pretty face was calm. 'They were married, that's the main thing. John Craigie . . .' she hesitated and Maeve saw the slight blush, '. . . that's the new young minister who's taken the Reverend Murdoch's place – spoke to me about it. He's very broad-minded, isn't he, Mother?'

'A grand young man,' Maeve agreed.

'"Those who are without sin," he said, '"let them cast the first stone."' Isobel raised her chin.

'He sounds eminently sensible,' said Kate. And then, 'How did Terence react to it? I used to think he would marry Bessie Haddow.'

'He got drunk at the wedding to drown his sorrow.' Maeve saw the look that passed between the two sisters. They'll get together and talk when I'm not here, she thought.

'Bessie says Elizabeth Maeve's a little like me,' she said. 'Her hair looks fair, what there is of it, but it has a wee hint of red.'

'I'm glad you like being a granny,' Kate said, 'because there will be another one, God willing, in October.'

'Oh, Kate!' Maeve looked at her, her eyes filling. What are those new attacks of emotion in me, she thought, and me only forty-four? Again, as so often, she was aware of the swift passage of time. So much to be done, she thought, in one short life. 'That's grand news, but no shock with it.' She laughed. 'I thought a ready-made family wouldn't be enough for you. You've got plenty of room in your heart for some of your own as well.'

'That's what James thinks.' The radiant happiness in her daughter's face decided Maeve. There would be no going over any suspicions in connection with Bessie's baby. Expectant mothers had to be kept free from worry.

Kate's the success of my family, she thought, looking into the fire while the girls chatted together. Her loving nature has led her to happiness. She's uncomplicated, has always been. Maevy's and Isobel's futures are still unpredictable, and Patrick and Terence . . . God knows what will happen there. She felt a shadow fall on her and, despite the warm room a cold shiver made her straighten her back. This would be a resting time, to prepare her for what lay ahead.

10

Soon there was a visit to Springhill where they were to stay for a few days. They were welcomed effusively by Caroline. She was a pretty woman, Maeve thought at first sight, fair-skinned and inclined to plumpness, and quite unlike anyone she had ever met in Scotland. She had appealing feminine ways, and yet behind them she could sense some kind of uncertainty or even sadness in the pale blue eyes. 'I don't want to take you away from Kate,' she said, 'but you simply must let us see some of you on your short stay.'

'But it's a pleasure,' Maeve assured her. 'I've looked forward for years to meeting Terence's wife and daughter.'

'Then I hope you are not too disappointed, dear Maeve,' Caroline said archly, smoothing the ruffles at her throat with a bejewelled hand which trembled slightly.

'Go on, please, my darling,' Terence said, putting his arm round his wife, 'she does so like a compliment or two.'

'Then I think you are very lucky, Terence,' Maeve said. 'If you'd searched all Ireland you couldn't have found the likes of her and that's a fact.'

'What a charming sister you have,' Caroline laughed prettily. 'And I have another favour to ask of you, Maeve. Would you permit me to have Isobel's birthday celebration here? We'd adore to do it, and I want to spare Kate in her condition.'

'Oh, Aunt, you are so very kind!' Isobel clapped her hands. 'A party in this lovely house – not that Wolf House

340

isn't lovely, too – but this seems so well-suited for it with the river and everything . . .' She looked entranced, Maeve thought, not at all like the usual sharp Isobel. Was the worthy John Craigie having to take a back seat?

'Say you agree,' Caroline pleaded.

'It's very kind. Isn't that too much for you?'

'Too much?' Maria, who was listening, laughed. 'My dear Aunt, it will be meat and drink to Mama. She loves giving parties.'

'And she's very good at it.' Terence smiled fondly at his wife. His attitude was quite unlike that of Kieran, almost over-protective, and yet Caroline could not be called a pathetic figure in any way. She had a natural dignity underneath her girlish ways. Maeve remembered Kate saying she came from an old family in Virginia.

'I do flatter myself on that score,' Caroline said, fluttering her eyelashes. The affectation amused and touched Maeve.

'Well, what can I say but yes, and I thank you sincerely.'

'There, that's settled. Maria knows some of the most handsome and eligible young men in these parts, Isobel. I can assure you, you will be quite the belle of the ball.'

'A long way behind Maria,' Isobel said. 'Oh, life here is so different from Scotland!'

In those few days spent in that luxurious house on the banks of the Hudson, Maeve and her brother had many a talk in the evenings when he came home from business. It became a habit for them to stroll in the garden before dinner, taking the path which led down to the river.

'You have a beautiful place here, Terence,' she said on one of these occasions. She could see the lights beginning to twinkle in the houses on the other side and thought, one of these is my dear Kate's where she is very well placed with that excellent husband of hers and their own child on its way. It was a pleasant thought on this fine spring evening.

'Yes, my life has fallen into pleasant ways, I must admit. But I had to work hard for it. As *you* did, still do. I've read between the lines of your letters.'

'Oh, we don't live in such grand style as this, but I'm well content with Braidholme. Even if the business grows and prospers, I wouldn't change. Besides, the young ones need homes, too. Catherine particularly has high ideas.'

'You haven't had your sorrows to seek.' He put a hand on her arm. 'Neither have I. Some day I'll tell you . . .'

'I've always felt there's no good harping over what's been done,' she said, 'but our childhood, now that's a different thing. To step back into those long-ago days gives me the feeling . . .' she hesitated, groping for words, '. . . that time isn't a straight line leading to the grave.' She laughed. 'No, I'm not getting morbid – but that I can . . . walk about in my life, ease back and forth, so to speak.' She laughed again, 'Sure I shouldn't have run away before I got a proper education!'

'You've put into words what I feel, never fear. You've never regretted it? Running away with Kieran?'

'Never.' And then, since this was a time for truth, 'Well, once I got near to it.'

'Another man?' He was quick.

She nodded. 'But I was pulled up in time by circumstances, or Providence. No, it's the real past that interests me, Terence: Woodlea, our home. Isn't it strange that we both left it? I ran away because I fell in love with a groom and I knew they would never agree to us being married. What made you do it?'

'You were too young to be told.'

'I'm not now.'

'Well, I became restless. As I grew up I felt hedged in.

342

I had no proper job, was meant to be Father's understudy. There were constant rows – you must have heard them. And Mother . . . well, what can I say about her now, Maeve, except to feel sorrow; a discontented woman with no love in her heart. Maybe that's why you and I have so much.'

'And we wanted so much.' The grass was wet under her feet now. She felt the dampness of her skirts, the moisture creeping through the soles of her evening slippers. But what did it matter? To be with her own brother, to be walking beside this great American river sliding blackly past them, but at the same time to be with him in far-off Ireland, that was worth a soaking.

'Then there was a real blow-up.' Terence's voice had grown quieter. 'Nellie – you'll remember Nellie, one of the servants – came to me weeping one day and said she was in the family way.' Maeve caught her breath.

'I didn't know . . .'

'Oh, it wasn't me, though I was no saint.' He caught her look. 'It was our father.'

'Father!' She was surprised how the news shook her after so long. 'I knew about her, of course, thought he was heartless bundling her off, even taxed Mother with it. But Father . . .' So many things fitted into place – remarks in the kitchen, Mairi's reproving glances at the other servants: 'Will you mind that we have Miss Maeve here, if you please . . .' 'She thought it was a village lad.'

'He wanted her to think that. He tried to tell me the same thing, but I believed the girl. There had never been any gossip about her. And she gave me chapter and verse, said he . . . bothered her. Well, I challenged him about it during one of our rows and he laughed, said he'd shut her up with some money.' She heard his sigh. 'It's troubled me, Maeve – ' she knew he turned to her as he spoke – 'that I left home for such a sanctimonious reason as my

343

father getting a servant girl into trouble. But it wasn't that. It was a trigger. It gave me an excuse to have a rip-roaring row with him, tell him we couldn't live in the same house, and clear out. I'd wanted to go to America for a long time, I'd been on fire with the idea for years, but he was adamant. He wanted me in Woodlea, to trail at his heels like one of his dogs, to succeed him when he died. I can understand his feelings now, but couldn't at the time. You can't put an old head on young shoulders. I've often wondered about Nellie's child – well, it wouldn't be a child now, our half-sister or brother.'

'There never was one. I picked up the talk in the kitchen. She went to a back-street abortionist in Dublin. But I never heard any talk about Father in connection with it.'

'Maybe he paid her well to keep quiet, though where he got the money God only knows. Ah, well, that's a long step into the past, right enough. And yet there were sides to him I loved. He had a wry sense of humour at times, and when he started on horses and their ancestry, he fascinated me. He gave me a love of horses, for the look of them, the beauty of them, that I've still got and have passed on to my daughter. All his love went on horses when we could have done with some of it.'

'Now I see it was there, under all his odd ways, but he couldn't show it.'

'Well, we're lucky there with our partners.'

'Yes, indeed. I can see how fond you and Caroline are of each other.'

'Caroline is . . . special. She needs love more than most. She . . .' His wife's voice called to them from the lawn above them. 'Terence! The dew is heavy. What about Maeve's thin shoes? Come in now . . .'

She saw Terence's raised face in the dusk, the smile on

344

it. 'Coming!' He turned to Maeve. 'I told you she needs me.'

Sometimes, while Isobel was being introduced to the game of croquet by her aunt, Maeve would spend a pleasant hour or two riding with Maria on the mount which Terence had provided for her. Once they stopped on the crest of a hill to look down on the river. It always drew one's eyes.

'I love your leafy lanes,' she said, 'but this is better.' She swept her riding crop round the panorama of the wide expanse of water, backed by the low hills on the opposite side. 'There's something about a view that attracts me.'

'Because you're a free spirit, Aunt. I recognized it immediately I saw you. You're different from Mother. She's more . . . reserved.' It was a strange word to use in connection with Caroline, she thought. 'But she already loves Isobel. They get on so well playing croquet, talking about clothes. Croquet's too slow for me, and clothes for me have never been a topic of conversation. Although I like to look smart.' She looked smart enough, Maeve thought, in her well-cut habit and the straight back of her.

'It's a new world for Isobel and she's enjoying every minute of it.' She kept her eye on a small sailing-boat tacking across the river. 'She's had a more spartan life in Scotland. She works in our Sholton office every day, although we may close that and transfer it to Glasgow. Money is only now coming to us, Maria, and I've always felt women should understand business as well as men. She's got a good head on her. In the end she'll choose what's right for her.'

'You make me sound . . . useless. I should like to be involved with the affairs of . . . someone I . . . cared for.'

'So you shall when the need arrives. You're far from

345

useless. You've got spirit; you've had a good education. There will be a use for both, just you wait and see.'

'Oh, life is very pleasant here, I can't deny it. And Father likes me to be company for Mother when he's away so much.' She said brightly, 'Do you think any of those young men I'm introducing to Isobel will turn her head? I know one or two already who're madly in love with her. They'll be desolated when she goes away.'

'I wouldn't know. She's trying out her wings. It's all very exciting for her.'

'She says such quaint things to them in that soft Scottish voice of hers. One of her admirers, Jack Constantine, asked me the other day if I thought she was pulling his leg!' Maria laughed.

'She's always had a sharp tongue in her head, Isobel, a bit sanctimonious. We used to laugh, Kieran and I, and say she'd become a lady missionary! But maybe she'll be won over by all this . . .' She waved her hand. 'I know I am, and then I think of Kieran . . .' My love, she thought, how are you, so far away from me . . . ? 'Kate has suggested she should stay with her until the baby is born.'

'Is there anything at home waiting for her?'

'There's a young minister who pays her a great deal of attention, but maybe the temptation here will be too great for her. Kieran said it might well be a tussle between God and Mammon.'

'She's fortunate.' The girl looked sad. 'I've never met anyone who has appealed to my senses. Oh, they may ride well, or dance well, or sail well, but to be bowled over completely . . . sometimes I despair of myself.'

'Don't forget your intellect. That has to be employed, too. Isn't it strange that had you been a son you would have been helping your father in his business? You wouldn't have felt frustrated then. But I can tell you,

Maria, there will be someone for you at the right time. You have too much to offer.'

When Maeve said they must get back to Wolf House, Isobel pleaded to stay for a few more days. 'There's a party at the Constantine house, Mother, and Maria would like me to go.'

'And you want to?'

She bit her lip, shaking her head as if bemused. 'I don't feel it's real, somehow. It's like being in a play, a lovely play, with all kinds of lovely things happening, but I know the curtain will go down and in a kind of a way I'll be glad. I couldn't live like this all the time. It's not . . . earnest enough.'

Maeve smiled at the word. 'Earnest, she says. I hear that Mr Jack Constantine is earnest enough.'

'Too earnest.' Isobel smiled, too. 'I tell him that he's quaint. He says such funny things in that Yankee voice of his.'

Maeve laughed. 'You stay, my love, and have a good time. You're only . . .'

'. . . young once,' Isobel chimed in, giving her a hug. 'Don't worry, Mother,' she said, 'you know me.'

'Do I? No mother is ever sure.'

While Isobel was enjoying herself at Springhill, James seized the opportunity to show Maeve the countryside around Wolf House. He was proud of his adopted country, and took a great interest in its history, especially their great president, Lincoln, who had been assassinated just over a decade ago. He owed his greatness, James told her, to the reading of the Bible, Shakespeare, and especially Rabbie Burns. 'And what better combination?' he asked Maeve, his eyes twinkling.

Maeve had to admit she felt in her bones the youthfulness and the vitality of the country. There was none of the melancholy which one found in the beauty of Ireland, and that of Scotland had been largely desecrated, at least where they lived, by the pits and coal bings which had spoiled the contours and sullied its green fields and woods, leaving only pockets like Sholton and other small towns and villages.

She did not find oppressive, as Kate sometimes did, the heavy foliage of the woods surrounding them, but then, she reminded herself, she was seeing the countryside in its fresh springtime. She would like to come back again when those glorious forest trees were tinged with flame colours, and see the contrast they afforded with the broad sweep of the river. If there were any defects, the Hudson made up for everything, she told herself, greater and grander than the Clyde.

The two families took a trip on the *Mary Powell* to Kingston. It was a glorious blue and white day, and the ladies of the party were in summer muslins and large shady hats. Maeve wore the new Indian shawl Kate and James had given her.

'You can depend on George and Ernest to supply the running commentary,' James said when they were all settled in comfortable deck chairs. 'But I know what will be uppermost in their minds . . .'

'General George Custer,' Maria said mischievously.

'Oh, the enactments we've seen in the nursery!' Kate laughed.

'Mama,' George said, 'don't spoil it, please. You see,' he turned to Maeve, 'we're going to sail past the place where he was buried! He was a wonderful general, and two years ago there was this grand battle called the Battle of Little Bighorn, against the Sioux Indians . . .'

'They called him Long Hair,' Ernest put in.

George waved aside his brother's contribution. 'And

the chief was called Chief Sitting Bull.' He took a deep breath.

'He was also known as the Hunkpapa Medicine Man,' Isobel said.

'Who told you that?' George looked aggrieved.

'I can read as well as you, cousin George. I found a book in your papa's library . . . probably the one you've been reading!'

The boy took another deep breath. 'Well, I'll begin at the beginning. There were these three warrior chiefs called Gall, Crow King and Crazy Horse. Actually the Hunkpapa Medicine Man,' he looked at Isobel, 'wasn't a fighting chief. And Custer's Indian scouts warned . . .'

'Mitcher Bouyer and Bloody Knife,' Isobel said, her face straight. Maeve noticed the twitching mouth.

'Oh, Isobel,' Kate said, 'you're spoiling George's story.'

'She's only filling in the finer details, my love.' Maeve saw the mischievous glance that passed between James and Isobel.

'*Warned* him,' George went on, looking sorely tried, 'that the Indian camp was too large for him to tackle, but he pooh-poohed them.'

'This is where it gets really bloodthirsty,' his father said. George nodded.

'When he came in sight of the huge encampment, Custer sent his regimental trumpeter back to one of his captains with a message. "Benteen . . . come on . . . big village . . . be quick . . . bring packs." ' George looked around his audience, pleased with the attention he was receiving, then said to Maeve, 'And, do you know, Grandma, the trumpeter was the last survivor to see General George Custer alive.'

'That was sad, George, but on the other hand the Sioux Indians were there first, long before the white men. It doesn't seem fair that they should try to dispossess them.

The same thing happened in Ireland.' She looked across at Terence. 'Kieran's father thinks he should have been the owner of Woodlea.'

George looked bewildered. 'But he was the bravest man who ever lived, and even the Indians thought that! And when the battle was over and all the white men had been killed, the chiefs gave the order to look for the long-haired one amongst the dead . . .'

'To scalp him?' Isobel said.

'Oh, Isobel . . .' There was a chorus from the others.

'No, not to scalp him.' George looked down his nose at her. 'They wanted to find him to honour him. It's just *rubbish* what you said!'

'George,' James said peaceably, 'Isobel's only teasing you.'

'And she isn't American.' Maeve leant forward and patted the boy's hand. 'That makes a world of difference. But we've all got heroes, like General George Custer and Lord Nelson, whom you know, and . . . David Livingstone, the great explorer. He actually came from near Sholton!'

'Did he?' George was appeased.

'Did they ever find Custer?' Isobel asked.

'No.' George looked triumphant. 'Do you know why?'

Isobel's face was a study. Again Maeve saw the look passing between her and James: Don't steal George's thunder . . . 'No,' she said sadly, shaking her head.

'Because . . . because, although he was called Long Hair, he'd had it cut before starting on his last march!' He paused for effect. 'But later, *later*, he was found and eventually he was buried at the Military Academy. I'll show you when we pass it, Grandma.' He leaned back, well pleased.

'That's a really wonderful story,' Maeve said. She, like her naughty daughter, knew when to keep her tongue

350

quiet. There would be no more mention of the poor Indians being driven out of their own country. It was too perfect a day to spoil. 'Come and sit beside me, and you and Ernest try one of the sweets I bought at your Wanapeake store. They are as near to humbugs as I could get. Do you remember them?'

Perfect, she thought, as they sailed up the river with its changing scenery – sometimes wooded cliffs, sometimes fields with cattle grazing, the occasional sight of a mansion half-hidden amongst the trees. It would be even more perfect if Kieran were here to share it with her. Scotland in her mind seemed to hover in a grey mist. In that grey city, Glasgow, Kieran and the boys would be working hard as usual, and in Sholton Maevy would be holding the fort . . . as the Sioux Indians had done . . . and Bessie would be crooning over her baby. It will be good to be back with them all, she thought, but I'm not going to waste this precious time by moping. George gave a loud, satisfied suck beside her. 'Grandma?'

'Yes?'

'Did you know the *Mary Powell*'s a sidewheeler?'

'Is it? Where's this, George?'

'The Hudson Highlands. You'll have to keep looking. I'll tell you when we reach . . . it!' She nodded and smiled at the boy. He had taken the black and white sweet out of his mouth and was examining it. Terence and Patrick had done the same thing when they were children.

'It makes our burn at home seem like a trickle and its banks like toytown,' she said. It was as if a giant's hand had been at work. No wonder the people living here had an extra zest, as if they were aware of being caught up in some great plan; no wonder the Old World, viewed from here, seemed tired.

'Look!' George had sprung to his feet. 'There it is! That's where General Custer is buried. Over there! That's

351

the Military Academy. It's called West Point. They brought his body there in this very same boat. Oh, isn't it exciting, Father?' They had all crowded to the rail.

There were exclamations, laughter, much talk, but eventually they settled down in their seats again as the *Mary Powell* sped along. George and Ernest were on either side of Maeve. George was at last quiet, Ernest close to her, drowsy. I am a grandmother, she thought, it's different, there's none of the anguish of motherhood. It's like coming into calmer waters, like this beautiful river which is flowing under me as I sit.

She drifted into a pleasant dream, half-formulated thoughts and images filtering through her mind; the varied landscape slid past, the light, fresh wind soothed her. After the burst of talk and laughter they had fallen into silence. On the edge of her vision she saw James' hand over Kate's, the tulle veil from her hat half-screening Isobel's fragile profile. She wanted to go on like this, to be her own person, divorced from reality, from caring for others, just for a time; not for ever, because Kieran was not with her . . . she thought of the *Mary Powell* as her life, cleaving its way, steadily . . .

There were movements around her. She opened her eyes and saw James on his feet. 'Poughkeepsie,' he was saying, smiling at her, holding out his hand. 'This is where we all get off to see Maria's school.'

Terence was gathering rugs together, helping Caroline, talking. 'They did well for Maria at Vassar. Taught her to have her own opinions. You should have sent your girls there, James.'

'Sometimes it's safer not to allow girls to have opinions.' He was lifting Kate's shawl from the deck chair, putting it round her shoulders, tenderly. 'Don't look at me like that, Maeve, I know what you're thinking.'

'Then you're a very clever man, but I'll tell you all the

same. I don't think it will make a scrap of difference where your girls are. If they have opinions they'll air them.'

'There speaks the new woman.'

'She's right,' Maria said. She linked arms with Maeve. 'Come with me and I'll show you my old *Alma Mater*.'

She enjoyed walking through the pleasant streets shaded with maple and acacia trees, exclaiming with Maria over remembered haunts. Isobel joined them. 'You look pensive,' Maeve said.

'Do I? I was just thinking . . . there never was any question of my going away to school. I wonder if I should have liked it.'

'You would. They like clever girls,' Maria said.

'I'm not clever. I've not had a good enough education to make me clever. It took my father all his time to keep us in food and clothes. There was no money to spare for education.'

'Schools have very little to do with it in the end,' Maeve said. She looked at her daughter. There was no envy of Maria in her eyes. 'This is education,' she wanted to say, 'to see the other side of the coin, the other side of the world.' But she knew better. 'Don't preach, Mother,' she'd be told. Coming from someone who might in the end marry a preacher, that amused her.

They made their way to the river-side where the boys and James had been busy spreading rugs and setting up chairs, and Caroline and Kate laying a tablecloth held down by a cornucopia of food which they'd brought in a great wicker basket.

The girls were chatting together. Maeve sat with Caroline and talked idly, her eyes held by the river. George and Ernest were on the bank, hoping to see the sturgeon leap. James had said they were as big as dolphins.

It's a day without tomorrow, she thought, and yet a day when my life is spread around me so that I have the prescience to see behind me and ahead, an all-round view of the good and the bad, with me in the calm centre and yet aware that I am living, in the fullest sense.

She said aloud, 'Today I am happy.' Smiling faces turned towards her. The two boys, as if it was a special moment, turned and waved. The image was caught in the sunlight for her to remember, for ever.

11

The great day arrived: Isobel's twenty-first birthday. Gradually its title had changed from party to dance, to ball, as the plans being made by Caroline revealed themselves in their true magnificence. They had all to go to Springhill the day before which would enable them to dress in comfort and thus avoid arriving windswept on the day of the great occasion.

Besides, Caroline wished Isobel and Maeve to give their approval to the final arrangements of the table and the floral decorations in all the public rooms. She was at pains, with true American hospitality, to make them feel that they were taking part in all the preparations.

Maria and Isobel shared a room so that they could help each other in their *toilettes*. Judging by the laughter which came from it, Maeve, who was next door, thought there were girlish confidences taking place as well as sartorial advice. They complemented each other beautifully, she thought – Maria so outgoing, Isobel less so, but with her own wicked sense of humour. It was a friendship that would last, and it had been well worth coming for that alone.

She was not ill-pleased with her own costume when she joined Caroline and Terence downstairs to await the guests. She had chosen a dress in an exclusive shop in Wanapeake recommended by Kate, saying that she had nothing grand enough with her and this was an occasion never to be repeated. The corsage was of bronze-coloured velvet, cut lower than she would have dared wear at home, the skirt of taffeta of the same colour, with a flounced train sweeping the floor. She had dressed her red hair high at the back in convoluted rolls and ringlets which she had practised the night before. Terence came forward and took her by the hands as she appeared in the drawing-room.

'What a sight for sore eyes! You look magnificent, Maeve!'

'It's the earrings that are doing it.' She moved her head, smiling, and the jade pendants swung and glittered. 'You were far too generous, Terence. It's not my birthday.'

'No, but it makes up for all the years I've been unable to give you anything really *dacent*.' He laughed, emphasizing his brogue. 'I like to see a fine woman with jewellery on her.'

'He makes a point of giving me a piece of jewellery each year,' Caroline said. 'He's the soul of generosity, my dear husband.'

'I can see that.' It was difficult to look at Caroline without blinking. She sparkled at throat, wrist and ears; even her elaborately dressed chignon had a glittering point or two. And surely such an abundance of curls and ringlets and rolls must be false, Maeve thought, secure in the knowledge that all hers was her own. 'And your dress is very beautiful, Caroline. So becoming.' Perhaps the deep blue of the Hudson would have been better than the baby-blue her sister-in-law had chosen, so intricately cut with flounces and waterfalls of lace that she bore the semblance of an elaborately-tied parcel.

'Because there is beauty inside it,' Terence said, and she felt ashamed of being critical. It's a Scottish trait I've acquired, she thought.

Kate, James and the two boys had joined them now, and the adoration in James' eyes as he looked at his wife was worth coming to America to see. She was radiant in lemon net, with a great sweep of flounces to the back which echoed the sweep of her hair with the dark ringlets falling to her white shoulders.

'It's high time the men were taken notice of,' Maeve said when the feminine compliments were over. 'Will you look at the elegant cut of James' frock coat, and those suits Ernest and George are wearing! They might have stepped out of *Harpers' Bazaar*.'

'Aren't they just splendid?' Kate said. 'I've three escorts tonight, if you please.'

'Splendid isn't the word,' Maeve smiled at the boys. 'You'll break every girl's heart in the room, the two of you.'

'It's only the supper we're here for,' Ernest said.

'Ernest lives up to his name,' James said amidst the laughter. 'I shall remind him in ten years when he's swooning with love-sickness what he said tonight.' He turned as he heard the girls' laughter. 'Here they come. Don't you think we should applaud?'

The wide staircase, of course, was made for a grand entry. Down they came, Maria, in white satin, a head taller than Isobel; Isobel in palest pink chiffon, a pearl, Maeve thought, gleaming as softly and delicately as the single string round her neck, which had been Terence's gift to her.

Caroline clapped her hands. 'You were right, James. We ought to applaud.' And to Isobel, 'My dear child, come closer till I see you. Did you ever see anything so fairy-like, Terence? A dream of delight! And that corset top! Well, only someone as slim as you could dare to wear that! Turn round and let me see the general effect.'

'You'll make me blush, Aunt,' Isobel said, turning for her benefit.

'It will only tinge the general pearliness – ' James struck a pose, arm raised – 'set off by this vision,' he bowed to Maria, '"clothed in white samite, mystic, wonderful . . ."'

Terence held up his hand. 'Stop! I can't compete!'

'Well, you could go into rhapsodies about the paying for these wonderful confections.'

'And worth every penny, twice over. Now, I think we should go into the hall and fortify ourselves against the onslaught. Do you remember when we used to have the hunt in for a stirrup cup at Woodlea, Maeve?'

'Indeed I do, although a habit was a lot easier to get into than this.' As well as the dress she had bought a corset a size smaller than she usually wore. 'Come along, Ernest and George, perhaps we can have a peep at the table at the same time.'

Parties, Maeve remembered from those days back in Ireland, were like a balloon going up. One minute you were waiting apprehensively, and the next, it seemed, the background of music and noise seemed always to have existed. She met many grand people, louder voiced than in Scotland, where people had to be coaxed out of their shell, but all universally welcoming: she watched the young dancing and saw how fêted Isobel was; she danced with James, Terence and several of the young men who, she told herself, were only passing the time with her until either Isobel or Maria should be free.

They were so self-assured, so full of life, so different from Patrick and Terence. Once Terence had been like them in his gaiety, singing with his father in the evenings as they washed in the scullery, racing about the village with his young friends, playing in Tweedie's barn. In the midst of all the music and dancing she had a sudden acute attack of homesickness, and then, as if Terence had guessed, he was at her side. 'I saw you looking pensive, Maeve. Is it too much for you?'

'No, no. It's all grand and beautiful, and I can't thank

you enough. I was only wishing for a second that Kieran could be here to enjoy it with me.'

'Ah, I can understand that. You miss him, don't you?'

'You know how you'd be if you were separated from Caroline.'

'That's true. I should have crossed to see you long ago, but she has a terrible fear of the sea. She's a little girl at heart, my Caroline. I have to guard her. Not like you . . .' he looked away, but not before Maeve had seen the sadness in his eyes. 'She doesn't like me to discuss her . . . weaknesses, as she calls them.'

'Nor should you. There are private things in every marriage, not meant for outsiders.' She thought of the times when she had comforted Kieran after the pit accident, even bolstered him, and earlier than that, his understanding when, after John's death she had turned away from him when he had offered his love. And how she had gone looking for it elsewhere . . . 'It's strange,' she said, 'how everyone has to shape their own destiny, but even the strongest of us need some help at times. I expect Caroline has given you that when you needed it.'

'Yes, by *her* need . . . sure and isn't that an Irish-like thing to say.' He gave his jovial laugh.

'You're Irish through and through.' She looked at him fondly. 'Your heart's still there.'

'And I'm not denying it. Isn't yours?'

'Some. But most is with Kieran and my family, wherever they happen to be, and maybe that's as dangerous as leaving it in Ireland.'

Caroline was at their side, fluttery, flushed, glittering like a Christmas tree. 'Terence, I've been looking all over for you. Supper is served.'

'Well, then, my dearest love, let us lead the way.' He offered an arm to each of them, rosy-faced, apparently without a care.

The food was as elaborate as the gowns of the women and as prettily coloured. Looking down the long table, Maeve thought of their meals long ago in the Row, the kale soup dished up from the pot swinging above the fire, the simplicity of everything they ate, like their lives. Food reflected one's style of living. That at Braidholme was much simpler than this table laden with silver platters of roast goose, sucking pig, pies of every kind, ice-puddings, towering gateaux, and the elaborate silver epergne of fruit in the centre, fruit such as she had never seen before.

Braidholme took the middle course, right for her. Catherine would be the one who would go in for the grand living when she got her mansion in Glasgow, and perhaps Isobel, if she made her life here. There was Jack Constantine . . . And Maevy? She would live simply. She had no aspirations except the wish to find out why she was here at all, a girl who questioned. She heard Terence's voice.

'And so I ask you to rise and drink a toast to my niece, Isobel, on her twenty-first birthday.'

'Isobel!' Everyone was on their feet, she heard the American voices with the different intonation, repeating the name, 'Isobel! Isobel!' She looked at her daughter, flushed, tremulous, and admired the way she raised her chin, smiling. You had to rise to the occasion.

'And now – ' it was Terence again – 'I'm going to ask my sister, Maeve, to reply as the mother of our birthday girl, as the representative of her family in far-off Scotland, because there is no one better fitted for the task. Maeve!' He raised his glass to her, and she got to her feet, her knees trembling. He should have warned her, the Irish double-dealer that he was

'Terence has sprung this on me,' she faltered, 'because he knew it was the only way to get me to my feet . . .' She looked round the table and saw the smiling faces wishing her nothing but goodwill. What was there to be afraid of? She took a deep breath. 'At our monthly meetings back home . . . I should say our family are haulage contractors . . . I usually take a back seat.' She smiled. 'Although I may have told Kieran, my husband, what to say before.' The roar of laughter surprised her, and she made an important discovery. If you can make them laugh they will take you to their hearts. 'But since he isn't here, I'll have to speak for him and say how much we appreciate all Terence, Caroline and Maria have done for us in giving Isobel this wonderful party.' There was loud clapping, and she made to sit down.

'No, Maeve, you're not getting off so easily!' Terence called from the end of the table. She saw Isobel beside him, her pale hair, her delicacy, her pale pink beauty, and the sudden rush of love she felt for her made her go on.

'I think Isobel's a fortunate girl to celebrate her twenty-first birthday under my brother's roof, and I know I'm speaking for her, too. Indeed, you've won her heart with your kindness, and whether she remains with her sister or goes back home with me, I know for her it has been the highlight of her life and something she'll never forget . . .'

That should have been the end of it, she knew, but suddenly it was easy, she was at ease, even liked the feeling of standing there, looking around the smiling faces raised to her. This is how men feel, she thought, confident, a feeling of power, of being in the forefront. Women can do it, but nobody ever asks them in Scotland. Here in a young country they're more willing to experiment, their women have pioneered with them, men recognized their value, not only in the usual tasks of running a home and rearing their children. The thoughts rushed through her mind as the words came to her.

'Our firm is small as yet compared with the mammoth

ones you have here and which James, my son-in-law, and Terence, my brother, are part of, but we're proud of it because it was our own idea born of necessity after a pit disaster and, Terence will understand this, born of a love of horses. In nine years we've seen it grow, and now we're in the process of setting up business in our neighbouring city, Glasgow. We all know that horses will become a thing of the past, perhaps in another ten years, but I have forward-looking sons, and perhaps they will come here, too, and see how you do things . . .'

She looked round the table. Would they think she was boasting, 'sprowsing', they called it back home? But no, the faces looked respectful. Praise them, something inside her said, they like to be praised. They're simple, kindly, in spite of their wealth.

'What an example you are to the world! The New World, we say in Scotland, the land of opportunity, first in everything; the Western Union Telegraph Company, and now, if you please, cables running under the Atlantic connecting us with you! James informs me you now have a telephone machine, but I must tell you,' she smiled, 'that although Mr Bell came to live here, he was born in Edinburgh, Scotland's capital!' There was an outburst of clapping, of laughter. Stop while it's good, the inner voice said.

'But in case all this praise goes to your heads, I'll sit down with my sincere thanks on behalf of Isobel and myself to all you good people . . .' There was a discreet knock at the door and she saw Mrs Schuyler, the house-keeper, enter and stand behind Terence's chair, taciturn – a good face for a housekeeper, she thought. '. . . and to my dear brother and sister-in-law, Caroline, my niece, my Kate, and James, her husband, not forgetting George and Ernest, their sons.' She finished hurriedly and sat down, felt James' hand on hers.

'Well done!' he whispered. 'You've set them by the ears.' She bowed her head at the admiration in his voice, at the applause all round her, raised it to see Mrs Schuyler whispering to Terence, his attentive face, and then he was on his feet, bowing to the table and going out of the room.

'Perhaps his mare has started to foal,' James said. 'That's the only thing that would drag him away.'

The music struck up again, people left the table, strolled about the hall, the young danced, Maeve was surrounded by the guests congratulating her. 'Mrs McGrath, you were wonderful! No wonder your business back home is such a success!' And one man, whose face was flushed, bent to her ear and whispered, 'Beauty as well as brains!'

Terence seemed to be gone a long time, and then she saw that he was back again, mingling with his guests. She heard his laugh ring out, but then was whirled out of hearing by a young man who said he would be honoured if she would dance with him. She felt the years slip away, and it was only when the guests were beginning to take their leave that she came up against Terence in the alcove made by the huge bay window.

'Has anything happened, Terence?' she asked. 'James thought Starlight might be foaling. I saw you go out . . .' He looked at her without answering and fear grew in her. 'It's something to do with me, isn't it? Oh, tell me if it is, please.'

He put his hand on her arm. 'It was a telegram addressed to me, Maeve, from Kieran. You must brace yourself.'

'Tell me.' The fear was in her throat now.

'They would send it to me so that I could break the news gently.'

'Tell me.' She heard her voice, faint, not like her own.

363

He took the telegram from his pocket and handed it to her. She read it, read it again to make sure. 'Bessie very ill. Come home.' She swayed and felt his arm strongly around her. She had never fainted in her life.

'Sit down, my dear. The shock . . .'

'No, I must get home.'

'Sit for a second.' She knew she was in the cushioned window-seat. 'There has been no time wasted. While I was out I made all the arrangements. A telegram has been sent booking a passage for you from New York tomorrow. You can leave early in the morning. I knew the captain of the ship, fortunately. It's all taken care of, as you would have wanted, and as quickly.'

'Thank you, Terence.' The full implication of the telegram hit her. Kieran would not have sent it needlessly, unless he thought . . . She put her hand to her mouth. Was she now going to scream, or burst into tears, spoil this lovely occasion so carefully planned, so much enjoyed until Mrs Schuyler had come into the room? But it had been spoiled for ever more for her. She would no longer remember it as Isobel's twenty-first birthday celebration, but as the day when they had got the telegram. 'Thank you, Terence,' she said again, controlling herself. 'You've done everything I would have done, only better.'

'Do you think Isobel will accompany you?'

'She must make up her mind. Oh, what can it be with Bessie? She was so well . . . and the baby, such a beautiful child. I should never have left them.' She took out her handkerchief. She must not weep.

'Now, that's foolish.' He patted her hand. 'Would you like me to fetch Isobel now and tell her?'

'No, let her finish the evening in happiness. I'll go up and start packing.'

'I'll ask Caroline . . .'

'No, please, I prefer to be alone. You go back to your guests. I'm all right now.'

She managed to walk past the few remaining groups of people, to smile, to accept further compliments about her speech. Pride goes before a fall, she thought, but this was far greater than any blow to her pride. It could well be a tragedy. Kieran would never have sent the telegram if she had not been needed back home urgently.

She was sitting at the window watching the occasional light from a freighter gleam on the dark river when she heard the rapid patter of feet. The last carriage had rolled down the drive. The door burst open and Isobel was on the floor beside her in a spread of silver-pink flounces, her anxious face raised to her.

'Mother, Uncle has just told me. Oh, what has happened to her, do you think? Are we leaving right away?'

'Tomorrow morning.' She took the girl in her arms. 'At least I am. There's no need for you to come. I'm sure it will be nothing. She's a strong girl, Bessie . . .' She heard her voice falter.

'You know that's not true. Father would never send a telegram for no reason. I'm coming with you. I couldn't bear to be separated from . . . knowing.'

She looked into the girl's upturned face. There was anxiety there, and regret, and why not? A wonderful life had been unfolding for her. But she knew better than to argue with Isobel. Her face was pale, her narrow lips firmly set together. Isobel had always known her own mind.

12

It was fortunate in a way that, unlike the outward crossing when the Atlantic had resembled the Pacific in its serenity, now, nearly a month later, the journey homeward was a buffeting nightmare with huge running seas lashing them most of the way.

It may have been because it was an older ship and their quarters were more cramped, or because their spirits were lowered by the thoughts of Bessie, but almost from the time they stepped aboard they were both unremittingly seasick and were confined to their cabin more dead than alive.

The good fortune lay in the fact that the peculiar effect of seasickness is the terrible concentration on self that afflicts the sufferer. Bessie disappeared from their minds, or very nearly. All they could do was minister to each other as far as possible and wish they were dead.

A whey-faced Isobel said to Maeve on the fifth day of the crossing, 'Did it ever happen, Mother, that visit to Kate and Uncle Terence? Those days in their lovely gardens, the croquet, the sail on the Hudson, and my twenty-first birthday dance? Was it all a dream?'

'It happened. It will come back to you later. But reality's facing us. All I ask at this moment is to be on my feet to face it when the time comes.'

'She may be better. It may be a terrible false alarm. You know Father. He's a worrier without you.'

'I'm counting on that, Isobel.' She did not say that the boys were not worriers, as a rule. Besides, it was not true where Bessie was concerned. They were both in love with her, always had been. Nor did she mention Maevy, the practical daughter who would never have allowed her mother to be brought back home unless there was good cause.

They were on the deck before the ship berthed at Greenock. It would be a longer journey for whoever was meeting them than to the Broomielaw. Perhaps Kieran would not manage to be there.

'I don't see your father, Isobel,' Maeve said, scanning the quay-side. 'Do you?'

'No.' Isobel had her hand above her eyes. Perversely, now that the ship had docked, the sun was shining with an early summer softness. 'Nor the boys, nor Maevy.'

'Oh, dear.' She tried to be light-hearted, to ward off the anxiety. 'What a sight I'll look! My clothes feel as if they're falling off me.'

'Mine, too. Aunt Caroline praised my "slim figure",' she mimicked her aunt's accent, 'she wouldn't recognize this scarecrow. Maria should have been with us. She's always talking about losing weight . . .' She was looking straight ahead as she spoke, not smiling. Now she stopped, pointed. 'There's Maevy! Away at the end beside the sheds, look, that one with the lifebelt hanging on it. No, it can't be her, there are two men . . .'

'It's your father!'

'And John Craigie!' Maeve looked at her daughter's pale face as she heard her voice lifting. 'Why would *he* come? Look, they've seen us! John's waving his hat. It's good of him to come, Mother, isn't it?'

'Yes, decent.' Their eyes avoided each other. 'Very decent. He must be anxious to see you.' That's what it is, she told herself fiercely, that's all it is.

But she knew it was more than that when she saw Kieran's face, ran into his arms. 'We came as soon as we could. Is she better? Oh, is she better, Kieran?' She stood

367

back to look at him, saw his pallor, how his eyes sought John Craigie as if for support. But it was not the young minister who answered. Maevy forestalled him.

'You've got to know right away, Mother. We buried Bessie yesterday . . . oh, don't, don't. Father, hold her . . . you couldn't have done anything for her. We knew when we sent . . .' Maevy's eyes went to Isobel who was already weeping on John Craigie's shoulder.

In her terrible grief Maeve could spare a thought for the girl standing alone. She herself had Kieran; Isobel was being comforted by John. He had eyes for no one but her.

'We're blocking the traffic,' she said harshly, disengaging herself, 'you lead the way, John. Kieran will see to the luggage.'

It had been too far to come by carriage to Greenock in one day, Kieran explained. They boarded a coastal steamer as different from an Ocean Greyhound as night from day, and sailed up the river to Glasgow, disembarked there and caught the first train to Sholton. Their luggage would be taken care of. After all, Maeve thought wearily, we're haulage contractors. She was surprised at the fatigue that possessed her, like a blanket dulling the keenness of her grief. At least it saved her from making a fool of herself before the other travellers, and Isobel seemed to be affected in the same way. She sat quietly beside John Craigie, her arm through his, her face ashen. Perhaps their systems had been depleted so much by the sickness that they were unable to react. Perhaps the news had only been a confirmation of their worst fears.

In the train she said to Maevy, 'You must tell me what happened. I have to know.'

'Yes, it's better. I'll whisper, Mother. You can tell Isobel later.'

'Yes.'

'We never thought . . . even when she was bad, that it was . . . *serious*. Or of trying to get you home. Father and I have reproached ourselves . . .'

'Don't ever do that.' She touched the girl's hand. 'Just tell me.'

'Well, she was fine after you left, just that wee cough that didn't leave her, and sometimes a runny nose. We laughed at that. I went every night as you asked me to, and once I stayed because Patrick had to be up in Glasgow for the signing of the documents for that place they're buying in the Gallowgate.'

'That's done, then?' Her interest in the business surfaced for a second.

'Yes, they've started on the renovations. Patrick will show you the plans. He worked night after night on them, but, oh, Mother, they were happy together . . .' Her voice broke. Perhaps the other people in the carriage helped to make her go on, speaking softly. 'The night I stayed I thought she was a bit flushed, but she said she was all right, just a slight headache. I asked her if I should get the doctor, but she said no, she would sleep it off. I wakened in the middle of the night with her moaning. I ran in, and oh, Mother, the difference in her was terrible! She said there was . . . a lot of, you know . . .' she spoke even more softly, glancing across the compartment at Isobel and John, '. . . dirty . . . you could smell it.' Maeve wondered at the way this young daughter of hers could say things like that, like a doctor, or a nurse. 'But the worst thing was the pain in her stomach. She was nearly mad with it. I wakened the wee lassie we'd got to do the rough work and sent her off for the doctor. Elizabeth Maeve was crying something terrible as if she knew there was something wrong . . .'

'Who's looking after her?' The shock of Bessie's death had made her forget about the baby.

'Mrs Robinson found a woman nearby who could feed her. She had a child still-born the week before. She's called McDonald. You'll remember her husband, Wally McDonald. He worked down the pit with Terence and Father.'

'Yes, a nice young fellow. Poor soul, losing her first-born. Is she willing to keep her for a time?'

'Yes. Dr Gray's arranged it, till we get her weaned on to cow's milk. She's as happy as Larry, the wee thing.' Maevy's eyes met her mother's. 'She's lucky. She doesn't know her mother's gone.'

'That's true enough. Let me hear the rest of it.'

'She got worse, fair demented with the fever and pain, yet she was fighting it, you could see that. The doctor said she had caught an infection somehow, and it got into the womb. "Septicaemia", he called it. I asked him if I should let you know somehow, but he said she was a healthy girl. He told me to bathe her to reduce the fever, and Mrs Robinson had to give her douches . . .' Maevy stopped.

'What is it?'

'I can say this to nobody but you, Mother. It's easy to try and blame someone else, but I think Dr Gray didn't realize the seriousness of it. He's an old man now. He doesn't notice things the same. And another thing. Mrs Robinson had a bad cold when she was nursing Bessie at the birth. I keep wondering if she could have passed it on to her somehow.'

'But that was in her nose and throat, Maevy.'

'Well, germs are the same wherever they are, and they could travel, couldn't they? Oh, I wish I knew more about it! I wish I could have . . .'

'Don't reproach yourself, nor anyone else for that

370

matter. It won't do any good. Besides, nobody could have done more than you did.'

'But I was doing nothing, just running back and forwards to Mrs McDonald with clean hippens and to see that wee Elizabeth was all right, and sitting with Bessie. She wandered awful in her talk, it got worse every day, and she said a lot of things she maybe wouldn't . . . sometimes she thought she was in Tweedie's barn. She would laugh out loud, you know the grand laugh she had, as if she was having a great tare . . . Oh, she was a lass for enjoying herself, wasn't she? And sometimes,' Maevy's voice dropped, 'she thought she was in the Sholton Woods. "The bluebells," she would say. The tears would roll down her face and she would be smiling . . .'

'The poor lass . . .'

'I was with her when the shivering started. Patrick was sitting in the parlour and I got him to come in while I ran for the doctor. Oh, Patrick's face, Mother . . . he was nearly as demented as Bessie, though he didn't rant or rave. It might have been better. The doctor came back with me. "Rigor", he called it. She went on and on, shaking. Patrick held her in his arms. He wouldn't budge. The doctor could hardly get near her. But there was nothing to be done. The poison had spread too far.' She turned to look at her mother. 'She died that night.'

It was a good thing about the other people. She wanted to raise her voice like an animal's at the unfairness of it. That lovely girl gone, Patrick bereft, and what were Terence's feelings. She had to sit rigidly upright until she managed to control herself. She put her hand on Maevy's. 'Patrick couldn't have done without you. That'll comfort him.' And you, she thought. It had been hard for a young girl.

Maevy shook her head. 'Nothing's going to comfort Patrick for a long time.' She looked away.

The carriage was waiting for them at Sholton Station, and when Kieran helped her into it she saw again the signs of strain on his face. He did not manage well without her. I shouldn't have left him to go gallivanting, she thought. They all need looking after. I'll have to get busy. Patrick will come to Braidholme for a while and get properly fed. And I'll get him back into the business. Work's the best thing for a broken heart.

In their bedroom when she went up to change, she went into Kieran's arms. 'What a time you've been through, my man, and without me.'

He kissed her. 'You're our strength, that's true enough, but don't waste your pity on me. It's Patrick.' He shook his head sadly. 'And there's Terence . . .'

Supper that night was a silent meal with only Maevy, Kieran and Maeve to toy with the food Susan had prepared for the travellers. 'Oh, we're that glad to see you back, Mrs McGrath,' she said, putting down the great steak and kidney pie that was her *tour de force*. 'You're sorely needed here.'

Patrick had called to greet them, but had refused to stay, saying he was working on plans for the new stables and that he would have to get back. The change in him was dreadful, Maeve thought; his youth had gone, and she knew that even to suggest his coming to Braidholme would be a mistake. He was distraught. No one could help him. All he wanted was to be alone.

When they were finishing the meal Terence and Catherine came in, Terence like a ghost, but exuding a false cheerfulness that was almost worse than Patrick's lack of pretence.

'Good to see you back safe, Mother, Isobel.' He went round the table, bending to kiss them in turn. 'No, don't get up. We're not waiting. Catherine insisted on coming to welcome you home. I said you'd be too tired but she'd have none of it.' He spoke as if there had been no telegram, no death. It took his wife to mention it.

'A sad homecoming for you, Mother.'

'Yes, Catherine.' She thought the girl looked softer. Maybe it had been that old curmudgeon of a father who had made her so difficult. Or was it relief that Bessie was gone? No, she must not think that.

'It was a terrible blow for us all. I can hardly believe it yet. She was getting on fine and then the life seemed to drain out of her . . .'

'I'm grieved I wasn't at the funeral.'

'We kept it small. Mr Craigie did the arranging and I helped Maevy with the tea here. We gave them a good one, nothing you would have been ashamed of. I boiled a big ham in my own kitchen. Susan did the pies. She's a better pastry hand than me.'

'You don't have to go into details,' Terence said, interrupting her. 'It's over, *over*.' He emphasized the last word almost wildly.

'Yes, it's over,' Maeve said. 'Let her rest in peace. Stop pacing about, Terence. You've just missed your brother. He couldn't wait.'

'We can't wait, either.' He ignored her remark. 'It was Catherine who thought we should look in tonight, just to see . . .'

'It was good of you both. Have a cup of tea at least, while you're here.'

'Well, we might . . . ?' Catherine looked at him.

'No, I told you . . . there's a lot to be done.' He got up from the arm of the sofa where he was sitting, as if he were on springs. 'A lot to be done. Well, you're home safe, the two of you, that's the main thing, the main thing . . .' He looked round vaguely. 'Well, we'll get on our way. Come on, Catherine. It's an early start for me tomorrow. I'm off to Glasgow first thing.'

'Your father tells me there's a meeting in the morning at the Sholton office.' Maeve looked at Kieran. 'You'll want us all?'

'It's a big agenda,' Kieran nodded, looking uncomfortable. He, more than anyone else, she thought, feels the tension in the room.

'You'll be expected to attend, Terence.' She spoke firmly. 'You can go to Glasgow after that.'

He nodded hurriedly. 'Well, I might look in, but I'll have to get off to Glasgow. I told you that . . . are you *coming*, Catherine? You look as if you're settling down for the night.' She had taken the empty seat beside Isobel and she got up quickly. 'You can have all the talk you want with Isobel another time.' He was at the door, holding it open. 'Good-night to you all,' he muttered as he went out. He could hardly be heard.

Maeve looked at her youngest daughter when the door closed.

'He was like that at the funeral,' Maevy said. 'Like a hen on a hot griddle, wouldn't sit down, didn't wait to eat. He makes you nervous just looking at him.'

'Did he speak to Patrick?'

'I never saw them together, but then Patrick didn't speak to anyone. He looked as if . . . he had been carved out of one of those big stones in the Sholtie. Oh, it was terrible, terrible! Catherine was a help, although she likes a pat on the back, but she did speak to the folks there, and she did act . . . normally.'

Maeve got up. 'We're all tired,' she said. 'Things will look better in the morning. I'll go to the office with your father but you have a lie in, Isobel.' The girl looked exhausted. Not for the first time the thought crossed her mind that she was a delicate lass, not as robust as the rest of her family.

'Oh, no, Mother.' She smiled wanly. 'I'll go, too. In a

way I'm glad to be back if it weren't for . . . Bessie.' She burst into tears and put her head down on the table. Maeve signalled to Maevy with her eyes and she got up and went to her sister.

'You've had a long day, Isobel,' she said, bending over the weeping girl, 'come away to your bed.' She helped her sister to rise, and they left the room together, Maevy's arm round her waist. Maeve watched them go, tears in her own eyes.

'She was a tower of strength, that Wee Rascal of ours.' Kieran got up. 'And you come away to your bed, too. You've had a long day.'

She said to him later, 'The only two this terrible business hasn't affected are Elizabeth Maeve . . . and Bessie's mother, no doubt.'

'Yes,' he said. She was lying in his arms and that was a grand comfort. 'I heard tell that when the Matron told her, she just laughed.'

13

The meeting next morning was brief. Patrick had his plans with him for the new stables and got up to explain them when called upon by Kieran. His face was gaunt, his eyes sunken. If I could only help him, Maeve thought, knowing herself helpless in the face of such grief.

'We're not going to stint on space at the Glasgow end. There's plenty of it. As far as horses are concerned I'm thinking in terms of stabling for anything up to three figures, not two. We have thirty here in Sholton, and that gave me something to work on. I'm planning for two hundred right away. Who knows what it will be by 1880.' He looked round the table. 'There will be more outlets than just railway and dock carting, as well as iron and steel works. There's general hiring and passenger transport – buses and trams drawn by horses. If we get in there we're made.'

'We'll have a busy enough time buying horses,' Kieran said, 'but I'm wondering where you're going to get the men to drive them?'

Patrick shrugged. 'The country folk are flocking into the town, Father – crofters, farm servants, unemployed miners, miners who've been forced to come above ground because of sickness. Oh, there's never any shortage of men. They're easier to come by than horses. We'll give them a fair wage, 24/- a week, and decent hours. That's been the firm's policy all along. We don't want them working from five in the morning till eight at night for a pittance.'

Tom Johnson was on his feet, precise as always. We'll

bring him into the firm this year, Maeve thought, otherwise we'll lose him. 'The office side will have to be gone into at this stage. We'll need at least three wages clerks in Glasgow if Patrick's plans come to pass, and a bookkeeper with an assistant to keep accounts for Bob. Isn't that the way of it?' He appealed to Bob Carter.

'That's right, but if you give us a free hand, Mr McGrath, we'll see to that side of things. It's just a bigger edition of the Sholton office, and maybe a bit more up-to-date.'

'I'd be glad if you'd take that over,' Kieran said. 'You know me. Horses are my department. The buying and the victualling of those will be a wholetime job.' He looked at Maeve and she nodded. 'We'll need stable lads, outlets for the dung, a good tack shop, a blacksmith of our own . . .'

He looked at Maeve again and she encouraged him, smiling. 'Mrs McGrath and I had a talk this morning.' She had wakened early, depressed, and, to take her mind off Bessie's death, she had turned to him and said, 'I'm going mad with thinking about Bessie. Tell me about the business . . .' 'We think I should confine myself strictly to that side of things. You can think up a title for me.'

'Livestock manager,' Bob Carter said, smiling.

'Aye, maybe. Patrick will take charge of the overall planning for the firm – he's the one with his eye on the future – with maybe a young apprentice to help with the drawing of the plans and such-like. Terence will be the man in the front office, the negotiator, the one on the lookout for business. His mother used to say he could charm the birds off the trees.'

Maeve looked at her eldest son. His whole body showed an inner agitation, he drummed with a pencil on the table, he shrugged, shook his head briefly as if irritated by his father's facetiousness. Kieran must have seen it, too, because he went on more quickly.

'All we need at this stage is a general division of duties so that we know where we are. Mrs McGrath is confident that it will fall into place . . .' He appealed to her boyishly, 'What was that thing you said this morning?'

She demurred. 'It was nothing. Just something that came into my mind, a saying. "Tall oaks from little acorns do grow".' She smiled. 'Goodness knows who said it.' She found herself on her feet. 'All I was saying to Kieran was that if the spirit to work and go forward is there, if we all work as a team, each sticking to what we know best, there will be no stopping us. It calls for sacrifices, putting personal worries aside, being single-minded.' She did not look at Terence or Patrick. 'When I was in America I saw all around me evidence of this in their prosperity. The spirit and the vitality is there, and we've got it, too, I'm sure of that, just as, like Patrick, I believe we're on the edge of great times. And even if Patrick's belief is right and we'll be scrapping horses before the turn of the century, we can be ready for that. We have the premises in the right place, we've got them at the right time . . .'

She stopped. 'Oh, I'm sorry. You can see what America has done to me. They're great talkers there. I must have caught the bug. Go on, Kieran . . .' She sat down. You caught it at Isobel's party, she told herself, don't let it go to your head.

She had a word with Patrick when the meeting broke up, putting her hand on his arm as he was gathering up his drawings. 'Patrick, I hate to think of you lonely in that house. Will you not come to Braidholme for a time? There's a fine bedroom you can have, and we wouldn't get in your way. But at least you'd get fed properly and looked after.'

'No, no.' He shook her hand away. 'I want to be . . .'

378

his head was lowered . . . 'where *she* was. I'm not fit company. I've got to do it this way.'

'I see that, but don't shut yourself off, son. Your family are there, ready and waiting to help you. You'd see them at Braidholme as they came out and in. Terence . . .' she was going to say he had been there last night, but he interrupted her, his head jerking up, his face surging dark red with anger.

'Don't mention his name to me! Just keep out of this, Mother. Keep out of it!'

She drew in a breath, feeling her heart ache with the rebuff. 'That's the second time you've told me off. Some day I'll learn.' She turned and left him. He did not try to stop her, and that was a greater rebuff.

She did not allow herself to brood because it was not in her nature. She went to the office in Sholton most days with Maevy and Isobel, and once a week she travelled to Glasgow with Kieran to see how the new place was progressing. She was impressed, especially by the fine façade with its large lettering above the gate, 'The McGrath Carting Company', and in smaller lettering underneath, 'General Hiring'. The stables going up were roomy, with a good yard for turning the horses and carts; the offices were bigger than she would have thought necessary, but Patrick said there had to be room for expansion everywhere.

'Expansion is the word he uses more than anything else,' she said to Kieran. 'He's obsessed. He works morning, noon and night, sometimes he sleeps here, I think. Terence is just the same. But they work even harder at avoiding each other.'

'I know. There's going to be trouble there. It's poisoning them. And there's no talking to them except about work.'

'Maybe they'll work it out of their systems, then.'

'I hope so.' He looked miserable. 'I can't understand their natures. You know me, Maeve, I'm not one to bottle up anything. Once when we were standing in this yard talking about drainage, I saw Patrick looking at Terence and there was . . .' he shook his head, '. . . I can hardly bring myself to say it, murder in his eyes.'

'Don't say anything like that,' she said. 'Don't even think it.' But she thought of it. The words came back to her at odd moments of the day, to torture her.

There were pleasant things, too, Elizabeth Maeve being one of them. The cottage at the gate, which Colonel Naismith had occupied, had been standing empty since his death last winter, and she offered it to Jess and Wally McDonald. 'Maybe if Wally gets enough of the pit, he'd like to take over the garden at Braidholme,' she said to Jess. 'Old Robert's getting past it with his arthritis, and there would always be work for you, as well.' With her talent for recognizing the virtues in people, she saw in the couple a devotion to duty which had no ambition except that of serving contentedly. Everybody could not be obsessed by the McGrath Carting Company, she told herself.

But her real reason for wishing them near her was to be able to see the baby every day. She was already a beautiful child, indeed she told herself, like a fond grandmother, which she was, that she had been beautiful from the first day. Her hair was turning red like her own, and she had the same intensely blue eyes. Maybe, she had to admit, she loved Elizabeth Maeve the more because everyone commented on how like her grandmother she was.

The McDonalds moved in willingly. Wally thought he would give the pit another year or two and then he would be glad to take on the Braidholme garden. Jess had been working at the Hall before she had lost her baby, and confided that she did not want to go back there.

'Mr Alastair's all right,' she said, 'I should say Lord, shouldn't I? Far kinder than the old laird ever was. But his wife's a terrible woman to work with, that pernickety you've no idea. Now that they've got a wee yin they've hired a children's nurse just like your Kate was but no' so bonny, and a special room for it done out with rabbits frolicking on the grass and such-like. Nigel, he's called, a daft-looking name for a wee lad, but I think she's English by her yammering tongue.'

With the baby at the end of the drive, Maeve felt comforted. You had to look for your own way out of grief. The summer-house had been completed, and when she could spare the time, she would fetch her grandchild from Jess and take her there to enjoy her on her own. She loved to sit sewing, or reading, with the child playing happily at her feet on a rug. She had her view, a vista of the Sholtie Burn purling beneath them and the still pool with the alders round it. Kieran had followed her advice and had steps cut in the banking to reach it. She had plans there, too.

'Maybe we'll stock it with trout,' she said to him, 'and I can buy you a rod like the gentry. We could have a seat down there, and I could bring down a picnic of your favourite things, a beef sandwich or two, a currant cake and some ginger ale, and we'd have a fine time together.'

'Aye, when the horses go,' he said. 'Or maybe we'll go back to Ireland. I still hanker for it.'

'We will,' she assured him, 'when I see those lads talking to each other again, when Isobel makes up her mind about John Craigie, when . . .'

'When the cows come home,' he said. His smile was sad.

14

It was the height of summer, a glorious Sunday when they ought to have gone to church, but the garden had proved too great an attraction. Each week was busier than the last. The constant travelling to Glasgow tired Kieran, and he relied on Sunday to let him indulge in a good lie-in. Looking at his exhausted face as she got up, Maeve had thought how much he needed it.

She had a leisurely breakfast on her own. The girls were still in bed, but Isobel would be going to church, and no doubt she would persuade Maevy to accompany her. 'Either Isobel's got an attack of religion or an attack of love,' Kieran had said when he watched her setting out twice every Sabbath on the long walk.

Maeve had stopped worrying about how this affected Maevy. She was thinner, quieter, calmer, looked older than her sixteen years. She seemed to have accepted John's frequent presence, his patent interest in Isobel, his love-lorn looks in her direction. Or maybe the talk she had had with her had borne fruit. Or, more likely, Bessie's death had made her realize that heartaches could be endured if not cured, and were not to be compared with the loss of someone young.

She went into the kitchen and helped Susan to get the leg of pork in the oven – she still liked to keep her hand in, as she called it. Then she went upstairs with a tray for Kieran. He was sitting up in bed, tousled, young-looking, as he always did in the morning, refreshed from sleep.

She put the tray on his knees and bent to kiss him. Her gown fell open and his hand went to her breasts. He was always more lusty, too, in the morning, she thought, smiling.

'My, my,' she said, 'you're sprightly this morning. Your lie-in has done you good.'

'Take this damned tray away and get back to bed, woman.'

'I'm up to dress, then I'm going to bring the baby to play in the garden. Oh, I'm looking forward to a long, lazy day.'

'You can spare half-an-hour of it, surely.' He whipped back the bedclothes. His nightshirt had ridden up over his knees and she felt lust rising in her, welcomed it.

'We should be at the kirk,' she said, slipping off her gown and lying down beside him.

'It'll feel all the better, knowing you should be listening to John Craigie's sermon.'

'Oh, you're a wicked man!' She gave herself up to his loving, thinking that she was in that as she was in the Company, backwards at coming forwards until she was needed.

'We're good at it,' she said later, resting on his shoulder, her heart pleasantly palpitating, her cheeks flushed.

'Long practice.' He laughed like a boy, fondling her body. He might be quick, but he never wanted her to leave him. He enjoyed her body, running his hands over it as if to remember the places where the joy had sprung from. Their love, she thought, was as strong as ever, if not so fierce.

'I wonder what Isobel will be like when she marries John, *if* she marries him,' she said. 'I can say this to you, and no one else. I put myself in her place, and I wonder if John will think she's a fragile wee thing, too fragile.'

'Thin bodies can be passionate,' he said, surprising her.

'Now where did you get that information?' she said,

caressing his body in the places where he was caressing hers.

'Stable boys and grooms pick up things. Do you think she'll marry him?'

'She's in love with him, there's no doubt about that. All Isobel has to do is persuade herself that he's right for her. She's having a tussle with herself. She knows if she had stayed on with Kate her life would have been changed. That was the watershed.'

'She could call it divine intervention. Was she reluctant to come back with you? I never asked.'

'If we hadn't got that terrible telegram . . .' she faltered, 'I can hardly bear to think of it even yet . . . I think she might have stayed on. It was all new to her and there's a feeling of vitality that's difficult to explain. You'll have to go there yourself. But when the news came she didn't hesitate. No, there's plenty of character in that slight frame. She'll work it out for herself and then we'll know if it's to be John Craigie or back to America.'

'You always knew it was me, didn't you, mavourneen?'

'Always,' she said, turning to him. Alastair Crawford had gone from her heart now. He had a wife and child. Someone had persuaded him into marriage at last, or he had persuaded himself it was time to settle down. I could meet him now and talk with him, she thought, pleasantly, coolly, like a friend. For a moment she toyed with going to church to test her theory – there was always the chance they would meet there – but Kieran's warm body won. 'I can spare another half-hour,' she said. 'I'm not in a great hurry.'

Maevy and Isobel had left for the kirk, Susan told her when she went down. 'Will the Reverend be coming back today, Mrs McGrath?' she asked.

'I'd set his place as usual. And one for Patrick. He's

promised me to come. I worry about that lad, Susan. I don't think he ever gets a decent meal except when he comes here.'

'Patrick has to work out his own salvation,' the woman said, 'like the rest of us.'

Maeve looked at her. She must be well over thirty now. She had worked in one of the big houses on the other side of the Glasgow road before she came to them to be near her ageing mother in Sholton. Not the marrying kind, she had told Kieran. What went on in her mind while she went about her duties, while she watched what was going on around her? 'You're happy with us, Susan?' she asked.

'Oh, I am that. If God is pleased to call me as a servant down below before he calls me to serve him up there, there's nowhere I'd rather be than with you.'

'But that's not to say you wouldn't rather be something else than a servant?'

'Aye, maybe, but I'll have to be like Patrick and accept what comes.' She bent to the oven to baste the joint. 'And like Maevy,' she said. Maeve, looking at the black-covered rump, thought that servants knew more of what went on than one realized.

She walked down the driveway towards the cottage at the gates, enjoying the sun on her bare head. Her hair was thick and she had never been a parasol carrier. Besides, she would have the baby in her arms walking back. Jess would offer to get out the perambulator, but she liked the feeling of the small body against hers. Especially this morning, she thought, when I have been loved. It was natural and right, somehow, as if she had given birth without pain. Only now, at forty-four, was she able to admit to herself that she had got rid of the ache for another child growing up at her knee. It had taken a long time.

Jess welcomed her. Wally had gone off with some of

the pit lads to race whippets, and she would slip round to visit her mother if Maeve was going to have the baby. 'Another six months and she'll be off the breast,' she said. 'Oh, I'll miss her! I think I would have gone off my head with wearying for my own bairn if it hadn't been for her. You saved my sanity, Mrs McGrath.'

'You saved her life and we couldn't have done without you. But don't worry. You'll have another one, I'm sure.'

'Sometimes I think I've started again.' Jess looked shy. 'When you're feeding you canna be sure.'

'So much the better. And in between times, because I know there isn't a lazy bone in your body, we'll be glad of extra help at the house. I'm up in Glasgow quite a bit.'

'My, you're a wonder, Mrs McGrath.' Jess was deftly changing the baby's napkin. 'Wally says it will come to the time when men will be doing jobs like this.' She looked up with a safety pin in her mouth, took it to push through the napkin, laughing and shaking her head. 'My Wally likes a joke.'

'Maybe he's nearer the truth than he thinks. My belief is that people should do what they're best fitted to do, man or woman. I've given my girls the chance of the business, too, but their hearts aren't in it like mine, though they work well enough. Maevy has other plans.'

'And maybe the Reverend has other plans for Isobel. There, now,' she spoke to the baby gurgling on her knee. 'You're all ready for your Granny.'

'What a place Sholton is for gossip! Come on, then, wee one.' She took Elizabeth in her arms. 'They know what's going to happen before the folks concerned know themselves.'

'That's village life. You'd have to live in the city to avoid that.'

'No, I'm content where I am. My, you keep her nice,

386

all in her Sunday best. You've been busy with the goffering iron, I see.'

'A bonny baby like her deserves the best. Are you sure you won't have the perambulator?' The baby carriage was a gift from Maeve, and Jess took great pride in it.

'No, it's good to have her near me. You know about that, Jess. I'll bring her back in time for her next feed.'

Peace lapped her in the summer-house, sitting inside with Kieran and the baby, to keep out of the sun. At midday it was fiercely at its zenith, but they were cool under cover with the door and windows open to let the soft breeze blow in. She imagined she heard the singing of the Sholtie below them.

'This minds me of the days when we just had Terence,' she said, looking across at Kieran in the basket chair. She thought his face in repose was sad, but he brightened as she spoke.

'You were no bonnier at seventeen than you are the day, sitting with the sun on your hair like that. And those eyes of yours! You're a picture, wife.' His eyes spoke of this morning, of their loving.

'I know what's softened you,' she said, smiling at him.

'Maybe so, but I'll remember this, you in that white dress, and the wee soul on your knee. Nothing happening, special just because it's ordinary and because there's you and me together.'

She saw Maevy coming across the lawn towards them. She walked slowly, but of course the heat was great, and it was a good mile and a half from the church.

'Come along, Maevy,' she called, 'I've got some home-made lemonade here for parched throats. Where's Isobel?'

'John asked her to stay back with him for a minute.'

'Did he?' She strove to be casual. 'Is he coming here for dinner?'

'I think so. He didn't say. Oh, you've got Elizabeth! Oh, you wee beauty!' She scooped up the baby in her arms. 'It's my turn. You've had her long enough.'

'You've a way with children, Maevy. Look at her looking up at you. She trusts you, that's why.'

'I'm a trustworthy soul, didn't you know? Hello, Father, you heathen! John asked me where you were. I think he wanted to have a word with you.'

'Well, he knows where to find me. And don't you try to make me feel bad about not worshipping. Your mother and I had better things to do.' He chuckled as he got up and poured out the lemonade. 'Put the child on her rug while you drink this, pet. You look fair wabbit with the heat.'

There could be no mistaking the joy in their faces when they came across the grass together. Isobel had her arm through John's, and her luminous look reminded Maeve of her appearance at her birthday dance. Her eyes were glowing, her skin was delicately pink under the parasol. Isobel liked parasols since she burned easily. But no shade could disguise the happiness in her face.

'Well,' Maeve said, getting up, 'you don't have to tell us. It's in your face, and that's without looking at that ring you're waving under our noses.'

'Mother . . .' Isobel went into Maeve's arms. 'Oh, I can't get this parasol down. You come under, too, Maevy, oh, I'm so happy!'

'I was hoping to see you this morning, Mr McGrath.' John was shaking hands with Kieran. 'I knew I had your blessing, but then, I thought, what if Isobel will have none of it?'

388

'But she did and you look the happiest pair in the world.'

Maevy left Isobel and went to John. 'I hope you will be very happy, the two of you,' she said.

'Thank you, Maevy.' He put his hands on her shoulders and kissed her cheek. 'And I hope you'll let me think of you as my sister from now on.'

'Of course.' She was calm. 'You'll be one of the family, won't he, Mother? You'll be able to give Patrick the news when he comes for dinner.'

'And I took the liberty of whispering to Terence and Catherine on their way out that I'd have something to tell them at Braidholme later.'

'Curiosity will bring them,' Kieran said, straight-faced, 'they'll not have the least idea what you meant.'

Maeve laughed, and the girls joined in. John looked sheepish. 'A man in love thinks it's his secret. It seems the whole of Sholton knows.'

'Yes, there will be a mighty sigh of relief when the news gets round. Come on, now, we need a bite of dinner after all this excitement. Patrick will be here any minute.'

Curiosity did bring Terence, or perhaps he had been forced to it by Catherine. Maeve watched them coming towards the summer-house where they were sitting again after dinner. The sun was as fierce as ever – as bad as America, she said – and she had sent Maevy back to Jess with the baby. They were sitting quietly, Isobel and John looking through a photograph album. Patrick had taken himself off on a walk to see the kitchen garden and old Robert's greenhouses.

Catherine looked pretty in a sprigged muslin dress, a magenta velvet ribbon at her waist and the same colour trimming her small hat. She was not beautiful, like Isobel, but she was smart, with a neat ankle . . . Kieran had often commented on that . . . a wife anyone would be proud of. Terence was the handsome one, but he had lost weight and he was paler than usual. He looked like someone who had been coerced into coming as he greeted them. And sounded like it.

'It was Catherine's idea,' he said ungraciously. 'She said we should come.'

'Isn't he the limit, Mother? As if we shouldn't! I had to drag him here.' She was the correct one, Maeve thought, kissing her, never puts a foot wrong in affairs of the family. She'll make a good society hostess if it ever comes to that.

'I'm glad you came. Isobel and John have news for you.'

'You're engaged!' Catherine turned to them. 'Am I right? What a lovely ring, Isobel! So small and dainty, like yourself.' She embraced her. 'Well, I'm not surprised, although Terence said he hadn't noticed anything. For goodness sake, Terence, kiss your sister or something. Am I permitted to kiss the bridegroom-to-be? It's special for me, John, you taking father's place. I can't think who I'd rather have in the manse than you and Isobel.' Yes, she did not let the family down. You could rely on Catherine.

Maeve persuaded them to wait for a cup of tea, and Terence reluctantly agreed. Patrick was still in the kitchen garden. She suspected it was to keep out of the way until he could reasonably say he was leaving. The sight of Isobel and John's happiness must have been a bitter reminder to him of Bessie.

They were sitting now in the shadow of the summer-house, but near enough to the steep bank so that they could look down on the Sholtie, and beyond it to the rolling fields and woods. Not exciting compared with the grand vistas on the Hudson, Maeve thought, but domestic, pastoral, her own. She had adopted this country because all she cared for was here, with the exception of Kate. Kieran still longed for Ireland. That was how it was.

When the rift between the boys had healed, she would go with him to Boyle. The autumn would be nice (the Fall, she remembered they called it in America), so that she would be back in time for news of Kate's baby.

Kate's letters were full of her happiness. Everything was fine, she felt well, Terence, Caroline and Maria were frequent visitors, the girls would be home in time for the arrival of their new little brother or sister, or both. 'I'm like the side of a house now, and James teases me and says it's sure to be twins. But whether it's he, she or they, Mother, you can be sure there will be a grand welcome on the mat.'

At least there was nothing to worry about with Kate, Maeve thought, not for the first time. It was necessary to count one's blessings. Isobel was settled, and Maevy would go into nursing when she was old enough. That was her destiny, and maybe where her happiness lay, too. Only the boys . . . she looked at Catherine talking to Isobel and John, at Terence discussing business with his father. It was their only common ground.

Now that we have a minister in the family, she thought, I wonder if I could ask him to speak to Terence and Patrick? It was like a revelation. He was a worthy young man, too worthy, maybe, for her liking, but he was young, like them, and ministers also knew passion. Why else did they want to marry and have children? She would draw John aside and open her heart to him, see if he could help . . .

Patrick came from the back of the summer-house and almost stumbled on the little party sitting round the table which Susan had set with the Sunday tea – scones, pancakes and seedcake, her usual offering.

'Sit down, Patrick.' She welcomed him. 'Here's a seat beside me. Terence and Catherine have looked in to give their congratulations to Isobel and John.' He nodded tersely, muttered something, Maeve only heard the word 'happy . . .', hesitated, then sat down.

'What's the verdict, Patrick?' She admired John at that moment, 'Have you decided to pull down old Robert's greenhouses and put up the very latest? You're the man for that, I hear.'

'No,' said Patrick.

Maeve poured him a cup of tea, then held out the plate of scones. He waved them away and her rare Irish anger rose at his rudeness. 'Please yourself,' she said sharply. She breathed deeply, and turned to Catherine. 'John was saying the greenhouses at the manse are falling to bits. He's not a gardener like your father, of course.' She smiled at the girl and she took the bait.

'Yes, my dear father made all kinds of experiments in his time. Rare bulbs were his special interest. He said it took his mind off the problems of running the parish. The lily family were his speciality, especially the sweet-scented ones. I believe I can remember one or two of the names . . .'

Terence rose. 'I think we'll have to be going.'

'I never heard the like,' Maeve said. 'You're in the middle of your tea. Sit down, Terence. Catherine's cup's half-full. Shall I warm it up for you, Catherine?'

'Just a spot. No more milk, thank you.'

'Maybe you could teach Isobel about those bulbs when she goes to the manse. It would be a nice pastime for her as well.'

'Yes. It's a ladylike occupation, although *my* interest lay in the pianoforte. I miss it.' She smiled bravely.

'Perhaps I'll take it up again when we go to Glasgow . . . when is the wedding to be, Isobel?'

Isobel laughed, blushed, looked at John. 'John doesn't believe in long engagements.'

'I was thinking of Christmas,' John said. He beamed round the table. Everyone was silent. No, I won't ask him for help with the boys, Maeve thought. How had he forgotten that Patrick and Bessie were married then?

'Not Christmas, John.' Isobel's voice was low. *She* had remembered.

'Christmas, is it?' Patrick said loudly, looking up. 'Yes, I can recommend Christmas. It suited *us* fine!'

'Patrick . . .' Maeve said under her breath.

'Mother doesn't like me to make remarks like that,' Patrick said. He gave a short laugh. Maeve looked at Kieran across the table. Why didn't he speak? Was it that he was still slightly over-awed at having a minister for a prospective son-in-law?

'You *could* have made it earlier.' Terence's voice dropped between them like a stone in a well.

'What's that?' Patrick's head went up. 'What's that, eh?'

'I said you could have made it earlier.' He leant across the table towards his brother. 'She was in that miserable place in Glasgow looking after herself when she should have been taken care of . . .'

'I shouldn't like to be in Glasgow on a day like this,' Catherine said, fanning herself nervously with her hand. 'Would you, John? When we go to live there I'll make sure we have a fine big garden with a summer-house like this. Kelvinside would be ideal . . .'

'*How* could I have made it earlier?' Patrick said, ignoring her, 'when I didn't *know* earlier. Answer me that, will you? Answer me that!'

'You're a damned liar!' Terence was on his feet, pointing his finger.

Patrick jumped up, too, and, pushing past his father who tried to block him, met Terence face to face at the other side of the table. 'Say that again!' He grabbed Terence by the lapels. Kieran was beside them immediately.

'What is this?' He tried to pull them apart. 'I've never seen anything like it, shaming your mother and me before the minister! Bessie's dead, poor soul. Let her rest in peace.'

'We have all to accept death when it comes,' John murmured miserably.

'Accept! Accept!' Patrick was shaking the struggling Terence whose head went back and forwards. 'That's all I hear! I would have married her long before if I'd known. Looked after her! Taken care of her! She got run down working on in that shop when she should have been resting . . .' He was half-weeping. 'Oh, I realize that now.' He thrust his face even closer to Terence's as he shook him. 'Do you know what you did? You killed my wife!'

Somehow Terence had freed himself, and they were at each other, fighting, punching, falling to the ground, rolling there while they fought. Isobel and Maevy had their arms round one another, whimpering, Maeve stood up, but could not make herself move as she watched. Patrick had Terence by the throat now, and was shaking him like a rat. John and Kieran were trying to separate them. The scene seemed like a nightmare, then it was suddenly real, galvanizing her into speech. 'For God's sake!' she shouted. 'Separate them, Kieran, John!'

'You killed her!' Patrick's voice drowned hers. 'Killed her, you bastard. You're to blame!'

They were on their feet again, facing each other. She

saw Terence's face blooded, twisted with pain and rage, unrecognizable. 'You can't bear it, can you? It sticks in your craw that I was the first, that the child is mine! Well, if it's any consolation to you, brother, I can't bear it either that she's gone . . . gone . . .'

They were at each other again, pummelling, grappling, swearing. Maeve felt sick. This madness could not go on. She pushed back her chair and ran towards them. Kieran and John were still trying vainly to separate them, dancing around like referees, she thought, and she saw a glancing blow from Terence's fist land on John's face, making him rear back. She took Kieran by the arm. He was shaking, his face was deathly white.

'You'll only get hurt.' It was terrible for him, a father, to see his sons like this. She braced herself. 'Terence! Patrick!' She did not shout. 'That's enough.'

Patrick dragged himself free and stood panting, and she thought, thank God, it's over, but at that moment she saw him stiffen as Terence sprang at him, fists clenched. The blow swung wildly past his ear, Terence swayed with the misplaced force of it, tottered backwards a few steps to the edge of the banking. She rushed forward but it was too late. His arms flung out, he rolled out of sight.

'What are you staring at?' she shrieked at Patrick. 'Go and get him!' He turned and looked at her as if he was not hearing, one eye partly closed, his face covered with blood, either his own or Terence's. 'Go and get him! By God, I've lost one son in the Sholtie, I'm not having two!' He went down the steep slope like a stag, slipping and sliding; she watched for a second, then she and Kieran hurried down the steps that they had had cut out of the bank. She knew the girls were behind her. She could hear John's comforting words to Isobel, 'It's all right, my darling, it's all right . . .' She met Kieran's eyes and was again alarmed at his appearance. He was shivering as if with cold, as if it was winter instead of a balmy summer Sunday.

Patrick had Terence on the bank when they got down and was bending over him. She pushed him aside and knelt down.

'Sit up, Terence,' she said sharply, 'and get rid of that water in your lungs!' He sat up meekly, and the movement made him retch. She thumped him on the back, getting rid of some of her anger and fear in the process. He had never liked water. Patrick had been the swimmer, fortunately. He stood dripping, silent, his chest heaving. She looked up at him, including him in her anger. 'You've given everybody the fright of their lives. He could have drowned in that pool. I'm so ashamed of you I don't know where to look, and on Isobel's engagement day, too!' The others had joined them, were standing awkwardly, silently. She turned to John. 'You'll be thinking it's a fine family you're marrying into, fighting on a Sunday forbye.'

'I know all about families,' he said, and he went up in her estimation. 'You come with me, lads. You'll have to get out of those wet clothes. Can you supply dry ones, Mrs McGrath?'

'Yes, ask Susan. We've been gathering Kieran's old ones for Catherine to take to the kirk.' She looked at the girl. Her face was paperwhite. The biggest shock had been hers.

'Come back to the house with me, Catherine.' She put her hand on her arm but she drew away.

'No, thanks. I'm going home.' Her face was closed against her.

'You go with her, then,' she said to Maevy and Isobel. 'And take good care of her.' They nodded. They were not stupid. At least the truth was out at last.

She made Kieran sit down for a minute or two, alarmed at his appearance. 'Let them get back to the house first.

There's no hurry.' He nodded but did not speak, and her mind went back to the time when he had been horse-whipped by her father. No wonder he hated violence, had hated to punish the boys when they were young. She said to him when they were walking back to the house, 'Don't take it to heart so much.'

'It blew up so quickly.' His voice trembled. 'I couldn't believe it. Like a boil bursting.'

'That's just what it was. Maybe it's best. It'll clear the poison.'

He shook his head. 'I don't think so. Only time will do that, if ever.' She looked at him. Was he remembering, too? She wished his mouth would not tremble like that. He was a different man from the one who had been in bed with her this morning – was it only this morning? – so sure, so confident in his love. Love was everything to Kieran. This fight had been an offence against his love of his sons.

'Tell me,' she put her arm through his, 'tell your old wife . . .' She wanted to make him smile.

'I was humiliated . . .'

'Because of John? Ah, don't let anything like that worry you. He's in the family now. He has to take the rough with the smooth.'

'No, no, it's not that. He had a difficult upbringing, reared in the Glasgow slums. He's told me about it. He knows all about that. It's the humiliation to *me*. I can't seem to believe that my . . .' his voice broke, '. . . lads would fight like that after all the love they've had, like animals, like beasts, snarling at one another.'

'But they're grown men now, with men's passions. They're no longer the lads we knew back in the Row. We're different, too.'

'Maybe.' He looked at her, unbelieving.

When they went into the house Susan met them in the

hall. She looked excited. Had she seen anything? 'Those two lads,' Maeve said, 'frolicking at the side of the burn like bairns till they fell in. Still, it's the right day for it. Will you get them some dry clothes from the manse bundle, Susan?'

'Did you say the two of them, Mrs McGrath?'

'Yes. Why?'

'There's only Terence with the Reverend in my kitchen. Standing shivering at the fire and a' bluidy. I didn't see Patrick.'

'Then he'll have walked home. The sun will soon dry him.'

She went into the drawing-room and sat down. It was empty. Kieran must have gone upstairs. She'd leave him for a minute. He needed to be alone.

15

On the surface at least, Terence and Patrick seemed to put the fight behind them. They worked harder than ever in the business, they avoided each other, which was comparatively easy to do, were terse at the monthly meetings. Where there had been a burning rage there now seemed only a smouldering hostility. Perhaps Kieran was right. Only time would heal it, and not even that.

But she put them at the back of her mind when Kieran came home towards the end of August from Glasgow looking so exhausted that she said he was to go up to bed and she would bring him his dinner there. She went immediately to the kitchen and asked Maggie, the new help she had engaged for Susan, to run and fetch Dr McNab.

'I've thought Mr McGrath wasn't looking like himself,' Susan said, 'ever since that Sunday.' There was a significant pause which Maeve did not fill and, defeated, she added, 'It's a pity it's the young one.' Dr Gray, in his sixty-fifth year, had taken on an assistant. He would see anybody who came to his house, but he had ridden on horseback to his patients for thirty years, and he was worn out. Only in the last ten had he invested in a cab.

'Well, we must just make the best of Dr McNab.' Maeve turned and went out. She was not in the mood for Susan.

Dr McNab was a spruce young man from the East Coast who had come with great credentials from St Andrews University. 'He knows things I've never even heard about,' Dr Gray had told Maeve when she had called one day for a cough bottle for Kieran. He was certainly spruce, a spring-heeled Jack, she thought to herself when she opened the door to him.

'Good-day to you, Mrs McGrath. Where's the patient?'

'He's upstairs. I'll show . . .'

'No. I prefer to examine him on my own.' She bridled, but he flashed her a smile as he made for the stairs, which made her forgive him. Old Dr Gray had often made it more of a social call than anything else and had lingered too long over his dram. This one was business-like, at least.

She was waiting anxiously in the drawing-room when Susan showed him in. She jumped up from her chair.

'Sit down, Mrs McGrath, and I'll take this one. This is a fine room.' His eyes swept over it. 'Your husband's heart isn't in good condition,' he said. 'He tells me he had a fainting turn in Glasgow. Indeed, I'd say he was on the edge of heart failure.'

'Oh!' Her hand went to her mouth. 'He didn't tell me he'd had any turn.'

'Now, don't distress yourself. We'll do our best for him. Did he work down the pits?'

'Yes. How did you know?'

'We've plenty of miners in Fife as well. My father was one.' *Was* one, she noted. 'How long was Mr McGrath down?'

'We came here in 1851 and he had to take the first job he could get. He was in the pit explosion and after that we started the carting business.'

'That may have been his saving grace, but I'm afraid the damage had been largely done by then.'

'What damage?' Her own heart was beating rapidly. She tried to calm herself.

'To his heart and lungs. He'll have to take things easily from now on, no worries, no getting over-tired.'

'Will he have to give up working, doctor? He's fond of the horses. Oh, I knew the pit was never for him.'

'We'll have to see. For a man who's been active all his life, there's nothing worse than sitting at home worrying.' He bent a keen glance on her. 'I should think Mr McGrath is a sensitive man. Has anything upset him recently?'

She made up her mind. 'Are you married, Dr McNab?'

'No.' His smile flashed, and she thought, I can trust him. 'I haven't had time for that indulgence. I came to this practice to be near the Royal Infirmary in Glasgow. There are great things going on there. You'll have heard of Lister?'

'No. I haven't much truck with infirmaries, although I have a daughter who wants to be a nurse.'

'Is that so?' He nodded. 'Then, if you haven't heard of Lister, no doubt you'll have heard of carbolic acid?'

'Yes, we put it down the drains.'

He laughed. 'Well, Lister used it on a lad's leg and it healed without the usual complications. That was the beginning of it. A great man.' His face shone. 'Aye, the Royal's the place. I wouldn't mind working there.'

'You'll not get much time in a busy practice for infirmaries.'

'You can always make time for anything you want.' He looked at her. 'You were going to tell me if anything had worried your husband, Mrs McGrath.'

'Yes, I was. My two sons have quarrelled bitterly, doctor. There's no need to tell you why.' If he stays long enough in Sholton he'll soon hear, she thought. 'It hurt their father, still preys on his mind. His family mean everything to him.'

He nodded. 'I thought that was what he was like. Well, it's up to you now.'

'Up to me?'

'Yes, you'll have to watch over him till this hurt heals.

It's as bad as a physical wound to a man like him, but carbolic acid would be no good there.' He smiled. 'I often wish that you could just see *inside* a man's body, then you'd know the extent of the damage.' She thought he was talking sense.

'I'd noticed, don't think that. I was planning to take him to Ireland for a holiday in a week or so. We'd always said we'd go this autumn.'

He shook his head. 'Out of the question. He'll have to rest at home quietly for a few weeks, maybe longer. And then you're into bad weather. He must be guarded against colds and chills at all costs. You're fine here, a lovely place.' He looked out of the window. 'Maybe next year. Is Ireland your home?'

'It is,' she said, smiling. 'But it seems to get further and further away, as if we weren't meant to go back, as if it was a far-away dream . . .' A fragment of the old song that Kieran used to sing drifted through her mind, stirring sleeping images, Crow Wood, the morning rides on Blackthorn, old Mairi's warm kitchen: 'Gone at last, like our youth, too soon . . .'

'Sometimes it's better not to go back, to keep your dreams.' He seemed to see into her mind. 'Do you know Keats?'

'Keats?' she said, 'the poet?' Unbidden came the memory of the young man who had tutored her at Woodlea, who had given her books to read, 'I think you will find this interesting, Miss Maeve . . .' Some day there might be time for reading.

'Yes. I read him in bed at nights to stretch my mind. There's one that says . . .' He quoted, without self-consciousness, a hand resting on either knee, his head to one side as if listening to the words.

'Heard melodies are sweet, but those unheard
    Are sweeter; therefore, ye soft pipes, play on;

402

> Not to the sensual ear, but more endear'd,
>   Pipe to the spirit ditties of no tone.'

She looked at him, slowly smiling. Yes, she liked him. She liked him very much.

That winter she devoted herself to Kieran, spending many hours upstairs in their bedroom beside him. Dr McNab had forbidden him the stairs. She had Maggie light a cheery fire every morning and bring their meals up there, although Kieran demurred, saying he was not used to being waited on.

'Maggie likes it,' she told him. 'She's your devoted slave. Hadn't you noticed?'

The girl they had taken from the nearby orphan home, unlike Susan who was her own mistress, only wanted to serve. 'It's like heaven here, Mrs McGrath,' she said, 'compared with that place with its stane flairs an' caul parritch. And this braw room of yours up amang the trees, it's like a palace.'

The bedroom faced south, looking over the garden and, because of its elevation, the view was better than downstairs. Sometimes in the short winter afternoons they would sit without the lamps being lit and talk in the firelight, Kieran in a chair beside her at the window.

'This is a queer like thing to say,' she told him, 'but I'm happy – oh, not you being ill – but it's the first time in our lives that we've had a chance to be together on our own. We're cut off here from the business, from the world, it's like a halfway house in our lives, the first chance we've had to look backwards and forwards.'

'Maybe it's been given to us so that we'll remember it.'

'What do you mean by that?' He looked frail. It was his hands, chiefly, she noticed, no longer work-worn, the hands of an ill man. She was afraid.

'When we're back in the hurly-burly again.' He smiled at her and she was reassured. 'It's almost as good as going to Ireland.'

'We'll get there, never fear, maybe next year. All you have to do is get better.'

She went up to Glasgow once a week, and looked in at the Sholton office most days. Tom Johnson and Bob Carter had left it now, but Maevy and Isobel were there to deal with their contracts with the pits and ironworks. Now that the Railway had installed a direct line, even that would be coming to an end.

Terence and Patrick were 'working all the hours God sent them', in Tom Johnson's words, and Terence had netted several big contracts already, especially with the Cleansing Department in Glasgow, which meant a regular income of several thousands of pounds per year.

They were competing with a firm which already ran omnibuses, working out routes it did not touch, cutting the time by employing better horses – 'that's thanks to Mr McGrath's good buying' – and Patrick was busy designing a new type of omnibus that would be more comfortable. The ladies of Glasgow complained especially about the colds and the smelliness of the damp straw on the floors of the rival buses. In summer they would extend their services, taking people for a day's outing to the Clyde coast, or to the Glens.

'The strange thing is they work quite independently,' Tom Johnson told her. 'You never see them conferring together, and yet there's a blood link there, they complement each other – Terence with his business flair, Patrick with his far-sightedness and his gift for planning.'

'It's evident to everybody they don't get on?' she asked him. She could say that now.

'Oh, aye, everybody knows it in a kind of a way, but it doesn't make a ha'pennyworth of difference. People forget, when a family tragedy hits them, how little lasting impact it makes on other folks. They're too concerned with their own affairs. The McGrath brothers are known in the haulage contracting business for their acumen, not for the fact that they fell out over Bessie Haddow. Life goes on. But you be sure and tell Mr McGrath that neither of them has an eye for a horse like his. When do you think he'll be back?'

'The doctor says not before the end of December.'

'Well, you keep him to it. His health's more important.'

He was a great comfort, Tom Johnson, a capable man, confident now that he was a partner. A man grew to suit his position.

'I was speaking to Tom Johnson today,' she said to Kieran after this talk. 'He says you're sorely missed, that no one has an eye for a horse like you.'

'I'm not the only man in the world who can buy a horse.' Perhaps he was beginning to realize, like Maeve, that delegation was necessary.

'It's always been our policy to pay well and treat our employees fairly,' she said. 'It's paid off with Tom.'

'And Bob. We couldn't be served better. All the same, a lot of the spark comes from the McGraths, though this member's blinking a bit.'

'Don't talk like that,' she said. She smiled so that he would not guess at the fear in her heart.

The news about the failure of the Glasgow Savings Bank spread like wildfire, even before Terence came to see them that same day in October. Patrick would come in when he got back to Sholton. 'The city's in an uproar,' Terence said, 'there are crowds round their Head Office at Virginia Street. You should see them! My God, the stories that are going the rounds already. Managers and directors taking off for God knows where. And they say there's been one or two shootings . . .'

'Maybe it's not as bad as you think.' Kieran's face was as white as his.

'You'll read all about it in the *Herald* tomorrow, Father. I'm sorry to bring you news like this and you not so well.'

'Sit down, Terence,' Maeve said. She could not bear to see him in such a state. How badly was he involved, or how badly had he involved the company? She went to the sideboard and poured out a stiff whisky for him. 'I never thought to see me encouraging you to take a dram.' She tried to smile as she gave it to him.

'Maybe I didn't need it before, but, by God, I need it now.'

'How do we stand?' Kieran's voice was steady.

'That's just what we don't know. Bob's been at their office all day. He's been pretty canny, never borrowing more than we needed, making sure he paid back as much as we ploughed into the business. But the bank's been daft, he says. Their discounts are concentrated with too few firms. If they disengage they'll be ruined.' His voice dropped. 'We have to face it, maybe *we*'ll be ruined.' He did not look at them. 'Bob says they've been too heavily dependent on the London money market, not to mention discounting a good deal of paper connected with America, India and, something the Western never did, financing a large-scale speculation in New Zealand, as well as investment in an American railroad. It beats me how . . .' Kieran cut across his recital.

'How much do we owe them?'

'I don't know yet. We're not one of the big fish, thank God, but you know as well as I do, we've got a lot of outlays. Well, you *have* to with a thriving business.' He had always been flamboyant, Maeve thought, but then his

406

flair was needed. And there were three steady men behind him, Tom, Bob and Patrick. When Kieran's better, she promised herself, I'll know what's going on, I've been neglecting things . . . *if* he gets better, a voice said in her head, *if* there is a business to see to . . . She lifted her chin, seeing Kieran's stricken face.

'There's no need to cross our bridges till we come to them. Tom's careful. So is Bob. They'll let us know as soon as they can. Will you stay and have a bite with us, Terence?'

He shook his head impatiently. 'No, thanks, I have to get back. Catherine will be worried. She'll have heard . . .' Worried in case she lost the chance of her fine house? You're doing the girl an injustice, she told herself.

The *Glasgow Herald* next day confirmed their worst fears. 'A more melancholy picture of wreck and ruin has never been given to the public,' it said. Seven directors were arrested and were in Duke Street Gaol.

There were conflicting reports in the various newspapers. Three firms owed the bank £5,379,000, as against total loans of twelve million pounds. But against that there were between twelve hundred and thirteen hundred shareholders, all wealthy. There was no need for alarm.

The hard facts began to emerge. Against liabilities of twelve million pounds there were assets of only seven millions. The shareholders, in addition to the destruction of their paid-up capital of one million pounds, had to find another four million. Calls totalling £2,750 per £100 share were made.

Maeve's head was dizzy with figures. Like Terence, she worked largely by intuition, an inherent business sense. She had always left the management of the finances of the company to Bob Carter. He was gloomy. It was a terrible mess, he said. They would not be ruined, like some, but it would cripple them at the most important time of their career: the move to Glasgow and the expansion of the whole business. There were outstanding bills. Stabling and the purchase of a new fleet of horses were a large part of it.

Patrick was non-committal as usual, but his haggard face showed his anxiety. 'We must wait and see, Mother,' he said, 'it's no good speculating. But the sooner we can do without the enormous expense of livestock the better. We'll see to that in the future.' But would there be any future? she thought.

After a few days she could bear the suspense no longer and took herself off to Glasgow to gauge the mood of the city. She was urged on by Kieran. 'I'd go if I thought I could get away with it, but that young doctor puts the fear of God in me.' He was scarcely eating. His face was bloodless except for his lips which had an unhealthy purple tinge.

She did not tell Kieran what she found. In the business quarter there was an unmistakable feeling of uncertainty tinged with gloom. People were milling about the streets. Others were standing in little groups, their faces grim, on others a smugness. The Free Kirk element amongst both directors and depositors was well-known, also that the seceders of 1843 had taken as their objective 'the raising of the moral standards'. 'Hypocrites' was a word she often heard amongst the more blasphemous epithets.

When she reached the Glasgow office she found it even more dispiriting. There was very little work being done. Business had ceased in the city, and the staff were not bent over their desks as usual. There was a buzz of conversation that stopped when she entered. The fear and uncertainty was proving infectious. Even the junior clerks knew their livelihood was threatened.

She played down the situation to Kieran when she got home, saying that they would have to trust Bob. He was a man of few words. He had refused to make any statement until the extent of their loss was sorted out. 'There will be no scaremongering,' he'd said to Maeve, 'and keep Mr McGrath out of it. He's too sensitive.'

Fortunately he did not ask too many questions, although Sholton itself was agog. Everyone was rushing to Crannoch, which was larger, to draw out their deposits if they could, now that the news of suspension had reached them. Those holding notes, Kieran said, had set out to get them changed by the other Scottish banks, but many had been too late.

They scanned the papers thoroughly morning and evening, sitting over the fire until late each night, talking endlessly about the crash. Neither Patrick nor Terence had been to see them for a few days, and that in itself seemed ominous. Kieran read aloud any comments he came across by experts, pondered over them. One in particular seemed to sum up the situation. 'While it is the business of the banker to assist traders to engage in sound commercial transactions, it is not their business to give facilities for wild speculation.' 'That's it in a nutshell,' he said, his face grim.

They hardly slept, lying silently beside each other, exhausted by fruitless talking. Never count on anything in this world, Maeve told herself. Just when we were congratulating ourselves on our move to Glasgow and the growth of the business, a blow like this falls on us. She thought with shame of her speech at Terence's table in America. There was one golden rule she had forgotten: you should never 'sprouse' in case you had to eat your words.

About a week after the crash, Kieran insisted on going downstairs. He said shortly that he was better able to face bad news on his feet. They both felt that it would come that day. Bob had promised not to keep them a minute longer than was necessary. They were sitting pale and speechless at the breakfast table when they heard Susan talking to someone in the hall. For the first time Maeve wished that the dining-room, which had always seemed so secluded with its garden view, faced to the front. It could be anyone. She did not know what form the bad news would take, who would bring it.

Susan knocked and came in with an important face. The *Herald* disappeared with regularity into her kitchen so that she could keep herself fully appraised, as Maeve well knew. 'A telegram for Mr McGrath,' she said. She seemed to part with it reluctantly, and remained at his side, looking pointedly into space.

'Go and see that the porridge isn't boiling over, Susan,' Maeve said.

When the door closed behind her she looked at Kieran. He was holding the telegram, making no effort to open it. Whatever it is, as long as he can bear it, she thought, meeting his eyes. They were dazed. 'Open it,' she said. He nodded, tore at the envelope, took out the yellow sheet.

'It's from Terence in America,' he said. He read slowly. 'Heard bad news. Feel partly responsible. Railroad here financed by the bank's money. Mine following to reimburse you for possible losses.'

They looked at each other for a long minute, then she said slowly, 'There's a brother for you . . .'

Kieran got up and came to her, put his arms around her. They were silent for a second, then both began to talk, interrupting each other in their excitement. 'We'll have to tell the boys.' 'Bob Carter.' 'I'll go.' 'No, we'll both go.' 'Yes, we'll both go . . .'

Susan knocked and came in again, her face alive with curiosity. 'Will you be wanting your porridge now, Mrs McGrath?' Maeve stared at her, unhearing, unheeding.

'Your *porridge*, Mrs McGrath?' Susan's eyes went to the telegram on the table.

'Yes, oh, yes. And some cream to go with it, if you would, Susan.'

'You never take cream, Mrs McGrath!' She looked outraged.

'We're taking it this morning,' Kieran said, 'and, Susan?'

'Yes, Mr McGrath?' She inclined her ear, noticeably.

'How long have you been with us?'

'Well, now, it's quite a time . . .' She threw the words away, her eyes on the telegram.

'Well, you can expect a rise at the New Year.'

'Huh,' she said, her chin tilted, then she remembered herself. 'Well, I thank you, Mr McGrath.' She went out.

They kissed, a thing they rarely did at the breakfast table. 'She'd rather have had the inside story than the rise,' Maeve said.

They had a meeting at Braidholme that evening to pass on the good news. Bob told them the extent of their losses. They were not as large as he had feared, but he had been thinking in terms of selling up at the Gallowgate to realize some money to pay off their loan, of sacking the staff there and retreating to Sholton. That would not be necessary now. 'This generous offer of your brother's will save our bacon,' he said. 'We must see that he's paid back as soon as possible. That's our aim now, a reason for working harder than ever before.'

Nobody would stay for any food or drink. They looked exhausted. The sight of Patrick's haggard face made Maeve's heart ache. He was going back to that lonely place with only memories of Bessie. Terence at least had Catherine, who had always had a good head on her and was a ready listener, even if it was only where her own welfare was concerned – that is, if they had made it up after the boys' fight, and her discovery about Elizabeth Maeve. And *she* had Kieran.

'You'll get back up those stairs right away,' she said, 'and not come down again till Dr McNab gives you permission.'

That month they had word from James that Kate's first-born had arrived, a little boy to be called Kieran James. He wept at that, and she knew the bank crash had taken its toll and he was not well yet.

She had never told Kate about the trouble between the boys, but one day when she was sitting quietly, she got out her pen and paper and wrote her a long letter.

My dear daughter, I was glad to hear that you were feeling fine, and that little Kieran is a bouncing healthy baby. Also that Emily and Victoria are back with you, even though you think Emily may have left her heart behind her in Paris. My goodness, what if we had a Frenchman in the family! But what a full, happy house you have. I read out your letter to your father, and we were both pleased to hear how attentive Maria is to you.

Terence will have told you of the failure of the Glasgow Savings Bank, if you haven't already heard from James, but maybe not how he came to our rescue. I can't tell you the difference it made to us to have him rally so quickly to our help. Fortunately we came out of it better than we expected, largely due to the cautiousness of Bob Carter, but the boys are, if anything, working harder than ever to repay their uncle. They know how lucky they've been. Many of our business associates have been ruined. There are some heart-breaking stories going around.

Your father's mending, Kate, there's no need to feel anxious about him, and we're all well, Isobel and Maevy still working in the Sholton office, although I see an end in sight for that. Maevy hopes to go as a trainee nurse at the Royal Infirmary when she's old enough, and Isobel and John have fixed their wedding date for the 23rd March next year. She's very happy about it, and is planning to change the gloomy manse furnishings bit by bit so that she won't annoy Catherine. She's not a very robust girl. I hope marriage will suit her, but the love in John Craigie's eyes should assure me. A marriage without love is no marriage.

Catherine and Terence are busy looking for a house. This may surprise you considering the financial trouble we've been in. Catherine came to see us one day last week – she's been very attentive to your father . . .

She put down her pen and stared at the summer-house through the window, thinking of that visit. They had been going downstairs together after Catherine had chatted to Kieran. 'Mr McGrath's still pale,' she said.

'Yes. We've all been going through a worrying time, perhaps your father-in-law most of all.' She stole a look at Catherine's face. It was set in a sadness that touched her. They had reached the hall and were going towards the door.

'Could I have a word with you before I go, Mother?' The girl stopped. 'I didn't want to upset Mr McGrath.' It was strange how she did not call him 'Father', but that was her way. Maybe her own father had not meant very much to her.

'Surely you can. Come in here and we'll be cosy.' She led the way into the drawing-room where a bright fire burned. The downstairs rooms were always kept warm for Kieran's brief sorties.

'You know we were looking for a house before the bank crash?' Catherine said, immediately they sat down.

'Yes.' She put her hand on the girl's wrist. 'I'm hoping that won't be put off for too long.'

'But it will have to be put off, I take it?' How tense she looked.

'For the time being, yes. My brother has said there's no need for repayment, but Bob Carter will have none of that. We don't want debts hanging round our neck.'

'That house meant a lot to me. I'd been counting on it.'

413

'Yes, I know that. I'm just asking you to be patient.'

'I've been very patient, Mother.' She spoke rapidly, taking her hand away. 'I've put up with Terence for a long time now, and his moods, even worse after that dreadful fight. No one thought of me! I don't suppose you've any idea what it's been like. You and Mr McGrath always seem so easy with one another . . .'

'Oh, we have our differences.' She smiled, wanting to break the tension.

'It's not the same. Mr McGrath has eyes for no one but you. But Terence . . . he looks anywhere but at me. He can't sit still when he's in the house. Sometimes he comes home late from Glasgow, reeking with drink. Oh, he's not as bad as he was, I'll admit, because he knows it clouds his judgement and the only thing that matters to him now is the McGrath Carting Company.'

'Don't say that, Catherine.' She had guessed at the misery. Now she was hearing of it at first hand from this unhappy girl. 'It's a bad time for you and him, but you've been a good lass. He'll come round to seeing that.'

'He can't forget her! In bed I know it's her he's thinking of, not me! Not the child! Her, her, her! She's between us all the time.' If she would only weep it would be easier, not this stony face, those bleak eyes. 'I want this house we've seen. We had looked at it before the crash. I've got the money my father left me. Oh, I can see by your face you're wondering why I didn't offer it to help you out, but what did Terence ever do for me? I'm going to buy it, with *my* money. It will be mine. It's the only thing I want.'

'Will he agree?'

'Oh, he'll agree all right. He's got big ideas, Terence. He'd like a fine place. But you see, Mother, don't you?' She turned to Maeve, dry-eyed, miserable, her cheeks flushed, 'I'll know it's *mine*. Do you understand that?'

'Yes, I understand.' It was the wrong time to say, 'What's yours is his,' quote the marriage service at her. 'Believe me, Catherine, things will come right for you both. You were the only girl he ever thought of all his young years. He had eyes for no one else. Try to remember that. Maybe you'll be able to build up a new life with him in your new house, in a new place, make it a home.' She met the girl's eyes. They seemed to soften.

'Maybe I was to blame . . . at the beginning. I wasn't . . . ready. My father always made me feel ashamed of my feelings. And then, when we were married, I thought he'd been right, my father. Terence . . . I was shocked at his roughness, his . . . lack of consideration . . .'

'Oh, Catherine, I blame myself. I should have . . .' The girl interrupted her, speaking quickly, her eyes hard again. 'But then *she* made herself available. It's difficult to forgive that.'

Maeve spoke sharply. 'Well, you must try, because she'll never make herself available again. You have to face that as much as Terence. You go ahead with your house, buy it, call it your own, but remember it takes more than that to make you happy . . .' She took up her pen again.

They've seen one in Kelvinside they like, and the last time I was at the Glasgow office we went in one of Terence's new tartan buses to see it. I said he'd laid it on specially to suit his new house, and he smiled a bit at that. I can tell you, it's been difficult to get a smile out of him for a long time.

I can't pretend to you they're happy, Kate. They thole each other, and Catherine, who has a fine sense of family, would never leave him, although I wouldn't have blamed her if she had. I've kept this from you, my Kate, because of the baby, but it's only right you and James should know. There were secrets in my own family back in Ireland, trouble between my father and mother which I could only guess at, much unhappiness. That's why I feel there should be no secrets in ours.

Patrick married Bessie because he loved her, had always loved her, although he knew she was bearing Terence's child. When she died he was heartbroken and blamed Terence for her death. They went at each other like animals in the garden here. I'll never forget it, although I'm better at taking blows than your father. I grieve for them, and for Catherine who has to live with the knowledge that her husband had a child by another woman. If the boys could only come together because of their grief instead of it separating them, they could make their peace with each other yet.

Time will heal – your father and I hope so – but there's a great sadness for us and especially for your father who dotes on the boys. Sometimes I think the solution might be for one of them to leave the business, and then I realize that they're wedded to it and that their sanity lies in it. If the McGrath Carting Company becomes a name to contend with in Glasgow and beyond, it's a terrible thing to think that it's grown out of hate, not love.

There, it's out, and I feel the better for it. I don't mean to distress you, but it's as well for you to know that families can be a sorrow as well as a joy, although something tells me you'll know mostly joy. There's that in your character that attracts it.

One good thing that comes out of all this – although I'm convinced this feud between the boys is partly the cause of his illness – is that your father and I have become closer, if anything. Here we are in our little eyrie, warm and snug, and we talk about going to Ireland, that far green place, and what we'll plant in the garden here, and Isobel's wedding, a real village one with all the kirk folks turning out to see their minister wed. And sometimes of that fine house of Catherine's in Great Western Terrace.

I thought she would have a large detached mansion, but she has a mind of her own. She pointed out the architecture of the Terrace to me, the fine columned entrance in the centre, and the grand drive for the carriages. 'It's got style, Mother,' she said. 'Greek Thomson built it in with the stones.' And I'm sure she'll make it as beautiful inside as out. At the back it looks like a bit of the Botanic Gardens with its fine shrubs and stone urns and the like. I tell you, you and your Uncle Terence will have to look to your laurels when Catherine moves in there . . .

It was true what she had said to Kate about herself and Kieran coming closer together. Braidholme was cosy;

there was a happy atmosphere about it. She still over-looked the Sholton office, still made a weekly trip to Glasgow, and sometimes she brought back copies of *Punch* so that they could have a laugh together at the Tenniel cartoons with Dr McNab when he came. He breezed in regularly like the wind, but always had time for a joke.

They tried to understand the disputes with Russia, and they argued about the relative merits of Disraeli and Gladstone. It was the first time in their lives they had had time to talk, and Maeve enjoyed sharpening her wits. She said once to Dr McNab, 'You'll have to hold the jackets, I'm thinking,' and he flashed his smile and said, 'Only dull couples never argue. So long as it isn't acrimonious.' When she repeated this to Maevy she sniffed and said he sounded as if he had an old head on young shoulders.

The plight of the Zulus caught Kieran's imagination, especially the courage of Cetewayo, their chief. 'The papers would have us believe *he* was the invader. But they were there first. All the trouble in the world is to do with the possession of land. It was the same in Ireland. My family were dispossessed.'

She was amazed that he should bring this up after so long. 'Does it still rankle?' she asked him.

He shook his head. 'No, mavourneen, the Ireland I long for has no bitterness in it, it is the Ireland of my youth, a green dream.' She did not say he would have difficulty in finding it. 'Heard melodies are sweet,' Dr McNab had quoted, 'but those unheard are sweeter.' The words were full of meaning for her.

16

Nobody in the family, least of all Kieran and Maeve, looked forward to Christmas. Patrick and Bessie had been married during the festivities a year ago, and memories were too painful. He had promised to come for dinner, nevertheless. Isobel, Maevy and, of course, John, would be there, but Terence and Catherine declined. They were too busy with their move to the new house in Kelvinside.

But Christmas was Christmas, Maeve said to Kieran, even although Hogmanay would be celebrated in true Scottish fashion with visits to and from friends, the richness of black bun and the mellowness of whisky, the ritual of cleaning the house from top to toe so that not one speck of dust would remain to usher in the New Year.

They would have one of those new-fangled Christmas trees that Prince Albert had brought into vogue during his lifetime, and they would have Elizabeth Maeve. It was a time for children. Jess brought her to Braidholme warmly swaddled against the winter cold, and Maeve carried her in proudly to sit on her knee at the dining-room table.

'Just look at your mother,' Kieran said, 'smiling fit to burst with that wee soul.'

'Her dear wee Lizzie,' Isobel said, and everyone laughed.

'Dear wee Lizzie,' Patrick repeated, his face softening for a second.

The name suited her. Elizabeth Maeve was too sedate for such a rumbustious, chuckling little baby. She might be like Maeve in appearance, but she had all Bessie's joy

418

of living in her, as if she carried her mother's vital spark. Her name changed to Lizzie from then on.

Kate's letter came in February, a bulky envelope. Maeve read it out to Kieran in the drawing room one evening when Maevy and Isobel were at the manse hanging curtains. The wedding was only a month away.

Your last letter reassured me about Father, and I hope by this time he's on his feet again and back with his beloved horses.

The dreadful business about the Glasgow Savings Bank would be a great shock to him, indeed to all of you. Uncle Terence came to see James as soon as he heard the news in New York, and said he was going to send immediate assistance to you. James offered his, and if there is still need of it, believe me, Mother, he would be more than willing. He says it would be a small price to pay for me – you know James with his sense of humour – but he has asked me to assure you, seriously, of his willingness to help.

Oh, Mother, we're so happy with our little Kieran, now nearly three months old and the spitting image of his grandfather, tell him, so much so that Uncle Terence says he wouldn't be surprised if he'd been born with a shillelagh under his arm! Our happiness is shared by the rest of the children. Emily and Victoria oust the nurse from her duties whenever they can, although I must admit to seeing Emily with a far-away look in her eye, which means only one thing.

There are letters flowing in from Paris, and Victoria tells me he is as handsome as Emily says, as well as rich. He is the son of a *notaire* in Paris, which is the same as a lawyer, and they also have a country house. They met through Miss Arbuthnot, of all people. His mother was an old friend of hers, and it was she who helped Miss Arbuthnot with an address of a nice private hotel where the girls stayed.

However, James has had a talk with Emily and said if Monsieur Charles Barthe – I didn't think his name seemed at all French until I heard Victoria pronounce it as 'Sharl Bart' – wishes to pay court to her he must write to him. She's just nineteen, after all.

He's very broad-minded, my James. He has no objection to

any person of different nationality, and says we are all citizens of the world, and what a great opportunity it would be for George and Ernest to have a French brother-in-law or, for that matter, a Hottentot! We laughed at that. I think he thinks it won't last.

Emily, Victoria and Maria have been constantly at balls and soirées over the Christmas season, and now that the snow and ice are here, there are skating parties and sleigh rides and all manner of fun. James had a brazier put in the garden for roasting chestnuts when the young people came back from skating on the Wanapeake pond.

Once Uncle Terence and Aunt Caroline were here overnight, and Uncle Terence said because I had a baby I hadn't to act like an 'auld wife', and sent me off to the pond as well, escorted by James. It was so pretty with the flares round and the bright colours of the skaters, and there was even a man playing a hurdy gurdy for the waltzing. Do you remember Joey long ago, and his monkey? Sometimes I miss you all so much, but perhaps next Christmas we'll be together. James talks about coming back to Scotland to visit old friends, but I wouldn't leave my dear little Kieran as yet.

And we have talked long and earnestly about what you told me concerning the boys. What a tragedy that Bessie should die, so young and full of life . . . if only there had been something to combat the poison. She always loved Terence, I knew that, but his obsession with Catherine blinded him. We can only hope that happiness will come to them in time.

She had a different upbringing from us. Her father never let her have young friends, and I can say this to you, Mother, a woman has to go into marriage with understanding and a great deal of love. A close relationship brings its problems. There must be give and take. I was lucky, not unlucky, that James had been married before. He understood me, the way a young man might not have done. I hope Catherine will be able to throw off her father's influence, it was narrow-minded, bad for her – what a thing to say about a Reverend! But all the same, precept is better than sermons, and you and Father always set us a good example.

Then there's the baby, and that little life mustn't be blighted. I wouldn't blame Catherine if she didn't wish to take her, nor Patrick, at first, if she is too hurtful a reminder of the wife he lost. But if there's any difficulty about a home for her, we would gladly welcome her here. James has asked me to say that, because we both feel you must put Father first, and his health.

But what to do about the boys, ruining their lives in this stupid feud? Well, we have an idea, or rather James had it, and he's talked it over with Uncle Terence. It is that you should try and persuade Patrick to come and stay here with us for a little, on the pretext that they might be able to put some business his way. I put that badly. It isn't a pretext. It's a reason.

James looks at it from a logical point of view. He thinks a sense of obligation to his uncle might make Patrick accept and, apart from that, his visit might help to break the tension between the boys. They've both had a hard time, culminating in the bank crash. They need to get away from each other.

Anyhow, Mother, you test the water. There are three lovely girls here who would swoon over a young cousin from Scotland. It's just a pity that he's not fond of riding because Maria would have had him rigged out in no time. But who knows, he might persuade her to go back to Scotland with him. She's not fearsome about travelling, like Aunt Caroline.

And now my little Kieran will be requiring his supper, so I must stop. I shall look forward to having your letter telling me that you have been successful in persuading Patrick, and all about the wedding. Our gifts to Isobel and John are speeding across the Atlantic towards them, and I shall want a full description of the dresses from Maevy if you are too busy to write.

> Your loving and very happy daughter,
> Kate

Maeve said to Patrick at Isobel's wedding. 'You're such a busy man these days that I never get the chance to speak to you.'

He looked at her, a hint of a smile at his mouth, not in his eyes. 'Well, you wouldn't like it if we weren't, Ma. You're the one that gave us a taste for hard work.'

'Hard work never killed any man,' she said, smiling at him. 'But worry does.' She thought of saying 'bitterness', but stopped herself.

He sighed, looked away. 'Fine cheery talk for a wedding.'

'Yes, I'm sorry.' She looked across the room at Isobel standing with John, like an angel, she thought, so delicate in that gauzy veil and voile dress she had chosen, and those clusters of white flowers at either side of her sweet face – stephanotis, they were called, weren't they? They did not grow in the Braidholme garden, that was for sure.

John was the better choice. She could not have kept up with the life in America, the quickness and vitality of it. She was better in a backwater like Sholton with a loving husband who would always put her first.

'I had a letter from Kate saying I was to try to get you to visit them,' she said to Patrick. He turned to her.

'Me?'

'Well, it's not so daft. You would be able to thank your uncle in person for helping the company out of its difficulties.'

'The money will be paid back.' He bridled.

'You don't have to break your neck over it. Your uncle has plenty.'

'That's real Irish. It's the principle of the thing, don't you see?'

'Oh, yes, I see all right, but you have to learn to take as well as give. There I am again, lecturing, and at Isobel's wedding, too. Well, then, you'd be able to see your sister – you were always fond of Kate – and that wee nephew of yours called after your father, and your uncle and aunt and cousin. Terence could tell you a lot. He might be able to put some business in your way or give you ideas, not to mention James. It's a grand country, Patrick, so . . . alive!' She saw the interest in his face.

'I wouldn't mind going when the time's ripe. But there's too much on just now, new contracts pending. We're hoping to get an agency from one of the big firms down south and that will mean working with the railways.'

'Will they not do you out of work?'

'No, this is the age of the urban carter. We've moved to Glasgow at the right time, short hauls . . . railways can't run up streets into warehouses. We'll be the go-between. There will be a bigger demand for feeder services than ever, and we can supply that. We'll close down the Sholton office gradually . . .' His face was alive. The business is his salvation, she thought. 'Besides,' he said, 'you're always talking about going to Ireland with Father. We couldn't both be away.'

'Dr McNab will tell us when he's fit.' Make Isobel's wedding a trial run, he had said. If he stands up to that you can think of it in the late spring.

'Well, he looks fine today.' Kieran and Maevy were coming towards them. 'By God, he must have been a handsome man when he was young!'

'What are you talking about?' she said, pretending indignation. 'He's the handsomest man in the room this very day by a long chalk.'

Kieran was beside her in his black frock-coat, his grey satin cravat, Maevy clinging to his arm, flushed and laughing, pretty in her sky-blue silk. Maeve remembered Caroline in her baby-blue at Isobel's dance. If she could see my daughter . . . she thought proudly. 'Oh, Ma!' Maevy said, 'I've had to rescue Father from all these women. He's flirting like mad with the lot of them!'

'What did I tell you?' she said to Patrick. The smile touched his eyes this time. That was an improvement, at least.

Terence had come with Catherine in their new carriage, both smart, both elegant. She could see the influence of the fine house, or was it his grandfather Muldoon? It's in him, she thought, and Catherine was always supposed to have distinguished relations. They make a fine couple.

'I have to collar you separately from Patrick,' she said. There was nothing like taking the bull by the horns. He looked at her coldly, and she felt rebuffed. To cover it she said the first thing that came into her head. 'At least you don't have the worry of travelling to the office now you're in Kelvinside. Do you like it there?'

He nodded, looking around the room as if only half-listening. 'Catherine's made a fine place of it.'

'Come on, Terence,' she said, being foolish again, 'let yourself go.'

'What do you mean, Mother?' He turned back to her, looking down his nose.

'You like it. Admit it. It's in your nature to like it. You take it from my side.' She rarely spoke to the children about her Irish home. Something had always stopped her, a feeling that since she had deliberately relinquished her life there and all it stood for, it was over and done with. She had made a new one. 'I've been in many fine houses in my time,' she contented herself with saying, 'your uncle's in America, oh, you'd like that, and Kate's, and once long ago I was in the laird's . . .' did he tense at that . . . ? 'But none of them have been as stylish as yours and Catherine's.'

'Catherine's,' he said, 'not mine.'

'But you live in it with her, don't you?'

'There will soon be enough money to put it in my name. If it hadn't been for the bank crash . . .' she interrupted him.

'Maybe she won't have that. It's the only thing she has of her own. Don't make her suffer too much, Terence.'

He looked coldly at her. 'Would you like some more wine?'

'Yes, please.' She sighed, watching his straight back as he walked away from her. She had had no more success with him than with Patrick, and made a fool of herself into the bargain. Children could never understand . . . or was it she who could not?

Spring came like a benison to Braidholme. The trees were a fresh, tender green, the banking down to the Sholtie was yellow with daffodils. Kieran was so much better that he was going every morning to Sholton to see to the stables.

'That man Crichton who's been in charge while I've been away is like Peters come home to roost,' he told her. 'He treats the lads in the same high-handed way as he did, with the same results. Although at least Peters did me a favour.' He smiled at her. 'Made me run away with the Major's daughter!' He was nearly his old self, she thought thankfully.

'The best thing you ever did, my lad. Maybe it is that Crichton sees you're running down the place and he's afraid for his job.'

'Maybe.'

He did not tell her of his encounter that morning with Crichton. He had walked into the stable yard and found him, whip in one hand, the other pulling viciously on the bridle of a horse he was backing between the shafts of a cart. His face was livid with rage and he was applying the whip about the animal's legs. 'You bastard!' he was shouting, 'Back there, get back!' The horse was pounding its great hooves in confusion, there was foam on its chest. Kieran could hardly contain his rage as he strode over.

'Go easy, for God's sake, man!' he said. 'That's not the way to treat a horse.' Crichton looked up, his face dark red, but he stopped using the whip.

'You've got to show them who's master,' he muttered, 'he's been the very devil to deal with all day.'

'That's no excuse. I don't want to catch you using that whip again. Don't forget!' He had turned on his heel,

425

surprised at how his heart was hammering. And Dr McNab warned me, he thought, not to . . .

'Mr McGrath?' The man's voice stopped him. He turned.

'Yes?'

'I hear tell you'll soon be shutting down this place, moving the stock to Glasgow? What about the men?'

'You'll know when the time comes.' He walked away before Crichton could say more, but he could not get the memory of the malice in the man's eyes out of his mind all morning. I made a mistake in the first place in hiring him, he thought, I mistook hardness for efficiency . . .

'You're glowering at me,' Maeve brought him back. 'You know what Dr McNab said. "Don't get upset . . ." '

He managed to smile. 'It's not you that's making me glower, it's the thought of Crichton. Nothing would make me take that man to the Gallowgate. He'll have to go.'

Dr McNab came one afternoon on a day so mild that Maeve had asked Maggie to take the tea-tray to the summer-house, and then walk down the drive to Jess McDonald's and ask if she could push out Lizzie in her pram. She had smiled at the joy on the girl's face.

'We've got a nurse ready and waiting in Maggie, then,' he said when she told him. He sipped his tea. She had persuaded him to join them. 'My, this is good.'

'Yes, Jess has had the baby now for a year. She'll be handing her over any day.'

'She'll tell you when the time comes.'

'I'd never thought I'd corner you like this, doctor. You're always so busy. Are you still going into the Glasgow Infirmary?'

'Every minute I can.' He smiled his quick smile. 'I only drink a cup when I'm signing off a patient, and here comes the man himself.' Kieran was walking across the lawn towards them.

'Hello, doctor,' he said, shaking hands. 'My, position's are reversed, I'm thinking. Me working and you dawdling with my wife.'

'And in paradise. It's grand here. You've both made this place a picture. I looked in to sign you off and find you back at work already.'

'Well, that's proof that I'm better. Thanks, mavourneen.' He took the cup of tea Maeve offered him. 'This will wet my thirst.'

'I shouldn't go at it too hard, though. And you might like to think of that holiday in Ireland to complete the cure.'

'How about it, Kieran?' Maeve asked. His smile was sufficient answer.

'You'll have to tell me what the attraction is sometime,' Dr McNab said.

'It's home, doctor, that's all.'

'Ach, well, I can understand that.' He nodded. 'I'm a Fifer myself.'

Jess McDonald came to see her the next day with Lizzie in her perambulator. 'She's getting quite a lump to carry, Mrs McGrath.'

'She'll soon be walking to the front door of Braidholme herself. I know it's going to be a break for you, Jess, when we take her away. But the time has to come . . .' She had hesitated to mention it, knowing how much she was attached to the baby.

'That's why I came to see you.' She took the cup of tea Maeve offered her. 'I don't know whether to laugh or cry, to tell you the truth.' She took a sip. 'My milk's been drying up and I've been giving Lizzie some boiled cows' milk backwards and forwards. I should have told you, but

I wanted to get used to the idea of parting with the wee soul. Well, I went to see Dr McNab the other day and he told me I was pregnant!'

'I thought he was a bit cagey when he was here last. Well, that's fine news, Jess. I would be laughing if I were you.'

'But it's wee Lizzie . . .'

'Now, just look at it this way. It couldn't have happened at a better time. She's beginning to know her place in the world, maybe wondering where she belongs, either with you or with us. There's nothing worse. Does Dr McNab want her completely weaned now?'

'Yes.' She shook her head comically. 'I always thought you couldn't get pregnant if you were feeding.'

'So they say, but the exception proves the rule. Auld wives don't know everything.' She made up her mind. 'We'll take her right away, Jess. A clean break's the best. But come as often as you like to see her. You'll soon be busy preparing for your own one, and that will take the hurt away.'

'Aye, it'll be a hurt all right. It's been the happiest time of my life. If my own baby is half as good as wee Lizzie, I'll do fine.'

Lizzie was welcomed by everyone like Queen Victoria when she arrived, but ecstatically by Maggie. Deprived of her task of ministering to Kieran, she became her devoted slave. 'You get on with whatever you have to do, Mrs McGrath' – Maeve's sojourns to 'Glesca' were treated by Maggie with the same awe as if she had said she was setting off in the footsteps of David Livingstone – 'and I'll take good care of her.' She guarded the baby ferociously, fed her carefully under Maeve's instructions, and there was no greater joy for the girl than to be allowed to push

428

the perambulator to the village to 'show her off', as she put it.

Even Susan fell victim to the baby's charms, Maeve noticed, and carried on long, ridiculous conversations with her as she sat in her high chair in the kitchen. Maevy rushed home from the office to play with her, Isobel took her to the manse often when Maeve went to Glasgow.

Never was any child more loved, she thought, watching her blossom daily under their care. She managed what Maeve had never been able to do, to bring Patrick to Braidholme every evening on some business pretext or other. She grew to recognize his voice. He would take her on his knee and play with her. 'You're always there when you're wanted, Mother,' he said once. 'I don't know how I'll ever repay you.'

'When I see you happy,' she said, 'that will be enough payment.' This time she had the sense not to mention Terence.

She said to Kieran one evening when they were sitting together after supper. 'I don't hear you mentioning your trip to Ireland.'

He looked shamefaced. 'Oh, I haven't forgotten it, don't think that. But there's such a stir about the place since Lizzie came. I'm surrounded by cooings and feeding bottles and baby clothes flapping in the breeze and God knows what else. It's like being back in the Row when you were nursing Terence.'

She laughed. 'I was a bit quick snatching her away from Jess, but I thought it best at the time. Maggie's a bit of a harum scarum to be left in charge. Unless we took Maevy away from the office?'

He shook his head decisively. 'I depend on her more than ever since Isobel left. She runs the place while I'm outside. And we can't ask a minister's wife to come back.'

He smiled. 'The village folk would throw up their hands in horror.'

'So would John Craigie.'

'It's a big undertaking, closing down a business, and a sad one. The horses have to be got rid of, unless they're young, the tackle and the carts – they're too old-fashioned for Glasgow – they're talking about sprung vans now. We've to maintain the service to our old customers while they make other arrangements. I've to pay off some of the carters. I'm handing out notices just now, not a pleasant task.' She saw his grim face.

'Do you think we should postpone our visit? I feel badly about it.'

'I can be patient. "Wait horse and you'll get corn", my mother used to say. Anyhow, I'm only too thankful I'm able to be back at work again. For a time, lying in that room upstairs, I began to wonder if I was finished.'

'You finished,' she said, 'and not yet fifty! You're in your prime.'

It became a time for quiet enjoyment, for savouring each day, but a time for looking back. If the one fly in the amber was the continuing coldness between Terence and Patrick, they decided without discussing it that it should not be allowed to taint the happiness of the little girl growing up under their care.

They were both busy, Kieran at the Sholton office, Maeve going to Glasgow every morning by train. She had not forgotten the Savings Bank disaster. This time she would be at the helm, know what was going on. Both boys were outside a great deal and she worked amicably with Bob Carter and Tom Johnson. She saw to it that they had a well-chosen, well-paid staff, and felt that her regular appearances contributed to the feeling of progress and optimism. She took the trouble to know them individually, and took pleasure in seeing the faces raised to her, the chorus of 'Good-mornings'.

She sat in again at the weekly meetings and took an active part in the discussions. There were always decisions to be made and she enjoyed 'putting in her pennyworth', as Kieran called it. She it was who suggested chain horses on West Nile street because of its steep hill, and who proposed they should go into the parcel service. Business always slackened off towards the New Year, she pointed out, and that would fill a gap.

The trouble that occasionally blew up between staff at station yards and their own employees was her special forte. She dressed in her best to call at the railway offices, as if it were armour, and knew she was good at sorting out the trouble. Any dissidents usually gave in when she talked to them, because she treated them like equals. And she knew about the schooling of horses. She could stand with Kieran watching a Shire in its traces with the coachman walking behind, or a young horse teamed with an older companion, and give him her considered verdict on its worth. Her Woodlea days came back to her.

But she was always back at Braidholme in the late afternoon. She and Kieran stopped having midday dinner and concentrated on a leisurely supper with Maevy about seven. When she came home, if it was fine, she would take Lizzie with her into the garden while she worked there. The child was now walking, albeit unsteadily. Maeve assured Kieran that she would soon be toddling down the drive to meet him.

They would have tea in the summer-house and, while Kieran read the *Herald*, or studied bills of sale, she would let her mind wander over the years as her eyes fell on the Sholtie purling below, up towards its source in the Lanarkshire hills, down towards the Falls where they had lost John. She had no bitterness about his death now. If only

431

Terence and Patrick would realize that in time they would feel the same about Bessie.

She would think of the hard early years in the Row, the rearing of the children, and the abundant energy that had gone with it, of the happy times sewing for them, playing with them; that Sunday School Picnic when she had met Alastair Crawford . . . 'Alastair . . .' She would repeat the name under her breath to see if it would bring back that turbulence of spirit she had once known, but it could not be resurrected, only some kind of sad sweetness that had something to do with Dr McNab's poem, 'Heard melodies are sweet . . .' – the might-have been.

Kieran talked about Crawford's sometimes. The pits and ironworks were now serviced by rail and they were using their own locomotives, wagons and brake vans. He relayed the young laird's words to her: 'We've to search far afield for ironstone nowadays, East Lothian, even the Midlands of England. Horses and carts would be of little use to us now.'

'He's an agreeable man,' he said, 'not like the old laird. There's give and take about him. You can have a crack with him. Approachable. "You and I have seen great changes, McGrath," he said to me.'

'And what was your reply?'

'I said my sons had foreseen that, especially Patrick, and that was why we were moving to Glasgow. Then he asked how you were keeping. "Your wife was a great favourite of my mother's," he said.'

She smiled at that. An elegant gentleman, Alastair Crawford, diplomatic to the last. 'I've never forgotten her,' she said, 'and how she used to come through our back garden at the Row with that loping walk of hers, like a shy animal . . . And I remember how she louped over the stile on the way to the Sholtie Woods, and how once we sat at the back door and I gave her a white rose . . .'

She would think of her like that, rather than the wasted face on the pillow when she had gone to see her at the Big House. Annabel, my one true friend, she thought. 'If you love your husband, don't let him accept this post,' she had said. Those strange eyes. Her face had been all eyes.

It had been good advice, but, oh, those fretful, enchanting days she had spent with her son, those morning rides with him, the wind streaming through her hair. Had she seen a picture of herself like that, a romantic one, a young Maeve Muldoon? 'Does it help to say I love you?' It was the tone of voice that came back to her, the elegance of it falling on ears used to the rough Scottish dialect of the Lowlands.

And she would think of that morning when those three viragos had flung themselves on her, humiliating her to the core so that she had to lie to her family about the bruises. Patrick had guessed. Trust Patrick. 'That must have been a hell of a fall.' Well, much good it had done them after all: Beenie Drummond dafter than ever, poor Bessie's mother still locked up in the Asylum, and jecoe Mrs Brodie scrubbing out the kirk hall every Friday for Isobel, no less. There was a fine piece of irony, to be sure. But she owed them a debt. They had brought her to her senses, and it had led to her going to see Duncan McGrath after the explosion.

That had been a bad time. Kieran's long illness, the forerunner of this latest one. Dr McNab had theories of the damage it did to men's lungs working down the pit. She would think instead of her visit to America, of the joy of meeting her brother and his wife and daughter, of seeing Kate so happy. When she and Kieran were rid of their responsibilities they would move about the world to stretch their minds. Long ago in Ireland, that had been her ambition, too.

* * *

433

One rainy evening when they were comfortably installed by the fire, Patrick called as usual. Lizzie had been put to bed and he said he would go up and see her. When he came down he took a chair beside them, a smile lingering on his face.

'How's it going, Father, the clearing up?'

'Fine except for that man, Crichton. He crosses me in everything.'

'He's got his month's notice like the rest we're getting rid of, but why not tell Maevy to pay him off and get rid of him if he annoys you.'

'No, we must play fair. The old ones are retiring, but he's got to find another job.'

'There's no place for sentiment in business. A month's only going to give him more time to brood about losing it.' He looked at them both, embarrassed, half-smiling. 'If you two haven't any plans, I'm ready to go to America now.'

17

It was a voyage of discovery in more ways than one, Patrick thought. The unaccustomed leisure of the ship gave him time to think. Some nights his mind was so full of Bessie that he had to rise and pace the decks. If he heard a burst of laughter from the crowded steerage it would remind him of her. She had taught him how to laugh in the short time they had had together. 'Don't put a ring round yourself, Patrick. You frighten people off. I know how tender you are, how good and kind. Let others see it.' Her face would rise before him, the laughing mouth, the strong yellow hair, the eyes that darkened when they made love.

And then perhaps the wailing of a baby would change his train of thought, and his pace would quicken with the black bile rising in him. Only four months with her. That brother of his was to blame. The child was his in name only, Terence's in reality. Bessie had been teaching him to accept that. 'Just wait till she says "Da" . . .'

'I had her first!' Would he ever be able to forget those words? By God, it had done him good to see that bugger, drookit and miserable, when he had fished him out of the pool in the Sholtie! He should have let him drown, that sprightly, womanizing brother of his, the singer of songs with Da, his bedfellow for all those years in the Row.

But he was not so sprightly now, living in that mausoleum of a place in Kelvinside bought by his wife. They would not get him to visit, even although he thought Catherine more sinned against than sinning. A hard man, but he brought in the business. 'It's your money or your life with Terence,' Bob Carter had once joked.

He would go back to his cabin and lie sleepless until dawn. 'Bessie, Bessie' – her name was stamped in his mind and on his heart, Bessie who had given so generously of her body and her spirit. In time she would have put away all lingering thoughts of Terence, and they would have had children of their own. What was the sense of struggling to build up a business if you did not have children to pass it on to?

Uncle Terence had met him at New York when the ship had berthed, and after he had been cleared, had taken him on a lightning tour round the city before seeing him on to the train. He would follow later. Business claimed him during the day. He had been as his mother described him, jovial, quite a dandy in his dress, but his handgrip had been firm. He would have known him by the family likeness, the same straight back, the red hair, the air they both had of the world belonging to them rather than the other way round.

He had been bowled over by the city, its vitality – Ma had been right – and its beauty. She had not mentioned that the tall, narrow blocks gave it a lightness which the sturdy buildings of Glasgow lacked. His uncle had laughed out loud at his enthusiasm. 'I see New York's putting its feelers on you already, Patrick.'

He had been impressed by his uncle's evident importance when he had shown him round the offices of his shipping company. They were much bigger than the Gallowgate ones, and much more splendid with their rows of typing machines and the great glass windows looking down on Fifth Avenue.

His staff, ten times as many as theirs, had been courteous and had treated him with a deferential politeness which was a world away from their Glasgow contemporaries. Scotsmen had no style, just hard drive and too much moral rectitude which was often hypocritical. Look at the directors who had gone to prison in the Savings Bank fiasco who had been pillars of the Free Kirk.

Before they parted, Uncle Terence had given him lunch in a big hotel on Fifth Avenue, all gilt mirrors and potted palms. 'You'll find a platform party waiting for you at the other end, Patrick,' he had laughed. He had eyes like Mother also, 'the colour of Irish loughs', he remembered his father saying. He always waxed sentimental when he talked about Ireland.

His uncle had been a fine talker, giving him his ticket and the itinerary so that he could follow the route. 'It would only have cost one dollar fifty in 1850,' he had said, 'all the way to Albany, but it would have taken twenty-one hours to get there. Look out for Sing Sing Prison, but don't let them keep you . . . !' He was still talking when the train drew out of New York Central.

All the same, his words stayed in Patrick's mind, and he kept his eyes open. He had told him that the original plans for the track to go overland had been abandoned in favour of following the course of the Hudson and, looking at the great expanse of water so near the railway, there was no doubt it was a magnificent sight, dwarfing anything he had ever seen.

It had not been easy to lay the track, according to Uncle Terence. Cuts and tunnels had had to be blasted through highlands, and along portions of the river so deep that tools falling into the water were lost to the workmen. At Montrose – he located it on his map – the grades were so heavy that pusher engines had to be used. 'We owe it all to Vanderbilt,' Terence had said. 'He was the power behind the operations. Guess what his stock was worth at his death? One hundred million!'

'Even the McGrath Carting Company can't equal that,'

Patrick had said, and his uncle had laughed uproariously.

He was fired with a rare excitement as he watched the sun set on the water, a lifting of his spirits. A new world, he thought, a land of opportunity. His eyes fell on a sentence in one of the pamphlets Uncle Terence had given him. 'The raging, tearing, booming nineteenth century, the glorious age of steam, electricity and progress.' He had lived in Sholton all his life, and he had had to come to America to realize his place in history, the times he lived in. For the first time since Bessie's death he was not obsessed by her, he was aware of the challenge of the age. It was like an iron band being lifted from his heart. He drew in his breath, settled down to watch the panorama unfolding itself through the window.

The train was slowing and, suddenly nervous, he got to his feet and lifted down his baggage. But it was not Wanapeake, he saw by the noticeboard. The other passengers were looking at him, half-amused. He sat down again, feigning a nonchalance he did not feel. Was it the cut of his clothes, or the way he had been studying the leaflets? Or that he looked too anxious? 'Take things easy, Patrick,' Bessie had often said.

He looked out of the window, and the scene charmed him again. However Ma had tried, she had not been able to convey to him the breadth and grandeur of the river, its traffic of ferries, yachts and the occasional freighter, the small fishing-boats. Its width made the Clyde look like the Sholtie in comparison, he thought, smiling to himself. He remembered she had told him about a sail she had taken up it with the two families. 'A red-letter day,' she had said, 'to be remembered for ever. I knew I was happy on the day itself, not in retrospect. That was a valuable discovery.' This, too, was a kind of red-letter day for him.

Now the train was slowing down again. He put on a disdainful look for the benefit of the other passengers.

Earlier he had gone to the small toilet and checked his appearance carefully – his grey silk cravat embroidered with a discreet maroon sprig, the correct black of his frock coat – smoothed his hair, made sure the centre parting was as straight as a die. Details mattered. He had found that out in their own business. He was the man for detail, Terence for the grand effect. They were a good team together . . . don't think of him, you'll not enjoy a thing.

Now the train had stopped. 'Wanapeake! Wanapeake!' the station master was shouting. He gathered his valises – the trunk containing all the presents so carefully chosen by Ma was coming on later – opened the door and stepped down.

Almost immediately he heard, 'There he is! Patrick! Patrick!' and Kate was running towards him. In a moment she was in his arms.

To his dismay he felt tears rush to his eyes. His sister, Kate, the sister no one had a bad word to say about, dark-haired, rosy-cheeked, instantly recognizable and yet different because she was smarter and her voice had a faint American twang. She was making no bones about crying, mopping at her eyes with a lace-trimmed handkerchief. 'Oh, Patrick, I knew you right away!'

'I knew you.'

'Did you see Uncle Terence?'

'Yes, and New York. And the Plaza Hotel where we had lunch. He had me fair dumfoonered.' He joked to hide his emotion at seeing her.

'Well, come and meet the others. They're just *dy*ing to see you.'

The girls, Emily and Victoria, were as different from Isobel and Maevy as night from day; softer, dressier, gigglier, they seemed to be all ribbons and bows, pouts and laughter. Victoria, he noticed, was quieter than her sister, but Emily threw her arms round his neck and

kissed him soundly on the cheek. She smelled of lavender.
'You're even more handsome than Kate said. Oh, I love
you already!' Her two brothers looked ashamed of her as
they shook hands. One of them spoke earnestly.

'We're off back to school tomorrow, cousin Patrick.
We're very happy you arrived before we left.'

'But shouldn't I have been seeing you every morning in
any case?' He was surprised when everybody laughed.

'Not unless you want to swim up the Hudson for a
hundred miles,' Victoria said.

The tall dark girl shook her finger laughingly at her.
'You're naughty, Victoria.' And to Patrick, 'I'm Maria.
Welcome to Wanapeake. And don't let those girls tease
you. The boys go to boarding school at Albany. That's
what Victoria means.'

'Aren't you going to kiss him?' Emily said. 'He's your
real cousin.'

'Only if he wants me to.' She had mischievous eyes.
'You're too solemn,' Bessie had said . . .

'But I do want to,' he said in an agony of embarrassment, and aimed a kiss which landed on Maria's nose.

'They're wicked, the three of them,' Kate said. 'Pay no
attention. James is very sorry he couldn't be here to meet
you, Patrick, but you'll see him at dinner. Aunt Caroline's
come over with Maria as well, and Uncle Terence will
join us here.'

'We've killed the fatted calf,' George said, jaunty in his
knickerbockers. Was he at it, too, for God's sake?

'Come along, Patrick. The carriage is waiting.' Kate
linked her arm through his. 'George, Ernest, you take his
valises. That's right, Maria, you walk beside him and
protect him from those awful girls.'

Patrick stole a look at his cousin and intercepted her
wry glance. 'I was just thinking how like my mother you
are,' he said.

440

'But she's got beautiful red hair, Irish hair, not like this horrible dark stuff, like a squaw's.' The 'dark stuff', he thought, looked very fetching in a chignon. Her clothes were well-cut but not beribboned like those of Emily and Victoria. 'Do you ride?'

'Ride?' he echoed.

'On a horse.'

'Oh! No.' He shook his head. 'There hasn't been time for that. But my mother's talking of teaching wee Lizzie, that's . . .'

'Your daughter?'

'Yes.' The simple words moved him. 'His daughter'. Well, his name was on her birth certificate, wasn't it? He it was who had married her mother.

'You have to start when you're young. Your mother's got a fine seat. We had some lovely rides together when she was here.' She smiled at him. 'She was a great success with everyone.'

'She's a great success with everything she tackles.'

She nodded in agreement. 'How is Isobel?'

'Happy.'

'She did the right thing. I always fancied there was a religious streak in Isobel.' They had reached the carriage. He liked his cousin. Her directness reminded him of Ma. You knew where you were with her.

He seemed to be taken in hand from then on. Where it had been hard demanding work at home, here it was relaxed pleasure. They seemed devoted to making their lives pleasurable, just as he had been devoted to hard work. James was a fine-looking man whom he had liked the first time he saw him at the dock-side, but grew rapidly in his estimation because of his evident love of Kate and his easy manner with the rest of the family, entirely different from Father who took his duties seriously. You always worried about hurting Father. But this man had a smiling tolerance of all those surrounding him, and yet there was an inner strength. Watching him with Kate and their little son, Kieran James, he would think, that is how we should have been if Bessie had lived.

'You've had a hard time, Patrick,' James said to him one evening when they were sitting on the verandah having an after-dinner cigar together. The heavy trees partially blocked the view of the river. I would have cut some of them down before now, Patrick thought.

'No more than most.' He should have jumped at the chance to speak freely to this urbane man, so different from Father who was almost too sensitive, who felt your hurt as keenly as you did yourself. Someone who could stand outside the problem was better. How much had Mother told them about Bessie and the child not being his? It was all right for James with a settled family and a wife like Kate, never any worries.

'You get through things in time,' James said into the well of silence. 'There are no easy words. I grieved deeply when my first wife died, but then I had the luck of few men – that your sister was prepared to join her life with mine, battered and bruised as I was.'

You were never battered and bruised, Patrick thought bitterly. Your life has run in quieter channels. 'Yes, there aren't many like Kate,' he said, getting up because he could not sit still. I only knew one . . . he did not know whether he said the words aloud or not. He turned, his back against the rail of the verandah. 'Now that I'm here, James,' he said, with a show of brightness, 'I'd like to hear about your export business. Sometimes I dream of expanding ours, even having overseas branches in time. Could you give me an idea how the land lies?'

'Ask away,' James said. He had taken the hint. He would keep off the subject of Bessie.

* * *

442

The atmosphere at Springhill was different again when he went at his Aunt Caroline's insistence to stay with them for a few days. She reminded him of Maevy who, by her capacity for getting her own way, could recall to you that she was the youngest of the family and should be indulged on that account. Although she was different now. At one time he had wondered which of his sisters John Craigie would choose.

'Don't judge your aunt at first sight,' Mother had said. 'Underneath her fluttery ways there's something else. It's a kind of façade, to hide a hurt, maybe. Was everyone hiding a hurt, even Maevy? But Ma could be right about Aunt Caroline. He saw how his uncle treated her like a delicate piece of china, and how her eyes strayed to him from time to time as if for support.

'Now, I know you want to have serious conversations with your uncle, Patrick,' she said, 'but all work and no play never did anyone any good.' She put her hand on his arm and he saw her pale blue eyes were suffused with tears. 'I can sympathize with you, believe me, I also lost a loved one, but you're young. I can tell you, it will pass.' And then she was her fluttery self again: 'Maria, take this dear boy into the garden and have a game of croquet with him. He needs some fresh air. Look how pale he is with all that travelling. Oh,' she clasped her hands, 'you and your mother and sister are so brave crossing the Atlantic. I would never dare . . .' The little bows marching down the front of her bodice quivered.

Nothing was too much trouble for her to arrange. Maria teased her. 'Mother sees herself as a great society hostess,' she said, when he protested that they were doing too much for him. 'She's determined to have your visit written up in the *Wanapeake Gazette*.'

'I wish she wouldn't put herself out.'

'She's used to entertaining. Dinna fash yourself. There,

443

isn't that good? I practised it for you coming. She comes from the old South, open house, piceaninnies and all that.' She laughed like Bessie, he thought, not sure whether she was teasing him or not, open-throated, open-mouthed. 'Have you got the picture? But, dear cousin, if you want to keep on the right side of her, just don't mention the Federals!'

There were trips laid on to see the Catskill Mountains and to Lake George, to Saratoga and the racing there – the latter being Maria's idea – and to Hartford to see Mark Twain's house; days sailing on the Hudson in her friends' yachts. She was surrounded by young men but had no special beau. There was a remoteness about her that puzzled him, made him curious.

Why was a beautiful, rich young woman like her not married? She was grand company, extremely popular, that was evident. She teased him out of his dark moods when he became remote and distant. 'Leave me be, Maria,' he said to her once. She drew back as if he had struck her, and he turned on his heel and strode through the garden gate to walk till he was dropping with tiredness. When he came back he found her in the stables.

'You're in a muck sweat,' she said, looking at him. 'You would have got rid of that black dog quicker on the back of one of those horses.'

'And risk concussion when it throws me at the first tree stump?' he said. She met his eyes and then they were laughing together.

'You . . . sailing over Starlight's neck . . . oh, Patrick . . . one thing, if you laugh like that tomorrow all the young ladies of New York State will be fighting to be the partner of the Scottish lord.' His aunt was giving a small dance for him – 'just a few young friends, Patrick. Not enough to weary you . . .'

'I'm no Scottish lord, as you well know,' he said. 'Six

444

years ago I was washing my back in my mother's scullery to get the dirt of the ironworks off me.'

She looked unimpressed. 'Anyone with Muldoon blood in them is an aristocrat. You should have seen the impression your mother made on the folks around here. You'll do the same.'

She never mentioned Bessie, but she restored his belief in himself. For the first time in his life he took pride in his ancestry, and that at least was something. Maybe there was something different about being Irish and half a Muldoon.

There were also strictly masculine outings when he went up to New York by train with James and Terence, returning with them at night. He was introduced to many of their associates, and given an insight into how they ran their businesses. Mother had been right. There was little of the cautiousness so often displayed by the Scotsmen he had to deal with, those stern men (Terence called them 'those thrawn buggers') who dug in their heels and would not be budged until they had looked at a proposition from every angle. 'Aye, maybe,' was their invariable response. Here it was. 'Why not?' There was nothing to lose, everything to gain.

Uncle Terence only spoke obliquely about Bessie once when they were on their own. He had stayed at Springhill for the dance his aunt had given, and in the morning had gone to New York with his uncle.

'Don't harp back too much, lad. I watched your face last night. Your mother and I are both forward-looking, and I'm not sure if you have that characteristic or not.' He shrugged. 'It's no good expecting a young man to benefit from an older man's experience – you have to go through the whins yourself and yours have been pricklier than most. But go forward. Get possessed and obsessed with the future of your business if you can hold on to nothing else; plan for it, work for it, and one day you'll find you're a whole man again.' He nodded briskly, looking away, but not before Patrick had seen the sympathy in his eyes. 'There is no reason why in time you couldn't extend your business to the other side of the Atlantic. Maybe join up with James and me. There will be motorized transport before long. We've already land and sea to choose from. Who knows there may not be the air as well?'

He was captivated by such boldness, but his Scottish upbringing made him cautious. 'We're going to go cannily for a few years, Uncle, after that bank debâcle. Consolidate our position.'

'Now, that's the wrong way to look at it.' Those were his mother's eyes, surely, the bright face. 'Take things on the rising tide. Depression will follow this upsurge, it's the rule of the universe. When you're riding high that's the time to make enough money to weather the recession. You must be constantly looking forward. Look how far my company has progressed from the days of sailing ships, and yet that's only a decade away.'

'We still have to repay you, Uncle. That's a debt of honour.'

'No, no, Patrick.' He leaned across the table. They were in the Plaza Hotel again. 'I look on that as an investment for my old age.'

And always there was Kate in the background, loving, happy, surrounding him with love and making no bones about talking about Bessie. 'She was my friend as well as your wife, Patrick. I grieve for her. Oh, I know it's nothing like the bond which exists between a man and his wife, but don't push her out in your bitterness, make her part of your life. She'd like to see you happy, she'll rest easily if she knows that. And you have a bit of her left,

446

don't forget that, in Lizzie. Give her the love you would have given her mother.'

'She's not my child, Kate,' he said, agonized.

'She's got your name, hasn't she? So what if your brother fathered her? What could be closer than a brother? Remember the good times in Colliers' Row, you and Terence sharing a bed; remember the time you got drunk together? Oh, how our mother and I laughed at that when she told me! I was at Blythswood Square then. Lizzie's a McGrath. Don't forget that. I've a feeling something will bring you and Terence together. I don't know what it'll be . . .'

He felt this to be a healing time. He had smothered his grief back home, his bitterness had kept the family away. Everyone needed to let their grief work through.

Kate encouraged him to take the ferry over to Springhill when she was busy with the baby and household tasks. Too much of a women's household this, she told him, with James working such long hours away, and the girls coming and going. Maria seemed always to be at home, as if she was expecting him.

'I've given up trying to teach you to ride, Patrick,' she said one sunny afternoon. They were sitting on the lawn looking across the Hudson. In the far distance they could see the occasional flame of the maple trees, the first ones to lose their green, she had told him.

'What are you going to do with me, then?' He was lying at her feet on a rug. He looked up and thought how her appearance pleased him – the intelligent face with the mischief in the dark eyes, the cloud of dark hair, today unbraided.

'I've decided to educate you. You're woefully ignorant when it comes to books. When the Wanapeake belles and Emily and Victoria can spare you, I thought we might read aloud to each other. There's Washington Irving whose house you've seen and who is a favourite of your sister, Kate, and Mark Twain. I've got his *Innocents Abroad* here.' She held the book up.

'That's me, to a tee.'

'Except you didn't sail into New York on the *Quaker City*.' She smiled. 'But in return you must read something to *me*.'

'I didn't bring any books. I knew you were all going to rush me off my feet.'

She clapped her hands. 'Now, that's better! You can be quite humorous when you like. Well, you must rack your brains, and for every chapter of *Tom Sawyer* I read to you, you must recite something you remember from *your* schooldays.'

'I didn't think I was visiting America for the purpose of going back to school.'

'My dear cousin,' she said, laughing at him, 'you have a lot to learn. How to play as well as how to work. Now, don't close up like a clam, when I'm doing my best to entertain you.'

He turned from her and looked across the river spreading away from him. She did not understand. Her life had been too sheltered.

But such was her sunny nature that the following afternoon he found himself sitting beside her again. He had declined Emily and Victoria's invitation to visit friends of theirs whose chief attraction, it seemed, was that their house had six marble fireplaces and was the talk of Wanapeake for its magnificence. He was intrigued by Maria. He wanted to be hurt again, to be picked by this girl who was like his mother and yet not like her, who was his age and yet seemed older, who had a lightness and sophistication he had never encountered in any woman. 'I'm ready to begin my education if you are,' he said.

'Do you remember our pact? An eye for an eye?'

'I'll try,' he said. Mother had always recited poetry to him, his father had sung songs. He would have to see that he did not let them down.

He had never known anything more pleasurable than to sit on the lawn beside Maria while she read aloud to him. He was sure he would not have the same flavour from the book if *he* had read it, he told her. It took an American voice to give it full justice. And yet all childhoods were the same. He remembered sunlit days playing in the field at the back of their house, fishing for baggie minnows in the Sholtie Burn, scuffing the gold and copper leaves with his feet as he went down the Sholtie Brae. Always with Terence. There was little of that laughing-faced boy left now . . . 'What could be closer than a brother?' Kate had said.

Sometimes, however, a word or phrase would make his mind stray to Bessie loving, laughing . . . Bessie living. He would be sunk in his misery, not listening, uncaring, and then her bright eyes would notice, her bright voice would recall him, and he would drag himself reluctantly from the black depths of his grief. Once she shut the book.

'Did you like it?'

'Yes, he can make you see it. Missouri or Sholton, it doesn't matter.'

'It's your turn now. Come on, you promised.' He said the first thing that came into his head, without embarrassment, as if the young Tom Sawyer had taken away his inhibitions.

> 'Wee, sleekit, cow'rin tim'rous beastie,
> O, what a panic's in tha breastie . . .'

She held up her hand, laughing, 'And what kind of foreign gibberish is that, pray?'

'Braid Scots, the tongue of Rabbie Burns, no less.'

'You must teach me it immediately. I shall ask James to let me say grace the next time we visit them, and surprise him with it. Can you imagine his face?'

'Yes, I can.' He had to smile.

'I hope it won't be as lugubrious as yours was a short time ago.' How clear her eyes were, full of intelligence, and something more. 'What do you think of my mother, Patrick?' she said, surprising him.

'Aunt Caroline? Well, she's a . . . kind . . . hospitable lady . . .'

'You're taken aback, aren't you? I can see it in your grim Scottish face. Oh, yes, I'm sure you think she's kind and hospitable, but I've seen you looking at her when she's being unsuitably . . . "girlish" . . . is that the word you'd use? And I know what you're thinking.'

'Tell me, then.' She was too smart by half.

'That she's a foolish woman, not a patch on your own mother.'

'You're wrong.'

'Mark Twain said, "When in doubt, tell the truth." Shall I tell you about my mother, cousin dear?'

'If you wish.'

'Ten years ago, when I was seventeen, my mother's dearly-beloved brother, Gaylord, drowned himself on the beach near their home.'

'You mean . . . drowned himself?'

'Yes, I mean, committed suicide. His clothes were found, and a note.'

'Where was this?' He was shaken.

'Tidewater Virginia. She took it very badly, so badly that she was under the doctor's care for a year. I was so upset at the effect her illness had on my father that I gave up my beau to devote myself to him and to visiting my mother.'

'Visiting?'

'Yes, she was in a rest home for six months. That's what we call them here. I loved them both very much, you see.'

'But not your beau?'

'I thought I did. Now I know I couldn't have given him up if I'd truly loved him.'

'I'm sorry.'

'Sorry I gave up Harold, or sorry about my mother?'

'About your mother.'

'That's better. You see, Gaylord was her twin. They were very close. They grew up together and he'd never really settled after she left home and came here. She'd met my father in New York when she was visiting friends. She's quite recovered now, but that's why my father can't do enough for her. He knows how she suffered. The good thing that came out of it is that he and I have a great deal in common because of what we went through together.'

'What are you trying to tell me?' He did not like the creeping sense of shame inside him, making him feel . . . unworthy.

'Nothing. I'm . . . *showing*.' She smiled at him, her eyes deep.

'Tidewater Virginia . . . you said on the beach . . .'

'Yes, the Atlantic Ocean.' Her eyes were still on him.

'And that's why she won't make the trip to Scotland with your father, any trip, fear . . .'

'No one is without fear.'

He got up abruptly and walked about the lawn, thinking of his Aunt Caroline and Uncle Terence, a Southern belle and an Irish gentleman, of their gaiety and their kindness, and of the sorrow behind it. And how *he* compared with his bitterness and his black moods. He had a small share of that gaiety, a very small share, so noticeable in his mother and her brother.

451

And Aunt Caroline had it in her own fluttering kindness, her desire to please and make others happy. Maria had it, Bessie had had it, Lizzie, please God, or perhaps it was up to him, would have it, too. A kind of gallantry.

He walked about for a long time, and when he went back and sat down beside Maria she looked at him smilingly. 'Do you want some more Tom Sawyer,' she said, 'or do you prefer to talk?'

'I prefer to talk,' he said.

The holiday was drawing to a close. They sailed up to Albany to enable him to say good-bye to Ernest and George, a great slap-bang wallop of a sailing party, as Uncle Terence called it, even including Kieran James in his bassinet. And it was a beautiful, calm autumn day with a hint of the coming snows in the wind as they sailed back.

'Has Mark Twain anything to say about this?' he asked Maria, standing at the rail beside her.

'Well, it would apply to the Mississippi, of course, but then all rivers are the same, if different. There's something about water that moves human beings.' She leaned over to watch the steamer's ruffled wake. 'My father and I are very grateful to you and your mother, and Isobel, for coming to visit with us.'

'It's the other way round.'

'No.' She turned to face him, her cheeks rosy under her fur bonnet. 'You see, Mother had never taken a sail on the Hudson until she went with your mother on the *Mary Powell*, and now she's done it again with you.'

'That makes her a very brave lady,' he said. She put her hand on his sleeve, her eyes widening with pleasure.

'How pleased she would be to hear you say that. Perhaps I'll tell her. She's a little afraid of you, did you know that? She thinks you are a Scottish genius like

452

Thomas Carlyle, that you go around thinking great thoughts.' He burst out laughing.

'Me!'

'Yes, you!' She turned away from him. Her voice was low. 'She's always lacked confidence, just as her brother did. Those parties and dances she gives, she suffers *dreadfully* before they begin but she makes herself . . . The act of suicide is the ultimate lack of self-confidence, don't you think?'

All the lonely nights he had spent in that house at Sholton came back to him, the getting out of bed in the middle of the night, the walking about until dawn. But he had never been near that, thank God. 'Perhaps now that she's got her sea-legs she'll come and visit us next year?'

'Perhaps.'

'She could send an envoy to spy out the land.' He touched her elbow and her face turned to him, smiling, lively again.

'Do you know, I feel the same sense of pleasure as a prospector discovering his first nugget of gold, when you make a remark like that. There's a playful laddie – is that Scottish enough for you? – under that grim exterior.'

'No' so wee, cow'rin, tim'rous as ye thocht?' He spoke broadly to amuse her. 'But *would* you become her envoy, cousin?'

'If you ask me nicely, kind sir, I might.' She put her forefinger to her chin, her eyes laughing under the bonnet.

He asked her nicely when they were all on the station platform at Wanapeake once more, this time to see him off. He was travelling up to New York with James and Terence to embark on the *Caledonia* for home.

' "Caledonia stern and wild," ' Maria quoted when the name of the ship was mentioned. 'Who said that?'

'Sir Walter Scott,' James said. 'Now it's a strange fact

that Maria knows more about the literature of Scotland than anyone else in America, with the possible exception of myself, and yet she hasn't been there.'

'She will have to rectify that,' Kate said. 'Why not become a stowaway on Patrick's ship, Maria?'

'I would if he would suggest it.'

'Go on, suggest it, suggest it!' Emily and Victoria chorused. 'She's *dying* for you to suggest it.'

'Come to Bonnie Scotland,' he said, smiling at her, 'afore long.'

'Aye, I maybe will.' Her dark eyes smiled back at him.

They were the last thing he saw as he stood at the compartment window, waving.

18

Maeve noticed a difference in Patrick when he came home. He was more relaxed, although he would never have the effervescent quality that Terence had, or used to have; but then he, too, was not so tense recently. Strangely enough, the Kelvinside house seemed to have had a good effect on him.

He had always liked nice surroundings, nice clothes – she remembered the care he had taken in his dress long ago when he had been going to meet Catherine – and he evidently enjoyed the gracious purlieus of Kelvinside, the important people they met. They even had an invitation to go to the Kibble Palace on the 5th December, no less, to see Gladstone being installed as Rector of Glasgow University!

'It looks as if we're moving with the gentry now,' he had said to her, trying not to look impressed.

And as far as Patrick was concerned, there was the strong bond that was springing up between him and Lizzie. She toddled to meet him now when he came each evening – he still could not be persuaded to move into Braidholme – and the only improvement Maeve could make there was to send Maggie periodically to his house to give it 'a good redd up'.

'Here's Daddy,' she would say to Lizzie when they heard his voice in the hall, and her little face would brighten with anticipation. Maggie had strict instructions not to whisk her away before Patrick had had a play with her. At a year and nine months she was a rollicking little

girl, a delight to everyone at Braidholme, but still guarded
ferociously by Maggie. She saw Maeve off to Glasgow
every morning with what could only be interpreted as
relief. 'Now, you take your time in Glesca, Mrs McGrath.
Wee Lizzie'll no' take any harm while you're away.'

She went with an easy conscience. Even in her youth
her children had never completely absorbed her mind. It
was too active. She was now immersed in the daily
running of the office, and the only remaining sorrow to
her was that while Terence and Patrick no longer pointedly avoided each other, they never seemed to exchange
any conversation except on business. Once or twice she
thought she detected a slight overture on Patrick's part,
but it was always rebuffed.

She invited Terence and Catherine to Braidholme for
her usual Christmas dinner – 'I don't care if they don't
celebrate it here,' she had said to Kieran, 'we always did
in Ireland' – but Catherine refused politely. 'It's no good,
Mother. I would come willingly, but Terence won't if
Patrick's going to be there. We've been through it many
times.'

Catherine now looked and was a grand lady. She had
developed a quiet but stylish manner of dress, patronizing
only the best shops in Sauchiehall Street. She had her
own dressmaker, her own bootmaker, she took an active
interest in various societies, especially the Temperance
Movement. The latter must have had some effect on
Terence, because Maeve noticed he had become a moderate drinker only, in accordance with his new position as
a man of substance. It was as if they had both taken their
lead from the elegance of Great Western Terrace.

They now had a wide circle of friends, important people
in the city, and even Patrick admitted to Maeve that they
were useful to the business. Great Western Terrace, with

its columned porticos, its stylish air, was becoming McGrath's shop window.

The stumbling block, of course, as Maeve said to Kieran, was Lizzie. The boys could now communicate on a business footing, they could meet at banquets, assembly halls, smoking concerts and the Corn Exchange eating houses, but what neither of them could stomach was to be at Braidholme together where Lizzie was now, with her laughing face, and already so like Bessie except for her red hair, that they would have been constantly reminded of her.

Just before Christmas Maeve had a letter from Maria which arrived with the usual generous gifts.

No doubt Patrick will have told you his impressions of us, perhaps not all flattering, but at least I hope we cheered him up a little. My heart bled for him, Aunt Maeve, when he stepped off the train at Wanapeake, so tight-lipped, so sad, but determined to put a good face on it. And so handsome! I should have known, remembering you.

But after a while I don't think he could resist Kate's and James' kindness, little Kieran's crowing, the girls' teasing, and I even think he enjoyed himself at Springhill once he knew we weren't going to bite him!

We had many a long talk. Sometimes I think it's easier to talk to someone outside the family, and yet part of it. He's been deeply hurt, as you well know, and he has nothing but praise for the way you and Uncle Kieran have supported him, but what he still can't wholly accept is Terence's part in Bessie's life, and the fact that Lizzie is his child. I don't think he ever will until they get together and discuss, not what has happened to *them*, but what's going to happen to Lizzie. It can't be put off for ever.

Do I sound a managing kind of girl, writing to you like this? Well, of course I am, or maybe circumstances have forced me to be. I was going to confide in you had that terrible telegram not arrived when you were with us, but Patrick will tell you how worried we were about Mother for a long time. Father was against writing to you. He said you shouldn't be burdened, and indeed I only told Patrick in the hope that it would take his mind off his own troubles. He's inward-looking, as you well know. I wanted him to realize that things do right themselves in time, or, failing that, that we adjust or make compromises.

You will be wondering why I'm writing this to you, but I've been invited by your son to come and visit you all, and I feel I can come now, and, oh, I'd like to! We'll be going to Norfolk, Virginia, for Christmas. Mother now feels she can face seeing her old home again with all its memories, and after that the weather gets pretty bad here, but I thought of the spring of next year. Eighteen eighty. What a propitious sound that has!

Would this suit you? Could you put up with your devoted niece Maria for a little while? What good times we could have talking together, riding together, perhaps, playing with Lizzie . . . and then, I should see Patrick . . .

Maeve put down the letter to smile. What a long time she had taken to get to the root of it! If you wanted to know why someone was writing to you, you should read the last sentence first. She took up the letter again. '. . . and then, I should see Patrick . . .'

19

It would be a good Christmas with wee Lizzie there, but not the one she had longed for, the whole family gathered round the table at Braidholme. Isobel and John were sympathetic, John, as minister, diplomatic. 'What might be the best idea would be for us to ask Terence and Catherine to come to the manse,' he said. 'If we came to you, then *they*'d feel left out. Besides, it's a busy time for me with the kirk.'

'But they needn't feel left out,' she protested, 'it's the season of goodwill. Surely they could bury the hatchet and come to Braidholme? Couldn't you say something to them?'

'I've spoken to Terence. It's no use. Patrick too. He seems, if anything, less adamant, but he says it's no good. He tried once when he got back from America and was rebuffed. I even quoted Ephesians 4, verse 32.' He smiled. 'But they're my brother's-in-law, don't forget. I don't want to lose their friendship and become their conscience.' She had to admit he took the sensible view. You could not force two people to shake hands, any more than you could get anyone to kneel at the Lord's table if he did not want to.

Isobel consoled her. 'Once they're with us and the Christmas spirit gets going, and maybe some of John's punch, who knows, we'll maybe all arrive at Braidholme and surprise you.'

She had to accept it. There was still wee Lizzie. She would rely on her to save the day with her childish delight in all things Christmassy. So they took her visiting on the morning of Christmas in the new brougham which had taken one hundred pounds to build, laden with gifts, and driven by Kieran who enjoyed feeling the reins between his hands and a high-stepping pony at his command.

The first call was a stop at the McDonalds' cottage at the drive gates to see the new baby there, a healthy boy this time, then on to the manse to drink some punch with John and Isobel. Terence and Catherine had not arrived yet; they were being entertained by their own minister and his wife to morning sherry and cakes. They were staunch attenders of the big church near them on Great Western Road, and counted the Reverend and his lady amongst their personal friends.

After that Kieran drove them at a spanking pace – possibly helped by the punch – through Sholton which was going about its usual workaday life. The men were down the pits, the shops were open. Only the school was closed. Heathens, Maeve thought smugly. But the Cranstons at Crannoch were all there, and Maeve suffered a pang of envy to see the sons joking with each other. The green ginger wine helped to soothe her spirits.

Arthur was 'well up' in Glasgow with the Labour movement, as Bob put it, and a staunch supporter of Alexander MacDonald, the Holytown schoolmaster. 'I'm convinced we're nearing the time when the whole idea of the truck system will be entirely abolished by an Act of Parliament,' Maeve heard Arthur say. 'It will be superseded by the cooperative societies run for the benefit of the men, not the owners, contractors or unscrupulous clerks.' The men were gathered in a group at one end of the room. She shamelessly listened. The women were engrossed in the bevy of children on the floor, Lizzie amongst them, to her entire delight.

'Those were the days back in the pits, all the same,'

Bob said to Kieran. 'You get to having a kind of yearning, although it was hard and dangerous work.'

She saw Kieran nod. 'It's not the pits we yearn for, Bob. It's our youth.' 'Gone like our youth too soon . . .' The words came back to Maeve as she listened to the two older men talking about the old days. It was no good looking back. Their house in the Row had meant hard, demanding work for her. No wonder Alastair Crawford had seemed like a knight on a white charger, an escape. Did she regret that period in her life, her temporary unfaithfulness which might have become absolute if it had not been for the three women? She did not know. Middle-age is a time for questioning, she told herself. Soon I won't even be doing that . . .

But going back to Braidholme she laughed and was happy to be with Kieran and wee Lizzie in her new white fur coat, white fur muff and white fur bonnet. As Kieran said, you did not know where the fur ended and wee Lizzie began. 'Kissmass, Kissmass,' the child sang in her own version of a carol. You had to see it through her eyes.

To fill up the table somewhat, Charlie McNab had been invited to join them, and he proved to be a good guest, playing with Lizzie in her high chair, teasing Maevy. 'I thought you would have gone for a nurse by this time,' he said to her. 'I keep hoping I'll bump into you in the corridors of the Royal.'

'Next year,' she told him. 'I'll be eighteen then. Mother and I will be going for an interview after the New Year.'

'And do you hope to become a nurse, too, Mrs McGrath?' He was dark, had a bold nose – a Jewish look, although he came from Fife.

'Not me. I would be far too impatient to minister to the sick. Maevy's the one with the patience.'

'What made you decide?' he asked her.

461

'It's a long story,' she said. She was as non-committal as Patrick at times. Charlie turned to him.

'I haven't seen you to have a word with you about America yet. What did you think of the poverty in New York? They tell me it's something awful there, folks dying on the streets from the bitter cold.'

'To tell you the truth, I didn't see much of it,' Patrick said, 'but you don't have to go to New York to see poverty. You should see the back of the Gallowgate where our stables are. Men and women in rags, children bare-footed. But they still find money for drink, some of them. They haven't heard of the Temperance Movement there.'

'I've seen it. I'm going round the houses collecting information for a book I hope to write some day.'

'Is that a fact?' Patrick looked interested. 'On what subject?'

'That's a long story,' he said. Maeve saw her daughter give him a look of appreciation.

The day passed pleasantly after all. Charlie McNab left about three to do his usual round of patients, and Patrick, Maevy, Kieran and Maeve, with little Lizzie, sat round the tea-table placed near the fire. Maggie and Susan had been asked in to drink a cup with them and taste the black bun, and they sat on the edge of their chairs in their starched uniforms, Susan primly, but with a pleased expression that indicated it was only right for a trusted servant like herself to be asked 'ben the hoose' once a year; Maggie, cup and saucer held with a pinkie stuck well out, following Lizzie's every movement as she played on the rug.

Maeve put a small table beside the girl. 'Put your cup there, Maggie. If you're going to dash to Lizzie's help every five minutes I don't want to see my best china in smithereens.'

'I'm watching it, Mrs McGrath.' She did not take her eyes off Lizzie. 'Will you look at her, though? She's got that wee dolly's claes off already, drawers and everything. My, she's that clever!'

Maeve smiled at Kieran. He looked contented in his big chair at the fire. How many years now is it, she thought. Getting on for thirty? We've been lucky . . . there was a loud knocking at the door.

Her heart leaped. Had Terence decided to come after all? Was the loudness of the knock to hide his embarrassment? That would be typical of Terence. When his mind was made up there were no half-measures. Rat-tat-tat-tat. Loudly. 'Go and see who that is, Maggie.' The girl dumped down the cup and saucer unceremoniously, was on her feet and out of the door as she spoke. It had been an imperative kind of knocking, more than just loud. She looked at Kieran, face calm. It had not been a happy sound at all.

Wally McDonald burst into the room, followed by a frightened-faced Maggie. 'I can see flames from my cottage, Mr McGrath! In the direction of the stables! I ran to tell you. The sky's awfy red . . .'

Kieran was on his feet. 'It wouldn't be the ironworks?'

'No, that's the other side of Sholton . . .'

'We'd better go.' He turned to Patrick. He was standing beside them, his face anxious.

'Yes, right away.'

'Get out the brougham, Wally,' Kieran said. 'It's quickest. We'll help you.'

'You'll have to let Terence know as well.' Maeve had picked up Lizzie. She felt the need to hold the child close to hide her fear. 'You pass the manse. Pick him up.' She saw Patrick hesitate. 'Do as you're told,' she said sharply, 'it's his business, too!' And, turning to Maggie and Susan,

463

'You two get away to the kitchen now and get on with the dishes.'

'Oh, Mrs McGrath,' Maggie wailed, 'what will happen to the puir horses gettin' aw burned . . . ?'

Maeve looked at Kieran. 'What about Crichton? Shouldn't you let him know?'

'He'll have heard.' He shook his head with impatience. 'Come on, Patrick.'

'The vet . . . we should get the vet there.'

'We'll send someone when we see the damage.' Kieran was halfway to the door. 'We're putting off time. Come on . . .' They were gone, and Maevy and Maeve were left looking at each other in disbelief.

'Maybe it's just some hay that's caught fire.'

'Maybe.' Lizzie began to whimper and Maevy took her from her mother's arms, put her down on the rug and sat down beside her. 'See, Lizzie, your bricks.' She began to build them, putting one carefully on top of the other. Lizzie clapped her hands and the bricks toppled. Maevy began painstakingly to rebuild them.

Maeve, watching her, marvelled at her patience. Here I am, she thought, burning inside with anxiety, and there she sits, building *bricks* . . . The flames must have been pretty high before Wally could see them from the gates . . . Someone knocked at the door. 'Come in, please,' she said. She sat rigid, straight-backed, preparing herself.

Susan showed in Cochran, the village policeman, a fat and perspiring Cochran. His uniform was half-buttoned, there was a currant sticking in the corner of his mouth. He had been in the middle of his clootie dumpling, she thought. His wife had the name of being a fine cook. 'Yes, Mr Cochran?' She did not have to ask.

'There's a fire at the stables, Mrs McGrath!' he panted. 'I came right away.' He was living up to his reputation of always being last on the scene.

'I know. Mr McGrath and Patrick left a quarter of an hour ago. But thank you for coming.'

'Who told them?' He looked aggrieved.

'Wally McDonald. He saw it from the gates.'

'He might have told *me* when I cycled past his house.'

'He went with them. How bad is it, Mr Cochran?'

'Bad enough. Well, now you know . . .' He looked around.

'Does Crichton, the stableman?'

'Aye, somebody will have told him. I expect.' His forehead furrowed. 'Well,' he said, 'I'd better get away to the scene of the crime.' The lodged currant wobbled. He remained where he was.

'Thanks for coming, Mr Cochran,' she said again.

'What a day for a fire!' He sighed.

'Yes,' she said, grimly this time. He was as bad as old Dr Gray had been for lingering.

'Susan will show you out,' Maevy said, looking up from the rug at the man. Their glances locked. He drew himself up and went out without another word.

Maeve shook her head at her daughter. 'You scared the life out of him the way you said that. Well, never mind. We got rid of Susan, too . . .' she tut-tutted impatiently, looking at Lizzie, then at Maevy, then sprang to her feet. 'I can't stand this a minute longer, hanging about here, wondering . . . I'm going, too.'

Maevy had scrambled to her feet as well. 'I was wondering how long it would take you to say that, Ma.'

'Were you? Well, you know now. You take Lizzie to the kitchen. I'll get our coats.'

'Right.' Maevy went out of the room carrying Lizzie, a lot quicker than Cochran.

It was about a mile to the stables, but they covered the distance in just over a quarter-of-an-hour. On the way they met people hurrying either to or from the fire, and they tried to gather some information. It had been smouldering for a long time, evidently. Some said they had smelt smoke in the air all day, but nobody had thought much about it until the flames had leapt into the sky. 'Like Dixon's Blazes,' a man said. 'You could hear the horses screaming . . .' They redoubled their steps, fearful of arriving, yet having to arrive quickly. Maevy put her hand through her mother's arm. 'Don't worry too much,' she said, 'people always exaggerate.'

But there was no exaggeration. The whole stables was alight when they got into the yard, and the fire engine was already there, steam rushing from the pump. The Chief knew her. 'I wouldn't go too near, Mrs McGrath. There's a danger from flying sparks.'

'Where is my husband, Jimmy? The boys are with him.'

He shook his head. 'I can't get any of them to keep back. They're doing their best to get the horses out with the help of some of the stable lads.'

'None of them are hurt? The lads?'

'No. But Dr McNab's been warned. He's at a birthing . . .'

'Is Crichton there?'

'No. He couldn't be found. He's not in his house. I'll have to get on.' He went back to his men.

They managed to get near enough to see what was going on. Someone had hung wet sacking over the stable doors, and every now and then it would swing forward and they would see a horse being led out. Some of the animals were docile, but others were screaming, their heads back in terror, their hooves flying. Occasionally they would recognize who was leading, hear the reassuring tones of one of the stable lads. 'Whoa, there! That's it, nice and steady . . .'

Smoke hung over the stables in a heavy pall, and every now and then, out of its clouds, great tongues of flame would leap up in the darkness. In the lulls Maeve began to catch glimpses of Kieran, then Terence, then Patrick. Once she saw them running to one side as a horse came tearing out through the sacking like a ball of flame, drew itself up on its hind legs screaming horribly, then fell to the ground, rolling in agony. The screaming cut through Maeve's head like a razor – the bared teeth, the foam escaping from its mouth was something to turn away from. There were shouts of terror from the people watching, then a loud report. The horse's legs flung out, the whole body writhed, and then was still. The horses inside set up a terrible noise as if in sympathy.

'Oh, Mother . . .' Maevy was in her arms, the tears running down her cheeks.

The firemen kept a steady stream of water playing on the stables. There was another engine on its way from Crannoch, Maeve heard someone say. Still, men went in and out through the hanging sacks; once, in the glare of a shooting tongue of flame, she saw Kieran's anguished face as he led out a horse, its mane blacked and singed. Every hurt will be his hurt, she thought.

It was like a nightmare that seemed to go on for ever. The onlookers did not speak to each other. She knew Charlie McNab came and went, only stopping with a few brief words of sympathy to them and to bandage the forehead of a stable lad who had been kicked getting a horse to its feet.

The scene seemed to claim everyone; the terrible sounds from the horses, the occasional thunder of their hooves, was like a drug that stopped tongues. Once, when Patrick appeared with a plunging horse's bridle in either hand, there was a rustle of appreciation from the watching crowd. Patrick was well-known in the village for his lack of interest in horses.

And then, as quickly as it had started, it seemed to be

over. The stables were a shambles; in some places the blackened corrugated iron of the roofs was intact, supported by a brick wall, or the remains of it, but for the most part the place was a ruin.

Mr Masters, the vet, was walking round examining the horses that lay on the ground. Occasionally a shot rang out. Maeve tried to be quick enough to turn her head away at the crucial moment, but she could still see the rolling horse in her mind's eye, smell the burning flesh. When she turned back again it would be still, except for the singed mane lifting slightly in the wind, and that seemed even more horrible. She and Maevy held on to each other, shuddering, speechless.

The fire Chief was at her side, carrying a paraffin lamp. 'It's all over bar the shouting, Mrs McGrath.' Suddenly it was cold, she noticed. The flames had died, only the sullen smoke hung over the stables. 'Your husband and sons are waiting in the brougham round the back of the inn. They had to leave it there because of the horse.'

'How did they know we were here? *Did* they know?'

He shook his head. His face was streaked with dirt, his shoulders sagged with exhaustion. 'I don't know. Maybe I told them. Maybe they saw you. You get home now.' He drew his hand over his eyes as if trying to blot something from his mind.

'It'll take a bit of forgetting, Jimmy.'

'Aye . . .'

'Come on, Mother,' Maevy said. She put her arm round her. 'We'll go and get Father and the boys.'

Bob Cranston was with them, his face as black as theirs with smoke. I haven't seen him like that, Maeve thought, since they used to go down the pit.

'Oh, terrible, terrible . . .' She went to Kieran, 'But you did your best.' He looked exhausted.

468

'Bob's kindly offered to take the horses that aren't injured to his barn for the night. It's nearer than our place.'

'We'd better get them round as quickly as we can.' Terence spoke.

'Where's Crichton?' She looked around. '*He* should be organizing that.' No one spoke.

'God knows.' Kieran shrugged. 'We'll manage without him.'

'We'll help you to ride them there, won't we, Maevy?'

'Yes.' She nodded. 'Don't worry, Father.' She was as keen on horses as Patrick.

'So will I,' Patrick said. If it had not been so tragic Maeve could have smiled. How often had she seen that expression on his face when, as a boy, he had been asked to do something that went against the grain. 'It will take a few trips, though.'

'You've got your stable lads, too,' Bob said. Where is *Crichton*? Maeve was thinking. She looked at Terence but his face was a mask.

'Come on, then, Kieran.' Bob put his hand on Kieran's shoulder. 'The sooner they're fed and watered and quietened down, the better.'

'You're a friend in need, Bob,' Maeve said.

It was a sad procession that made its way not once but three times to Bob Cranston's stables. Not like the last time I was in these parts, Maeve thought, riding with Alastair Crawford, my hair streaming in the wind, my heart beating with excitement at his nearness. There were so many coincidences in life, as if there were only a limited number of situations that had to be used again and again. But the circumstances were always different. She patted the poor animal's shivering neck, and her hand when she looked at it was black with soot.

* * *

469

When they got back to the house, Catherine, Isobel and John were in the drawing-room. They jumped up to greet them.

'Come and sit down here, Mr McGrath,' John said. 'I've been keeping it warm for you.'

'And you take this one, Mother.' Isobel plumped up cushions.

'All right.' She smiled. 'Don't fuss. It's your father and the boys who've been in the thick of it.' In spite of the shock she was feeling, one part of her mind was registering that Terence and Patrick were in the same room, her room. 'Pour out a drink for them, John.'

'I will indeed.' He went to the sideboard. No one spoke for a second, as if there was too much to say. Maeve looked across at Kieran. Was he still seeing the leaping shapes of the animals in his mind's eye as she was, smelling the smell of burnt flesh? There was a flush high on his cheekbones, his eyes were very bright.

'Here you are, then, Mr McGrath.' John was at his side. 'You deserve this.' He had a tray with glasses of whisky on it. 'I was sorry I was with a dying parishioner when you called at the manse.'

'Oh, yes?' He took a glass. 'Who was that?'

'Old John Stevenson, the roadman.'

Kieran nodded. 'Ah, well, his time had come.'

'And Dr McNab looked in to see everyone was all right,' Isobel told Maeve. 'He's at the bedside of Carrie Gibson with her ninth. She's having a bad time.'

'Ah, poor soul.'

Kieran said, sipping his whisky, 'By, this is welcome, sure enough. Better than a doctor.'

'Was it a total disaster, Mr McGrath?' Catherine said. She was as neat as usual in a navy-blue dress trimmed with bands of navy-blue satin, a white frill at her neck.

Like out of a bandbox, Maeve thought. She would be like that on the Day of Judgement.

'No, no, Catherine.' Kieran had always had a soft spot for her. 'We saved half of them. Some were in a state, though. Masters had to . . . shoot them.' His voice shook.

'He saved old Dobbin, though.' Terence spoke to his wife. 'You won't remember him. We took him over with the stables. He had a smile on his old face when Father led him out, stepping quite jecoe.'

The talk suddenly flooded as if a tap had been turned on. Maeve sat lapped in it. She heard Terence talking to Patrick.

'When you went in that time I thought you were chancing your arm a bit. Especially as you hardly know one end of a horse from the other.' She looked at Patrick and saw his mouth quirk over his whisky.

'I had no option with my own father dashing in and out as though he was at the Sunday School Picnic.'

'I can't get over them . . . being shot,' Kieran said. His voice was low. He looked rosy in the firelight.

'Where was Crichton in all this?' Maeve asked him. It had to be said.

He shook his head. 'That's what's been puzzling me.'

'I've bad news for you there, Mr McGrath,' John said. 'You'll have to prepare yourself.' He hesitated. 'He was found dead at the back of his house with a bullet through his head. There are rumours that he . . . well I'd better not say any more till the fire's investigated.' There was a shocked silence. Terence broke it, his voice rough.

'Maybe the vet shot him. Good riddance to bad rubbish.'

'Hush, Terence,' Maeve said, 'that's no way to talk!'

'Well, we all know how he had a grudge . . .'

'I believe he hasn't been a well man for some time,' John said. 'His wife had been to see me.' Did he suspect, too, that Crichton had set fire to the stables? Maeve met Maevy's eyes. They both looked away from each other, quickly. She said briskly,

'Tea and sandwiches. Plenty of hot tea. That's what we need. I'll go and tell Susan.'

'She's doing it, Mother,' Isobel said. 'Sit still and rest.'

'Yes, sit still, Mother.' Maevy smiled around the room. 'Do you know, she made three trips to Mr Cranston's barn to stable the horses we saved?'

'So did Maevy, they must have seemed like thirty-three to her, considering she's more at home on her feet than a horse's back.' Everyone laughed as if to relieve the tension.

'At least you got Katie out safely.' Patrick turned to his brother, and Maeve thought, he's showing his father that things are all right, to cheer him, and not to mind too much about Crichton. 'Her being in foal. But she came to no harm. Masters examined her.'

'Did he?' Kieran said. 'Yes, he did a fine job, Masters. Wouldn't have had it for the world. The sight of those horses . . . lying on the straw in their stalls . . . burning . . . not able to get up when you pushed and shoved . . . and on top of that, Crichton!' He let out his breath. 'Who would have thought . . . ?'

'Where's that girl with the tea and sandwiches?' Maeve said crossly. 'It's not like Susan not to be in when there's something going on.'

'Maybe we're better off with a dram,' Patrick said. He had got up and was leaning against the mantelpiece. His face looked stern. Maria had spotted the vulnerability behind the sternness. 'Good thing you were at Sholton.' His voice was shy as he looked at Terence.

'Aye, maybe it was meant.'

'We'll have to get word to Tom and Bob.'

'Catherine and I will call at their houses on our way back.'

'They're near you?'

'Yes, at St George's Cross. There's some fine tenement property there. Neither of them wanted gardens.'

'You like yours?'

'Yes, it sets off the house. You haven't been to see it.'

'Maybe it's because you haven't asked me.' There was no rancour there. Had it burnt out with the ruined stables? It was a pity Crichton had to set fire to them to bring about a reconciliation. And kill himself.

'Oh, surely you don't have to wait . . .' Maeve smiled '. . . your own brother . . .' Patrick interrupted her.

'What's wrong with your drink, Da?' The slight smile was still on his face. Maeve watched it fade, alarm take its place. He crossed quickly to his father's chair, bent over him. 'Terence . . .' his voice rasped. He did not turn.

They were both there now. What were they going on about, frightening her to death when they were here together at last in spite of the fire, in spite of Crichton, frightening her . . . ? She watched them turn towards her, saw their faces.

'I think he's gone, Mother . . .' Terence was weeping, his face breaking up, the lower lip trembling. He had cried like that as a baby. They came towards her like one person, to comfort her. The girls were round her, and Susan was there with the tea and sandwiches. Susan had always been in at the kill.

20

'We *would* be too early, of course,' Maeve said. She had come to the Royal Infirmary with Maevy for her interview. It was March, three months since Kieran had died.

Sometimes it seemed like three years, at other times the wound was so raw that she could not bear anyone near her, even the family. Her role had always been to console *them*. She had to hide away until she could face them again.

Lizzie had been her saving grace, because she was too young to grieve for Kieran. Grandpa had gone away to Heaven, she had been told by Maggie, and possibly she equated it in her mind with some kind of celestial stables and accepted it utterly.

All she wanted was to be played with, cuddled, pushed through the country lanes in her fine upholstered perambulator with its leather, kid-lined hood, its large shining wheels. The bright face smiling at Maeve as the little mittened hands waved at a glancing bird or the furry pussy-willows, was the only antidote she could accept.

John Craigie supported her as a priest. 'Let the grief out, Mother. Don't hold it in for the sake of the family.'

'It's not like grief, John,' she told him, 'it's like an amputation, something missing.'

'So there is,' he said, 'your husband. But when it heals he'll be there again. In the next room. What you were to each other cannot be destroyed.' She was grateful at least that he did not quote the Scriptures at her, although she did not believe him. Being in the next room was no good to her when she wanted a loving body beside her. John, the husband of Isobel, would know that. He had been too shy as a minister to say it.

And worse still, what if there was no next room? What if she found that the whole of Braidholme as she had known it with Kieran had dissolved, been swept away, and she was left in a kind of emptiness where only ghostly figures swam past her, where no one, no place, had any meaning?

'Do you feel like a walk, then?' Maevy said. She looked trim in her black broadcloth coat, the bit of fur at her neck. Her curls were bright gold escaping the blackness, escaping from the small black hat perched on them. Far too pretty for a nurse.

'Yes, anything's better than sitting in this waiting-room smelling of carbolic . . .' Carbolic. Charlie McNab had spoken of that.

'We could walk along Cathedral Street and see the shops.'

'No, I'm not interested in shops. I've never been in the Necropolis, though.'

'But that's a cemetery, Mother. You don't want . . .'

'I like cemeteries.' Grief made you perverse, like a child. 'I'm more at home in a cemetery than in a shop. People . . . jostle me. They want to talk. Dead people can't talk.' She felt Maevy's glance.

'Come on, then.'

They crossed the Bridge of Sighs and bent to the steep hill. Had they built it like Gethsemane, a Gethsemane with John Knox at the top? Jesus would not have approved of a woman-hater, would he? She was still feeling perverse. 'There should be a fine view when we get up. Maybe we'll see Sholton.'

Saying that, strangely enough, brought quick tears to her eyes. Sholton, where Kieran was *not*. Black veils were a blessing. All the girls were in black, the boys, too.

475

Kieran would be pleased with their respect, in that other room John talked about. Wally McDonald had worn a black band on his arm when he had driven them to the funeral. It was the biggest turnout Sholton had ever known.

John had said they were to treat it as a joyful occasion, a respected, beloved figure of the parish going quickly and peacefully to his rest. 'So much accomplished in his full life,' he had said, 'so much valuable work to rectify some of the iniquities in the pits . . . the building of a fine business with the sterling help of his wife and family . . . a tender, affectionate man who loved his family, loved the countryside, all living things . . . horses.' He made it sound like Kieran, and not like Kieran, like one of those important men here with their grand mausoleums.

Kieran would not like to have one of those grand erections like the Tron Church on top of him. He had always hated going down the pit.

The only person at the funeral who seemed to know what she was like was Alastair Crawford. He had come up to her at the end, black-coated, a wing of grey on either side of his fine, narrow face, his top-hat held respectfully as he bowed. People had stood aside, had walked away that the laird might speak some consoling words. He had taken her hand in his. 'You must miss him, Maeve.' Maeve. The dark eyes spoke of love, rich, abundant love, the kind of love she had lost when Kieran died.

'Look at this!' Maevy said, stopping. 'It's the grave of the man who wrote "Wee Willie Winkie"! I always thought you made it up!' She read from the inscription. '"To the memory of William Miller, the Laureate of the Nursery". Do you remember?' She turned to Maeve, '"Wee Willie Winkie rins through the town, Upstairs and doonstairs, in his nicht-gown . . ." Oh, I wish we were all

476

back in the Row, with Da.' Her eyes widened, filled up. Now Maeve was strong.

'Here's a nice seat. We've gone far enough.'

'All right.' They sat down. Maevy stretched her legs in front of her like a child. Their shape could be seen under the black skirt. Surreptitiously, the back of her hand wiped away tears.

'Do you really want to go in for this nursing?'

'Yes, I do.' Her voice was low. 'I've never changed.'

'It's a long time since John drowned.'

'Yes, I know.'

'And John Craigie's married to Isobel.'

'He was my first and only love.' Her voice made Maeve look at her. At eighteen there should not be sadness like that.

'He won't be your last one. Take it from me.'

'Maybe he will. I'm not interested in men now. I want to devote my life to my work, like Florence Nightingale.'

'You can do both. I did.' She put her hand on Maevy's clasped ones. 'You need love in your life. There's nothing more important. A girl without it becomes dry . . .'

'Not if she's nursing.' She turned to Maeve, her tears gone. 'Don't try to dissuade me, Mother. I've made up my mind.' She stood up. 'We'd better get back now.'

'All right.' She had had to say it, and she had not said, 'I'll miss you.'

They walked in silence, but crossing the bridge Maevy spoke again. 'Will you stay on at Braidholme?'

'Yes, Patrick's moving in. There's plenty of room. And I'm going to do up a bedroom for Maria coming.'

'We're all dying to see Maria. You liked her, didn't you?'

'Yes, she's a grand girl. Spirited. We had some fine times together.'

'Do you think . . . ?'

477

'I don't let myself think.'

'So you'll keep Lizzie?'

'She isn't mine to keep. But I'll guard her. Isobel said she'd have her when I go to the Glasgow office.'

'She won't be so keen now. She's pregnant.'

'She might have told me.' She felt hurt.

'She only saw Charlie McNab yesterday. I expect she told me right away because I'm going to be a nurse.' She squeezed Maeve's arm as they walked.

'Anyhow, Lizzie might go occasionally to Catherine, now that things are different between Terence and Patrick.'

'*She*'s pregnant.'

'Catherine?' She was shrewish for a second, then surprised, then pleased. She had thought the girl looked blooming, and had put it down to the reconciliation between the two brothers. 'You seem to be their confidante. Maybe I should have been a nurse, too.'

'She was just being cautious. You know Catherine.'

'Well, it looks as if we're all going to be pretty busy.' She meant 'they'. She tried hard to subdue the feeling of desolation. All busy with their own concerns, all slipping away from her. If Kieran had been here . . . tears filled her eyes. She recognized them for what they were.

'We were wondering . . .' Maevy's voice was too casual. She knew they'd been discussing her, '. . . if before you start working full time in the business again you wouldn't think of a wee holiday? I could go with you before I start. To Ireland, maybe?'

They were kind, but they did not understand, could not understand the regret she felt that she and Kieran had never been there before he died. 'Wait horse and you'll get corn,' he had said once. He had yearned for his home so much, dreamt of it, longed to feel its softness on his cheek . . . oh, he had been a grand man with words.

'No,' she shook her head. 'I missed going with your father, and that's hard for me to thole. Very hard.' She drew in her breath. 'But I'm not ready for sailing into the sunset yet.'

Maevy laughed. 'Oh, Mother, you're the limit.'

'Am I? Well, I haven't reached it yet. Ireland is another chapter, another book.' The words came to her and she said them softly: 'Heard memories are sweet, but those unsung are sweeter . . .'

'What's that, Mother?' They had walked past the fine Cathedral door, were at the entrance to the Royal Infirmary.

'Something Charlie McNab once quoted to me. In a different class from "Wee Willie Winkie", perhaps. It's from "Ode on a Grecian Urn". I asked for it in the Crawford Library . . .'

But Maevy was not listening. She was looking around like Miss Florence Nightingale entering the British Hospital at Scutari. There was the same kind of light on her face.